CHHATTĪSGARH REDISCOVERED

(Vedāntic Approaches to Folklore)

CHHATTĪSGAṚH REDISCOVERED

(Vedāntic Approaches to Folklore)

By

H.L. SHUKLA

Aryan Books International

New Delhi

Chhattīsgaṛh Rediscovered

Published in 1995 by
ARYAN BOOKS INTERNATIONAL
4378/4B, Pooja Apartments
4, Ansari Road, Darya Ganj
New Delhi-110002 (India)

ISBN-81-7305-058-9

Computer Typeset at Aakriti Graphics, New Delhi.
Printed in India at Efficient Offset Printers, New Delhi.

CONTENTS

APPENDICES

PREFACE

The conventional idea of *Chhattisgaṛh* as a great arid plain chiefly populated by the "*depressed*" classes forgets the great diversity of scenery and population in this little known but fascinating part of Central India. The plain itself is drained up by the upper Mahānadī and its tributaries. The broad expanse of level country, which includes Rāipur, Durg, Rājnandgāon, Bastar, Bilāspur, Rāigaṛh and Surgujā districts of Madhya Pradesh is thus shut up on all sides by hills and forests. The country originally known as *Kosala* (600 B.C. to 1700 A.D.), changed itself to *Chhattīsghar/Chhattīsgaṛh.*

The people of various groups in *Chhattisgaṛh* resemble each other to a greater or lesser degree in standard of living, dress, and in social custom. Most of the tribes or castes, however, have certain characteristics that distinguish them and naturally there will be a great difference in sectarian life between a *Satnāmī* and a non-*Satnāmī*. Many of the apparent differences between a *Satnāmī* and non-*Stanāmī* is a matter of sect than of tradition.

So the book is about *Satnāmīs.* It is concerned with Guru Ghāsīdāsa, who created a new world, a new way of seeing things. Ghāsīdāsa was the architect of cultural renaissance of Central India. He was deeply committed to the oral tradition and worked within the framework of the psychology of the depressed. *Ghāsīdāsa* (1756-1850) was a *kameyā* (labourer) in a *Marār* community in *Chhattīsgaṛh.* He drew upon his symbols to model the making of *Chhattīsgaṛh*, symbols which have a rich heritage in his oral tradition.

A question arises, 'What did Ghāsīdāsa understand by *Satnām* ?' In order to begin looking for answers to this question we spent more time in visiting the *Jait-Khambhas.* After all, religious experience does not arise in a vacuum, and the very term *Satnām* has a wealth of associations, memories and meanings which apply to the tradition of Guru Ghāsīdāsa. To explore the way in which the Guru 'saw' things we had to start with the religious alphabets he used to describe his experiences.

Satnāmī religious beliefs and doctrines are formulated in metaphorical and symbolic language. In seeking to understand what the *Satnām* meant to Ghāsīdāsa, we have been involved in relating the use of symbolic language to his theological world-view. To explore this symbolic language is to engage in religious interpretation, which, like any other form of interpretation, involves listing to what is being said, identifying patterns of meanings, and translating these for the *Satnāmīs.*

If symbols stand for, represent or denote something other than themselves, and religious symbols function in relation to *Sat,* then we can be sure that the *Satnām* when viewed as a symbol, 'hides' and 'reveals' knowledge regarded as sacred.

The purpose of this book is to present a new method to explore the 'hidden' meaning in *Satnām* by applying semiotic approach. Semiotics is commonly known as a structural analysis and cognitive science, because it is closely related to structuralism and epistemology. Using some of the basic concepts and theories of semiotics, it is possible to investigate the structure and cognitive process in *Satnām.*

This book then presents a semiotic approach to the history of Chhattīsgaṛh. It is the *Dalit* history which betrays the anguish of a community, and demands the shaping of a just and realistic future for the under-privileged and the outcastes in society. It is our faithful concern for a neglected region of this vast country and thus rediscovering Chhattīsgaṛh.

In order to bridge the gap between the urban and rural consciousness, between directions past and present, a new trend may be visible in this book. It is the use of mythology to present history. One cannot deny that the operative sensibility of the most personalities of this country retained the mythical origin of their historic sense, and as a result a new history has been filtered from the mythical data.

Mythical thoughts of Guru Ghāsīdāsa mediate the gaps between the continuity and change, thereby authenticating the idea of 'total history' of Chhattīsgaṛh. Myth has been accepted as a meaningful unit of the historic text.

In the Indian context there is a dividing line between the elite (*Śāstra*) and the folk (*loka*). Folk or *laukika* elements are very much a part of "Chhattīsigaṛh Rediscovered." It is a combination of intra-cultural (*Śāstra* and *loka*) and inter-cultural relations; therefore inter-textalism is connected not only with historic texts but also with folkgenre. It expresses both the tradition and the actual. It may give a broader dimension to the present-day realities and past happenings. I hope that this book will be a cause for collective action. I also hope that freedom and human dignity will continue to be the central concern of all works of history.

I conducted my research on the semiotic design with the *Satnāmīs* of Bilaspur and Raipur districts. In my work with them, it seemed to me that they were extremely intelligent. They grasped readily the points of any enquiry upon which I entered, and often showed a marked appreciation of my work. They were interested in the behavioural patterns of other philosophers and appeared to grasp readily the essential differences between their own thinking and those of other peoples. They have the realization of the interdependence between *psyche* and *soma*. I am indebted to them. I hope the book in its entirety will be found useful as a study in Dalit history and its *Ādiguru*:

Ajñānatimirāndhasya Jñānāñjanaśalākayā I
Cakṣurunmīlitaṃ yena tasmai Śrīgurave namaḥ II

H.L. Shukla

LIST OF ILLUSTRATIONS

MAPS

PLATES

CHAPTER I

INTRODUCTION

1.1 *Kosala: The Ancient Chhattisgaṛh*

Kosala, the ancient name of Chhattisgaṛh, literally means the 'land of treasure'. The name Kosala was given to this area much before Gupta period. This is evident from the two great epics and inscriptions.

General Cunningham (1884.68) has also described it as *Mahā Kosala* and says that it comprises the whole of the upper valley of Mahānadī and its tributaries from the source of Narbadā at Amarkaṇṭaka on the north, to the source of Mahānadī near Kānker on the south, and from the valley of the Wain-Gaṅgā on the west to the Hasdo and Jonk rivers on the east. The frontiers given are the most acceptable ones and other scholars like R.B. Hiralal (1933.161) and C.V. Vaidya (1940.348) have accepted these boundaries.

The boundaries of *Kosala Janapada* varied from time to time. The name of its capital also bore the name of the kingdom. During its heyday as depicted in *Kosalānandam Mahākāvyam* (written by Gangādhar Mishra and edited by the author), the kingdom included major parts of Chhattisgaṛh of the present Madhya Pradesh and south-western parts of Orissa. Several trade-routes passed through the region, which had some important towns, such as Śarabhapura-Mallāla-pattana (Malhār), Aṣṭadvāra (Aḍbhār), Shrīpura, Saṅgama-grāma (Tālā), Rājim, Prasanna-pura and Cakrakūṭa (Bajpai 1985.92-94).

The rivers Mahānadī, Arpā, Līlāgar, Śivanāth and others flow through this region. They played their role in making the land fertile and also as media of commercial communication. As now, so also in the past, there was paucity of water in the area. Hence numerous ponds and wells were dug out at necessary places. Rulers of the Śarabhapurīya, Somavaṁśī and Kalacurī dynasties paid special attention in this direction.

The Purāṇic legends enumerate seven Kosalas, *Sapta Kosala* (Shukla: 1977). Literary and epigraphical evidence indicates that adjoining (south) Kosala was the *Janapada* of Mekala, which included major parts of the present districts of Satnā, Rewā, Sīdhī, Śahḍol and Surgujā. To the south and south-east of Mekala was the region of Kosala. Subsequently, Mekala was merged with Kosala, which was appropriately designed as *Mahākosala* (Bajpai 1984. 30-33).

The name of the region, Kosala or Dakṣiṇa Kosala, is the most ancient one. The modern name, that is Chhattīsgaṛh, was assigned to it in the eighteenth century. The word was first used in official papers in 1795 by Blunt (Nelson 1909).

There are different conjectures about the origin of the name 'Chhattīsgaṛh'. According to a story given by J.B. Beglar (Russell. 1908.410). "The real name is not Chhattīsgaṛh but Chhattīsghar. When I was in Bihar, and long before I had any notion of visiting this district, I must confess, did not even know of its existence. I heard a tradition saying that ages ago about the time of Jarāsandha, 36 families of the Dalits[1] (leather workers) emigrated southward from Jarāsandha's kingdom and established themselves in a country which after them is called Chhattīsghar. Neither my information nor I at the time knew of the existence of a real Chhattīsgaṛh, and I looked upon the legend as an idle tale — could not be made to apply to any known locality — I got no clues; here however in a Chhattīsgaṛh, south too, of Magadha, and, what is of the utmost importance as conforming to the tradition, inhabited mainly by the depressed caste who further speak a dialect which resembles even in colloquial terminologies and abbreviations, the dialect now spoken in Bihar; and more than this, the very costume of the people and their physique are identical with, and nearly similar to, those of Bihar."

1.2 *Chhattīsgaṛh Revisited*

Too many people have struggled too long to define legend. I shall not enter the lists at this time. For our purpose chapter, a legend is a tale that has an air of veracity about it, a narrative in a real setting with real persons as the doers, a tale that is told as the truth and that is heard as the truth (Jansen in *Alan Dundes* 1978.123).

Chhattīsgaṛh — legend, recorded by Beglar is a local legend because the setting and the real persons — characters, are known only to the residents of Bihar. This localized legend is close kin to such folk fictional genres as the tell-tale and the realistic tale. Indeed, in performance many folk narrative genres are made by their performers to resemble legends, particularly local legends, in an effort to maintain as long as possible the illusion of veracity.

Indeed, I believe that most of the Dalits in Chhattīsgaṛh did emigrate from Bihar[2]; most of the memorable remarks were made, most of the socio-religious movements did occur, and the speakers, actors, and settings were just as they are specified. The thirty-six families of the Dalits are well known. This is illustrated in the first place by the fact that most of the sub-castes of the Dalits are found fairly in well-defined areas, and these may be described as local groups.

Dalits are scattered well over Chhattīsgaṛh tract, under one name or another. Dalits are most numerous in Chhattisgaṛh. The Census figures for 1991 show the Dalits as the first caste of Chhattisgaṛh in point of numbers. This type of generalization proves the hypothesis that the thirty-six families of the Daltis designated the name Chhattīsgaṛh. The *Satnāmī,* a religious group in Chhattīsgaṛh, has become practically a new caste. These *Satnāmīs,* who make up the largest group in this part of India, have given up their traditional work entirely, and have become cultivators. Many of them have tenant rights, and a number of them were landlords. Their guru, Ghāsīdāsa (1756-1850) has been unique in many ways. His voice "*Satnām*" has stood alone against every kind of attack and has been the greatest manifestation of the real "Chhattīsgaṛhiā" for those who believe in the triumph of truth and truth alone. It is probable that due to his spiritual power this tract was known as the 'abode of the 36 families of the Dalits . It is probable in the sense that modern Chhattisgaṛh emerges with the emergence of Ghāsīdāsa. It was known as Kosala before the *Digvijya* of this true believer. Guru Ghāsīdāsa had faith in the triumph of truth. He was not opposed to or inimical towards others. He was, as Kabīr said:

Kabirā khaṛā bajār me sub ke māngē khair,
nā kāhū se dostī nā kāhū so bair.

Semiotic[3] explanation to the above legend goes back to the basic properties of Chhattisgaṛhi. One of the important ideas of this century is that language organizes itself according to opposites. Thinking in opposites has gone so far that if, while reading in the history, one meets with an opposite pair of ideas like this, one may suspect that the creator is familiar with semiotics: was it thirty-six forts or thirty-six families?

What are the opposites in the etymology of Chhattīsgaṛh? They are such thoughts, as though by force, evoke another thought: the manner in which the idea of "forts" calls forth the idea of "families", or the idea of "good" evokes the concept of 'bad', or the idea of day gives the thought of "night". Here we can speak of typical Bihari behaviour or can we identify a Chhattīsgaṛhī on forts in Chhattīsgaṛh ? What is *Chhattīsgaṛhīness?*

It is difficult to catch these meanings in an unequivocal and clear way, but it works. This is one of the fundamental myths which is based on the fact that we are socio-economically different: the advantaged and the disadvantaged. It means that Chhattīsgaṛh belonged to both the people.

The material good is only one part of emotional charge: most of the planning for the Golden Age is immaterial, refers to spiritual gods, and goes back to the old beliefs which people keep in their collective consciousness.[4]

Very often the Golden Age is tied to forts. It was a spiritual thing, an image or symbol that is sought for. With its opposites it became the Kali Age with the advent of Britishers and the analogy was shifted from forts to the depressed families.

What people want to hear are the myths of the Golden Age. In a sense they are right. This is why first of all, P.N. Bose (1890) attacked the hypothesis of 'thirty-six families' and he along with other historians, propounded the theory that 'Chhattisgaṛh' may be due to so-called 36 forts or it may be a corrupt form of *Chedīsgaṛh*, meaning the political seat of the *Chedis.*

1.3 *Major P. Vans Agnew, The contemporary of Ghāsīdāsa*

Major P. Vans Agnew (1818-1825 A.D.) was the contemporary of Guru Ghāsīdāsa. He was the most important of the superintendents who ruled and managed the affair of Chhattīsghaṛ during the Protectorate. Major Agnew, before joining the Nagpur service, was attached to the Holker court of Indore and was an extremely able officer. He has written the most authentic and monumental work *A Report on the Subah or Province of Chhattisghur* in the year 1820 A.D. Instead of using the word "*Chhattīsgaṛh*" in this report he has used the word "*Chhattīsghur.*" It means that during the period of Agnew "36 families" were on the records. Later on they shifted to "36 forts". The first act of Major Agnew was to change the seat of the Government from Ratanpur to Raipur (Grant, 1870.371). Thus, ended the political career of Ratanpur which was a seat of Government from 1100 to 1818 A.D. The Report of Major P. Vans Agnew is reproduced in the Appendices so that one may have a look on the cultural scenario of Chhattīsgaṛh when Ghāsīdāsa was very much active in revitalising the Daltis.

1.4 *Problems and Methods*

Since the establishment of Guru Ghāsīdāsa University at Bilaspur many scholars have been facing problems to write the authentic history of the *Satnāmī* movement. All of them have up-till now failed because of the reason of the paradoxes involved in the movement. Even the University authorities tried to publish a booklet on "Ghāsīdāsa" (1986) but it was banned from publication due to the protest of *Satnām*-followers. At this point we must consider the problem of mythological analysis.

Just as there are many meanings in the *Satnām*, many themes that may be extracted, so there are many theories of interpretation that might be applied to Ghāsīdāsa-myths. There may be metaphysical interpretation of the Hindu theologians. The mythologist, like the myth- makers himself, cannot be too proud to accept diverse scraps from dubious sources. It is interesting to take note of Freudian overtones in analysing certain parts of the *Satnām*-cycle. Levi-Strauss himself, though objecting to the widespread Jungian interpretation of mythological functions in absolute terms, nevertheless assumes that a myth is a kind of collective dream expressing unconscious wishes. Similarly, one need not stubbornly refuse the assistance of the ritualists in analysing *Satnām* myths.[5]

The ambiguous relationship between myth and reality produces another logical circle, for ethnographic observation must decide whether this image of a myth corresponds to the facts. The main source of explanatory material for any myth is not in ethnography but in other related myths. A myth must be analysed in terms of its relationship to the total myth structure of the culture. Each myth taken separately exists as the limited application of pattern, which is gradually revealed by the relation of reciprocal intelligibility discerned between several myths. This theory is particularly well adopted to the variants of *Satnām* myths.

The latent structure of the *Satnām* myths can only be grasped by working through a large corpus of myths which express in many different ways, certain similarities of structure, the repetition itself emphasizing the form behind the slight variations. The ultimate conclusion of the analysis is not that all the myths say the same thing, but that collectively the sum of what all the myths say is not expressly said by any of them. Thus each myth within the cycle is a variant of every other myth.

The very delimitations of the episodes and symbols can only be identified by the comparison of several versions: integral units are those which appear in one version, but not in another, on the principle of minimal pairs. As in algebra, the more terms (characters, episodes, symbols) involved in a myth, the more 'equations' (variant myths) are required to isolate the terms.

There are many myths dealing with each theme, and many themes within each myth. There is no way to begin with any 'basic' myth or any 'basic' theme, for the entire corpus interlocks and feeds back so that the total fabric resembles a piece of chain-mail rather than the brachiated, family-tree structure sought by the text-historical analysts and some structuralists. I have, therefore, selected certain myths best suited to illustrate certain motifs, while indicating in the margin other motifs which also occur therein. At some point, the reader will have to reread myths cited before their component motifs have been discussed; the chicken must precede the egg, and *viceversa.*

In analysing the myth on its various levels, in seeking patterns and in seeking meanings within these patterns, it is necessary to rely upon a basic principle of *Itihāsa.* In the Indian context it is imperative that we should have our own critical frameworks for the study of oral literature. The oral narrative tradition has come down to us mostly by word of mouth. The *Satnāmī* oral poet describes events for the exteriorisation of the worldly process, and therefore selects a vantage-point in the time past or the time present or the time future which enables him to frequently change his axis in time as well as in space. This mobility gives him a holistic vision; time turns circular for him, and he talks with his total existence which may be described as orchestration of all senses.

Malleability is the characteristic of *Satnām* oral culture. The *Satnāmī* oral culture (nine million followers) takes the help of *Itihāsa* and *Purāṇa* to explain the Vedic *Truth.*[6] Here history changes into *Purāṇa*, so one cannot find a unity which one deserves out of cause and effect relationship.

Itihāsa does not mean history as we generally understand the term. It may be deduced that *Itihāsa* is not a simple narration of past events as 'history' signified in western concept; rather those narrations of the past events are regarded as *Itihāsa* which have some bearing on the fourfold goal of human life. Since *Itihāsa* does not assert 'so it was' but only reminds us that 'so it has been' in the Indian view, the 'so it was' aspect remains neither relevant nor real; the most it can achieve is to stimulate one point in continuum whereas the 'so it has been' view remains continuously relevant and real.

In *Itihāsa* the emphasis is not on the happenings, however true they may be, but on some teaching, on some ideal. In this sense *Panthī*-song is the real *Itihāsa* of Ghāsīdāsa and his *Pantha.*

It is because the *Sat* (Divine Truth) is always existent, so the past and future are merged into present making the axis of the present very important for the folk-singer. This attitude has helped in the development of cultural syncretism, moral and religious humanism and the rising stature of the free human personality. This truth of Indian cultural ethos is expressed in *Mahābhārata*:

Logical argument is inconclusive;
the Vedas are dissimilar;
there is no sage whose doctrines
can be taken authoritative;
the verities of Dharma lie hidden
in the inacessible recesses of the soul;
the traditions followed by the many
show the true way.

Vedā vibhinnāḥ śrutayo vibhinnā
naiko muniryasya vacaḥ pramāṇaṃ
dharmasya tattvam nihitam guhāyām
mahājano yena gataḥ sa panthā

REFERENCES

1. Jheriā Satnāmīs still trace their descent from Bihar.
2. As students of folklore, we are interested in semiotics for what it can tell us how people use language, to help us in making progress toward greater comprehension.
3. The task typically calls for more than adroit symbol formation and transmission. It may call for modifying the object as well as the reader's perception.
4. The truth of some members' statement about the social world is one way of producing studies of social organization.

CHAPTER 2

SEMIOTIC BREAK : THE PROCESS OF ADHAROTTARA[1] IN CHHATTĪSGAṚH

Let us imagine a highly unlikely scenario. The majority is forced to a disadvantaged position, partially as a result of caste-system and partially as a result of unfavourable economic conditions. In large areas it is at the beck and call of others, and dares not lift its voice in protest lest it might be beaten or driven away. Not only is it under the heel of the landlords, who it fears may deprive it of its cultivating rights and of houses, but it is also under the influence of *baniyās* and the landlord, from it whom borrows to purchase seed-grain, leather and oxen. Debt becomes a heavy shackle and often the labour of the whole family is employed in satisfying the claims of the creditor. Over the centuries many of its sons and daughters are lost to it, due to persecution, forced conversion; nevertheless, a huge proportion remains identified with its ethnocultural heritage. The people whom we are imagining are therefore triply miraculous. Its conquerors perish and pass into oblivion while it itself somehow 'muddles through' one cataclysmic reversal after another. In its dispersion, its non-communicating branches become greatly dissimilar and, for periods, even unaware of each other, and yet they do not lose their sense of ultimate unity.

To overcome the basic antinomies of existence is associated with the attainment of godlike or supernormal powers, and with the exploration of the most elusive phenomena of the space-time-continuum. According to Indian religious systems, the transcendence of opposites is a state which can be attained by a human being and is indeed the goal of human life. The unique social status of absolute oracular authority is ascribed to the individual who attains this liberation. The consequences of positing a hypothetical transcendence of opposites are important in the domains of thought, ethics and social organization.

The movement which Rāmānuja started in south India was carried into northern India by his great disciple Rāmānanda. He brought with him the conception of God as a person who cares for all men and who rewards their devotion. He also spread the revolt, against caste-exclusion, insisting that men of a low caste, and even the "untouchables" are capable of *bhakti*[2] (spiritual religion). He, who himself had been outcasted for the supposed violation of the strict rules of commensality, became the missionary of popular Vaiṣṇavism in all northern India, preaching the worship of Viṣṇu under the name of Rāma. And thus started different socio-religious movements in Chhattīsgaṛh.

2.1 *Kabīr and Kabīr Pantha*

Perhaps the greatest of Rāmānanda's disciples was Kabīr (Westcott. 1907). The real importance of Kabīr[3] rests in the enormous influence which he has exercised upon subsequent religious thinking, specially as it has affected the masses, because of his use of the vernacular. His attitude towards caste drew to himself a large following from the lower levels of society.

Kabīr Panthīs[4] are better known in Chhattīsgaṛh. They are largely recruited from the dalits (Briggs, 1920. 205). Nowadays, the members of the sect are divided on caste lines, which are not broken except in the presence of the Chief Guru on the anniversary of the birth of Kabīr, and amongst the lower castes of the sect. All who desire to become members of the *Panth* are required to renounce polytheism and to acknowledge their belief in only one God (*Parameśvara*). They must also promise to eat no meat and drink no wine; to bathe daily and to sing hymns to God both morning and evening; to forgive those who trespass against them up to three times; to avoid the company of all women of bad character, and all unseemly jesting in connection with many subjects; never to turn away from their houses their lawful wife; never to tell lies; never to conceal the property of another man; and never to bear false witness against a neighbour, or speak evil of another on hearsay evidence (Westcott, 1927.112).

Members who renounce the world and attach themselves permanently to the monasteries belonging to the order are called *bairāgis.* Women as well as men may become ascetics.

The *Kabīr Panthīs* of Chhattīsgaṛh are the decendants of Dharmadāsa, who was one of the disciples of Kabīr. Dharmadās established the *Panth* here. So the Chhattīsgarhī branch of *Kabīr Panth* is also known as Dharmadāsī branch or Bhāi-branch. The main monasteries of the *Panth* are at Kawardhā and Dāmākheṛā. There are also other monasteries in charge of mahants, such as Kudurmāl, Kharasiā, Chāmpā, Hardī, Bangolī, Bamnī, Dhamdhā, Pāndā Tarāī and Ratanpur.

The doctrines of the *Kabīr Panthīs* are similar to those of *Satnāmīs*: like the latter, they are enjoined upon to abstain from flesh-food and spirituous drinks, to observe no caste distinction and not to worship idols. Both the forms of faith are a protest against idolatry and the caste-system on the one hand and the vicious habits of aborigines on the other. There is, however, one point of essential difference. *Satnāmīs* forcibly enjoin belief in one guru[5] and the ordinary village deities like Ṭhākurdeo and goddess of smallpox. But the *Kabīr Panthīs* do not have any object of worship.

Kabīrism, notwithstanding its anti-caste tenets is not in such a bad repute amongst the Hindus as *Satnāmīsm* is. This is probably due to the fact that the latter is professed by the depressed only, whereas among the followers of Kabīr are many Hindus not excepting Brāhmāṇs and Rajputs. The Pankās form the greater majority of the *Kabīr Panthīs* of Chhattīsgaṛh; there is not a single Pankā who is not a *Kabīr Panthī.* The Gāṇḍās, Telīs, Marārs, Kunbīs etc. contribute large numbers, the Telīs especially. In this cases, those who become *Kabīr Panthīs* are not ex-communicated, but continue to live with their caste people.

Though the *Satnāmīs* and the *Kabīr Panthīs* equally profess a disregard for caste-distinction,[6] the latter do not carry their regard, into practice or do so to a limited extent. The *Kabīr Panthīs* usually observe caste-restriction.

The ceremony of conversion is very simple, consisting in blowing the *mantra* into the ear of the convert and placing a necklace of wood-beads round his neck.

The constitution of the order is similar to that of the *Satnāmī* sect. There is a Guru who is venerated and worshipped. The Guru lives at Kawardhā and like the *Satnāmī* Guru he occasionally goes out on tour in great pomp. He has got his deputies called *Bhaṇḍāries* and *Mahant* dispersed all over the country, who make converts, collect contributions and officiate at social ceremonies.

The dead are buried. The grave is dug and the corpse laid in it with the head to the north, a *Mahant* or in his absence, some elderly *Kabīr Panthī* blows into its ears some sacred names and pours into its mouth some coconut-oil, after which every member of the party with his back to the grave throws a handful of soil into it, then turns towards the grave and fills it up. Those who can afford, raise a memorial pillar over it. After three days, the head is shaved entirely by near and partly by remote relatives. The kinsfolk assemble at the house of the deceased and squat round a raised dais (called *Caukā*) and sing sacred songs (Bose, *ibid.*).

2.2 *Ghāsīdāsa and Satnām-Panth*

The *Satnāmī* movements have their rise in teachings of Kabīr. The word means the "True Name" and indicates that they worship the One Reality under this title. The first known movement bearing this name appeared in the seventeenth century at Narnāl, seventy-five miles south-west of Delhi. The sect had a reputation for esoteric doctrines, and for uncleanliness in morals and in eating. They came into conflict with the Government of Aurangzeb, and were sanguinarily overwhelmed in 1673 (Sarkar, 1916.385).

A sect by the same name (*Satnāmī*) appeared in the next century, but there is no evidence to show that it was a revival of the earlier movement. Its founder was Jagjīwan Dās (*Oudh Gazetteer*, 1977, Vol. I, p. 361), a *Ṭhākur,* born in a village not far from Lucknow. He died in 1761. Jagjīwan Dās preached the worship of God under the name *Sat Nām* and taught that the deity is both cause and creator of all things, but conceived of him in popular Vedāntic terms. His followers prohibit the use of meat, red *dāl* (*masūr kī dāl*), egg-plant and intoxicating liquors. *Satnāmīs* do not worship idols, but they do worship Hanumān, and pay reverence to what they consider manifestations of the nature of God visible in *avatāras,* particularly in Rāma and in Kṛṣṇa. They observe most of the Hindu festivals, and honour the family and caste customs of the members of their sect. Jagjīwan Dās urged that men should practise absolute indifference to the world, that they should be dependent upon no one, and that they should practise implicit obedience to the Guru. They are said to practise the horrible rite of drinking a mixture of human secretions and excreta (*gāyatri-kriyā*). They enjoy tolerance, charity, consideration for others, prayer, study and kindness to animals (Briggs, 1920).

Jagjīwan Dās was, as noted above, a householder. The sect has a superior order of *mahants,* some of whom are of low caste origin. Through a *Kōrī* (weaver) disciple many depressed and others of low caste were brought into the movement.

The principal works of this guru, written in Hindi, are the *Agha Binās*, the *Gyān Prakāś*, the *Mahāpralaya* and the *Pratham-Granth* (Briggs, 1920.222).

The *Satnāmī* movement was carried from Oudh into Chhattīsgaṛh by Ghāsī Dās, a depressed, and here it has produced notable results.

Ghāsīdāsa[7] was born in poverty at Girod, in Chhattīsgaṛh As a man he took to the life of a pilgrim;[6] later, he abandoned pilgrimage and began an ascetic life, and from that time retired to the forest regularly for meditation. The rocky hillock near his native village to which he repaired, is still a place of pilgrimage. His reputation as a man of supernatural powers grew, and miracles were reported from his place of retirement. Finally, he emerged from the forest with his gospel to the depressed. Ghāsīdāsa carried on his geat work during the decade 1820-1830. He was undoubtedly indebted to Jagjīwan Dās, for the teachings of the two men are well-nigh identical. It was in substance the message of Jagjīwan Dās. Ghāsīdāsa, like the rest of his community, was unlettered. He was a man of unusually fair complexion and rather imposing appearance, sensitive, silent, given to seeing visions, and deeply resented the harsh treatment of his brotherhood by the privileged. He was well-known to the whole community, having travelled much among them; and had the reputation of being exceptionally sagacious, and was universally accepted (Chisholm, 1888, 45).

Ghāsīdāsa died at the age of ninety-five years and was succeeded in office by his son Bālak Dās. The latter, however, managed things badly, and was assassinated in 1860. Since then the family had fallen upon evil times (Briggs, 1920).

A division has occurred in the movement over the use of tobacco, and those who smoke use a leaf-*chilam* and not a *huqqa*.

Satnāmīs worship the Sun, morning and evening, as representing the deity, crying out, "Lord, protect us". Otherwise they have no visible sign or representation of the Supreme Being. They are opposed to idolatry, and are enjoined to cast all idols from their homes. Theoretically, they have no temples, no public religious service, no creed and no form of devotion. They simply call upon the name of God and ask His blessing. They, however, do have temples, and they recognize the whole Hindu pantheon, especially revering the Rāma and Kṛṣṇa incarnations of Viṣṇu.

They profess to set aside caste and to receive all men as equals, but they do not admit into their community members of those castes which they regard as inferior to their own. The sect is practically a depressed one.

Depressed have died and *Satnāmīs* live today. A *Satnāmī* is put out of caste if he is beaten by a man of another caste, however high, or if he is touched by a sweeper. Their women wear nose-rings, although Hindu custom forbids it. They do not usually accept cooked food from the hands of others, whether Hindus or Musalmans. With them two months are taboo for wedding, August (*Shrāvaṇa*) and January (*Pūṣa*). An initiatory practice concerned with marriage has already been described by Briggs (*ibid.*). It is carried out within three years of the wedding and after the birth of the first son.

The *Satnāmī* movement is of considerable importance as a social revolt on the part of the depressed. As an economic and social struggle upwards it has met with a large measure of success. The history of the sect illustrates also how a theistic propaganda can live and transform a whole community.

2.3 The Rām-Rāmī-Panth or Rām-nāmī Panth

The *Rām-Rāmīs* are a small group of the depressed who were organized about 1890 (Briggs, 1920.219). They are found chiefly on the south side of Mahānadī, in the Chhattisgaṛh. They carry a flute, put peacock-feathers around their caps, and cry out "Rām-Rām." They mean always to keep Rām in mind. Their most distinguishing characteristic is that they have the concept "Rām-Rām" tattooed all over their bodies (Briggs, 1920). The idea is that 'Rāma' is the symbol of nature and scribing it on one's person and worshipping it every day keeping it on the clothes would help in keeping man's mind and heart, eyes and ears and the sensory organs constantly aware of the magnificence and munificence of nature. Rāma, they believe, mirrors nature.

The traditional way of saluting in Chhattīsgaṛh is Johār (*Gāthā Saptaśatī*, 300 A.D.). Rām-Rām came into vogue in the year 1651-52 A.D. during the period of Shivājī (Bakhara). The followers of Rām-Rāmī *Panth* are known as Ramramihā in Chhattisgaṛh.

2.4 The Raidās-Panth

One of the most noted of the followers of Rāmānanda was the depressed Rae Dās or Ravi Dās (Crooke 1896). A considerable amount of legendary matter has arisen concerning him, and in some legends an effort is made to give him a respectable ancestry.

Followers of Rae Dās believe that at the age of one hundred and twenty years he reached *Brampad*, the state of bliss, and then disappeared in the flesh. He took his *bānī* (sayings) with him.

Rae Dās, born at Varanasi late in the fifteenth century, came under the influence of the great Rāmānanda, and afterwards became the founder of a widespread religious movement. He was a monotheist, following the general lines of his master's teaching and of even purer faith than Kabīr. The influence of his teaching has been sufficiently great to give him the place of a *Brahmachārī* in *Bhaktamāla* (Lives of Viṣṇu-saints).

Followers of Rae Dās in Chhattīsgaṛh are known as *Rae Ḍās-Panthī*. Many depressed prefer to be known as *Rae Dāsīs*.

Rae Dās taught that the soul[8] differs from God only in that it is encumbered with a body. For him God was everything and he gave himself over to passionate devotion to the deity, believing that God is gracious to all and is accessible to persons of lowly birth. God alone can save a man from evil passions. His conceptions are based on the general principles that underlie the teaching of all the reformers.

One of the outstanding facts about the erstwhile depressed was their lamentable and abject poverty. Ill-clad and cold in winter, badly housed, and insufficiently fed, they belonged to the poorest of the land. In many instances the hovels in which they lived were repaired by the landlord, so that the depressed might not acquire any claim upon the property. To begin with, they were greatly in debt on account of loans both for the purchase of raw materials with which to carry on their traditional occupation and for seed and for cattle for their agricultural enterprises. Rates of interest were exceedingly high; in most cases their obligations were such as to keep them in perpetual bondage to their creditors; and as a consequence, they were never able to rise above the lowest economic level.

Another contributing cause to their poverty was the pernicious system of *begār*. The depressed lived at the beck and call of others, and were obliged to do a great deal of work for which they received no wage whatever. This is but a phase of the general condition of depression in which they lived. They had been so conquered and broken by centuries of oppression that they had little self-respect and no ambition. Their condition was in reality serfdom, and at times they were sore oppressed.

Another cause of their poverty was ignorance. Ghāsidāsa taught them "*gyān ke panth kirpān ke dhārā.*"

A further cause of poverty was vice and excess. They were notorious drunkards and to drunkenness both men and women were addicted. Liquor had an important place in much of the domestic ritual.[9] There was very little attempt to remove that evil until the *bhakti* movement.

Ignorance was more deep-seated than the mere inability to read or write. For generations depressed had been out of touch with even the best light that the village possessed and their mind was almost inert.

The public schools were virtually closed to the depressed. Besides the lack of educational facilities and their intellectual inertness, the environment in which the depressed lived was unfavourable to their advancement.

The depressed held a place very low in the social scale. He belonged to the "untouchables."[10]

The outstanding fact about the depressed religion was its lack of comfort and hopeful outlook. For the most part he lived in fear of malevolent powers and was engaged in propitiating them, and superstition gripped him with all its terrors. This ignorance concerning their religion led many of them to say that they had no religion at all. When these depressed followed the gurus, they were becoming ashamed of the grosser and more superstitious elements in their customs, and were professing not to style them depressed, instead they wished to be called by the sectarial names.

The progressive refinement of irrational psyche intervention in the cult of *bhakti* led the depressed not only to cultural expression of a high order but also to social changes which profoundly affected the course of Chhattīsgaṛh-history. In fact, *bhakti* is historically one of the main agencies of social fusion developed in Chhattīsgaṛh. In origin it is a non-Brāhmaṇ movement of popular religiosity which emerged in south India among classes which were resistant to the pressures of caste hierarchization; it is still very much a living force. True, as soon as any *bhakti* sect gained social influence it was incorporated into the social body; inter-caste as each successive wave has been, and emotionally appealing among low castes; for this very reason, the *bhakti*[11] sect which does not find a very large number of adherents tends to become just another caste as in the case of *Satnām Panth.*

It is evident from the ecstatic, sometimes orgiastic, nature of *bhakti* religiosity, that the states of feverish emotion it encourages, can be traced to the paroxysm of the social outcaste; devotees tend to merge the practices of *bhakti* with the erotic ritualism of *Tantra.* The very word *bhakti*, it may be remembered, can mean 'sexual desire' as well as 'religious devotion'.

Several distinct phases in the development of *bhakti* theology in Chhattīsgaṛh can be discerned (Shukla 1985). The key-figure in the expansion and ultimate triumph of *bhakti* is Rāmānuja. Rāmānuja's God is the first unambiguously ethical divinity in Hinduism, no longer the abstract pure being of Brāhmanism, but infinite goodness, mercy, and beauty. While Rāmānuja's loyalty to his own caste prevented him from taking the final step to abolish caste distinctions, his philosophy added weight to a movement which, in principle at least, cut across caste differences. The followers of Rāmānuja, and numerous gurus who were the fruit of the movement, occasionally proclaimed their antagonism to caste differences in a much more outspoken fashion, but in practice, this did not lead to a consistent offensive against the institution. Dharma Dāsa and Ghāsidāsa developed various aspects of the *bhakti* movement inspiring a large body of devotional literature in the emergent Chhattīsgaṛhī dialect of Hindi.

The streak of anti-intellectualism in the *bhakti* movement was its greatest weakness in spite of Rāmānuja's intellectual qualities. On the one hand, it led wto the glorification of the guru's charisma and thence to the cult of power by the more ambitious. On the other hand, the emotional climate of psychological dependence, even self-abasement of the devotees, and their extreme other-worldiness prevented them from transforming the social order within. In the changing circumstances of a multi-religious society during the Muslim period, these *Panthas* (schools) failed to meet the challenge of times and turned themselves into secular institutions.

Satnāmism was not an exception. But it created a *Satnāmī* awareness[12] in the region. There are *Satnāmīs* who are quick to refer the concept of *Satnāmī*-awareness and *Satnāmī* identity as stemming from a time when the depressed were forced into the *begār*-system. The *Satnāmī* is devoted to the task of demystification. They had been successfully victimized in the past because they had internalized alien concepts which defined them negatively. If *Satnāmī* studies is to be a viable and worthy endeavour, it must be devoted to the task of demystification. Unfortunately this is a long and difficult endeavour, and I have only scratched the surface.

REFERENCES

1. *Adharottara* is the theory of radical subversion proposed by Manu. It constitutes semiotic break. It challenges the basic code of discrimination. See my book '*Semiotica Indica*' (1994)

2. *Bhakti* cults challenged the moral values and attitudes of orthodox caste society. Most o them had their roots among the lower castes and there can be no doubt that they involved attitudes of a true reformatory nature.

3. Not until the fifteenth century do we find a Hindu sage who had the down-to-earth realism of the practical man. For the work of Kabīr gave him an understanding of matter-of-fact realities of life which we miss in the princely personality of Buddha and in the author of *Gītā*. Kabīr was the man who worked for Hindu-Muslim unity. So is Ghāsīdāsaho worked for the unity between lower and higher castes.

4. Strictly speaking guru is a person who gives *dīkṡā*, initiation into a sect.

5. Caste-disputes in India may be described as ritualized realignments, not rebellion against the caste system itself. Their functions are not to be sought in their relation to emotional needs alone, but in

the need to dramatize and uphold the principle of inequality in social relationships. Gluckman and others have shown how ritualized conflicts are built into social life.

6. His journey to Purī is not only a kind of descent int the underword but also a descent into inner self, a journey into human soul. As Ghāsīdāsa penetrates deeper and deeper into the Sōnākhān jungle and his disappointment increas he begins to look into his inner self until he reaches a serious state of morbidity and depression from which he is saved finally by *Satnām*. However Ghāsīdāsa's experience in this journey is a mixture of hope and disappointment. It is through this journey that Ghāsīdāsa learns much about secretsof *Satnām* and about human life as a whole but the note implied in the image of descent is that he ends as he began.

7. Raidāsīs believe in the survival of *jīva* and *brahma*. The one which represents a kind of life-force, is known as *jīva*, and this is believed to go to *Bhagvān*, who after sometime sends it into the body of an unborn child. According to Gonds, the other element to which the human personality is believed to be attached goes to an under-world where it joins the company of clan-ancestors and the clan-god.

8. Guru Ghāsidāsa preached his followers to abstain from alcoholic drinks: *māns madirā ke to chhor de adhār ga jehī khānā-pīnā ma bigare saṁsār ga.*

9. This immense sector of Indian people has an incalculable potential, particularly since it is the least affected by introversion, other-worldliness, and the world -as-illusion syndrome of the upper castes.

10. The brotherhood of mystical devotees of the *bhakti* sects originated in popular movements which attempted to cut across caste lines and to bring people from all walks of life together.

11. Although self-absorption is something we need to guard against, our capacity for self-awareness is our species' greatest assets. It develops naturally in infancy-but can be cultivated to advantage throughout life. Psychologists distinguish four elements of the self. First, we each have our own bodies and their automatic processes. Second, we each have our own experience of sensory stimuli. The two elements together are classed as parts of *passive self.* We are also, third, an *active self,* an agent responding to our environment. The fourth element of self-hood is the *reflexive self.* This is a type of experiencing. Human self-awareness, certainly, is typically triggered of by situations of self-presentation.

CHAPTER 3

GURU GHĀSĪDĀSA AND SATNĀM-PANTHA

The study of *Satnāmī* religious movement belongs first of all to mission-derived scholars. Presently the most valuable information we have on our shelves has been produced by them (Lawlor 1867, Chisholm 1868, Hewitt 1869, Grant 1870, Sherring 1879, Nelson 1909). This effort and contribution in part a testimony to their special interest in the subject and a certain collegiality of such scholars experienced with the leaders of many religious movements. This collegiality has its limitations, of course, and has tended to orient them towards the movement with a marked christocentric orientation.[1] We have much less material on the movement which is strongly traditional or nativistic. But this collegiality has made for a very productive empathy.

3.1 *Cultural Environment*

It can be said without prejudice (or pre-conception) and in all seriousness that the point of view of Ghāsīdāsa was all-embracing and his life was culturally highly significant.

Ghāsīdāsa had no direct connection with the Anglo-Marāṭha politics (1741-1854) which overpowered Chhattisgaṛh region during his time. During the period of Ghāsīdāsa this region was called '*Sūba* or Province' (Agnew 1820) and was directly ruled by the Bhonslās or Britishers from Nagpur. The agricultural castes together formed a very numerous community. The depressed were one of them at the time of Sherring (1879):

> The depressed are populous in Chhattīgaṛh, where they are chiefly found. As a people they are far superior to the depressed of Northern India, although doubtless of the same race. They are principally found in field-work, in which they display considerable energy and skill. Having discarded Brahminical influence they have a priesthood of their own. Many of them are rich, and most live in comfort, while as a people they have the character of being the best subjects which the British Government has in those parts (*ibid.*, 87).

Ghāsidāsa was disgusted with the Anglo-Marāṭha politics bereft of morality: political jugglery or trickery in plain terms. Having been dejected by British Government, Ghāsidāsa took in hand the task of uniting all the downtrodden persons to morally oppose the immoral politics of the Britishers. The people of Chhattīsgaṛh were terror-stricken by the colonial rule. Still they could not be united under one flag. Ghāsidāsa wanted to make them bold through the ideology of equality and non-violence.

An in-depth and unbiased investigation of the *Satnāmī* movement reveals that it has over a century provided a knowledge of nature and rules of natural-resource utilization that has enabled *Satnāmīs* to survive materially. Simplicity and non-voilence are obviously closely related in *Satnāmī* sect. The optimal pattern of consumption, producing a high degree of human satisfaction by means of a relatively low rate of consumption allows *Satnāmīs* to live without pressure and strain and to fulfil the primary injunction of *Satnāmī* teaching:

"Cease to do evil, try to do good."
yah mānāvata ki jaladhārā
isakā teja prahāra hai
isakī rakṣā karo sadā tum
yah śubha hai aur sundar hai

thoḍe men nirvāh karo
mat āḍambar phailāo
rūkhī-sūkhi khākar
apnē man ki śānti banāo

(Khare : *Satnām*)

As physical resources are everywhere limited, people satisfying their needs by means of a modest use of resources are obviously less likely to be at each other's throat than people depending upon a high rate of use. The teaching of Ghāsīdāsa enjoins a reverent and non-violent attitude not only to all sentient beings but also with a great emphasis on the birds and animals.[2]

3.2 *The Satnām Consciousness*

The Highest Reality is described by Guru Ghāsīdāsa, as the *Satnām*, the true name of the True one: *Raso vai saḥ.* Since *Satnām* is ever creative and is of sporting nature, it is the Blessing of Love, it is essentially one: *ekamevādvitīyam.* The religious act of *Satnām* consists of muttering the name of God (*Satnām*), and asking His blessing.

The *Satnāmī Dharma* was in reality a movement to reform the great Hindu *Dharma* in accordance with the principle of liberalism (or broad-minded). The Supreme Entity (*Akṣara Brahma*) became the single God. In *Satnāmī* faith importance has been attached to worship with an adoring mind.

3.3 *Cultural Performance: The* Panthīgīt

The kind of cultural performance which is closest in form and spirit of *Satnāmi* religious movement is a group of folk-songs called *Panthīgīt.* These are very informally organized as part of *Satnāmī* processions around the streets of the villages. The song is always accompanied by dance, which enlightens the soul of the *Satnāmī* folk:

Tannā nannā nannā nannā vāre nannā
ek penṛ anwrā dūsar penṛ dhanwṛā
nām leke āye Sāhab nām leke āye
mālā mugwā chūṭis kaṇṭhī pahināye
adhare ke nāgar adhare juārī
adhare ma dhotiyā sukhāye
aisan karnī kar nām lā kamāye
nām ke ḍaṇkā la girod mā bajāye
giraud lā chāṇḍi ke bhaṇḍār purī aye
jahān taynhā nām ke dhajā phahrāye
mare mare murdā lā tayn hā jiyāye
sānp chābe chābe lā amrit mā jiyāye
aisan aisan karnī lā duniyā hā dekhis
tabhe sabe đuniyā saran gati āis
jāke dekhe kono Telāsi nagar mā
jahān tore nām ke diynā jarat he

3.4 *The Moral Significance of Food and Drink among the* Satnāmis

Satnāmī practices regarding food are based on three assumptions: First, in the absence of the mind-body dichotomy prevalent in the West, food is held to be imbued with moral qualities which affect the mind and disposition of the eater such that certain categories of food cool the blood and dispose to virtuous thoughts while others inflame the passions and brutalize the character. This restricts the choice of diet, especially for the true *Satnāma Panthī*.[3]

Second, the cooking of food opens it, in varying degrees according to the method of preparation, to contagion from outside. Cooking is here to be understood as a relative term. All methods of preparation that conduce to the decomposition of food are classified as degrees of cooking. The use of fire further assists the process of decomposition, but food is only considered to be completely cooked when boiled in water. Permeability to contagion increases with the degree of cooking, which restricts the range of individuals from whom food can be accepted with safety. Raw whole foodstuff carries no pollution and is freely purchased in the market from the lower caste also, but the orthodox *Satnāmī* will not buy cut fruit.

Third, moral qualities are transmitted by contact with cooked food and internalized by the eater. A man is also believed to transmit his qualities to the food he eats so that its remains can only be eaten by those inferior to him.

3.5 *The Moral Properties of Food*

Nutrition as a biological process is more fundamental than sex (Freud's patients). In the life of the individual organism it is the more primary and recurrent physical want (as envisaged by *Gītā*; it is not the sex as presented by Freud), while in wider sphere of human society it determines, more largely than any other physiological function, the nature of social groupings, and the form their activities take.

The classification of foods as hot or cold is assimilated to the three spiritual categories and the *Satnāmīs* always use *sāttvika* (conducive to goodness) food. This has the property of inducing virtue and saintly habits. Sherring (1879: 110-11) wrote:

> "The Satnāmīs will not eat meat; nor will they take water from any one not of their own caste. They drink no spirits." "Women will not drink water except from one of their own and liquor is prohibited." (Nelson, 1909, 83) "Ghāsīdāsa prohibited the use of meat, of lentils on account of their red colour suggesting blood, of egg-plant, which was considered, probably on account of its shape, to resemble flesh and of intoxicating liquors" (Hiralal, 1916, Vol. I).

It means that in *Satnāmi Panth rājasika*[4] (conducive to passion) and *tāmasika*[5] (conducive to darkness and sloth) foods were prohibited, because they vitiate the system and brutalize the character. The positive evaluation of cooling foods that tend to detachment from the world is consistent with the ascetic emphasis in *Satnām Pantha.* The *Satnāmīs* became the people of *sāttvika* class.

Food transactions in India have been analysed chiefly in relation to caste-status. The intake of *sāttvika* food by the *Satnāmīs* places them at par with the Brāhmaṇ-caste, and this is why, in the Census of 1911 (Census Report of 1911, Calcutta), they returned themselves as the Brāhmaṇ-Hindu.

Here in *Satnāmī* sect a man's sect-altered when he took *rājasika* or *tāmasika* food. One of the precepts of Ghāsīdāsa was the prohibition of the use of tobacco and this led to the split in the sect as many of his diciples found the rule too hard for them. Sherring (1879:110-11) records.

> "But some smoke tobacco, and as others do not, two separate and important divisions of the tribe sprung up.... A few years ago a serious division arose among the *Satnāmī* on the subject of smoking tobacco. This and drinking spirits were both forbidden by their spiritual teacher. The latter was easily abandoned, but the former, although given up for a time by all the *Satnāmīs,* was after an interval resumed by some of them. These did not adopt the *hukkā* as formerly, but, in its stead, a broad *palas*-leaf was folded into the shape of a pipe, and tobacco was placed in the bowl, and thus smoked. This pipe is called *Chōngī,* and the smokers are designated *chongiyās.* The more orthodox *Satnāmīs,* however, have resisted the temptation; and the sect has split into two great sections—the smokers and non-smokers."

(See also Report of the Census of the Central Provinces for 1872, Appendix, p. xxii). Nelson (1909:83) says that in his later years Ghāsīdāsa withdrew the order of prohibition. But the *chongiyas̄* ultimately converted themselves to the idolatry which was against the preachings of the Guru.

Because the Chhattisgaṛhi *Satnāmi* replicated fully and completely the structural function of the Hindu Brāhmaṇ, and because the Chhattisgaṛhi *Satnāmīs* can therefore use a ritually determined caste hierarchy, it is possible for them and for outside observers to classify their social ranking system as a higher caste society.

3.6 *Changing Moral Values in the Context of the* Satnāmī *Movement*

While the relativity of morals in different societies and cultures is well-known from research, changing moral values over a period of time in Chhattīsgaṛhi society have not sufficiently attracted the attention of sociologists and social anthropologists. The complexity of Chhattīsgaṛhi society is evident from the existence of Great Tradition and Little Tradition. These contain elaborate traditions and codes of moral conduct, sanctioned through merit, sin, guilt, shame, honour and prestige. The values and sanctions have had for their sources of legitimacy the scriptures, the priests, and teachers who interpreted them, and kings and elders who safeguarded and implemented the norms.[6] However, established traditions have time and again been challenged by sectarian and other social and cultural movements. Protest movements either modified the existing value systems or established new ones with independent sources of legitimacy. The *Satnāmī* movement among the lower caste has challenged the moral values and attitudes of the peasant society of Chhattīsgaṛh. The present chapter is an attempt to trace the process of the emergence of new moral values, and to examine the impact on the traditional value system, with special reference to *Satnāmī* Movement (SM) among the depressed of Chhattīsgaṛh. But before I consider the emergence of the *Satnāmī* movement, we need to understand the traditional value system which underlay the Hindu caste system in Chhattīsgaṛh.

3.7 *The Traditional Hindu Value System of Chhatīgaṛh*

Chhattīgaṛhi society, like the wider Hindu society of which it is a part, was characterized by the general values of deference and hierarchy. Not only were social phenomena differentiated into different 'classes' but all were hierarchically arranged on the basis of birth and purity. Deference and hierarchy as general values were codified by scripture and enforced by priests, kings and elders. In the process of codification, specific norms were established and sanctioned, governing people's conduct in the context of intercaste relations in the religious, economic, political and civic areas of social life. Agnew (1820:8) remarks:

> Considering the uninformed state of the people their moral character seems to be superior to that met with in most other parts of India. Murders are rare and are in most cases occasioned by jealousy or supposed acts of witch craft, both which occasions are universally considered, if not a sufficient justification, at least a great palliation of the offence. Petty thieving seldom occurs, and the more daring robberies by gangs and on the high-ways are less frequent than might be expected from the facility to escape afforded by the surrounding jungles and zamindars. In regard to women their habits appear to be rather loose. On the whole they may be said to be honest, to be un-addicted to great crimes, and to have more regard to truth than is common in India, as an instance of which it may be mentioned that offenders very generally make an unhesitating confession of the crimes they have committed.

Now let us look at the expected behaviour patterns (norms) of the depressed in the traditional social system in Chhattīsgaṛh before the *Satnāmī* movement.

In the caste hierarchy, *Satnāmīs* were, we are told, low caste people. They were the lowest in the caste-hierarchy. The depressed was required to show deference by doubling up and shivering, with one palm closing his mouth. He was not allowed to call his dwelling a house, but only a hut, and he had to refer to his food as cow-dung. He was not permitted to wear any footwear or use an umbrella. *Satnāmī* women were not allowed to cover their breasts and *Satnāmīs* could not walk on the streets, than ran near upper-caste houses or temples. Nor could they bow to the idols in the temples. Most *Satnāmis* were landless labourers and survived on the meat of dead animals. As to religious beliefs and rituals, they were expected not to worship Hindu deities. The depressed[7] were not allowed to read *Śāstras* and other sacred scriptures, or to solicit the services of upper-caste priests. The washerman and the barber of the upper-castes did not serve them. These services were performed by *Satnāmī* craftsmen. A depressed violating the norms received a punishment which could range from having his head chopped off to a beating and fine. (Lawlor: 1867).

3.8 *The Rise of the* Satnāmī *Movement*

Against the foregoing background, I shall discuss in this section the genesis of the *Satnāmī* movement. Guru Ghāsīdāsa[8] (1756-1850) was the founder of the movement and being a charismatic leader, was able to attract the spontaneous response of a large number of following to his new philosophy, especially among the depressed. He developed his ideas from a knowledge of the preachings of the great saints of north India. According to R.B. Hiralal (1916):

> Ghāsīdāsa got his inspiration from a follower of the older Satnāmī sect of north India. This was inaugurated by a Rājput, Jagjīwan Dās of the Bārā Bankī District in 1761. He preached the worship of the true name of one God, the cause and creator of all things, void of sensible qualities and without a beginning or an end.

The creed of Ghāsīdāsa, enunciated subsequently, was nearly identical with that of Jagjīwan Dās and was no doubt derived from it, though Guru Ghāsīdāsa never acknowledged the source of his inspiration (Nelson 1909:79). Again we are told by Sherring (1879:111):

> The depressed of Raipur call themselves Raydāsa, being disciples of Rae Dās, a depressed reformer, who adopted the creed of the celebrated Rāmānanda, who flourished three or four centuries ago. The Raedāsis assumed the designation of Satnāmīs. Ghāsī Dāsa, in proclaiming the dogmas of this sect in Chhattīsgaṛh, seems to have revived the teaching of Raedāsa rather than to have originated a new creed.

Others say that Rohī Dāsa was the first depressed of Chhattīsgaṛh who was the disciple of Rāmānanda at the end of the fourteenth century. The plea of the proponents of this hypothesis is that the depressed of Chhattīsgaṛh also call themselves as Rohi Dāsa, a synonym to *Satnāmī* (Nelson, *ibid.*). But there is no evidence that Rohi Dāsa ever came to Chhattīgaṛh and there is practically no doubt, as already pointed out, that Ghāsīdāsa simply appropriated the doctrine of his *Satnāmī* sect of north India.[9]

Though Ghāsīdāsa was illiterate, even then he managed to acquire the *Truth* through the great saints whom he met during his wanderings in the woods stretched to Jagannāth Puri in search of *Truth* (Keyūr Bhūṣan 1982.70). Ghāsīdāsa rose to the level of a Brāhmaṇ through the path of devotion and not by chanting sacred texts.

Ghāsīdāsa insisted that idol-worship should be stopped and there should be no temples to propitiate gods. Rather he did not believe in any form of God except that of Supreme Being. He insisted that men should rise above the level of mere image-worship. The Sun[3] symbolized the Absolute by its light and a *Satnāmī* prostrates himself before the Sun, morning and evening, crying *Satnāma*, the *True Name* or the True One (Sherring 1879.110). He used the *Āgama* style of worship, using *Satnām* instead of Vedic hymns and offering only vegetarian food and non-alcoholic drinks. Here again, tradition held that it was immoral for the depressed to worship deities in the *Āgama* style; they were required to worship spirits and lesser gods and goddesses using only Chhattīgaṛhi oral texts and offering non-vegetarian food and alcoholic drinks. But he asked his followers not to worship any kind of god except the Absolute Being. He also evolved simple domestic rituals of marriage and bade them give up the meaningless puberty rituals. He created an order of guru (priesthood) to carry out his programmes and established a centre at Bhaṇḍār (Raipur district) to train them in philosophy of *Satnāma*.

Ghāsīdāsa's basic philosophy is contained in his oral statement: one caste, one religion and one God.[9] 'Ghāsīdāsa was against all types of caste distinctions. For him, man's humanity was marked out by the human species and not by Brāhminhood (Lawlor, 1867:40). Moreover, the Guru flouted caste and religious distinctions in his own day-to-day activities. He also advocated oneness of the caste, and asked his followers to drop caste name and use *Satnāmī* instead of the depressed one. He encouraged the patrilineal system of inheritance and monogamous marriage. He insisted on functional education and laid emphasis on the value and importance of action. Hence he advocated abandoning the traditional tanning or skinning occupation. The Guru's new moral system thus covered all spheres of social life. It was, in effect, a new system of religious belief and rituals, of agricultural activity, and of domestic behaviour, the whole being used with egalitarian values.

The message propounded by Ghāsīdāsa gave the *Satnāmī* movement its basic ideology. The leaders of the movement were in fact able to secure all the basic ritual and civic rights from which the depressed had traditionally been excluded.

Thus *Satnāmī* movement was able to challenge the traditional Hindu value system and create it anew within the Hindu fold, in accordance with the awakened needs and aspirations of the depressed and other untouchables. The Guru's ideology was religious but rational. His charisma provided the source of legitimacy for the new value system.

Ghāsīdāsa considered that the Hindu religion had only spread a superstition and magic which supported the caste system. Thus he developed a secular ideology. The Guru's ideology consisted of three major strands—the secular humanism of Buddhism, the worship of one Supreme God, and the ideology of equality (in a strict *Gītā* philosophy). To bring these views to the public and win support, Ghāsīdāsa initiated a programme to stop devotees from sacrificing fowls at the Devī festivals and from undertaking pilgrimages to various places. He stopped human sacrifice at Dantewāṛā (Keyūr Bhūṣaṇ, undated.42).

3.9 *Ghāsīdāsa's Value-system in the Wider Social and Cultural Context*

So far we have seen the emergence within *Satnāmī* movement of the value-system which established the moral[10] system. I shall now analyse the process by which it gained recognition in the groups; the manner in which its introduction was related to wider economic, political and social forces; and the implications it had for the traditional moral system.

Members of a group develop a common interest in an idea and begin to value it because it promotes their interests — material or non-material. Both values and norms then become constituents of a general value-system and moral order which requires a source of legitimacy. Orthodox Hindu texts, priests and kings provided the traditional source of legitimacy in Chhattigaṛh, with an elaborate system of sanctions to enforce conformity and punish deviance. The question is: how did changes occur in this traditional value system and what were the sources of legitimacy for the new system? The changes brought about by Ghāsīdāsa stemmed from his analysis of the situation in which he found the depressed and the strategy he adopted to improve their condition. In his view, his task was to challenge orthodox Hindu values which maintained a hierarchy based on birth and purity. This was the root cause of the acute relative deprivation of the depressed. How was he to induce society to honour, esteem and hold them worthy? The prevailing values which gave status, honour and worth were a knowledge of the Vedas and Vedānta, the worship of vegetarian and non-alcoholic deities, and the practice of puritan values such as vegetarianism and teetotalism. But all these were considered the monopoly of the Brāhmaṇs and the upper-classes. Instead of appealing to the mercy of the Brāhmaṇs, Ghāsīdāsa protested against the control of these values. He was illiterate and his fellowmen were also illiterate. Hence instead of acquiring Vedic knowledge he went in search of *Truth* which prevailed in the traditional folk of the region. He believed in naturalistic explanation based on sensory perception, without any faith in the godhead or the Vedas. It was just a Buddhist interpretation of the *Truth.* Ambedkar while realizing the caste-hierarchy turned to Buddhism and became, along with his followers, a convert to it as a protest against Hinduism which sanctioned untouchability. Ghāsīdāsa, however, did not advocate conversion to Buddhism but asked his followers to practise its basic values in their lives, as he himself did. He had his own interpretation of the Supreme Being which is orally transmitted to the *Satnāmī* society of Chhattīgaṛh through *Panthīgīt* (folk-songs of the *Satnāmī* sect). Some lines from the *Panthīgīt* are quoted here which tell the *Satnām* philosophy of existence and address to Ghāsīdāsa:

Ta na na na na na ho na bāre lalnā
tor man mohnā ki mor jag mohnā?
ek penṛ anwrā dusar penṛ dhanwṛā sāhab !
tehī mere Ghāsidās dhūni lā ramāye sāhab !
Sat ke nām sat lok lā lāye sāhab
chāron baran lā tain hā amrit piyaē sāhab !
chābe chābe sānp ke mankhe lā jagāye
mare mare murdā lā tain hā jiyāye
dhukī dāi khappar lā sātkos bhagāye
moṭrā dharā ke Himglāj la kudāye
jahān jahān Sāhab tor paug hā paṛat gis
tahān tahān hamar to tīrath banat gis
nām ke gaṇgā lā charan men bohāye
charan daras bar man lā lubhāye.
(Field-song)

Thus he interpreted *Satnām* in his own folkway. He negated the image-worship of the high-castes. And he himself provided the legitimacy for the value system he introduced. Since this legitimacy was accepted by hundreds of associations formed all over Chhattigaṛh to propagate his philosophy, there emerged a source of moral legitimacy parallel to and separate from the great traditional source of Chhattīgaṛh.

The new moral order[12] heralded by Ghāsīdāsa gave the depressed honour, worth and self-respect, as well as religious rights and privileges. The new value system and norms based on the principles of equality and achievement were formulated by Ghāsīdāsa in the context of a symbolic reinterpretation of the social and cultural environment. It was oral history of the sacred texts into *Panthīgīt* to suit new aspiration and realities; and this legitimized both by Ghāsīdāsa's charisma and by his knowledge.

3.10 *Conclusion*

I can now draw together the different strands in the argument. Social and cultural movements generally aim at constructing a more satisfying system of morality. However, a distinction has to be made with regard to the nature of the changes made and their consequences. The *Satnām* movement was a protest against the existing value system and the reconstruction of a new moral system by providing alternative sources of legitimacy.

Ghāsīdāsa's above ideology grew out of the interaction of the structural conditions of existence of the depressed and a perception of their needs, interests and resources. The depressed suffered from many kinds and degrees of relative deprivation in the traditional moral order. Ghāsīdāsa formulated a full-fledged and consistent moral system fulfilling the need of the people to participate in the highest form of the Brāhminical Hinduism. This gave them both self-respect and a realization of their capabilities. This meant that he rejected the value-system based on Hinduism and adopted one based on secular rationality rather than any other religion. Rejection of Hinduism, of which the depressed were a part, was a symbolic expression of their protest and frustration. He established and legitimized a different identity in order to acquire self-respect, worth and honour. It should be pointed out that although the immediate social situation provided the stimulus for Ghāsīdāsa, he transcended a narrow group-identity in seeking legitimacy for his new moral system.

The process by which moral values became internalized in people's thought and action involved de-socialization from the orthodox values and agencies of social control on the one hand and re-socialization in the new values with the help of informal and formal agencies such as new associations, new shrines and a new order of priests. When the negative sanctions were imposed, there was a danger of splitting the sect as in the case of *chongiyas̄.* In this sense the routization of the new moral systems was not complete.

Thus the ideology of *Satnām* movement contributed to the pluralism of moral systems in Indian society as a whole. The traditional moral system (of Great Tradition) came to co-exist with Ghāsīdāsa's systems of morals, since Brāhmaṇs and kings (*Bhonsalas*) had lost their authority to punish the deviants. Further, this ideology supporting egalitarian moral values provided the motive force for the organization of specific programme of action calculated to secure basic civil rights. This programme in turn caused a social transformation in Chhattīgaṛhi society and culture by changing superordination-subordination relationships and its pattern of allocation of rights and privileges.

Thus, *Satnāmism* that emerged as a school of religious thought in the more recent periods of Chhattīgaṛhi history, has demonstrated through the visible performance of its followers the most laudable virtues of protecting and enriching the natural environment, making the most efficient use of natural resources for man's sustained benefits in terms of food, nutrition, health and good living, and developing the true spirit of partnership and sharing in community life.

Ghāsīdāsa could discover his inner nature, made the most of everything he was capable of being and doing. Some psychologists may believe that his urge to achieve the *Sat* (the upper limit of his potential) was inherent in his human nature. They may believe that the ultimate truth of his life was the expression and full development of his qualities which were blended in a harmonious whole of Chhattīsgarh.

Studies of human behaviour often strike a pessimistic note. Psychologists who emphasize the environmental forces that shape our personalities can create the impression that we have no part to play in making ourselves. Others emphasize our drive to express an inborn nature, but many — Freudian psychologists especially — seem to have a negative view of this nature: we are seen as products of a conflict between unruly instincts and the restraints that society is forced to impose.

The "humanistic" style of psychology, pioneered by Carl Rogers and Abraham Maslow, takes a more positive view. Maslow (*Motivation and Personality,* New York, 1971), in particular, constructs a hierarchy of increasingly human natural needs. Ghāsīdāsa is strongly motivated to his basic deficiencies (of nourishment, security, love and acceptance, self-esteem). His struggle to overcome these deficiencies gave him the characteristics of the self-actualizer.

When Ghāsīdāsa became self-actualizer, he developed a positive personality. In fact, adversity and suffering often provided a rich soil for his further growth. Disadvantages became advantages because they were experienced as challenges. Perhaps even a sense of inferiority could not shake his self-esteem. He became the paragon of all virtues. His self-actualization was a continuous process of becoming, not an elevated plateau of being.

In fact, his attainment and success might be quite modest, but what distinguished him from the majority of the people is his determination and ability to get the best out of whatever assets and opportunities he had.

Achievement, social status and prosperity could come as by-products, but irrespective of whether they did or not, the essence of Ghāsīdāsa was living to the full, discovering his inner nature and being all that it was in him to be.

REFERENCES

1. Guru Ghāsīdāsa was against the process of Christianization which was very much rampant in those days, and even his brothers Nankū, Mankū, Gangā and Jogī could not remain in their traditional creed and were forced to embrace Christianity. Ghāsīdāsa could save his fellowmen by reforming the *Sanātana Dharma* as *Satnām.*
2. *Kono jīvkā jhan mār be. Jīv-mārab hā hiṁsā karab mahāpāp āy* —9th *Rāvṭī* of *Satnām.*
3. *Sattva* is that constituent of *Prakṛti* which is of the nature of pleasure and light (*laghu*) and illuminating (*prakāśaka*). It gives rise to happiness and love, tranquillity and modesty, health and lightness of body, patience and forgiveness, courage, magnanimity, self-restraint and the illumination of knowledge.
4. *Rajas* is the constituent of *Prakṛti* which is of the nature of pain and is mobile and stimulating.
5. *Tamas* is the constituent of *Prakṛti* which is of the nature of indifference and is heavy and enveloping.
6. The juxtaposition of the grossly physical with the structurally normative produces a profound effect: Norms and values become saturated with emotion while emotions are ennobled through contact with values.
7. A sense of helplessness was the characteristic of the depressed. They felt unable to cope even with problems that were well within their capabilities. Two aspects of habitual thinking style were important: their 'self-focus' and their 'attributional style'.
8. There is some controversy about his acual period; see Behar 1986.

9. The *Satnāmī* revolt of Narnaul occurred in the year 1672 which aimed at terminating the Muslim rule in India.

10. This one ness is the zero-concept in Indian philosophy.

11. Ginsberg (1974.119) considers the universality of morality as a human phenomenon in the sense that everywhere we find a recognition, implicit or explicit, that conduct has to be controlled or guided by reference to principle.

12. A more explicitly ethical aspect of Guru Ghāsīdāsa is the concern that no life is to be harmed and that all living beings are to be treated with compassion. This movement rejected the practice of animal sacrifice.

CHAPTER 4

THE SEMIOTICS OF SATNĀM

Ghāsīdāsa lived in Chhattīsgaṛh during the first half of the nineteenth century A.D., and the influences upon his thought were derived from the spiritual traditions he valued and incorporated within the authoritative lineage of Vaiṣṇavism.

Ghāsīdāsa's originality lies in his method, which integrated popular spirituality with the rather rigid structures of accepted Vedāntic tradition. He found a way of doing this while working as a labourer (*kameyā*). He is orally recorded as being the Guru. His teachings are found in the *Panthi-gita* — a poetic tradition orally transmitted from generation to generation. Stylistically, several folk genres display his school of thought. The sections dealing with *Satnām* are scattered throughout the oral and non-verbal traditions of *Satnāmīs*.

Perhaps one of the most exciting features of Ghāsīdāsa's depiction of *Sat*[1] is that he brings together different elements from different sources to communicate his spiritual vision. This reflects his own experience.

Ghāsīdāsa's *Sat* (i) belongs to a conscious being; (ii) is controlled and supported by that being; (iii) serves to further that being's purpose in all circumstances; and (iv) its proper or essential form is accessory to that being.

These four points will serve as guidelines for our enquiry, since Ghāsīdāsa's argument develops from this definition into a claim that the world (i.e. all conscious and non-conscious beings) comprises the *Sat*:

Sat ke nām Satloka lā lāye Sāhab
Cāro baran lā tain amrit pilāye Sāhab
(*Panthī*-song)

"Since everything is in all circumstances controlled and supported by the *Sat* (the Supreme Person), and always has the nature of being his subordinate, then all conscious and non-conscious beings are his body":

Sat ke nāh sahab
Kirvaria surtā ke bās

This claim, which summarizes Ghāsīdāsa's *Sat*-doctrine, can now be investigated in more depth.

(1) Firstly we need to understand what Ghāsīdāsa means by referring to *Sat* as a 'conscious being', before going on to consider how the world (*loka*) may be said to belong to him. In depicting *Sat* as the Highest Person (*Sāhab*), Ghāsīdāsa is affirming the authenticity of his tradition. *Sat* is *Brahman* in the real sense. Ghāsīdāsa desires to know *Brahman* (*Brahmajijñāsā*), concerns the Highest Person (*Sat*) as its object. The following passage from a *Panthī-gīt* affirms his claim:

tannā nannā nannā vāre nannā
ek pēr anwarā dusar pēṛ dhanwṛā
nām leke āe sāhab nām lēke āe

In this folk-form Ghāsīdāsa makes it clear that although the term *rām* refers to the outer Self of all things, nevertheless, strictly speaking, it primarily denotes Him who "possesses greatness, of essential nature as well as of qualities, in unlimited fulness". The method he advocates is a form of *bhakti-yoga*[1] integrating the *bhakti* of *Gītā* with the interior contemplation of *Upaniṣads* and a practice of meditation.

I choose to explain a little of Ghāsīdāsa's soteriological teaching at this point because it is the appropriate context for understanding a crucial aspect of his depiction of *Sat* as 'conscious being'. I am referring now to his references to the *rūp ke guṇḍariā son ke dauriā* (*rūpatatva*), i.e., divine form.

This descriptive passage depicting the birth of *Kṛṣṇa* may fruitfully be compared with earlier references to *Sat.* Allusions to seeing (glorious visible), the orb of the Sun (*Sūraj*) and 'rays of thousands of suns' are reminiscent of light symbolism in the Brāhmaṇs, as is the reference to *son ke daurā* (molten gold). The vivid description of the *Sat* (Supreme Person) which follows is remarkably similar to that of the Lord in the *Bhagavad-gītā* (as in these earlier passages the anthropomorphic imagery is counteracted by images of transcendence).

For Ghāsīdāsa's the form of *Sat* has specific functions. Firstly, it is this form that assumes a descent form (*avatāra* of Rāma and Kṛṣṇa*)* to protect and help all devotees. Secondly, it is the *Jait-Khambha* or abode attainable by the devotee. Thirdly, it is *nām* (means or *upāya*) to attain that goal, both as a manifestation of the Lord's grace and also as the object of meditation for aspirants.

The clearest exposition of these functions is given in the *Gītā* (chapter 11), where Arjuna attains a vision of Kṛṣṇa:

> *Paśyāmi tvām durnirīkṣyam samantā-*
> *ddīptānalā–rkadyutiprameyam.*
>
> "I see you, difficult to look at anywhere effulgent like the brightness of the blazing fire and Sun".

This Sun *of Gītā* symbolizes the *Sūraj* of *Satnām.*

The teaching on the divine form of *Sat* (*Brahman*) is profound. It encapsulates the heart of Ghāsīdāsa's spiritual vision, and indicates the nature of transformation experienced by one deeply committed to the task of self-realization — *adharē mā dhotiyā sukhāe* (*Panthī-gīt*). It is not, for Ghāsīdạsa, an undifferentiated experience, but one which integrates each facet of a person's world-view (*mankhē lā jagāya*) into a sense of divine and personal presence. Ghāsīdāsa's description of Kṛṣṇa refers to the self-manifestation of his essential form. To refer to *Sat* as a 'conscious being' is to indicate his essential form as the Self of all beings.

Ghāsīdāsa explains this ontological dependence by having recourse to the *Sāṁkhya* doctrine of *Satkāryavāda,* by which a substance or cause (*kāraṇa*) is transformed in time into a new form or effect (*kārya*), but not into a new substance. In this case, *Sat* in this casual state is transformed into the world, his affected state, without changing the essential nature. As *Sat* (literally 'being'), *Brahman* is the material cause of the universe; in his affected state, he is the operative (or efficient) cause, guiding each new creation in its emergence and dissolution.

While explaining the doctrine of *Satnām,* Ghāsīdāsa describes the world's dependence on *Brahman* in metaphorical terms as a mode-possessor relation. The world belongs to *Rāma* as his 'mode'. His illustration is depicted in the following *Satnāmī* funeral-song:

> The dancing horse is tethered
> in the house with seven stories.
> We were watching by the flickering lamp.
> How the thieves came I do not know.
> From outside they bring the vessels.
> From the house they carry out the corpse.
> Four men have gathered and camp by the lake.
> The messenger has come
> from the land of death.
> You must break the cord and go.
> In the forest your body must
> make its camp.

He illustrates here the characteristics of the body and soul. A body is a 'mode', since it serves as a distinctive feature for a certain substance, namely, a self. And a body can have no function apart from the self.

Thus the *Satnām*-doctrine provides a theological structure to hold together a vision in which the divine and the world are fully integrated, one with the other. It also provides a model for spiritual practice leading to knowledge of *Sat* through coming to know the true nature of one's self and the world.

4.1 *Functions of the* Satnām

While explaining the functions of the *Satnām* I shall take for consideration two hypotheses: first, that the function of the *Satnām* is metaphorical; and secondly, that it becomes a conceptual model for the way Ghāsīdāsa believes things to be.

What does it mean to speak of the *Satnām* as a metaphor ? By metaphor I mean a figure of speech which refers to something in terms of something else, thereby creating a new mode of perception. In this context, the *Satnām* is a metaphor with two sets of association drawn from understandings of the terms *sat* and *nām*.

Metaphors are powerful tools of communication, and religious language abounds with them. This is partly because some things simply cannot be said in a literal way. Metaphors are non-literal ways of presenting things, and none-the-less 'true' for being non-external. The truth of metaphors can only be assessed by their relative appropriateness as interpretative perspectives on reality. And metaphorical expressions, such as *sat mā dīvāl rangāy, sat ke nāh sabad* evoke responses in the hearer which confirm or deny their appropriateness: the 'truth' or meaning of the expressions is realised through appropriating a new way of seeing.

Talk of *Satnām* is similarly powerful as a form of communication. It has a disclosive and evocative character in the preachings of Ghāsīdāsa. He uses it to communicate his visions of the world, his ways of seeing. It becomes for him a method of spiritual teaching, which is his ultimate purpose.

The *Satnām* has a particular role to play in the theological framework of Ghāsīdāsa,[2] and the role is associated with what may be termed a 'root-metaphor'.

This is a metaphor which has become dominant within its contextual usage to the extent that other interpretative perspective of reality has become subordinate to it. Most world-views, consciously held or otherwise, have certain root-metaphors which act as keys to the total perspective. Comprehending such a root-metaphor can lead to an understanding of the world-view as a whole. So in explicating the function of the *Satnām* as root-metaphor in the theology of Ghāsīdāsa reflects his theological world view.

4.2 *Key to* Satnām

Let us look first of all how the *Satnām* in Ghāsīdāsa serves as a root-metaphor. We saw how he defined *Sat* in terms of the Highest Person:

The true guru has come and
built his temple amid the waters
and ensouling the universe;
They made 3608000 divisions
of the temple
And through it
a path for wind.

For Ghāsīdāsa, knowing *Sat* is equated with being granted a vision of transcendent form, and this arises through *caran-darasa,* i.e. *bhakti* and the practice of devotional meditation:

tēhī mēr Ghāsīdās
dhunī lā ramāyē sāhab
Sat kē nām
Sat lok la lāyē sāhab.

In such a vision, or meditative insight, the Lord's form is seen to be of great beauty, incorporating all the elements that together comprise the world, which then appears as his 'body'. This vision of the Lord seen in terms of the world Ghāsīdāsa takes as his key for interpreting the *Sat*-tradition: for us he seems to be a Vedāntin.

4.3 *Gyān ke Panth Kirpān ke Dhārā*

Let us consider firstly the epistemological function of *Satnām*-metaphor. Ghāsīdāsa presents that the means to approach the knowledge (*Sat*) is the means to walk on the edge of the sword: *gyān ke panth kirpān ke dhārā*[1]. This is why he presents the *bhakti-panth* (means of devotion) to attain Him. He presents the Lord in all his transcendent beauty, with the world as his body. The reason for this symbolism, however, is to communicate the possibility of knowing the Lord. This object of reverence, awe and beauty, he says, is the described goal of meditation.[3] To know Him means *dhunī ramānā* (meditating on Him) and worshipping him (*caran me girthē, daṇḍavat karthē*), because *gyān* (the divine knowledge) has the form of direct vision, received through loving devotion (*bhakti*). Continuous sweet remembrance (*Suratā ke bās*) is thus the way to attain the Lord, the means to final release, and Ghāsīdāsa's descriptive picture of Rāma and Kṛṣṇa in all their beauty and glory symbolises this attainment.

4.4 *The Function of* Haṁsa

The ontological function of the *Sat* becomes apparent as Ghāsīdāsa articulates a structural relationship between the two trees, one *anwarā* and the other *dhanwarā: ek peṛ anwarā dusar dhanwarā sāhab*. This relationship is homologous in the sense that there is a parallelism between the two sets of relations. In other words, it is a relationship between different sets of relations, yet the structure of both is identical. In this context we can speak of micro-macro correspondence.

An example of this is to be found in *Satnāmī* death-founds. It explains how the coordination of *tor* (*tvam*) and *mor* (*tat*) expresses both oneness (identity) and difference between the two terms:

> Haṁsa, you must leave the village.
> The five messengers[4]
> have come to his courtyard.
> They have brought the ox-goad
> With the goad they beat the soul.

They break its ribs
and spread it on the way.
O *Jambhạiyā* wait a moment.
The net of love is spread
throughout the world.
Let me tie it in a bundle
Then Haṁsa may leave the village.

As we can see from this, Ghāsīdāsa's precision with language enables him to express the full significance of his analogy. Since Haṁsa is the self of everything, having all this as his village (body), word denoting Haṁsa, for example, refers ultimately to him in the parallel way that word denoting the village refers ultimately to those individual selves. The reason for this is ontological: the body (village) stands towards the embodied self in the relation of a mode of *māyājāl*. In this sense, the body is ontologically dependent upon the self for its very existence.

It is significant to note that Ghāsīdāsa refers to the world as *māyājāl*. This metaphor reveals the world manifesting the *tie* of the *Sat*. The *māyājāl* metaphor thus discloses a vision of the world as divine. Ghāsīdāsa indicates that self-knowledge takes the form of a transformation of awareness or consciousness.

As we have seen, the *Sat* is developed to become a key concept in the framework of Ghāsīdāsa's theology. The *Sat* serves as an analogical model for the true nature of reality. The structural relationship between the *Sat/asat* (*māyājāl*)[5] and the world is presented as homologous to the relationship between the individual person and his or her body. However, the primary defining relationship is the former. In other words, comprehension of the nature of the *Sat* as person determines an understanding of the nature of the human being and of the cosmos. In addition, there is considered to be an ontological continuity between the two sets of relations in the sense that the individual is viewed as a microcosm of the *Sat* totality. Thus there is both a structural correspondence between the divine and human and also an identity of form or nature (*rūpa*).

REFERENCES

1. *Bhakti* is intense love for God. This involves attachment on one side and continuous remembrance on the other. The two are, as it were, the two sides of the same coin.

2. Guru Ghāsīdāsa is famous for the way he had overcome disadvantaged position. For example he had first to overcome consequent depressedness he experienced as an infant. He was fortunate in having his teacher Jagjiwan Das to show him the True Path.

3. The mind of man was compared to a mirror. The extent to which we know really depends on the state of our mind. An impartial and impersonal attitude is necessary to refine the mind and improve the mirror. It is only through meditation.

4. Five vital airs: *prāṇa, apāna, vyāna,* udāna and samāna.

5. The different schools of Indian philosophy have advanced different theories of illusion. According to *Advaita,* illusion is neither real nor non-real. In the illusory perception of silver, it is silver that appears in consciousness, so silver must be the object of this illusion. But this sliver is neither real (*Śat*) nor unreal (*asat*), nor both real and unreal (*Sadasat*), but is undefinable (*anirvacanīya*). This theory is called *anirvacanīyakhyāti.* Māya in the thought of Ghāsīdāsa is not the cosmic illusion of classical Vedanta. The world is indeed *māyājāl,* but it is far from unreal, for it is an illusion only in the sense that it is accepted for what it is not. Delusion is a more appropriate word. The essence of the world is its impermanence. It is real, but it is impermanent, both in the sense that it is itself perishable and in the sense that its attributes cannot follow a person after his physical death.

CHAPTER 5

THE MODEL OF JAIT KHAMBHA

In this chapter it is intended to to present the model of *Satnām* consciousness[1] in Chhattīsgaṛh. The *Satnām* metaphor, when articulated conceptually, provides a key to understand *Satnāmīs*' theological world-view.

In this context it is appropriate to refer to the *Satnām* as a 'model', in that it represents connections made between things in order to help us structure and interpret what we see. Like metaphors, models are intrinsic to our thought-processes: we look on things in terms of other things and act upon their perceived connections. Janet Martin (1985:50-51) makes the distinction: When we use a model, we regard one thing or state of affairs in terms of another, and when we use a metaphor, we speak of one thing or state of affairs in language suggestive of another." Models are thus maps of inner processes. The potential relationship between a model and metaphor is brought out by Janet Martin's (*ibid.*) definition of a model. She says, 'it is an object or state of affairs viewed in terms of its resemblance, real or hypothetical, to some other object or state of affairs' (*ibid.*). She distinguishes two main types of models: those in which the subject of model is also its source, as in a model aeroplane (homoeomorphic models), and those where source and subject differ, as in a discussion of the properties of gases in terms of billiard balls (paramorphic models).

A model is made through its function, or functions, in relation to other things (occurrences, events). Paramorphic models have a particular type of relation to other things in that they provide explanations through their structure, like the billiard ball model of the properties of gases. Of course, the explanations emerge from culturally determined perspectives. Thus a Buddhist may find a model of the wheel, which represents more accurately his or her view of life. A *Satnāmī* may not find this a helpful model, and may prefer, say, a model of the *Jait Khamba*[1] (pillar of victory) which is a useful model because she or he believes this to represent the way things are.[2]

In this sense a model represents a particular way of looking at things. It serves as map of a world-view. As a map, it interprets things in terms of certain features or relationships. It has the potential to create meaning.

Models indicate the structure of things, their constituent interrelationships. Whether in a 'homeomorphic' or 'paramorphic' way, they are intrinsically informative; they are either models 'of' something (a structure) or models 'for' understanding and creating meaning — or both.

In Ghāsīdāsa the S*atnām* metaphor serves to model, in each case, a relational view of reality. The *Satnām* becomes, therefore, a model of consciousness. What we find when we hear *Panthī-gīt*, therefore, is that *Satnām* is a theological model for the differentiated and unitive structure of the consciousness.

Before looking at how the *Satnām* works as a model in the oral poetry of the *Satnāmī* community, let us consider how others have understood this important theological function.

Eric Lott, in his book *Vedāntic Approaches to God* (p. 27), provides a useful Introduction to modelling function of Rāmānuja's body-self-teaching. Julius Lipner perceives body-self model in Rāmānuja to be more complex (1986. 7).

It is precisely in relation to the symbolic power that we can see why metaphors make good models. Metaphors feed upon symbols and express them.

Indeed it is their symbolic roots which give metaphors the power of evocation: they call up associations and experiences which arouse the hearer's own creative imagination. A model which has not first been a metaphor has not the same epistemological potential. It does not have the same power to disclose a way of seeing things. The *Satnām* model is for Ghāsīdāsa a theologically indispensable metaphor. It encapsulates the spiritual insights Ghāsīdāsa wishes to communicate concerning the interrelatedness of all things and, furthermore, in defining the nature of this interrelatedness it provides a structural model of reality which can be appropriated as a model of viewing, and hence experiencing, the world.

The key to the power and realism of Ghāsīdāsa's use of the *Satnām* model is to be found in the fact that it serves as an analogical structure of the consciousness.

The structure of consciousness revealed in Ghāsīdāsa's *Satnām* model is a symbolic structure in which the *Sat* is disclosed to be innermost set or heart of the universe and each thing within it. Ghāsīdāsa actually acknowledges this by referring to *Satlok cali—dehanva-gā.*

It is the symbolic function of the *Satnām* model which gives it power to communicate truths about the way things are. This is because symbols represent and suggest things to us in a language which speaks to the depths of our experience. We can not only 'hear' what is being communicated by symbols, but we have the ability to respond to recreating and resonating with that which is 'heard', thereby consciously aligning ourselves more fully with what is 'given' in our experience of the world.

In other words, *Satnām* not only teaches about the nature of the *Sat*, the nature of the way things are in the world, but also reveals something of this nature to our own consciousness. This is the most powerful form of the theological language because it is potentially transformative. It does not separate the ideas it seeks to express from their symbolic roots. Renewal of spiritual life remains a possibility through such discourse.

In the case of *Satnām*, we can see the application of this structure to individual growth: there is a movement implicit in the model, from the outer spheres or layers of consciousness inwards, towards the common centre of integration. In Ghāsīdāsa, this is presented as an orientation towards the individual's true self (*Haṁsa*), within which *Sat*, the Supreme Self, is to be realised. This is the goal of the individual's spiritual quest.

As a symbolic structure, the *Satnām* is not unique. In fact, it exhibits features of *Jait Khambhas,*[3] which are symbols arising from a collective unconscious. It may be interesting at this point to consider the structure of *Jait Khambha* and its possible relationship with human consciousness, since this may have some bearing upon our understanding of the *Satnām* symbol in Ghāsīdāsa.

The round-shaped pillar in every *Satnām* village forms the concept of *Jait Khambha*. The structure always includes cosmic symbol. These *Jait Khambhas* serve as exterior aids to inner practices of transformation. When visualized, they represent the elements and energies which together constitute ourselves and the world. The practitioner recognises these elements and energies by the white flag and shapes of the *Jait Khambhas*, often matching them with specific sounds. She or he integrates them by progressing gradually from the outer rim of the *Jait Khambhas*, through the gate to the inner 'realms' and finally to the flag—a process involving specific techniques in the transformation of consciousness. White colour here represents Truth. Sometimes round-shaped boat also resembles Truth. This pole or *Jait Khambha* stands for memory. Chanting of *Satnām* is the pedal of words. The creator or the carpenter of the pole is *Brahma*.

In theological terms, the language of metaphors and symbols is close to the apophatic tradition. We cannot say that the *Sat* is X or Y, but we can create symbolic pictures to evoke and communicate our 'sense' of it. This 'sense' of the *Sat* can lead to the creative use of symbolic means of communication which draws upon the very depths of our existence to fashion forms for what is perhaps at the level alone fully known. Ghāsīdāsa drew upon the depths and richness of his receptive spiritual heritage to create a language which would transmit and disclose truth at the levels of symbolic understanding. He used a metaphor of consciousness to communicate the inseparability and integration of the *Sat* (divine) with the *nām* (world): the *Satnām*.

When we analyse the symbolic structure he formed for this purpose, the micro-macro homology is notable. Learning to grasp the significance of this teaching involves total commitment to the spiritual[4] path which leads, ultimately, to a transformed knowledge of perception: a transformed consciousness. From this perspective all things are seen to belong to Rāma, and to manifest his *Satnām*. This vision represents an integration of the differing elements which make up physical and psychological existence, and in this sense the *Satnām* presents holiness in terms of integrated consciousness. The following pages will address the questions of how the *Satnām* also serves as a model of such holiness.

II

I have shown how Ghāsīdāsa in presenting his visions of the world has drawn upon rich symbolic understanding inherent in his tradition. Representations of the *Sat* whose *nām* is the world date back to the Vedic tradition.

One reason why certain symbols appear in different times is quite simply their 'workability'. If a religious symbol is prevalent, it works well for people. By this I mean it has transformative power.

Perhaps the symbol of *Satnām* is of key significance in the *Satnām Panth* because for *Satnāmīs* it has proved to work. In the previous section I said that the *Satnām* presents holiness in terms of integrated consciousness. In this section I would like to consider how it does this, and how the *Satnām* actually works as a model for the transformation of consciousness leading to integration and wholeness. What concerns us now is the way in which Ghāsīdāsa uses the *Satnām* symbol as a tool for attaining the *Sat* and becoming part of it.

5.1 *The Symbol of* Sat[2]

We saw earlier how 'attaining' or knowing the *Sat* is depicted by Ghāsīdāsa in terms of seeing him:

binā dekhe tolā ankhiā jhurāy

This is what the aspiring individual longs for: a vision of the *Sat.* But what does this desired vision comprise? A study of the *Panthī* folk-songs suggests that the *Satloka* (divine vision) is conceived by both in terms of the proper form of *Sat.* It pervades, encompasses and illuminates the world, his *nām.* If we go through the *Satnāmī* oral literature we find passages with a vivid description of *Sat* as a Person of incomparable beauty and splendour (compare the episode of Kṛṣṇa *or* Rāma in *Panthi-gīt*). The two most prevalent themes are of light and lotus blossom. The splendour of the *Sat* is like a mountain of gold; his brilliance is that of a sun; he "shines" in his majesty throughout the three worlds:

tor nām ke diynā jarat hay

The lotus metaphor develops the theme of the *Sat*'s pervasive presence: not only are his eyes and feet like lotus flowers, but the *amrit* (nectar) of his 'loveliness' fills and overflows the whole of existence; and his fragrant holiness 'perfumes' the entire world. The *Satnām*, therefore, comprises a cosmological structure in which the different hierarchies of existence are held together.

Each picture has its own code or symbolic language. For example, the *Satnām* in Ghāsīdāsa is seen "within the sun"[5]. Ghāsīdāsa means that the *Sat* seen "within the sun"[5] is none other than *Brahman.* It is coterminous with the universe.

On closer examination, the *Sat* in each passage is found to have certain features in common. Ghāsīdāsa's Sun image also explains the five divine names. Ghāsīdāsa draws upon a rich symbolism when he speaks of *Sat* having the splendour of a sun. In addition, there are other references to *agni* (fire), denoting purification and contemplative devotion (*dhūnī ramāye*).

The symbol of light is associated in Ghāsīdāsa with the vision of the *Sat.* The focus of vision is a *Satnām* of light, whose beauty evokes awe and adoration. The images of fire and the sun are connected in Ghāsīdāsa's mind, with divine creativity, sacrifice, and the human response of devotion. There appears to be a fundamental link between all of these. They represent different aspects of reality of the material universe.

Light symbolises for him, pure consciousness. Ghāsīdāsa, therefore, discloses the divine vision of the *Sat* (or Rāma) through light symbolism. This is associated with divine consciousness. To see the *Sat* is to see from an enlightened perspective, an illuminated world which is revealed to be *Satnām.*

Such a vision implies a transformative process by which the viewer is enlightened. It represents the transformation of consciousness involved in coming to know the *Sat.* Attaining the divine vision is synonymous with realising *Sat* or consciousness. The limited ego or self-centred world-view is opened out into a universal, infinite perspective, the focus of this new realm being the *Sat,* who is experienced as one's true 'Self' or 'centre' of consciousness.

If these descriptions of the *Sat Lok* (divine vision) represent a transformation of perception and consciousness, then how is this transformation worked out in the lives of individuals? What spiritual practices do Ghāsīdāsa recommend as valuable, or necessary even, for spiritual advancement and personal fulfilment? In the rest of this chapter we shall look at the ways advocated by Ghāsīdāsa to attain the transformation of consciousness effected in the vision of Sat.

The religious practices advocated by Ghāsīdāsa are broadly speaking, devotional in character: *nām* ke *dhajāla phahrāye.* Love of Rāma, and devotion to Kṛṣṇa, the *Sat* is believed, by both, to be a prerequisite for every believer or devotee. We could go further and classify these practices as riualistic, in so far as they entail prescribed acts,[6] physical and mental, pertaining to worship of *Sat.* The attitude and awareness cultivated in this way are intended to be carried over into everyday life.

In fact the individual offers himself and all he has at the *Satnām,* and is encouraged to praise, remember, meditate upon and adore the *Sat* continually, as a form of total self-dedication. Thus the *bhakti* develops in the individual towards the *Satnām,* which is valued for its own sake, which is uninterrupted, which is an absolute delight in itself and which is meditation that has taken the character of the most vivid and immediate vision. It is through such *bhakti* that the *Sat* is attained. Thus *Sat* is practised in daily life. It appears from this that some form of 'taking refuge' in the *Sat* initiates the aspirant (or *Satnāmīs*) into this practice of *bhakti-yoga.*

The spiritual practices advocated by Ghāsīdāsa as conceived, clearly lead to an integration of the individual with *Satnām* (divine consciousness). The results of such practices are referred to in terms of 'seeing' the *Satnām* in the world. This is described symbolically as seeing the *Satnām.* This type of 'seeing' can only be done through the practice of *dhūnī* (meditation).[6] The Lord reveals himself to those who has meditated. The Lord should be focused on continually, either through meditation or prayer. Using Ghāsīdāsa's term I call this a *kirpān ke dhārā.*

Through the practices of meditation, prayer and the sacraments the individual integrates the disparate elements of his or her life. During the act of meditating and participating in the sacraments, the 'true' nature of reality is revealed to the subject. This nature is experienced as a 'seeing' and a 'knowing'. It unites and liberates through the very act of perceiving the world and the *Sat* as one.

The *Satnām* symbolises the change of perception and consciousness. The devotee practises to surrender to the Lord and builds a new 'structure' or pattern of love in daily life. The *Sat* presence is felt to be everywhere, and the individual begins to perceive a correlation between the *Sat* as Self and the 'mass of light', or 'divine milieu' seen to pervade all things. By self-offering, therefore, the individual receives a new 'form' of consciousness, and realises his or her participation in the *nām* of the cosmos which belongs to the *Sat* who is its 'heart'. In this context the *Satnām* becomes both a means and an end. It is a symbolic model of that transformation, and a symbol for that transformation.

If, as I suggest, metaphorical and symbolic language can actually initiate a changed state of perception and consciousness, then these descriptions of the *Satnām* are indeed 'secret' teachings which have still not been explored by the scholars. They are potent symbols which have been proven to be useful in *Satnāmī* tradition.

REFERENCES

1. *citti* (Sanskrit) means consciousness and *acitti* means unconsciousness in Vedic literature. The Chattīsgaṛhi term *Cetāi* denotes the same.

2. The bottom in the *Jait Khambha* is wild and chaotic in appearance, while the upper part is calm and serene; hence the lower part represents *id* and the upper the *ego*, their spatial relationship symbolizing "the triumph of reason over passion".

3. *Jait* may be same as *caitya*, the *Satnāmī* sanctuary representing the *Satnāmī* universe, round with flag on the top. The word *caitya* is associated with *citā* or funeral pyre. *Satnāmīs* give much importance to the worship of the *caitya*. This was a feature unique to Buddhist religion also which means *stūpa*.

4. Ghāsīdāsa's discussion regarding the perception of space is very illuminating.

5. The central fact of man's being is his divinity. This is the bold declaration of *Upaniṣads*. Ringing through the corridors of time, their voice is still heard.

6. Gīta recognizes that human actions, like the animal action, are based on physical needs. They arise from the guṇas of prakṛti.

7. Mind and body are inextricably linked. There are many excellent meditation techniques designed to increase inner awareness and a sense of well-being. In exploring mental techniques it is important to use imagination and decide what is right.

CHAPTER 6

SATNĀM PARADIGM OF SATLOKA

It has been shown in the previous chapters how the *Satnām* symbol[1] functions in the preachings of Ghāsīdāsa. It serves, for both, as a metaphor to disclose an apprehension of reality in terms of the *Sat* (Rāma, the Highest Person). It also becomes an analogical model of an integrated world-view. In other words, the term '*nām*' is extended in its usage to apply to all aspects of reality which together constitute a model, or part of the *Sat*. And since the *Sat* is understood, in both cases, in terms of consciousness, the whole of the material world is presented as being alive and conscious.

The term *Satnām* acts as a root-metaphor for Ghāsīdāsa to disclose this non-dualistic vision. The world is perceived as a part of a *Satnāmic* totality. As a model representing a theological map, the *Satnām* reveals a way of viewing things in terms of relationships: it refers to the interrelated unity of the divine and cosmos at every conceivable level.

This vision encapsulates a pattern of cosmic wholeness. All the layers of life are integrated. The integration is represented symbolically through allusions to the beauty and the transcendence of a divine *Nām*. He is depicted as being both infinite and containable within the space of a human heart.

In the context of the continuing consciousness debate, the *Satnām* vision of Ghāsīdāsa may serve as an example of a useful paradigm for a conscious cosmos. And this is a paradigm with a respected lineage in the history of religion. It offers a way of seeing the world which relates all the elements and inhabitants of our world to one another. Each particular individual or thing is viewed in connection with others and in the context of the whole. Furthermore, consciousness, which is usually attributed only to certain forms of life, is recognised as an inherent structure of every cell, every atom. From this perspective the entire world appears as a multifaceted expression of consciousness.

For Ghaṣīdāsa, the *Satnām* is a symbol which can help transform existing ways of knowing and seeing things. Through practising love and devotion to Rāma, however, he is conceived, through visualizing him around and within us, and through attaining deeper insight and understanding of the sacramental nature of reality, it is possible to begin to perceive the world differently and to allow its inherent 'form' to shine forth. This language communicates the perception of a *Sat* (divine) universality in which all things are seen to be equal and illuminated. In this sense we can speak of a transformed perception.

The *Satnām* symbolises, therefore, the way of a self-transformation.[2] It serves as a cosmological map of consciousness to guide the individual committed to realising his or her *Sat* (truth). In fact, the practice advocated by Ghāsīdāsa reveals that the main object of *Satnām* is the cultivation of *bhakti*. It is *bhakti* which leads to and precipitates the divine vision.

REFERENCES

1. It should be obvious that cultural behaviour can be understood only if the code on which it is based is described, thus allowing us to know what is being communicated and how such messages are to be constructed. The major difficulty with these types of meta-communicative events—as distinct from simple communicative events — is that their reference is to aspects of the cultural code that are by nature quite abstract and, thus, not verbal.

2. Acting in a spirit of free choice, not compulsion, can help to resolve the seeming conflict between self and social expectations. Thus, the *Gītā* recognises two levels of operation in the

self, the lower and the higher. Let a man lift himself by himself. Let him not degrade himself. The (higher) self is one's friend and the (lower) self is one's enemy. For him who has conquered the (lower) self by the (higher) self, the self is a friend. But he who has not gained the higher self, is indeed an enemy of himself (*Gītā* v.5-6). Thus, according to the *Gītā*, the lower self consists of reflexes, bodily needs, feelings and emotions and the higher self manifests itself when the individual has gained full awareness of his needs and limitations.

CHAPTER 7

SATNĀMĪ SPEECH BEHAVIOUR

Chhattīsgaṛhi is the speech of the people of Chhattīsgaṛh who live in the eastern extremity of Madhya Pradesh bordering on Bagheli, Bhojpurī, Oriya, Halbī, Marathi, Gondi and Bundeli. Its speakers number is approximately 10 million.

Chhattīsgaṛhi is a delightful, vigorous and flexible language in its wit and punch, remarks Elwin (1946. XLVII). It often reminds him of Elizabethan English and especially of Shakespeare's prose. Technically it is a dialect of eastern Hindi, the language of Rāma, and its allied dialect *Awadhī* has a notable literature including the *Rāmacaritamānasa* of Tulsīdās.

Chhattīsgaṛhi[1] is the common, standard, name, but the language is also known as *Khalṭāhī*, the tongue of the lowlands, to the hill-people and as *Lariā* to the Oriya-speakers of the east. It is spoken in its purest form in Raipur, Bilaspur, and the west of Sambalpur. But it is also spoken in considerable purity, in Kanker, Nandgaon, Khairāgarh, Chhuikhadān, Kawardhā, in the north-east of *Chāndā* and in the east of Bālāghāt. The Chhattīsgaṛhi of Śaktī, Raigaṛh and Sārangaṛh, though slightly affected by Oriya, is of high standard. In northern Bastar, it is competing successfully with Gonḍī and Halbī. In Koreā, Surgujā, Udaipur and western Jashpur it appears as the Surgujiā sub-dialect (Grierson, 1904. VI.24). In the Bindrā-Nawāgaṛh and Khariār region Chhattīsgaṛhi is considerably mixed by Oriya and by vague recollections of Gondi; in the western areas Marathi and Gondi have been at work in it. Yet everywhere, as I know from personal experience, Chhattisgaṛhi-speaker soon finds himself at home.

The forms that strike a stranger who is familiar only with pure eastern Hindi, says Grierson (*ibid.*), are the sign of the Dative–Accusative which is often *lā* even in the Accusative and the plural termination *man.* But he considered that Chhattisgaṛhi did not differ from the Bagheli dialect so much as was commonly supposed and maintained that if a Chhattīsgaṛhi speaker was set down in Baghelkhand he would find himself at home with the language of the locality in a week. The termination of the past tense in *-is,* as in *Kahis,* (he said) or *māris* (he struck), which is what everybody notices in Chhatisgarhi, is pre-eminently the typical shibboleth of a speaker of eastern Hindi and is commonly heard in Calcutta from servants belonging to Oudh or in Bombay from the *Bhaiyās* of Uttar Pradesh. The use of *o* instead of *e* for the oblique of the personal pronouns —*mor, tor,* 'my', 'thy' — is found in all the eastern Hindi dialects, so is the past tense *bhaye,* 'was', and the use of *rahanā* for the past imperfect, as in *dekhat raheun,* 'I was seeing'. Other particularities are the instrumental in *-an* as *bhukan,* 'by hunger', and the addition of *-har* to a noun to give definition as *garhar,* the neck. To indicate the plural *sab, jamā* may be prefixed with or without *man.* Thus *jamā puto man,* 'the daughters-in-law'. An old form of the plural ends in *ān,* thus *bail,* a bullock, plural *bailān.* In declension the following postpositions are added to the noun which itself remains unchanged: *ka,* 'to'; *la,* 'for'; *bar,* 'for'; *se,* 'by', 'from'; *ke,* 'of'; *ma,* 'in'. The *ke* of the genitive does not change; for example—*laikā* , 'a boy; *laikā-kā,* 'to a boy'; *laikā ke,* 'of a boy'; *laikāman ke,* 'of boys'. There is no difference between the conjugation of the transitive and of intransitive verbs. The construction of the past tense is always active, not passive. The syllables *ech* and *och,* meaning 'even' and 'also', are profusely used in ordinary conversation. Thus *dāich-kā* 'even to the mother', *toroch,* 'thine also'.

Differences in Chhattīsgaṛhi speech distinguish at least 21 sub-groups in society from one another (Dube 1983). The social structure of Chhattīsgaṛhi villages is determined by Hindu caste membership with Brāhmans at the top, then Rājputs, Vaiṣyas, and several groups of artisans and labourers lower down. At the bottom are the untouchable castes. Previously *Satnāmīs* were restricted to living in certain neighbourhood and had less freedom to move in the village than did members of the upper castes. Upper caste-members who used to mix with *Satnāmīs* (as Sunderlal Sharma of Rājim) were indicted and humiliated.

So far as Chhattīsgaṛhi is concerned it has been promoted to serve as a 'standard' for the whole Chhattīsgaṛhi communities. It has come to be used as a model for speakers of other varieties. However, the *Satnāmī* variety of Chhattīsgaṛhi restricted only to *Satnāmī* group is quite unlike the variety (varieties) spoken by some other groups, while all the 21 varieties are still the varieties of Chhattīsgaṛhi dialect. In such circumstances we may appreciate why the influential groups in Chhattīsgaṛhi society prefer standard variety to another and why that has a favoured position in the society.

The standard variety of Chhattīsgaṛhi is 'better' only in a social sense; it has a preferred status, it gives those who use it certain social advantages, and it increases their life chances. *Satnāmī* variety tends to produce the opposite effect. These are some of the consequences that follow from elevating standard variety and denigrating the *Satnāmī* variety.

Many people in Chhattīsgaṛh believe that upper caste Chhattīsgaṛhi is better than the *Satnāmī* Chhattīsgaṛhi is, e.g., that standard Chhattīsgaṛhi is particularly beautiful, *Satnāmī* is a depressed jargon, standard Chhattīsgaṛhi is more expressive, *Satnāmī* is deficient, and so on. In other words, it is widely believed that one can be advantaged or disadvantaged not just socially or aesthetically, but also cognitively i.e. intellectually, by the accident of which dialect or variety of a dialect one happens to speak. Thus *Satnāmī* is the sub-dialect of a disadvantaged group in Chhattīsgaṛh.

So far *Satnāmī* is concerned, certain characteristics of it are clear indicators of *Satnāmī* group membership. For example, *Satnāmīs* do not make certain phonological contrasts that speakers of all other castes make. *Satnāmīs* and *Rāmnamīs* also lack certain phonological contrasts made by all others, and some, in attempting to make such a contrast, actually hyper-correct, that is, they over-extend a particular usage in trying to emulate others. *Satnāmīs* have a characteristic morphological variation in the past tense of the first person pronoun, such as standard Chhattīsgaṛhi *rahen* (we were) becomes *rehan* in *Satnāmī. Satnāmī* has a marked distinction at the accent system which places it as a distinct variety. *Satnāmīs* address2 in-group members by uttering '*Satnām*', while others say '*Rām-Rām*[1]'.

The isolation of *Satnāmī* community from other *Chhattīsgaṛhi* communities produced certain differences in verbal as well as non-verbal communication patterns with the *Satnāmī* culture.

Not every *Satnāmī* exhibits every feature in his non-verbal behaviour. However, these features occur with such great frequency in the *Satnāmī* population that they can be considered pattern behaviour. The same is true of the *Satnāmī* who speaks *Stanāmī* sub-dialect will have all the features of this sub-dialect in his speech.[3]

7.2 Satnāmī *Non-verbal Patterns*

Although much research has been done on verbal communication patterns[4] of the people of Chhattīsgaṛh, little research has been directed toward their non-verbal communication. The research of Grierson (1890), Hīrālāl Kāvyopādhāya (1880), Menzel (1939), Tailang (1966), Kāntikumār (1969), Naendradeo Vermā (1979), Shankar Shesh (1973), Tārā Shuklā (1976), Mannūlāl Yadu (1979), Vyās Nārāyana Dube (1983) and others on the verbal communication patterns of Chhattisgarhī has demonstrated that many *Satnāmīs* speak a variety of Chhattisgaṛhi that differs from other varieties of Chattisgarhi. The existence of *Satnāmī* Chhattīsgaṛhi or non-standard *Satnāmī* sub-dalect (it has been given these labels) has been conclusively demonstrated; thus it can be expected that non-verbal communication patterns in the *Satnāmī* sub-culture, too, differ from those in the dominant culture or other Chhattisgarhi sub-cultures. Indeed, many of those who have researched verbal patterns (particularly Narendradeo Vermā) have commented on this difference. The purpose of this section is to describe some of these non-verbal communication patterns of *Satnāmi* people and the meanings these non-verbal patterns convey.

The hypothesis that *Satnāmī* sub-dialect has a different base of development fromother varieties of Chhattisgarhi (even though it is similar to other varieties of Chhattīsgarhi and it shares many common features) can be extended to non-verbal communication patterns. That is, non-verbal communication patterns in the *Satnāmī* culture that are not commonly exhibited by other Chhattīsgarhians possibly have their origins in antipode-non-verbal communication patterns. This does not mean that all non-verbal communication patterns of *Satnāmī* people differ from those of other Chhattisgarhians. As with dialect patterns, *Satnāmīs* share many non-verbal patterns with other Chhattisgaṛhīs. Years and years of isolation of the untouchables from touchables could have produced alternations in these original non-verbal patterns, and separation could have produced entirely new patterns unrelated to elite patterns.

The focus here will be on those non-verbal patterns that have been labelled *āngika abhinaya* or (kinesics) by Bharata. Specifically, kinesics refers to how people send messages with their bodies through movement, expression, gestures, etc. Shukla (1993) has pointed out that these non-verbal patterns are a learned form of communication which are patterned within a culture, and that they convey a particular message. Some of these patterns that are unique to the *Satnāmī* population and the messages they convey are described below.

Not every *Satnāmī* exhibits every feature in his non-verbal behaviour. The same is true of *Satnāmī* sub-dialect features. Not every *Satnāmī* who speaks *Satnāmī* sub-dialect will have all the features of this sub-dialect in his speech.

In stress or conflict situations, *Satnāmīs* express with their eyes an insolent, hostile disapproval of the person who is in the authority role. The eyemovement here is in '*Vivartana tārā* (rolling eyes).

'Vivartana tārā' is a non-verbal way of expressing impudence and disapproval of the person who is in the authority role and communicating every negative label that can be applied to the dominant person. The movement of the eyes communicates all or parts of the message. The movement is very quick, and it is often unnoticed by the person, particularly if the other person is non-*Satnāmī.*

Satnāmīs will often roll their eyes when being reprimanded or 'lectured to' about some infraction of a rule. Rolling the eyes can also be used to express a kind of general disapproval.

Many *Satnāmīs* may have the "reluctance" through the eyes. They do not look another person in the eye, if the other person is in an authority role. To look another person in the eye (in the context of the dominant culture) is a non-verbal way of communicating trust worthiness, forthrightness, masculinity, truthfulness, sincerity, etc.

Avoiding eye contact to communicate respect and acknowledgement of one's being in a subordinate role is a common pattern in Chhattīsgaṛh.

The walk[5] of young *Satnāmī* males communicates the same non-verbal message as that of young non-*Satnāmī* males. In addition, the *Satnāmī* male is egoistic. Some young *Satnāmīs* vary the speed or swing of the head or effect a slight limp or alter any one or a number of the components of the *Satnāmī* walk to achieve elitism.

The walk is also used as a hostile rejection of another person in a conflict situation.

Another non-verbal behaviour pattern easily noticed in *Satnāmī* male group discussion is the way males punctuate laughter. Often when something funny is said by a *Satnāmī*, the audience will raise a cupped hand to the mouth and laugh. The non-verbal message is that the audience has acknowledged the particularly witty statement of the speaker.

One of the most friendly greetings that can be given to another *Satnāmī* is to walk up to him and verbally greet him with "*Satnām*".

The non-verbal behaviour described here provides some illustration of the non-verbal communication patterns of *Satnāmī* people that are different from those of non-*Satnāmīs.* We will discuss the *āhārya* language (the object language) of *Satnāmīs* in the next pages.

In *Sātnāmī* religious thought a sense of bodily aesthetics is linked to an inner harmony of the soul. Here in *Satnāmī* community, a whole language of body art has developed in which feelings, aesthetic sense and cultural attitudes are expressed by colourful designs, oils, fragrances and hairstyles. The body has become a kind of model of society, which aesthetically communicates customs and role relationships from individual to individual.

Hair is used in ritual and magic since it is seen as an extension of the whole person. Tattoos, scarification and painting provide signs of group belonging. Among *Satnāmīs,* the rules of hygiene and eating habits are closely connected with religious beliefs. Every *Satnāmī* wears the white-coloured sacred thread. White is the colour of purity, enlightenment, innocence for the *Satnāmīs*; the flag over their *Jait Khambha* is also white.

The matter goes even deeper. Body painting, sacred cord wearing, even hairstyles, are concerned with the perennial questions all human beings have asked: Who am I? Who are we? As long as there is an attempt to find an answer, people will continue to make up. A sane perception of self is closely linked with a sane perception of the body.

Beyond the tasks of understanding and interpreting the process of speech behaviour, we should also explain what passes between *Satnāmī* society and individuals. To put it in the abstract formula, we will find in Chhattīsgaṛhi a medium by which action reproduces or transforms social system. Chhattīsgaṛhi is also the medium by which the Chhattīsgaṛhi society constitutes meaning and limits of action. Much depends on whether particular speakers can learn the registers. The authority and credibility of particular speakers depends on the survival of traditional beliefs whose claim can match the authority on matters of life and death. The ability of an individual (say Guru Ghāsīdāsa) to challenge effectively the authority of a social system also depends on whether the individual's faith is spoken with the authority of a particular religious community (say *Satnāmī*) and not of the person alone. Being this, Guru Ghāsīdāsa provides the boundary between the *Sat* and *nām*.

Satnām has guaranteed the authority of speaker: a relationship between religion and language so common as to appear commonplace when put in so many words. Take, for instance, the traditional *Satnām* formula still used in Chhattīsgaṛh. Not only does the use of *Satnām* illustrate the operative function of religious speech: the name thus invoking the divine presence, the use of *Satnām* carries great authority.

REFERENCES

1. Scholars enumerate 21 sub-groups in Chhattīsgaṛhi with a distinct variety. These sub-dialects are emblems or badges of the dialect-aggregates and also are as badges of identity for Individual Chhattīsgaṛhi people. Badges and emblems of identity can be seen as a kind of message, the successful transmission, reception, and decoding of which is necessary to the interaction taking place.

2. In principle a greeting must occur between any two persons who are visible to each other. Out on the road, in the fields, or if someone is entering a compound yard, a greeting must occur if one party must make a wide detour (perhaps hundreds of yards outside the village) to accomplish it. In the village centre, a large open plaza which usually has many people sitting about, one must greet all those whom one passes within a distance of about a hundred feet.

3. The notion of 'speech' is vastly extended from its usual narrow meaning to encompass not merely verbal–non-verbal forms of human behaviour, but such cultural products as clothing style, architecture, cooking and so on; all are regarded as patterned sets that may be decoded, and may thus be regarded as analogous to human communication by means of signals, signs and symbols.

4. Standard non-verbal patterns may be enumerated as following: proximics, kinetics, paralinguistics, haptics, chronemics, oculesics, olfaction, gustation, music postures, orientations, etc. (Shukla 1994).

5. The average adult walks at a speed of three miles an hour. The way one moves is affected by a number of criteria—and watching the way people walk can provide interesting clues to personality. Posture, speed, and the kind of stride being taken all vary, not only with levels of fitness and body type but also with mood and emotion.

CHAPTER 8

THE FOREST OF SYMBOLS

Although it is clear that many *Satnāmī* folk-songs possess symbolic content, research on symbolic poetry tends to focus upon the meaning imparted by individual poems in isolation. It is proposed that meanings of many poems are in part derived from their occurrence, or expected occurrence, with other poems in the inventories of prototypical roles. Sets of poems, although functionally, unrelated, may none the less possess symbolic complementarity; these are used to define socio-religious roles and/or situations, and *Satnamis*' spiritual realities are structured according to the message communicated by Ghāsidāsa.

Although it is clear that many poems possess symbolic meaning for the *Satnāmīs,* it is also apparant that in many cases no single poem in isolation defines a *Satnām* concept. Instead, *Satnāmīs* look to the total collection of cues in the environment to decode the meanings present there and to structure their behaviour accordingly.

Group identity can be conceived as coalescing around forms of expressive symbolism. The self-definitions of *Satnāmī* group members are derived from the common symbol[1] system to which the group is dedicated: these symbols define the group's personality.

Finally, a brief description of symbolism is in order. Following Turner (*The Forest of Symbols: Aspects of Ndembu Ritual,* Ithaca, 1967), the symbol is the smallest unit of ritual retaining specific properties of ritual behaviour. Symbols are polysemous, their references are linked by association and their meanings are polarized. A denotational and connotational cluster surrounds a pole of gross physiological reference (say *Jait Khambha* in *Satnām*). This sensory pole arouses emotions, desires and feelings. A similar cluster surrounds a pole of cognitive or ideological reference. The normative pole promotes moral and social norms and values. The juxtaposition of the grossly physical with the structurally normative produces a profound effect: norms and values become saturated with emotion while emotions are ennobled through contact with values. The *Jait Khambha* is effectively condensing referents to vigorous *Satnāmī* approach. Thus, symbols function as both storehouse and power-house, encoding information which is ultimately authoritative. For Turner, symbols have ontological status, in so far as they precipitate social action.

Perhaps the most technical device of Chhattīsgaṛhi poems is their symbolism. This is only an extension into verse of the habits of ordinary life, for people actually do converse all day long in symbols. When a man has daughters to marry he tells his friends that he has *kodon* in his house; when he goes to ask for a girl in marriage he says that he has come for a gourd in which to put his water or for a flower to put in his hair. In Bastar a boy does not ask his girl directly for her favours but begs her to give him some tobacco.

This symbolic method is found everywhere in Indian folk-poetry. Two excellent examples come from the Punjab Rasalu legend. When Raja Rasalu returns home, he speaks to Rānī Kokilan in a way that closely blends reality and symbolism:

Who hath used my well Rani? The brim of my well is wet, Rani.
I was dying of thirst, Rājā; and thus brim of the well is wet, Rājā.
Who hath eaten my mangoes, Rānī? The rinds are fresh, Rānī.
The gardener's wife brought them, Rājā, and so the rinds are fresh, Rājā.

who hath bathed on my stool, Rānī? The splashing bath spread afar, Rānī.
I was hot and bathed, Rājā, and the splashing spread afar, Rājā.
Who hath lain on my bed, Rānī? The cords of my bed are loosened, Rānī.
I was in great pain and lay on it, Rājā:
and so the cord of thy bed are loosened Rājā. (Turner III, 224).

Another example of this symbolism occurs in the speech of Hīrā, the deer, after Rājā Rasalu had cut off its ears and tail because he was jealous of his wife's affection for it:

I am a deer of the dark mountain and have come down from it.
I have not drunk the water of thy well, nor have I eaten the grass of thy pasture.
Without fault hast thou shorn ears and tail, for no fault is proved against me.
Thou shalt know my name to be Hīrā, the deer,
when I bring a robber to my place.

(Temple III, 234)

Again in the Punjab version of the *dholā* story, the princess Marwan writes a letter to her lover (Turner II, 295). Here is combined direct statement, ordinary simile and symbolism.

The Chhattīsgaṛhi poem, besides helping to explain the image in the Chhattīsgaṛhi one, handles this image in a way that is stepping stone between the early Chhattīsgaṛhi method and that of modern poetry; for the comparison is linked to the question with which the poem ends only by a frail pharse *dosre,* which means probably 'so' or 'thus'. To put in a "like" or "as if" where there is none in the original, is to alter the whole character of a song.

Similarly long poems are given by Verrier Elwin in the *Baiga* (London 1939, page 257) and in the following dialogue between a boy and a girl the lover's wishes are at each stage demonstrated by parallel references to forest life:

Boy : You have drawn water from the well,
You are standing in your garden.
How am I to come to you, my friend ?

Girl : Wrap up your supper in parsā leaves,
And come and sit with me, O friend.

Boy : I want to cut my bewar, but I can't find an axe.
I have searched through all the village.
But there is not one girl unmarried.

Girl : When you take your pipe, how the smoke puffs
out of your mouth !
on yonder hill two Baiga boys are fighting
over me.

Boy : When I drive an arrow, I do not miss.
To-night I will make you cry
holding your head in your hands.

Girl : I can see your bones sticking through your skins.
Who are you to make me cry ?

Boy : Whenever I go to cut wood in the forest
I will always think of you, my friend.

Girl : In my red sāṛi I go there every day.
But all you remember is that
I belong to another.

Boy : I am going to the forest to get a beehive.
You have lovers inside your own clan.

Girl : I'm going to the bazar to buy a cloth.
You think of nothing but your own pleasure.

Boy : I'm going to the forest to dig roots.
Tell me truly, will you come or no?

Girl : You have climbed half-way up the hill.
And now for weariness you throw yourself down.

Boy : How silent and lonely is this jungle?
Who is there to see anything we do?

In this poem, '*cutting bewar*', '*driving an arrow*, '*cutting wood*','*getting a bee-hive*', '*buying a cloth*', '*digging roots*', '*climbing the hill*', are all images of the encounter of lovers.

Among the tribes of the Maikạl Hills, a whole poem is often only the pairing of two images — the first line symbolizing an aspect of the second:

He bent the mango branch and twisted it.
I have wept for desire of my slender-waist love.
The gun is crooked, the bullets are soft.
Though others think you mad
how sweet are your words to me.
The long-nosed rat wanders
all over the new house.
You wander everywhere after me.

(Elwin and Hivale, 1944, 102)

Similar examples occur again and again in the *Folk-Songs of Chhattīsgaṛh* (by Elwin, 1946):

You have broken
The golden pitcher.
where did you lose
your lusty youth? (1)
In the new field
I have sown *Kodon* and rice.
My uncle's daughter
Is a field untilled. (2)
I cut up and ate

the ripe mango.
I understand
The pretty girl. (3)
The ploughman is driving
his bullocks over there.
To enjoy its woman
The rat scampers to the bill. (4)
The flood comes down
In swirling eddies
My love, to see you
I have climbed a tree. (5)
O lovely girl
The flowers grow quickly.
And we who once were small
Are ready now for love. (6)

In many Oraon poems the actual subject of the poem was never referred to and one who was neither an Oraon nor versed in Oraon poetry, the poem apparently possessed a meaning quite the contrary of its actual signification:

In the fields at Sissai
The bear does not drink water
The bear comes
The bear comes.

(Archer, *The Blue Grove*, London 1940, 123).

The subject of this Oraon poem is not a bear but a bridegroom. Here, the traditional acceptance of certain symbols makes possible a sensitive relation between 'art' and the 'community'.

In a note in *New Verse* (February-March, 1936) Geoffrey Grierson referred to *Songs of the Forest* (by Hiwale and Elwin, London, 1935) 'as typically instructive' and added: 'Poems such as the Rain Song (86)':

Gently, gently falls the rain,
In the courtyard, moss has gathered,
A little orphan girl has slipped on it.
The old mother has run to catch her
But she has caught hold
of the branch of the mango tree.

Or Poem 106.

On the mountain of red earth,
A green parrot had its home.
On this side lived a pigeon,
On that side lived a mainā.
The one was sold for five rupees,
The other went for ten.
On the mountain of red earth,
A green parrot had its home.

are element poems. Blake turned the element of English folk-song into great poetry which was individual and communal.These *Gond* poems are elements for us in the same way elements, as Eskimo carvings or Azilian painted pebbles are now for the sculptor and the painter. Of Munda poetry Hoffman writes.

The Mundas exhibit a marked predilection for clothing their ideas so completely in similes and symbols always taken from nature as it surrounds them, that an alien might understand every word of a song without as much as guessing what idea the song is meant to convey. Songs of this kind they call *banitā kāji*, "fictions" or *jonoka kāji* "word measures", a piece where the ostensible words are used as a measure or counterpart of something not expressly stated. They will symbolize the idea by translating it into a different order of nature, sometimes in its more striking outlines, sometimes into its details and leave to the listner the task of applying the simile, and of feeling and dreaming himself into the emotion the poet intends to stir up by the picture he presents. Many of these similes are chosen with a genuine poetic instinct and with a correctness which reveals depth of feeling as well as a close and appreciative observation of nature." (Hoffmann, *J. Mundari Poetry, Music and Dance,* Mem. A.S.B., Vol. II, 1907, p. 105).

W.G. Archer (*The Blue Grove*, London, 1940, 100) has studied the Oraon method of symbolism with great insight. He describes how Oraon marriage poems use the twin-leaves of image system—the poems being apparently about subjects of nature, but actually referring to aspects what the different symbols mean and thus ensure that the people will always be alive to the method that is used. Sometimes a slight distortion is used to expose the second meaning. A fig tree blossoms becomes a girl because its scent spreads for forty miles. A calf become a girl because it belongs to mother and in this way part of the object symbolized is added to the image symbolizing it and the system appears through the distortion. In many poems however, there is no distortion and the second level is detected by the marriage context in which the poems are used and by the employment of pantomimic images.

Wild buffaloes and cobras are equated with opposing relatives because their actions are similar. The action of a bridegroom's party in descending on the girl's house is paralleled in a line of storks descending on a river or a flock of sparrows settling on a tree. A leaping member of the bridegroom's party acts like a frog. The action of negotiators in choosing round a girl resembles bees round a flower and spiders on a web. In these poems the marriage context suffices to show that the images are pantomimic and the accuracy of the pantomimic exposes the symbol.

> 'In the poems which relate to the bride and the bridegroom the clue remains in the context, but the types of symbol vary more widely. Those of the bridegroom consist either of colour analogies (the green parrot) or power images (the bear, the tiger, the other). In the case of the bride, certain images are based on the composition of qualities. Doves, pigeons, wild geese and fish for instance, possess varying qualities of elegance and speed which resemble the grace or flirtatiousness of a girl: while calves and fawns resemble a girl in their weakness and dependence. Certain other images such as brinjals, mangoes, figs and bamboos are based on sexual parallels — the connection being either visual or through a fertility power.

'In all the poems it is marriage context — the presence of an audience for a marriage purpose — which enables the images to be used without explanation and in fact to form an image system. They do not need to refer to the objects they symbolize because the occasion itself makes the audience see them as symbols'.

W.V. Grierson's beautiful version of a Muria poem consists entirely of a long series of parallel images:

Lejā, lejā, O dear vine,
take my one-stringed fiddle
To the flooded river,
plunge in and play with it. (1)

Lejā lejā, O sliced gourd,
in the long days that have passed
since I last saw you,
you have grown plump and lovely. (2)

Rain has fallen and fallen,
the pond is brimming.
But, dear one,
Do not touch me,
for my heart jumps to see you. (3)

We have been separated long,
too long, my darling,
And now, lejā, O lejā,
we must live together. (4)

Beloved I'm carried away by the pockmark
on your dark, shining face,
But the glossy hair on your dear head. (5)

Throw a fiddle at the plum-tree,
and the fruit will fall.

But who will soften the Englishman
to the tale of our love. (6)

My tender fern,
he is not our Bastar-born king
who would listen to our tale,
and you would walk before him. (7)

In your loveliness,
and melt him to sympathy!
Lejā, lejā, O wild berry,
would you leave me. (8)

Lejā, lejā, though, wealth of my heart,
I know that you are not mine,
nor for me touch, yet
Lejā, O lejā, desire will flare
in your heart;
will you then come for a while
to my house. (9)

Lejā, lejā, O wealth of my heart
the summer rains have soaked the fields,
the rains of June.
My heart blazes with passion,
my flower
Let go my loin-cloth a moment;
the white girl is coming. (10)

Lejā, lejā, sweet bug of my bed
what have you done to me?
I see you, and all our past love
leaps to remembrance. (11)

Why though you snuggle do you struggle,
why cry and try

To keep yourself back,
though I've tumbled you down. (12)

Lejā, lejā, give in, give in,
shining bow,
or, by the mother,
my love will become hate. (13)

Lejā, lejā, sweet saunterer,
Lejā, O love,
Lend me your jewels
for me to go to Jagdalpur. (14)

Lejā, lejā, O love,
you will remember your promise
For as the deer leaves tracks
I have left an itch in your body,
And I shall learn how to tell
English ruler about you. (15)

The wild beans and berries
have dried up under the hill,
But your memory came fresh
there to me at night,
And I could not sleep,
Lejā, O lejā ! (16)

ye de, O little gold fish
O shining brow,
Do not cry over
what happened last night;
Lejā, lejā come, dear vine,
let us enjoy ourselves first
And then, if you will, tell the foreigner. (17)

The rain is falling,
sweet bug of my bed,
Why should I listen
to your silly pleading?
Why are you striving and crying,
pulling and pushing?
You'll be all right,
yes, you' ll be all right. (18)

There, there, sweet bug of my bed
dear wild berry,
Lend me your plough and bullocks,
And I will sow
a crop of maize. (19)

Lejā, lejā, re lejā re,
who will play my one-stringed fiddle?
All night I thought about you.
Come and plunge
and play in my pool !
I will play with you,
as a shuttle flashes
through the warp of a loom. (20)

Listen, O listen to the pouring rain of June,
The wild beans and berries
have gone dry under the hill,
And you tell me to sing to you about God.
God is everywhere in the world,
but your singer,
your singer, my flower,
is with you in Bastar. (21)

Lejā, lejā, re lejā re,
sweet saunterer,

my berry, my plantain-tree
you knew,
One who walks on the edge of Gangāmuṇḍā lake
is bogged in the mud;
But that mud is the place
For sowing rice seeds,
Lejā, lejā, O lejā. (22)

ye de, burn, my berry, burn
my only jewel,
And think and long for the night.
The tall plantain-vine bears
a fine cluster of fruit.
Be ready for me,
dear bug of my bed,
Comb and decorate your hair,
my only jewel for tomorrow.
Desire will fire me
and I shall come back to you. (23)

(Grierson, "A Leja, or love-song of the Murias of the Amabal Pargana of Bastar State," *New Verse*, Feb-March, 1937, No.29, 17-19)

In the Bilaspur version of the Rasalu legend there are similar remarkable passages where the sexual act is indicated by symbols; unless the reader has the key to the method he can have little idea of what is intended. Here we find natural objects not only symbolizing the act of life, but providing a sympathetic setting for it. With these passages may be compared the beautiful account of people sleeping in the *Bengal Ballads*, 'The Blind Lover'.

'It was the dead hour of night. Reclining on its bed of leaf the flower-bud lay silently asleep, and on the bossom of the flower the bee slept sweetly. One of the breasts of the king lay the queen like a loose garland of flowers unconscious in sleep' (Sen, *Eastern Bengal Ballads*, Calcutta, 1923-32, IV.229).

In Chhattīsgaṛh we could not escape the conviction that sexual love has a deep and spiritual significance. There is nothing with which we can better compare the 'mystic union' of the finite with its infinite ambient — that one experience which proves itself and is the only ground of faith—than the self-oblivion of earthly lovers locked in each other's arms, where 'each is both'. Physical proximity, contact, and interpenetration are the expressions of love, only because love is the recognition of identity. These two are one flesh, because they have remembered their unity of spirit. This is moreover a fuller identity than mere sympathy of two individuals; and each as individual has now no more significance for the other than the gates of heaven for one who stands within. It is an algebraic equation where the equation is the only truth, and the terms may stand for anything.

Because the stages of human love reflect the stations of spiritual evolution, it is said that the relationship of hero and heroine reveals an esoteric meaning, and this *Sat* (truth) has been made the basis of the well known allegories of Rāma and Sītā, Rādhā and Kṛṣṇa in the *Panthī*-folk-songs of *Satnāmis.* Here love becomes the very type of salvation. The interpretation of this mystery, however, is so well-known as to need no elaboration. But there is a related cult, which is called *Satnām*, the adherents of which sing mystical songs also. These mystical songs are very much semioticized.

8.1 *The Songs relating to conception, child-birth*

Songs about pregnancy are not very common in Chhattīsgaṛh, but there are certain songs in Kharia during which people dance round wife and husband throwing ashes over them and fanning them with brooms and peocock's feathers while they sing:

O Sun, Moon ! O Rām-lakhan !
May the woman bear
twelve sons and twelve daughters.

The *Satnāmī*-song to avert miscarriage has been quoted by Elwin (1946.5). For this a magical remedy such as the string of a bed knotted ten times or indeed anything that is well tied up (it must, of course, be undone before delivery) is bound about the waist and the people sing:

Day and night the stream flows under the moon.
The true Guru has come
and built the temple amid the waters.
The river is very deep
no one can find the bottom
of the dark pool.
How has he built the temple
in the middle of the stream ?
Where has the boat come from,
and where the pedal?
O carpenter, how did you make them
in the middle of the stream ?
The boat is truth,
the paddle of the word,
the bamboo-pole of memory.
It was on the full-moon day
that the carpenter made the temple.
Where is the lime and whence the cloth?
How did they stick together?
The bricks are the father's
The stone are the father's
By the mother they were stuck together.
It was on the full-moon day
That the carpenter built the temple.
Where is the lime and where the cloth?
How did they colour the walls?
The lime is of silver
The cloth is of Rāma,

With truth they coloured the walls.
In the walls they set the bones, here and there,
and tied them inside.
They made 3608000 divisions of the temple
And through it a path for wind.

8.2 A Chhohar-mangal *Song*

After the birth of a child, the *Satnāmīs* perform a ceremony to ensure its happiness in the world and give it a name. They sing the following *Chhohar-mangal* song:

Where have you come from, little one?
Where were you staying before?
Today where have you made your camp?
I come from the sky
Till now I was staying in the belly
Today I have camped on earth.
You come down to the world
With your little fists clenched.
You have forgotten the five divine names.
You have forgotten them in love of your new home.
The *Semur* tree climbs up to heaven,
Its cotton flies into the sky
and whirls about the world.
Where will it find rest?

The expression of this song is made explicit in Chapter 6. The thought process is beautifully presented here. The child who is camping on earth, only camping on a temporary home: his forgetfulness of the divine names is love of this lovely but quickly passing world; the baby breaking from the womb as the silk-cotton bursts from the pod of the bombax-tree and is tossed and whirled through life by the wind of fortune. Every element is awfully semioticized.

8.3 *Satnāmī Death-dialogue*

In classical Hinduism, Yama is the God of Death. He lives in the underworld and his city is Yamapura or, as the Chhattīsgaṛhi peasant shortens it, Jampur. His messengers, here as in the classics, are the *Yamadūta* who go forth to fetch souls to the ghostly city. But there is no reference here to the two dogs of Yama who, with their four great eyes and gaping nostrils, also play the part of the heralds of death. Indeed, the people—especially the aboriginals— are not entirely sure about these messengers: many of them consider them to come from Bhagvān rather than from Yama, who introduced death into the world who punishes the guilty.

But it is difficult to generalize about the theological views of many types of people scattered over a great area. The general setting of the song is clear. The most remarkable of them are *Satnāmī* dialogues between a man's soul and his body and a man's soul and his widow's soul.

(1) The dancing house is tethered
in the house with seven stories.
We were watching by the flickering lamp
How the thieves come I do not know.
From outside they bring the vessels
From the house they carry out corpse.
Four men have gathered and camp by the lake.
The messenger has come from the land of death.
You must break the cord and go
In the forest your body must make its camp.

(2) When it is time to go
we put a new cloth on him.
The people sit around
his eyes are closed.

The life-servant has left the body
the whole place knows.
Four men lift the cot
They snuffle *suskat-suskat*
As they take the road.
They take him to the burning ground
they put him down
and pile the wood above him.
The bones bush like forest-wood
His hair like jungle grass.
Mother weeps *harar-harar*
Sister weeps for six months
His wife weeps for three days
Then seeks another man for her house.

On the tenth day after a death the *Satnāmī* perform *ārati* and sing a number of songs, of which the following are specimens recorded in the Mungeli Tahsil. In the following song the soul is imagined as speaking to the body it has so recently abandoned:

(3) Now there is nothing to link you and me together
Dumb corpse.
When you and I were together how proudly you went about
Dumb corpse.
Now why do you lie so still with gaping mouth?
Dumb corpse.
When you and I were together what enormous joys you had
Dumb corpse?
The tank was filled, the lotus bloomed
The boat swam to and fro.
Now the tank is broken
The lotus withered.

The boat has sunk in the mud
Dumb corpse

In the next song the idea is that a married man has died and his widow's soul leaves her body and addresses his soul:[2]

(4) Go go away, mad fool
There is nothing to link us now.
Why are you standing there
in the middle of the path?
I have cleaned rice in a little basket
I am doing *āratī* above it.
Go go away, go mad fool.
O my love is going to a foreign land
and who will teach him its language.
My lord is going to a foreign land
he takes with him all my joys.
In my breast is my door of sorrow
I have fixed the chain and gone.
The lime-tree branches are very long
The crow has spoilt the curds.
His body lies empty now
my eyes for ever weep.
Ram's *hukumdār* has come.
Goose, you must leave the village
The five messengers have come to his courtyard.
They have brought the ox-goad
with the goad they beat the soul.
They break its ribs and speed it on its way.
O Jambhaiyā wait a moment.
The net of love is spread throughout the world.
Let me tie it in a bundle
Then the goose may leave the village.

Haṁsa, which I have here translated 'goose' is more commonly rendered 'swan'. In fact it is a fabulous bird of great beauty, that lives on pearls, and is often used as a symbol of the mysterious invisible life of man.

REFERENCES

1. Every symbol that unites believers divides them from others who do not believe. Symbolization as defined here as the selection process, the choice of one aspect of complex array to serve as the top of the iceberg, a light weight mental token that can be substituted for the entire knowledge package for purposes of higher order congnitive operations.

2. *Sātnāmīsm* is a spirit—possession cult. This concerns a spirit who is said to 'seize' and cause symptoms ranging from mild hysteria to depression or sometimes organic troubles.

CHAPTER 9

THE FOREST-SONGS

The *Dadariā*, or *Sālhō* as they are called in Chhattīsgaṛh, are the true *ban-bhajans*[1] or forest-songs of the *Satnāmī*. They are sung by the people at work in the field or forest, by groups of girls on their way to bazar, by travellers resting by the fire at night. Young lovers sing them to each other, and many a proposal has been made and elopement arranged in verse. At weddings, the two parties sing them against one another competitively; while they are singing boys and girls throw rings to each other and exchange gifts of tobacco and betel. The *Dadariā* can also be used as taunt-songs; at one time a notorious criminal, in whose activities we had ventured to interfere, never passed our house without singing at the top of his voice a selection of obscene and insulting *Dadariā*.

These are the most spontaneous and original of the songs. There is a great corpus or floating reserve of *Dadariā* verse, on which boys and girls draw according to their knowledge and their fancy. But they also often improvise, a task which is facilitated by the rather cheap and easy rhymes that are in fashion.

The music is always fresh and thrilling, with a tilt, a joy, an excitement that never stales. The songs are sung very loudly, at night, at a high pitch; they are the radio messages of the aboriginal. They are usually sung antiphonally; one verse of a *Dadariā* expects an answer (Elwin and Hivale, 1944. 89-90).

Though the music is always lovely the words of the *Dadariā* songs are often cheap and facile, a fault forced upon them by their rhymed complet form and extempore improvised character. The singers are more interested in getting a rhyme at the end of the line than in what they say: that is why the second line of a *Dadariā* often has so little connection with the first. This is not always so, of course; there are *Dadariā* — some of them are in this collection — which have the grace and logic of true poems; but it must be remembered that the songs given here are only a tiny percentage of the great volume of *Dadariā* verse which is constantly being created and revised.

Certain stages in these rhyming improvisations can be traced. There are first the rhymed and punning songs of the children. There are other sayings and nursery rhymes, often very coarse, which teach children from an early age, the use of 'internal rhyme' and the technique of sound with the line which is used to such great advantage in the *Karma* songs. The rhymes need not be exact and sometimes the effect is obtained by the repetition of a word:

Tōlā pāton
to letōn Korā

If I get you
In my lap I'll seat you.

ṭaṭhiā kī bāsī
ṭhaṭhiā Juṛāi
binā dekhe tolā
ankhiyā jhurāi

The stale food in the pot
Cools in the pot
without seeing you
My eyes dry up.

From this it is an easy step to the *Dadariā* improvisations; both the rhymed catches and the *Dadariā* are used for the same purpose of love-making. They are often in fact 'love-epigrams'.

There are two main types of *Dadariā* — the *Jorphī* and the *Thaḍī.* In the *Jorphī* type, the first 'line' has little real connection with the second; it is a refrain referring generally to some homely familiar object of the countryside — the creeper climbing up the wall of the house, the mango tree silhouetted against the sky, the gruel cooking in the pot. The *Jorphī Dadariā* is usually sung competitively; a party of boys begin and while they are singing, a party of girls discuss and prepare the reply. They continue using the *Jorphī* line, each side composing additional lines to rhyme with it until they are tired, and then they change the rhyme and the tune. The second line often ends with the word *dos,* 'friend', a technical device which is useful for concealing any deficiency in the rhyme.

The *Thāḍī Dadariā* is a complete short poem; it may sing *piārke jhulaniā,* rather slowly with a dragged-out tune, in contrast to the simple *thaḍī* which is sharper and more concise in its music. This type of *Dadariā* can also be sung antiphonally, but not necessarily so; it can be shouted as a whole-hearted, delighted means of self-expression, even if there is no one to hear or answer (Elwin and Hivale, 1944. 92).

Throughout India two-line rhyming songs are very popular. These may either be sung as single poems or a number of them may be improvised, stung together, and bandied to and fro for a considerable time. In Chhattisgaṛh, the *Dadariā* is sometimes sung competitively between men and women, and it is said that if a man wins he can take the woman; if she wins, she can take the man and her own husband must go elsewhere (Elwin 1946. 189). I doubt, however, if this bargain is ever kept. Of a similar type are the *Ṭtappā* or *miśrā* of the Musalmāns.

The method is twofold. Sometimes the second line is a genuine extension of the first; sometimes it is merely suggested by the rhyme:

beherā ke khodrā ma pakṛē mainā
tor mastī jabānī ma galay lamsenā
mor Karelā re dos.

In the hollow of the *bahera*, you caught a mainā
For your strong youth you have kept a lamsainā.

Here the first line was probably inspired by the need to find a rhyme for *lamsainā*, yet here is a true *Dadariā* with correct parallelism between the lines. The *mainā*, the pet, in the hollow; the *lamsainā*, pet boy in the house, for the girl's lusty youth.

But this type of couplet is only for the rhyme:

Sāvan re bhādōn oṛhe la kamrā
Satnāmī ke maram nahi jānay chamrā

In Sawan and Bhadon, wrap yourself in a blanket
The *Dalit* does not know the ways of the Satnāmī.

There is no possible connection here between the two halves of the song; they have come together through the necessity of rhyming *Kamrā* and *Chamrā*.

But in many others the connection is subtle but true and their study throws a light on the mentality of the singers. For example take the following *Gond Dadariā*:

In Sawan there are mushrooms.
In Bhadon young bamboo-shoots.
How can I spend my days
While my body is green?

Here the first line creates the atmosphere: the young mushrooms are sprouting in August, the bamboo-shoots, young and vigorous, are coming up; mushrooms often symbolize the immature breasts of young girls, little bamboo-shoots are equally suggestive of youth. There in the next line *'How can I spend my days while my body is green'*, we see the mushroom-girl, green and immature as a bamboo-shoot, longing for maturity and the expression of life. Mushrooms and babmoo-shoots are things to eat, and the green body too will be eaten when it is ripe.

Take the following *Ahīr-Dadariā:*

Clouds to the east, the rain falls in the south,
you delight in the play of love, but you are anxious as you go.

Here, clouds and rain are conventional sex-symbols, and lead us direct to second line. The threat of rain, before which the traveller hurries home, matches the girl's anxiety as she tastes the stolen joy of love.

I have recorded one hundred stanzas of the *Dadariā* song that Chunnīlāl of Janakpur (Surguja) sang in 1967. It is clear that new stanzas are continually being added and old ones dropped. But an analysis of the following stanzas provides an incisive comment on the way of life of these children of *Kāma*. It is difficult to convey the content of these verses exactly. Some of the important verses are produced here in their original form:

(1) *navā re talwā bahut gahirā*
molā bhāgan bhal daile
pāchhū kar Jahirā.
navā re poirī lagāvay retī
tan rahay ki jāvay
tumhar sētī

The new tank is very deep.
Let me first run away
Then tell everyone.
To smooth a new anklet you need a file
For your sake my body may stay or go.

(2) *Umariyā ḍumariyā ḍūmar phūl ke darvājā le*
darvājā le bolai jhokai
Sītārām bungulaiyā re
nahi āvay mor piy
rājā māndī lagā ke
ḍolā sajā ke
jāthay barāt
lāde bailā
nadiyā la nahi nāke.

Flower of the fig peeps out from the cover of the leaves. So does this girl stand in her house and accepts Sitārām. He will not come. For my king is drinking, seated among his friends.

But the litter is ready decorated to go for the marriage.
And the loaded bullock cannot cross the river.

(3) *Nahi āvay...*
pāne lagāy, pansariyā re hāy
lavangē lagāy jarā mahkat āvay.
ānso ke amlī pharālā capṭī
lāne lagāy pansariyā re hāy
tor mukh par dayā bhitar kapṭī
He will not come...
O leaf-maker, when you prepare the *pān*
Put in a little cinnamon
So he will come with scented mouth.
This year's tamarind is spoilt.
There is pity in your face
But you are false within.

(4) *āmā ke ḍār la*
navāke bhanj ḍāre rām
mor patrelā
mayā ke māre robay ḍhāre
jaṛwālā kāṭay
chhāṛi ke chhādī
mor bāt la batāy de
kadi ke kādī

One bends the mango branch
And breaks it in the end.
Now has my love for this slim-bodied girl
Brought me tears.
One cuts long straight branches
From the thorn-bush.
Now quick and straight
Make answer to my song.

(5) *pātar mungā pātar ḍangī*
pātar havay sarīr
de daibe mārganī.
jaise ma debe taise ma lehūn
māngani ma nahi debe
paisā ma lehūn.

Slender is the mungo tree
Slender are its branches.
Slender is your body
O give it me delicious.
However you give it me
I will take your body.
If not for my desiring
Then give it at my purchase.

(6) *ek pēṛ āmā alag pāke ḍār*
pānī būṛ gaye chhokrī
bacay re dos
āy āy mārō tākō ga
pānī būṛ gay e chhokrī
bacay re dos.

The solitary mango tree
Cannot preserve its fruit.
Nor can anyone save this girl from me.
No, not even if she tries to kill herself in water.
No one can save her from me.

(7) *hāy hāy mor gelhā patrēlā*
nāgar phānday
bhai talvā ṭipan khāle pār
kāṭe lā ḍōrī ā jābē
ḍauā hamār joṛi

O my friend, my slim-bodied love
Is ploughing his field.
Beside the lake where our camp is

O love, come to cut the creeper
Come, little brother, my yoke-fellow.

(8) The youth speaks:
āmā la toṛe khaunch kahike
mōlā dagā ma ē chhokrī
bulāvay re dos.

She called me saying
If you go picking mangoes.
I will come to eat them
But it was all deceit, my friend.

His girl also speaks:

kon ban āmā
phin kon ban jām
ye bhanvarā nikal gay
re dos.

Where is the forest where the mango grows?
Where is the forest of *Jamun*?
And where has my bubble-bee flown away,
my friend.

(9) *gāle gāle...*
bāns ke to lāṭhī tor
chāndī ke gaṭhān dos ḍāri ke
milaunā to āmā ke athān
tor bōlī saṛak le
sunāy re dos.

Your stick is made of bamboo
And it has silver bands.
The meeting of friends is (sweet as) mango pickle.
I hear your voice in the street, O friend.

(10) *bhāt ke khabaiyā bāsī la nahi khāy*
saikal ke to chaṛhaiā
mor karelā paidal

nahi jāy re dos.
gaye bajāre laye la loṭā
ghar baiṭhe khelā le
āpan beṭā

A girl and a boy taunt one another. In the first verse she declares that she can do better than him. In the second, he replies accusing her of bringing home a bastard from the bazar.

He who has eaten rice
does not care for stale *bāsī.*
The cyclist does not care
to walk on foot, O friend!
You went to the bazar
and brought home a pot.
So sit in your house
and play with the baby.

(11) *gayē bajāre lihe gaghrā*
ghar panhucay na paō matābai jhagrā.

(12) *gaye pahāre kāṭain rohinā*
tain to ṭhagi ṭhagi rākhe
aṛhāī mahinā.

(13) *mārai re machrī halābai morbā*
din kahān ganvāye nadī-narvā.

(14) *khāye to jamtī tor to*
hajāron milaunā
kahi ma kamtī.

(15) *ārā chalāvai kaṭhvā ma*
arkasiā bahasi gaye ḍhoriyan ma.

(16) *roṭi ke palṭā sōhārī lai le.*
adhbuṛhiyā ke palṭā
biyāhī lai le,

(17) *chūlā pateuā chulahnī ma jāy*
mor basni rupaiyā
kalahalī ma jāy.

(18) *chāndī ke mundrī unārō kaise*
tain to dhanī ka aṛikā
bigāron kaise.

(19) *nadī to āve bahal āve ḍhūnḍh*
tor do rattī ma māyā
kaise lāgun pār.

(20) *chāndi kai mundrī*
vo hīrā jaṛī
to mo milan hoigaye
hajāron khaṛī.

(21) *nadiyā ke bālu*
nicaṭ kughrā
lūgā pahirain na pāvai
pāchū kai ughrā.

(22) *gaye pahāre toṛen simhār.*
sumer sālhō gāyē gānw ka sinvār.

(23) *aṭpaṭ ghaṭiyā phuṭai loṭiyā*
kusiyārī ka pāgā bāndhe
hamār rasiyā.

(24) *pīpar ke pān disai jhejhrī*
kaun san mor bāi disai panjarī.

(25) *pāke pīpar parevā nahi khāy*
binā māge jhūle bāi
kalevā nahi khāy.

(26) *nadiyā kināre lagāi gōbhī*
tor bahinī chhinariyā
paisā kai lōbhī

(27) *nadiyā ka bālū bahut chhalkāy*
chalkal jiu karai
gali ma maṭkai

(28) *nāvai to saṛakiyā*
piṭāvai giṭṭī
ābā nāhī banai
bhejāvā ciṭṭhī.

(29) *nāvā saṛakiyā ma rēnge rājā*
rāmlīlā dekhain jābe
dono sāthī.

(30) *tarī ke laukī ūpar dohinī*
cale ahiyā bāī
dono bahinī.

(31) *sājhā ke māre saraī binā*
devrā surāy gaye
bhaujāī binā.

(32) *bhāt to rāndhe, māngai baraphī*
tor bahirai ka māyā
jhiray kapṭī

(33) *pān to ṭorain pateriyan ma*
nīd bairī nahi āvay
semariyan ma.

(34) *kariyā hai bhainsī*
bhunvariyā hai sīng
mor palangā ma ābā
jhapaṭi ābā.

(35) *dhotī to pahirain*
araj nahi āy
mor painyā painyā loṭe
garaj nahi āy.

(36) *pāke to doṛī halāvon kaise*
sarkārī baredī
bolānvon kaise.

(37) *gānv ke gaunṭiyā*
painyā lāgū tor
bairī ka nikāl de
painyā lāgū tor

(38) *uṛai kaṛākul banai pankhā*
jiu jhamphkā na mānai
uṛai ho laṅkā.

(39) *harrā ke bikan ke*
harraiyā lai deun
jōṛā bailā bikan ke
kardhaniyā lai deu.

(40) *machhrī to mārai*
mārai kotrī
tohin jāne rahon
nanhe ke chodrī.

(41) *par bhar machrī*
talaiyā bhar jhor
kahān dhare burmārī
sataurī chodaun tor.

(42) *champā ke chāur*
chameliyā ke dār.
phulbagiyā ma jhūlai
hamār joṛīdār.

(43) *navā paṛeruā lāge nahi ḍor*
duei ṭhe gālī daile
māyā jhan ṭor.

(44) *nadiyā kināre chhuhi khadān*
main nahī mānevn
pai laṛikā adān.

(45) *pahile asāṛh mārai ṭiṭhī*
ghar jāy ke jhan batāve
tor ḍaukāī piṭihā.

(46) *māre to labdā girai gajbel*
tor kanihā bhar chūndī
lagāy le ḍorī tel.

(47) *kuṭkī kodaiyā ragaṛ dhoi le*
tor ābathai lebaiyā
nagad roy le.

(48) *pahile asāṛh chaṛhābai congī*
bich galiyā ma ṭhāṛhe
hamar man ley.

(49) *ponḍki to māre dhanrahī*
tose git na bane
le le mose udhār

(50) *gaye bajāre lihe ālū*
ghar pahunch na pāye
kudāven bhālū.

(51) *navā to ghailā bharai mirchā*
galiyā batāy pāchhe phirtā

(52) *dūdh re duhai kaseliyan ma*
nīd nahi āvai
akeliyan mā.

(53) *lakṛī re kāṭai lagāvai chaṭṭā*
chorī-lukkā piyā de bāi biṛī kaṭṭā.

(54) *kabai debe katthā*
kabai debe pān
kabai debe ḍoriyā
apan dil kā jān.

(55) *sānjh dehūn katthā*
bihāne dehūn pān
adhratiyā ke amal ma
dehūn jiu kā dān.

(56) *nāt lehī bokrā*
kuṭumb lehī bhāt
rānā to lehī
rupiyā pachās.

(57) *pānchis ke lāge pachās lagi jāy*
binā bole na chhoṛon
pulis lagi jāy.

(58) *nāke nathuniyā julaniyā to āy*
na hoy mor savatiyā
jiy ke jaraniyā to āy.

(59) *kunvā ka pānī kubāsī lāge*
paradesī nikar gaye
robāsī lāge.

(60) *ledrī ghoṛiyā kasain nahi dey*
tor sughī meheriyā
hasay nahi dey.

(61) *sānkar re kuinyā laram lejurī*
nihuraiyān pānī khīnchai
hamar bahurī.

(62) *nān nān ḍholiyā*
bovābai jīrā dhān.

puliyā ma khaṛe rahiye
khabaihaun bīrā pān.

(63) *kunvā ke pāṉī kunvārī piyai*
gangā-jamunā ke pānī
revārī piyain.

(64) *pāke re āmā halāvon kaise*
sarkārī hai baredī
bolāūn kaise

(65) *tor man chaṛhtī pai mor man udās*
jalhaniyā ma ṭhāṛhe pai marthon piyās.

(66) *āgī re bāre ageṭhan ma*
chit gāṛe hai ṭoraunā
baheṭhan ma.

(67) *gaye bajāre lihe bastā*
ṭhāṛhe baiṭhe nihāron
tohār rastā.

(68) *āvai re nadiyā bahai ghonghī*
koū dayā vāle hoihā
piyāle chongī.

(69) *āmā ke ḍāre baiṭhe runiyān*
baṛī durihā se dekhenv
ajab duniyā.

(70) *Gāndhī māre barchī*
Javāhar māre bān
Bhāratmātā ke kalapnā
dekhāthe hīrālāl.

(71) *ek phūl phulai mandir ūpar*
dil bas gaye rājā
tonhār ūpar.

(72) *sanjhā ke belā taroī phūlai*
tor chimṭī bhar kanihā
tōlā ke khūlai.

(73) *kaṇṭhī re bāndhe bāndhe mohrī*
āj din bhar nahi dekhehv
kahān rehe rī.

(74) *nāgar phānd nagarpur ma*
rājīnāmā bolāy de
Janakpur ma.

(75) *bāns re kāṭai phaṭik ajrā*
tohī ek to bolāyō
āyō na labrā.

(76) *āye re holī jarai re jiyā*
saṅg chalbe bajāre
lai dehūn phariyā.

(77) *gānjā kai thailī gānjā nahi āy*
tor utartī dehinyā
majā nahi āy.

(78) *chandā ke uge sūraj chal dey*
dono janghiyā ke bīch
marad ras ley.

(79) *khāye re bāsī dhare ṭangvā*
tohī origit gayon bhanvar talvā.

(80) *bajnā pairiyā nichaṭ hai rāt*
banai banai lāge
uṛhā ke rāj.

(81) *hānthī par haundā*
ghoṛe par jīn

joban par syāhī
kon dhar dīn.

(82) *makunā re hāthī*
bajai ghaṇṭā
kabai aihain lebaiyā
miṭai ṭaṇṭā.

(83) *gaye bajāre lihe balṭī*
tolā nichṭay bolāye
toray galtī.

(84) *Lachiman au Rām*
rath pe bīnā bajāmay.

(85) *mai patlī laph jānv*
gagariyā dui dui dharānve

(86) *jiylā lai ley re*
gore munh vālā godnā.

(87) *dukh robay banāy*
choṭe balam vālī dhaniyā.

(88) *chalī jaihon re*
jiyrā mār ke tunhār.

(89) *I brought you* channā *shoots in the evening*
My slender love, the child of your womb has a share of me.

(90) *The Kewat boy pushes the* pelnā *trap through the water*
There's no money in the house, we're going to play in the tank.

(91) *You have not cleaned the* kājal *from your eyes*
You have not yet taken the sendur *from your hair.*

(92) *With your lips you do not talk to me*
But you have called me with the words of your eyes.

(93) *My arms are covered with my husband's bangles*
But the two lovely silver bracelets were given by my lover.

(94) *The boy has sifted the chaff from the wheat*
You have sucked my body empty of its juice.

(95) *The cart is decorated, the bullocks are red*
How smart is the driver, how loving the passenger !

(96) *The virgin drinks water from the well.*
The young mother takes it from the river.

(97) *When the water is cold, you can make it hot*
When your youth is growing, keep it in control.

(98) *You have made bread with* mahua *juice*
O bird, you have taken me into your caste.

(99) *Come along, black barren cow, come along fat bull.*
Fire has burnt your grazing-ground;
They are sowing rice there now.

(100) *Along the hills the forest fires light up the lovely sky*
O lover hurry, for impatient night is longing to be gone.

This suggests that a fuller semiological meaning of the *Dadariā*-songs is self-explanatory. It seems that any object may change from being seen as a sex object of the physical extension of the sex. It also seems that the inherent asexuality has a sexual motive also. The meaning in these *Dadariās* is in relations between the man and woman. So is the music in the relations marked out by sounds and not in one note. The inherent signals in these *Dadariās* is : the love of other person.

REFERENCES

1. *bhajana* is the art of surrendering one's own self to the Supreme Being. The word also stands for devotional songs in Sanskrit. In the second sense it has a twofold significance — praise of the Lord and music of a particular type.

CHAPTER 10

PANTHĪ : THE SECTARIAN DANCE AND SONG

"*Pantha*" is a sect on common religious bond. In medieval reformistic religious movements this term acquired a wider significance. When the depressed in Chhattisgaṛh came under a centralized authority, the whole body began to be known collectively as *Satnām-panthī* and came to be regarded as an embodiment of the Guru. Also the sect of Kabīr was split into twelve different schools, each of which was known as a *panth.*[1]

The *Satnāmī* movement of Chhattīsgaṛh began with the illiterate authority and the community which adopted this school had no written records. While writing the history of Ghāsidāsa and his *Satnām-panth* we had to rely on the oral literature. Oral literature is the specific form of the historical source — the so-called oral history. The term means the use of oral testimony of participants of historical events that are not recorded in documents. However, due to the wide use of sound-recording, the data on oral history of Chhattisgaṛh are, as a rule, transformed into a variety of documentary sources for this book.

Oral history is of particular importance for the disadvantaged people who have no written language of their own. Data concerning the historical past of these people are often contained in legends transmitted from generation to generation by word of mouth. Apart from the legends other folk genre have also historical importance.

Panthī-songs as a type of oral sources always reflect the actual historical events that took place in the remote past. We may compare the protagonists of the *Panthī* songs with the persons that actually existed in history and, moreover, at synchronising the events described in them. Thus *Panthī-gīt* is a history recounted by the people itself. This is also a living history of the *Satnām* sect.

Panthī song is always combined with the dance. It is the feature of the *Satnāmī* life. It is very much distinctive dance as compared to other folk-dances of Chhattīsgaṛh. The dance leader actually leads the dancing while the Guru takes no active part in it. It has the dance leader who invents the steps and composes the words of the song, which is so important in the dance.

There are certain clear characteristics of the songs of the *Panthī* dancers. First, there is the element of the narration of the life-history of Ghāsīdāsa. A second feature of the songs is clear recognition of the epic heros —Rāma and Kṛṣṇa.

These myths[2] in *Panthī* dance have originated from the social rituals. Rituals in essence gave birth to myths whose purpose was to elaborate or provide an aetiology for the rite. G. Frazer (1915:153) in the *Golden Bough* says that myth was "a fiction devised to explain an old custom, of which the real meaning and origin had been forgotten."

More recently, scholars have largely abandoned the myth-from-ritual paradigm and returned, in part at least, to an extension of Malinowski's mythopoetic consciousness propositions. As Wheelwright (1965:159) states: "In the mytho-poetic mode of consciousness there is a strong tendency for the different experimental elements to blend and fuse in a non-logical way.... The selfhood of the worshipper tends to blend with them.... He becomes a full participant, not a mere observer...." These sentiments close to Cassirer's (1955) view that such thought is a synthesizing activity of emotion, cognition and evaluation "into the key of myth," and Watt's (1953:3) proposal that myths are those stories "which, for various reasons, human beings regard as demonstrations of the inner meaning of the universe and of human life".

Ghāsīdāsa's myths serve four interrelated functions: First, 'the reconciliation of human consciousness with the preconditions of its own existence, which is termed the mythical or metaphysical purpose. For example, Ghāsīdāsa shares the Hindu myth regarding the life after death.

A second function of myth is that of formulating and rendering an image of the universe, a cosmological image, of such kind that all things should be recognized as parts of a single great picture... the trees, the rocks, the animals, sun, moon and stars, all opening back to mystery. The cosmological function may be seen in the following lines of *Panthi* song:

Ta na na na na na ho na bāre lalnā
Tor man mohnā ki mor jag mohnā

A third function is sociological, that of validating and maintaining of some specific order, authorizing its moral code. For example, in seeking to establish the moral authority, the singer uses the mythic notion of *Gītā* in the *Panthī-gīt.*

A fourth function of *Panthī* myth is to provide psychological guidance, shaping individuals to the aims and ideals of their various social groups, bearing them on from birth to death through the course of human life. Rāma and Kṛṣṇa serve as models of personal conduct, for overcoming personal obstacles, for self-direction.

10.1 *Analyzing Myth in* Panthī-gīt

There are two basic aspects to *Panthī* myth — content and structure. Content refers to the actors and objects in the myth; structure to the way in which actors and objects interact. The view taken here is that the content element of the *Panthī* myth can be usefully examined as cultural archetypes — as entities embodying some significant, often primal, factor of concern to *Satnāmīs.* A very tall structure serves as a point of contact between mortals and gods, as for example, the way to Puri, where Ghāsīdāsa received enlightenment of *Sat.*

10.2 *Classifying Archetypes*

Although the notion of arche-types is most frequently associated with the writings of Carl Jung (1958), reference to archetypic symbolization is mode in writing both preceding and postdating Jung's work. Sir James Frazer (1915), Frans Boas (1911), Emile Durkheim (1961), F. Nietzsche (1967), Sigmund Freud (1953) and Bruno Bettelheim (1976) all posited the existence of unconscious ideational forms or symbols that were shared by members of a particular society or were even universal to all humans. Jungian archetypes have been fruitfully applied to interpreting the meaning of the mythology of Ghāsīdāsa.

10.3 *The Structure of* Panthī *myths*

In addition to their content, here viewed as consisting of archetypical entities, myths of Ghāsīdāsa may also be interpreted as to their structure that is, the relationship between archetypes depicted in the *Panthī* myths. Perhaps the foremost advocate and practitioner of the structural analysis of myth is Claude Levi-Strauss, who has used this approach to explain mythic themata as diverse as food preferences (1969), religious beliefs of the Winnebago Indians (1970), and the Wagnerian operatic tetralogy (1978). As Levi-Strauss describes it:

> "The structural approach—is the quest for the variant, or for the invariant elements among superficial difference...It's a problem, one might say, or translation, of translating what is expressed in one language of code... into expression in a different language. Science has only two ways of proceeding: it is either reductionist or structuralist.. When we are confronted with phenomena too complex to be reduced to phenomena of a lower order, then we can only approach them by looking at their relationships, that is, by trying to understand what kind of original system they make up."

Typically, a structural analysis proceeds by organizing the actors in the *Panthī* myth according to their relationships to certain outcomes. Next, I have attempted to discern an overarching principle that explains why some actors are consistently led to certain outcomes, while other actors are consistently led to other certain outcomes. In applying the structural approach to *Satnāmī* myths I have discerned the following propositions to characterize the *Satnāmī* metaphysic:

(a) Extraordinary people live their full lives and die their full deaths;
(b) ordinary people die earlier but live more fully;
(c) negative extraordinary people are able neither to live nor to die.

Application of the structuralist approach to *Panthī* myths does not guarantee the identification of the *Sat*, but it does provide a systematic way of examining the relationships between elemental categories (i.e., archetypes) and identifying consistent themes.

The root of *Satnām* sect lies in obtaining power from Ghāsīdāsa, who is also central figure in the *Panthī* music. *Panthī* music today functions importantly for the *Satnāmīs*, as a means of expressing the fact that they remain *Satnāmī* no matter what changes in their way of life occurred or how far-reaching these changes may be. The *Satnāmī* music is also means of relieving psychological tensions. Finally, the occasions for music provide various opportunities for self-expression through the mechanism of drawing the *Satnāmīs* together in one place at one time, thus reinforcing the social integration of the group; it is no accident that the 18th of December celebrations are again the occasion of evocation of the past. In music and dance, especially on the birthday of Ghāsīdāsa, people reaffirm that they are indeed, the *Satnāmī*.

10.4 *Towards a musical semiotics of* Panthī-*music*

The *Panthī*-musical text may be presented according to the following musical semiosis:

Satnām models
↓
technological models
↓
manifest level — | the musical discourse | —
immanent level
↑
Structures of communication
↑
Fig : Structures of signification

Satnāmī-discourse in music is ruled by two kinds of models which may be called *Satnāmī* and technological. In this context the term '*Satnāmī*' is to be understood to form an opposition to the technical aspects of music; it is formed by *Satnām* models determining all the symbolisms related to music. Again *Satnāmī* model itself is an aesthetic model. It regulates the production of meaning. The *Satnāmī* model is mythical by nature.

Technological models are oral representations. Here the technological knowledge in turn is transmitted orally.

The technological and *Satnāmī* models cooperate in several different ways. A musical style has emerged as a result of the cooperation of these two factors.

Does the *Panthī* composer, while composing, function exclusively according to the *Satnāmī* and technological models of his time? If this were so, hardly any aesthetically significant works would emerge, but a composer's production would be redundant, too socialized a speech (parole), manners and cliches, which could no longer fulfil their aesthetic function. From all this we can draw the conclusion that a composition like *Panthī-gīt* cannot be identified solely with its structures of communication, but that it is rather the structures of communication which in turn distinguish in a composition a certain area wherein the composer's fantasy can move in a relatively free manner and produce some unique signification. We may present here two poems. The first poem is based on the *Satnām* model, while the second poem distinguishes itself by transferring the model to the National Flag.

I *tain to rāndhī ḍāre jewan ho, āgī ke binā pānī ke binā*
ē āgī ke binā sāheb, pānī ke binā
ē dēkhā to mahimā lā pāpī khāyē hār,
tain to rāndhi ḍāre jewan ho āgī ke binā

ē ḍōngrī jāyē bar Ghāsīdāsa lā tiyārē ho bābā
jāny bar bābā ṭangiyā lā dhare ho
e māre bhūkh-piyās ham hōnge khās tain to

e saṅg-saṅgwārī chōṛē guru Ghāsīdāsa la
tain to rāndhi ḍāre jewan ho, āgī ke binā pānī ke binā.

II *lahrāye hamar des ke nisān*
pawan me yaho jay-jay kār
gagan me yaho jay-jay kār
kon kon raṅg ke jhaṇḍā lā banāyē ho jhaṇḍā lā banāye
kon kon nām ke khambhā la gaṛāyē khambhā la gaṛāyē
tor kon nām cakra he mahān
pawan me yaho jay-jay kār
gagan me yaho jay-jay kār
lahrāye hamar des ke nisān
tīn raṅg nām ke jhaṇḍā la banāyē ho jhaṇḍā la banāyē ho
jay Swastik tor khambhā la gaṛāyē ho tor khambhā la gaṛāye
tor Asok-cakra he mahān
pawan me yaho jay-jay kār
gagan me yaho jay-jay kār
lahrāye he des ke nisān
pawan me yaho jay-jay kār.

Regarding the primal processuality of *panthī* music one has to take into account that musical logic cannot be based on the logic of a static world where the phenomena are either this or that, but on a logic which depicts the constant changes of phenomena from one state to another. Consequently, the musical signification should be based on the continuous coming and changing of musical figures.

The Guru's increasing interest in popular music reflects his deepening sensitivity to the ecstatic spiritual aspect of dance, exemplified by the transcendent rhythm of dance which constitutes the flux and timeless, eternal order of the universe.

Ghāsīdāsa has in a different context, spoken about three birthplaces of man: first, the material world; second, the world of memory (*surtā*); and third, the

Universal Self (*Satnām*). These three worlds are closely intertwined and man is liberated when he comprehends the unified pattern of the three worlds. The birth of *Panthī-gīt* takes place in the unified state of these three worlds. The time and space-bound world of incidents is the basis, and when it is transformed into musical-subject matter it transports the human being to a level of spiritual consciousness. In this way two poles are created, the spiritual world and the world of material existence, and for *Satnām* the connecting link between these two worlds is the folk memory.

In *Panthī* songs, the rural speech (*Chhattīsgaṛhī*) progressively develops into heightened speech and then draws itself up into emotionally charged songs. Songs are an extension of dialogues, not having any separate role to play. In fact, Ghāsīdāsa wanted to develop a musical structure for his *Satnām*-teachings because he thought music has the potentiality of revealing man in his true self and therefore music is an artistic application of the theological form as well as its subject-matter. Songs for Ghāsīdāsa have always been a means to coming in touch with the trancendental. The pulsations of a song surcharge one emotionally, keeping one away from any connection with the incidents of life.

A symbol is developed when an image gets concretised. Ghāsīdāsa's imagery is created in an oblique fashion, and as a result it becomes difficult to understand it within the natural process of expression. The various images used in *Satnāmī* songs create a dramatic symbol, and thereby emerges a much deeper and more meaningful 'structure of feeling'. The movement in dance symbolizes not only a dynamic life but also a static road on which the life moves. These opposites are complementary to each other and sometimes in the process of syncretisation the road becomes the saga of life. The saga has a structure resembling a fair.

A fair indicates the folk life or the *panthī* image. *Panthī* also means a companion in journey and one needs a road to make one's long march. In *Satnām* it is nature which creates a road.

Thus in *panthī* dance the most dominating symbol is *panthī*—not only *pāntha* but *Chirapāntha* who is on his way to *Satlok* so that he may discover the ultimate truth. The discovery of the real truth (*Sat*) is possible if one knows how to trod on the true *pantha.* Ghāsīdāsa and his *Sat* both are *pathika* or *pāntha.* When one understands the profundity of the concept of the partnership of the man and deity, one realises that the history of man is not an alienation from the deity but his pursuit and fulfilment. It is also a search of man by God so that he may become part of bigger reality.

Satnāmis see Ghāsīdāsa as a divine agent coming to lead them back to a happier paradise they have lost because of the impact of outside world.

CONCLUSION: FROM SANĀTĀNA *TO* SATNĀM

Certainly, Ghāsīdāsa was not a philospher[3] in the strict sense of the word. He is essentially a guru and reformist, and above all a mystic. He stands in the direct line of Indian mysticism, and though less profound, speaks with the same voice as Rāmānanda and Kabīr. These three might, indeed, be said to voice the religion of modern Chhattīsgaṛh. If it were realised that his originality does not consist in an incomprehensible and unnatural novelty, but in a poetic (through *Panthī* oral songs) restatement of a very old position, it might be less needful to waste our breath in the refutation of theses he never upheld.

It is true that we find in his oral tradition certain protest and exaggeration: but its very nature is that of passionate protest against unworthy values, elitist virtue, and snobbery, and the fact that this protest was received with so much execration suggests that he may be a true prophet. The *Jait Khambha* is the emblem of *Satnāmī* in Chhattīsgaṛh — in true sense.

Amongst the chief marks of the mystic are a constant sense of the unity and interdependence of all life, and of the interpenetration of the spiritual and material — opposed to puritanism, which distinguishes the sacred from the secular. So too is the sense of being everywhere at home — unlike the religions of reward and punishment, which speak of a future paradise and hell, and attach an absolute eternal value to good and evil. "All things" he says, "are enlinked, enlaced and enamoured." "I conjure you, my brethern, remain true to the earth." This is characteristic mystic intuition. *Sat* is real. It is all-inclusive unity of the Absolute that imparts substantiality to all beings and thus sustains their value.

Ghāsīdāsa has certainly a contempt for untouchability — that is, discrimination on the basis of one's birth. In Chhattīsgaṛh a sense of identity was imposed on the depressed caste by those who had power over him by virtue of their class, caste and official standing. P. Vans Agnew, a contemporary of Ghāsīdāsa reports: "Distinctions not reconcilable to our notions were also made in reference to the caste of the parties as well as in determining the quality of offence as the punishment with which it was to be visited. For instance if a Brāhmaṇ killed a low caste man he was at most fined. If, however, a low caste man killed a Brāhmaṇ he lost his life." (1820.42) This was certainly the agony which stimulated *Ghāsīdāsa* for the liberation of his fellow-members.

It is hardly worthwhile to refer to those who bracket our poet-philosopher and mystic with the anti-Brāhmaṇa philosophy and would make him one of the prime instigators of 'anti-Brāhmaṇa' war. It would be easy to understand how he appreciated the *sāttvika* philosophy of Brāhmanism and detached his caste from all the ill habits. He was a true Brāhmaṇa professing the unity among all the people.

The teaching of Ghāsīdāsa is a pure *satkarma-dharma.* The highest duty is that of realisation of truth. When Ghāsīdāsa says that *Satnām* is the meaning of the earth he means what we mean when we speak of a *Bodhisattva,* or of a *Jīvan-mukta.* This type which represents the highest attainment and purpose of humanity is the most difficult thing for self-assertive minds to grasp. The pattern of man's behaviour is not to be found in any code, but in the principles of the universe, which is continually revealing to us — its own nature.

Those who have comprehended the decline and fall of the province of Chhattīsgaṛh will recognize in Ghāsīdāsa the awakening of the conscience of Chhattīsgaṛh.[4] Until relatively recent times the cultural image of the *Chhattīsgaṛhi* people has been that of a group of rather primitive and hostile peoples whose contribution to human thought had been negligible. With the publication of this book this image will change rapidly. My own research on the people of Chhattīsgarh has begun to reach a depth and breadth of enquiry that were formerly unthought of, and this newly gained insight is beginning to shed an entirely a new light upon the intellectual achievement of the people of Chhattīsgaṛh. It seems that the old stereotypes are disappearing at last; and instead we are presented with a new image; the Indian, not only as a highly pragmatic thinker and an individual with a sound sense of reality, but also, the Indian as an abstract philosopher, a builder of intricate cosmic models, and a planner of sweeping moral designs.

REFERENCES

1. Guru Ghāsīdāsa did also split his followers in twelve regions and a separate seat was given to the different twelve *mahantas.*

2. The definition of classes is the first step in structural analysis. This takes place through 'coding' process.

3. The three main schools of *Vedānta* are: *advaita, visiṣṭādvaita* and *dvaita.* While Śaṅkara's *advaita* appealed to reason, Rāmānuja's *viśiṣṭādvaita* appealed to emotion. Ghāsīdāsa followed the latter.

4. Shukla, Ḣ.L. 1993. Chhattīsgaṛh : Ātmamanthan kā daur (in Hindi).

APPENDIX-1

A Report on the Subah or Province of Chhattisghur written in 1820 A.D. by Major P. Vans Agnew : the Contemporary of Guru Ghāsidāsa [Some portion missing*]

* * *

But I have not had opportunities of visiting many of them of myself and am little qualified to do justice to subjects of this nature.

Inscriptions. — The inscriptions at Sirpoor, where there are many, are in a character not known to any of the natives I have shown them to.

Forts. — The Hills Forts of Chuteesghur are Saffee [Lapha], Kosgie (Kosgain], Kochur and Kakair [Kanker], the whole of which are said to be strong by nature, but the few works upon them are bad and very much out of repair.

On the plains there are no places of any strength, or which merit the names of fortifications although every large village has a Ghurry [Garhi] or walled spot attached to it. Such are what are called the forts of Ryepore, Ruttunpore and Bellaspoore. Both the former are commanded by adjoining heights and derive any little strength they may have from tanks which partly surround them. The latter is small and unfinished, but is perhaps the best fort in Chutteesghur.

Number of towns and villages inhabited and deserted. — Confining my reply on this point [to the] eight Kalsa Perganahs which have [come] under my charge since my first [arrival] in Chutteesghur to the exclusion [of Droog Sanjaree] which has only lately been [added to the] district and in which the requisite inquiries have not yet been made, there are, within the extent described, 3,300 villages inhabited, 1,300 wholly deserted, and 203 which were deserted and have been granted free of rent for a stated term to individuals who have engaged to people them.

HISTORY

Succinct account of the changes and revolutions that have taken place with their effects on the state of the country and its inhabitants. — The information to be obtained respecting the history of this Province is very unsatisfactory and so frequently disagrees with the few certain data which exist that it can be little depended on.

It would however appear that Chutteesghur was from a very remote period governed by princes of its own, who resided latterly at Ruttenpore, and at a more distant epoch at Jazepoor Pallee†, and that it was never subjugated until conquered by the Mahrattas in sumbut 1802, although Kallian Singh a former rajah is said, on the summons of Acbar, to have repaired in sumbut 1601 to Delhi where he was detained for 12 years, and was only permitted to return to his principality on becoming tributary to the Mogul Emperor, a condition which from that period appears to have been adhered to.

Of the predecessors of Kallian Singh I have received many lists, but the only information that can be relied on, is derived from an inscription upon a building at Ruttunpore which gives the names of the following rajahs, and the date establishes that the latter reigned in sumbut 915, A.D. 858—

Brumma Deo,
Roodra Deo, his son,
Prittee Deo, his son,
Sirree Deo, his son.

It seems also certain that a rajah of the name of Ruttun Singh was the founder of Ruttunpore, but the accounts I have received differ materially as to the date assigned to his reign.

I am told that much information might be obtained respecting the ancient history of this province by consulting three copper tablets which were found buried at Ruttunpore and were transmitted by the Soobadar Kaishoo Govind to Raja Vincojee Bonslah in sumbat 1859, A.D. 1802.

The common tradition is that the rajahs of Ruttunpore are descendants of one of the four great dynasties [which at] a very remote period, ruled in [this part] of India, and the history of which is connected by a variety of fables with the mythology of the Hindoos.

These were the Nurputtees established at Suttara, the Gajiputtees at Cuttack*, the Rutputtees at Bustar and the Ashwaputtees at Ruttunpore, all so called from the Sangskrit words (Nur a man, Gujee an Elephant) for the conveyances which it was the privilege of each family to use.

The rajahs of Ruttunpore are said to be the representatives of the Ashwaputtees although the family appellation has been changed to Hyhywance (or as it is more commonly pronounced Ecomunee†) but as Hy is also the Sangskrit for a horse, the alteration is not considered to impair their pretensions to the high descent they claim.

From Kalian Singh, before mentioned as having become tributary to the Emperor of Delhi, the succession is said to have been as follows:—

Kullian Sing Died 1653 sumbut, A.D. 1596.
Lutchun Saye, his son.
Triboan Saye, his son.
Sunkur Saye, his son.
Jagernaut Saye, his brother.
Tuckut Sing, son to Sunkur Saye.

Rye Sing, his son, but of a doubtful legitimacy.
Sirdar Sing, his brother do do
Ragonaut Sing, do do do

This latter prince was deposed in sumbut 1802 (A.D. 1745) by the Mahrattas and is said to have died in 1838 (A.D. 1781), being the last survivor of his family.

Members of the Ruttunpore family seem to have been occasionally deputed to rule at Ryepore, Lohun and in other parts of the province, but as far as I can ascertain they were never wholly independent of the Ruttunpore Government.

Thus Jagernaut Saye before his accession to the Gaudee [Gaddi] of Ruttunpore was Governor of Lohun and his grandson, Burriar Sing, subsequently became rajah of Ryepore.

On his [Burriar Singh] death in sumbut 1800 (A.D. 1743) he was succeeded by Ameer Sing, his son by a concubine, who 12 years afterwards was deposed by Ragojee, 12 villages being assigned to him for his support. He died in sumbut 1815 (A.D. 1758) leaving a son named Newrage Sing whose death occurred in sumbut 1872 (A.D. 1815). The wife of this latter, two sons and three daughters are now alive, and residing at the village of Nandgaon, near Ryepore, supported principally by a voluntary donation from certain villages of that Pergunnah, only two of the villages formerly assigned to the family in Mokassa being now in its possession.

I may here mention that an inscription in the fort of Ryepore dated in sumbut 1458 (A.D. 1401), proves the existence then of rajahs of Ryepore, but it may be presumed that they were also a branch of the Ruttunpore family.

Previous to the Mahratta conquest this country appears to have undergone no great revolutions and to have been little disturbed but by the internal quarrels of its own chiefs — some devastating incursions made by the rajah of Mandla in the time of Rajah Sirdar Sing are the only events which are now recollected. The assumption of the country by the Mahrattas was also gradual and unattended by any circumstances calculated to make sudden changes. The Mahratta Commander Baskur Punt, in sumbut 1794 (A.D. 1737) according to most accounts, took Ruttunpore by storm and compelled the Rajah Ragonaut Sing to accede to the payment of a tribute which he left Kullian Geer, a Gosain, to receive, himself continuing his march towards Bengal on the ulterior objects of his expedition. Seven years afterwards in sumbut 1801 (A.D. 1744), on Buskur Punt being treacherously killed in Cuttack and his army dispersed, Ragonaut Sing seized Kallian Geer and threw off the Mahratta yoke; but, on the arrival of Ragojee in the following year (A.D. 1745), at the head of an army of 20,000 men, he was finally deposed, five villages being assigned for his support.

Mohun Sing was left in charge of the Province by Ragojee, whilst the latter pursued his progress towards Cuttack, and appears to have been very successful in extending the Mahratta authority over the whole of Chutteesghur and in exacting tribute from Sumbulpure and the other surrounding Zemindaries. He died in sumbut 1812 (A.D. 1755) when his brother-in-law Ranogee, availing himself of that confusion then existing in the Government of Nagpur from the disputed succession to Ragojee, usurped the chief authority. On the settlement of that question, Chutteesghur became the appanage of Bimbajee Bonsla, who sent a bramin named Pandoo Rung to assume the Government, but he was resisted and defeated by the usurper Ranogee. In sumbut 1815 (A.D. 1758) Bimbajee himself arrived at Ruttunpore, seized Ranojee, and personally ruled the Province until his death at Nurrah in Kaondwan in sumbut 1844 (A.D. 1787).

After this event, his Widow Anundee Bhaye exercised the chief authority for one year when Eswant Row Bawanee came into power. He was succeeded by the following soobadars:-

		Authority commenced
Myputrow Dinkur	... ...	sumbut 1845 A.D. 1788
Veetul Dinkur	... ...	” 1847 A.D. 1790

Kondo Visnew as agent to Bowanee Kaloo	... ...	”	1853 A.D. 1796
Khisboo Govind	... ...	”	1854 A.D. 1797
Vinkojee Piddree and Dircow Kullulkur	... ...	”	1865 A.D. 1808
Beccajee Gopaul	... ...	”	1866 A.D. 1809

Succaram Hurry and Seetaram Tantia acted for 3 and 8 months each during the temporary suspension from authority of Beccajee Gopaul.

Jadoo Rao Dewakur	... ...	”	1874 (A.D. 1817)

who was displaced by the arrival of Captain Edmonds in sumbut 1875 or June 1818 A.D.

Judging from the present state of the Zemindaries, into which the direct authority of the Mahrattas has not been introduced, compared with that of the Kalsa lands most of which have been under their direct management for near 74 years, the effect produced by their conquest of the country must be considered to have materially promoted the civilization of the inhabitants, as well as the agricultural improvement of the lands.

POPULATION AND DESCRIPTION OF THE INHABITANTS

Gross amount of the population. — The Gross amount of the population of the eight Kalsa Pergunahs, formerly described as having been under my charge since my first arrival in this district, according to a census which has lately been taken, amounts to 494, 845 souls or 100,603 families, of which 33,177 are cultivators; 53,180 traders, merchants and servants; and 14,246 are unemployed. These eight pergunahs may be considered as forming an oval of 180 miles in length and 120 in breadth, which would give 16,964 square miles and an average population of less than 30 souls to each.

Estimating the population of Droog Sanjaree, lately placed under my charge and in which no census has been taken, at 70,000 souls, and that of the talook of Koojee [Khujji] at 2,000 souls, the total populaion of the Kalsa Lands of Chuteesghur would then be 566,845 souls.

I have no information which enables me even to guess at the population of the zemindaries; but it may be observed generally that it is much more scanty than in the Kalsa lands, unless perhaps in the zemindaries of Cowerdah [Kawardha] and Pundareah which are pretty well peopled.

Numbers and castes of each trade or profession. — Confining my reply on this head to the eight Kalsa Pergunahs already mentioned there are within them—

Hindoos

	Families
Silver-Smiths	594
Black-Smiths	964
Carpenters	321
Gardeners	2,236
Oil-makers	9,519
Sellers of Arrack	1,680
Fishermen	1,416
Boatmen	3,644
Weavers	1,157
Silk Weavers	89
Tailors	125
Washermen	1,651
Brasiers	246
Cowherds	9,941
Barbers	1,375
Potters	605
Shepherds	398

Lumhans [? a class of Banjara]	...	...	159
Gosaeens	...	...	628
Byragees	...	...	975
Rahets (? Raouts]	...	...	125

All of the caste are designated by the trades to which they belong, but which some do not follow:

Also:—

			Families
*Bramins	...	...	3,127
Rajpoots	...	...	1,843
Bunneiahs	...	...	672
Conbees [? Kurmis]	...	...	7,190

Mahomedans principally employed as Sebundees† and Boodkurs [Revenue peons] 2,040.

Goands

			Families
Goands	...	...	17,314
Beejwars	...	...	512
Cowers [Kawars]	...	...	2,024
Hullbahs	...	...	1,340

All these come under the general appellation of Goands and are principally cultivators.

Low Castes

			Families
Kundairs	...	...	220
Gandahs	...	...	6,445
Punkas ...	...	...	625
Mahrahs	...	...	1,820
Hullalkores	...	...	53

Gusseahs, etc.	...	...	5,234
Chumbars	...	...	12,306

A Description of any district tribe that may exist and what part of the country they inhabit. — The only tribe I heard of that are peculiar to this part of India are the Koands, or inhabitants of Koandwan Kakair, and Bustar, and the Binderwa and Pardeea castes found in the hills north-east of Ruttunpore.

The Koands are Hindoos and not particularly distinguished from the wild inhabitants of other jungles, except by the high character they are reputed to possess for veracity and fidelity. Their word, it is said, may be wholly relied on, and they will never desert those to whom they have promised to adhere or betray those they have engaged to protect.

The Binderwas reside in hilly and woody country near Ruttunpore, particularly in the Koorba and Sirgooja hills, and much resemble the wild savages who have been described as met with in other parts of India. They appear to be so seldom seen by the other inhabitants of the country that there is much reason to doubt the truth of all that is reported respecting them. They are, however, said to have scarcely any religion; but if they regard any idol, Daby (Debi) has the preference. They go entirely naked; are armed with bows and arrows; never build any huts or seek other shelter than that afforded by the jungles; feed principally on the mowa and taindoo fruits furnished by the jungles, but sometimes cultivate small quantities of the coarse grains; are said to destroy their relatives when too old to move about and to eat their flesh, when a great entertainment takes place to which all the family is invited. Their enemies, and the travellers they may slay, they are also said to eat. It is doubtful that they have the ceremony of marriage.

The Pardeeas are less wild than the Binderwas, come occasionally into the villages to sell wood tatties and jungle fruits, and are not accused of being cannibals. They and the Binderwas have languages peculiar to themselves which are not understood by the other inhabitants of the country.

The following peculiarities may also be deserving of notice. Amongst the Musalmans there is a class who make bangles and dye cloths. They are generally distinguished by the appellation of "Toorkarries", and are said to worship the Hindoo idols and to besmear their houses with cowdung in the manner of that caste. The women in particular observe all the Hindoo superstitions and have abandoned their own faith.

The Bramins of Chuteesghur have also departed from strictness of the observances enjoyed by the Shastrees, they eat fish and animal food, and are consequently looked upon with great contempt by their more precise brethren.

The amount of the military population — This is very inconsiderable if the Goands be not included, and, although it is their habit to take up arms upon any occasion that presents itself, they are so despicable as soldiers that they little deserve the name. Excluding them therefore from what may be termed the military class, that will be reduced to about 3,000 Moosalmen settled in this province, and perhaps double the number of Moosalmen and Rajpoots, but principally the latter who have come from the Bengal Provinces to seek employment.

Numbers employed as Sebundees, etc., and out of service with suggestions respecting their employment, etc.—There are at present only 168 Sebundees in employ, but I should not suppose that above 2,000 of the military class were now destitute of all occupation or means of gaining a livelihood. Moosalmen settlers since they have lost military employ, have mostly become traders or cultivators, and the adventurers from Hindoostan are daily quitting the country or engaging in agricultural pursuits, for which there is an ample opening from the quantity of waste land in Chutteesgurh, and the system pursued of granting cowls exempting the holder from the payment of any rent for four years upon such untilled lands as they undertake to cultivate. Subsistence is also very cheap in this quarter, and upon the whole the distrees upon this class of the population I conceive to be less great than in other parts of India, and not to require further relief than that above adverted to.

General condition of the inhabitants. — The general condition of the inhabitants appears to me to be good. Their wants are few and those are supplied with little difficulty or exertion.

This is proved by the excessive indolence of the people who, if they have food for to-day, will take no concern for the morrow, a confidence which must arise in their exemption heretofore from all hardship or want. Indeed, from all I can learn, the calamity of a famine has not for above 40 years occurred in this quarter, owing probably to grain being the principal production of the country, and to the climate and soil yielding with wonderfully little culture, as well the Rubbee as the Kureef crops both of which can scarcely fail. A larger quantity also being produced annually than is required for the consumption of the inhabitants, it is always cheap and abundant, and thus the inhabitants are relieved from all apprehension of a scarcity of food, and from all necessity to provide by activity and foresight against such a deficiency. To these advantages may be added the facility or obtaining a livelihood, afforded to all who seek for employment, by the quantity of unoccupied land fit for tillage. The people are healthy and stout, but their frequently effeminate appearance bespeaks the ease in which they live. Their towns and villages although of an unprepossessing appearance, consisting of thatched huts, are far from uncomfortable. Each family has two or three of these huts, the whole surrounded by a wall, which, with the interior yard, is neatly plastered with a whitish earth and has a clean appearance. Beggars are rare and those met with are generally so by profession.

Languages. — The languages spoken in Chuteesghur are the following.

The primitive inhabitants of Chuteesghur proper speak either Goandy or Chutteesghury, the latter being a mixture of Goandy and Hindoostanee. To the east and towards Sumbulpore some of the inhabitants speak Oorreeah which seems to be derived from the dialects of the Eastern Coast. In Koandwan, Kakair and Bustar and Karondee [Kalahandi] the Koand language is spoken which from what I can learn seems to be a mixture of the Goand and Oorreeah dialects. The Pardeea and Bindurwa tribes mentioned in a former part of this report also speak dialects peculiar to themselves. Besides these Hindoostanee, Mahratti and Telingee have been introduced by the numerous settlers from other parts of India.

Manners and Customs. — The manners and customs of the inhabitants of Chutteesgurh do not appear materially to differ from those of similar castes in other parts of India which have been described. The only points which attract particular attention are the prevalence amongst the Goands of human sacrifices to their Idols and the universal belief in witch-craft by all the inhabitants of the country.

The first of these practices has, I believe and hope, ceased since the introduction of our authority but I am assured that before it was not unusual although the Mahrattas had endeavoured to abolish it.

Culprits, and prisoners made during war, and sometimes innocent persons, were sacrificed at the shrine of Daby, by the Goands, and it was not an unfrequent mode of punishment by the chiefs of that tribe to direct an offender to be taken to pay his devotions before some particular Idol, and to cause him to be put to death at the moment he prostrated himself before the image.

The belief in witch-craft has no exceptions, the best informed and the most ignorant of the Hindoos and Moosalmen alike give credit to its existence. The art is however supposed to reside almost exclusively in old women, and the faith of this class in the general superstition is such, as actually to induce them to believe that they are possessed of the power imputed to them, and frequently to acknowledge themselves Tonees (as witches are here called) although the consequence [? confession] subjects them to immediate death, or at least to expulsion from their caste and severe punishment.

The usual test by which witches are discovered is that of plunging them tied up in a bag into the water. If they sink they are innocent, if they swim guilty, and they are punished sometimes by death, at others their teeth are drawn, they are made to drink the water in which skins of dead animals have been immersed, are beaten with the twigs of a particular bush supposed to have peculiar properties, and are turned out of their caste and sometimes out of the village.

In Chutteesgurh, as in other parts of India, little reliance is placed in the bare assertion of any individual upon a fact in which he is interested. This has

133 led to the practice called Deep, which was common until the introduction of our authority, of persons submitting the truth of their declarations to the following test.

One of the parties, generally the complainant, having seven leaves of the Peeple tree placed upon his two hands, and secured with cotton threads, and the whole rubbed with butter, receives into them a red hot ball of iron about the size of a 4 pounder shot, which if he carries seven paces without the flesh of the hands being burnt his truth is established, and he is entitled to the redress which his case demands. If his hands are burnt he is adjudged to have told a falsehood and is dismissed or punished.

It may also be remarked that the people of this province are particularly cleanly, none excepting of the lowest caste eating their daily meals until they have bathed.

State of their moral character. — Considering the uninformed state of the people their moral character seems to be superior to that met with in most other parts of India. Murders are rare and are in most cases occasioned by jealousy or supposed acts of witchcraft, both which occasions are universally considered, if not a sufficient justification, at least a great palliation of the offence. Petty thieving seldom occurs, and the more daring robberies by gangs and on the highways are less frequent than might be expected from the facility to escape afforded by the surrounding jungles and Zamindaries. In regard to women their habits appear to be rather loose. On the whole they may be said to be honest, to be unaddicted to great crimes, and to have more regard to truth than is common in India, as an instance of which it may be mentioned that offenders very generally make an unhesitating confession of the crimes they have committed.

The state of Education and to what castes generally extended and its expense. — Education in this Province is confined to very few children. Those are generally of the Bramin, Gosein, Rajpoot, Kaet, Sonar, Tumbair, Bunniah, Mahratta and Moossalman castes. Some are instructed in the houses of their parents by one of the members of the family or by a person retained for the purpose. Others by the shastry or principal Brahmin of the village. In the first instance the children present their tutor upon certain days of the year with a present but this is optional, and the value is not fixed. It also is seldom accepted and is tendered merely as a mark of respect. The remuneration of the tutor, if he receives any, consists in his living free of expense with the parents of the children and in the claim he establishes to their good offices, as well as to those of his scholars. In the latter case where the principal Brahmin teaches the children of the village, he has no other object than the performance of a praise-worthy and charitable act. Presents are occasionally offered to him by his scholars, but they are of no value and are seldom accepted. Ruttunpore is the only place where I have heard of school masters who instruct scholars as a profession, for a fixed remuneration. There they generally receive between 2 and 4 annas per month per month for each boy. No caste teaches their daughters to read or write. The languages generally taught are the Naggeree and Mahratta and some few are instructed in Persian and Hindoostanee.

Number of Schools. — The number of schools of the description I have mentioned does not exceed 4 or 5 at Ruttunpore, 3 at Ryepore and perhaps one at each large village.

Disposition of the inhabitants to the present order of things. — The disposition of the inhabitants to the present order of things is very favourable. Two classes alone may be considered as dissatisfied, those are the revenue servants principally Mahratta Brahmins, and the military, who have been thrown out of employ. All others seem highly to value the tranquillity and security to their persons and property which they at present enjoy. Even the Goands who are famed for restlessness show no disposition to revert to their former habits of insurrection and plunder.

PRODUCTIONS OF THE COUNTRY — NATURAL AND ARTIFICIAL

What kinds of and what quantity of grain. — The grains produced are rice, wheat, chenna, kodo, jow, kootkee, bajra; and pulses oorad, toor, buttana, musoor, moong, and lack [Tiura]. Both rice and wheat are produced in most parts of the province, but the former predominates in the northern and eastern Pergunnas, and the latter in the southern and western. Chhenna is grown everywhere. I have no means of stating the quantity of these grains produced annually, but it greatly exceeds the consumption and leaves large quantities for exportation.

Jewaree and coolty [kulthi] have both been tried and thrive well, but they are not valued or used, and are not sown.

The coarse grains such as kodo, bajra, kootkee, etc., etc., are grown in the Zemindaries where the soil is bad and hilly.

Spices. — There are no vegetable productions which can correctly be termed spices, but there are a great variety of medicines and curry stuffs of a somewhat similar description. The principal of these are the following:—

Dunneah	Adrack
Sope	Pimplamole
Bellanah	Dypool
Hirdah	Mooradoosaing.
Beeara	Sailudge
Owlah	Indierjow
Charolee	Pullass

Gums. — There are a great variety of gums produced in the surrounding jungles, and large quantities are exported, but the practice seems to be to mix all together and [not] to separate that of any particular tree, from which it may be inferred that the properties of all are nearly alike.

The dyes are lakh, buckoolee, coosoomba, kutta, cumeela, load, pullcasska pool, shaina, neel, munjeet rainudge and hurdah, but of these I should imagine small quantities produced, for coloured cloths are seldom seen in provinces, the common mungall being the only colouring matter which the inhabitants use.

Metals. — There are no metals produced in Chhutteesghur except Iron which is found in the Zemindaries of Matin, Ooprodah, Koorba, and Chooree. Abruck or Talk is said to be found in the Zemindary of Kaindah.

Oils.— The oil plants are the ulsee, till, errundee, akbaree, sirsa, and kirdy, all which are in abundance.

Other Productions. — The other productions of Chutteesghur are cotton which seems to thrive well, particularly in the Nawaghur Pergunnah and the Zemindaries of Cowerdah and Pundareeah, the sugar-cane, the sun and ambaree, arrowroot, tobacco, the beetle Leaf, considerable quantities of bees wax and a good deal of the coarse silk called tussar. The province, particularly Dumdah, is also famous for its ghee, but no large quantity appears to be exported.

The indigo or neel mentioned among the dyes grows wild all over the country, and might, I imagine, be cultivated to any extent. But the inhabitants do not understand how to extract the colouring matter and scarcely use it at all.

Horse, cattle and sheep. — No good horses are bred and the climate is said to be unfavourable to that animal but there are many tatoos. Bullocks and cows bred in numbers, but are rather small and are swept away by periodical distempers. Buffaloes are not numerous, but are large, fine and indigenous to the country, as they are found wild in the surrounding jungles. They are much more highly valued than bullocks. Sheep are bred and they are woolly and short legged, but are not in abundance.

TRADE

Manufactures. — The manufactures are limited to coarse cotton cloths, cloths made of the coarse silk called tussar, cumlies of sheep's wool, Tats or gunees made of sun or hemp, and small quantities of cotton tape.

Articles of trade. — The exports of Chutteesghur consist of manufactures of cotton and tussar clothes, cumlies and gunees; in raw materials cotton and tussar; in grains, of rice, wheat, chenna and mussor; of all the different grains for making oil; of the beetle Leaf, tobacco, sugar, arrowroot, all the various jungle medicines and curry stuffs, ghee, oil, gums, wax and iron; and in some instances of buffaloes and bullocks.

The imports are, from the Eastern Coast, salt, coconuts, sooparee, brass and other metals; from Mirzapore, silks, kincobs, broad cloth, shawls, salt-pepper and brimstone, glass bangles, the coarse metals, foreign spices, sugar, dried ginger, opium, hing, and other medicines and curry stuff, paper, elephants, camels and horses; from Mundla, cotton, chintz, karwa, cumlies of a fine kind, Iron vessels, metals, bullocks and buffaloes; from Nagpur, cloths of a high value, also coloured cloths, silks, shawls, metals, metal vessels, made up ganja, gold and silver; from Bastar and the Southern Jungles, buffaloes, bullocks, and gums.

Amount of imports and exports.— The customs in this District being farmed, I have no means of answering this question with precision, the contractor not being able to give me the required information, and being unwilling to submit his accounts to examination. There can, however, be little doubt that the imports greatly exceed the exports in value.

Suggestions for its improvement. — The only direct measures which occur to me as likely to improve trade, would be the opening of new lines of communication, particularly that by water to Cuttack, and the removal of the numerous heavy and vexatious imports levied, as well in Chhutteesghur as beyond it. The buying up the koots or tolls from the Zemindaries, and the regulating of the customs upon fixed and just principles would appear best calculated to effect the latter object.

MILITARY DEFENCE

What troops regular and irregular now stationed in the district, what numbers of each may be reckoned necessary to have permanently. — There are now stationed in the province two hundred of the auxiliary horse, one battalion of the Nagpur brigade 800 rank and file strong, with a brigade of guns attached, two companies of Madras Native Infantry, and the Chutteesgurh provincial battalion of 544 rank and file, also 168 sebundies.

Of these troops the two companies Madras Native Infantry and the sebundies may probably be dispensed with, but the remainder appear necessary to secure the tranquillity of the province. The greater part are stationed at Ryepore which is central and has as yet proved quite healthy. The remainder are stationed at Bellaspore, the nearest point to Ruttunpore which was found salubrious, and the locality of which was favourable to the object to keeping in check the numerous Zemindars of that quarter and of suppressing the bands of Freebooters who have not unfrequently appeared in the vicinity of Ruttunpore, the population of which likewise, being composed of a variety of adventurers attracted from other quarters by the cheapness of subsistence, requires to be controlled and overawed.

LAND REVENUE

A General account of the systems which have prevailed at different times. — Under the Hyhywane Rajahs the feudal principles of their rule precluded anything in the nature of a system of revenue. The rajah and the members of his family retained more lands under their own management than were necessary for their comfort and dignity, the rest were assigned to their chiefs, who, on their requisition, supplied them with whatever they required, with money according to their wants, and in war with quotas of troops proportioned to the lands they held. These petty lords seem, on their part, to have followed the same system, retaining but small tracts of land in their own hands and distributing the remainder amongst their servants who were at the same time soldiers and cultivators. The Judicial authority in important cases they personally exercised but in all inferior and common occasions they left the chief executive authority in revenue as well as other matters to the head of each talook or village, who, it may be concluded, did not act upon any general or uniform plan.

The conquest of the country by the Mahrattas changed this state of things and gradually led to the introduction of their revenue system in all those parts of the province which were sufficiently productive to repay the trouble of the change.

During the time of Rajah Ragojee Ist, little was done towards establishing any regularity, although Mohun Sing, who was left in charge of the province by him was very active and successful in subduing many Zemindars and either making their lands Kalsa or subjecting them to tribute.

After Bimbajee's arrival in sumbut 1815 (A.D. 1758), the first attempts were made to establish order; but it was not until the time of Veetul Dinkur, who filled the office of Soobadar in sumbut 1847 (A.D. 1790) that any regular revenue system was introduced; and that then adopted has continued, with but few changes, until the superintendence of the affairs of the District fell into our hands. It was as follows:—

The assessment was upon each village, was settled annually, according to detailed orders received from Nagpur, and was paid in three equal instalments.

In June the Fussili year commenced. At that season, the only measure adopted by the Soobadar of the District and by the Commavisdars of Pergunnahs was to encourage the ryots to cultivate the ground and to invite back any who might have absconded, but this they did merely as occasions offered, and did not assemble the ryots for the purpose. Indeed, their business at this time was to keep quiet.

If the ryots of each village as they usually did, complained to the Potail or Gowteah that the existing distribution of lands was unfair, he assembled them and a new division, which satisfied all parties, took place. If also any stated that they required aid in money, seed, or cattle; the Potail or Gowteah aided them if he had the means, or, if he had not, became their security with some sowkar. But for these purposes there was no particular day, nor were the ryots collected at all unless on their own application.

After the seed was sown (in the end of July or beginning of August) Commavisdars recommenced their *Tuckaza* for any balances on account of the preceding year remaining due to the Government.

In Zilkand (end of August) the Soobadar of the District despatched *Takeeds* to Commavisdars of Pergunnahs directing them to collect one-third of the annual Revenue according to the assessment of the last year and to remit the amount to the Public Treasury before the 5th Aswin (October). On receipt of these orders the Commavisdar immediately despatched *chitteess* to each Putail or Gowteah directing them to repair to the Kusba for the purpose of settling the *sall* or Annual Assessment and to bring with them the instalment then due.

The Putails and Gowteeahs complying with these directions assembled at the Kusba. If the Commavisdar thought a village could pay more than it had done the preceding year, he demanded about double the increase he expected, and after a good deal of discussion concluded an agreement with Gowteeah or Patail for the current year, taking from the latter what was called a *Wydah Poorjah* or receipt, in which the amount of assessment agreed upon was particularized, and an engagement entered into for its payment before the expiration of the year in certain *kists* or instalments. It also contained an agreement to pay such further sum as the Subadar or the Sirkar might impose on the country generally. Ten or twelve days were then demanded and allowed for collecting and paying the Kist already due, and the Patails and Gowteeahs returned to their villages. On these occasions, and whilst discussing the amount of assessment, they made various representations that their lands had fallen out of cultivation from epidemics amongst the ryots or their cattle, that the season had been bad, that disturbances had prevented the labours of the field, etc. Of these the Commavisdars who were most attentive to their duty, took notes which in some cases they made the Gowteeahs sign.

Thus one-third of the revenue corresponding generally in the total amount from each Pergunnah, but not in the assessment on each village, with the last year, was collected and paid into the Treasury before the Dussara (September or October). If any remained due by the Pergunna at that festival the Soobadar wrote letters urging its immediate payment, and if they were not attended to he gave a *Barrat* or order on the Commavisdar to some troops or others who exacted payment.

The Second Instalment also one-third, was collected by precisely a similar process, except that Commavisdars sent the Revenue Peons under their authority, who are in most parts of this Province called Boodkurs, sometimes with chits, sometimes without, to receive the amounts from each Putail or Gowteeah, and did not summon them to the Kushbah, the 5th of Poos (January) being the date within which it was to be paid into the treasury.

Between the collection of these two Kists the most active and zealous of the Commavisdars made a tour of their Pergunnahs in order that they might be prepared, on the coming of the Soobadar, to give him the fullest information, particularly as to the truth or otherwise of the various representations made to them by Patails and Gowteeahs of which in settling the *sall* they had taken notes, and had allowed to influence them in reducing or increasing the assessment of the past year.

At the sowing of the rubbee crop in October and November, as at the Kurreef, the Putail or Gowteeah of each village aided his ryots with seed and advances of money, but no new distribution of the lands took place.

The third instalment, or the remaining third, was payable on the 5th of Chite (April) and was collected in the same manner as the second.

The Soobadar having received the second instalment of the revenue commenced his tour generally about the end of January. He previously apprized Commavisdars of his approach, and directed them to assemble all the Putails and Gowteeahs. He visited each Kushbah, where he remained but three or four days, seldom making any tour of the Pergunnah. On arriving he called upon the Commavisdar and Furnaveese for the Kutcha accounts of the collections made in the last year, and having received these, he heard in public Cutchery all that the Putails, Gowteeahs or ryots might wish to state. From their representations, from the report of the Commavisdar, from his own public or secret enquiries and adverting to the orders he had received from Nagpur he determined whether to confirm or to alter (which he was understood to have the power of doing) the *sall* settled by the Commavisdar. When an increase was thought necessary, as was generally the case, that was enforced more by the weight of the Soobadar than by any compulsory measures, and was seldom carried into effect without the consent, although perhaps yielded reluctantly, of the Putails and Gowteeahs. If any particular Gowteeah, however, would not come into the general arrangement and complained of the sum at which his village was assessed, the Soobadar enquired into the payment it had made for the last year, and from the neighbouring villages into its present state, and decided upon the representation by the result. If that was not satisfactory to the complainant, the village was offered to another; and, where a candidate stood forward which was generally prearranged underhand, the objection was either withdrawn, as was commonly the case or the Gowteeah was changed.

The account of the Pandree or tax upon those classes not being cultivators, and of the *kut* or toll collected on cattle loaded with grain of merchandize, were examined in a general way; and the receipts on account of Sewayee (fines, etc.,) were particularly enquired into from the date of the Soobadar's last tour. This latter being a branch of revenue in which impositions were frequent, persons were encouraged by agents of the Soobadar to come forward and state the payments they had made, that it might appear whether the whole amount, deducting certain allowed fees to the Revenue Servants, had been credited to the public. Finally the Bakee Account, or arrears of former years, was examined. The Commavisdar's expenditure was also looked into and cautions given him, but its final settlement was deferred to the end of the year.

Thus the Bakee Account and whole assessment of the current year, was finally fixed, and a copy of the Terrow or Settlement, entered on the Dufters was taken by the Furnaveese of the Pergunnah. In it was stated the Bakee from the last year, the total revenue for the current year, the instalments in which it was to be paid, the expenses allowed for the Mall Muskoor, the deductions for Mokassa villages, Dirmadow, Devestan, and Nainmooks, the amount which had already been paid to the Circar, and the balance which would remain due. For this latter sum the Commavisdar's receipt, payable within a limited time, was taken.

The complaints of the ryots against Putails and Gowteeahs were also attended to by the Soobadar, but what the latter might have improperly collected was appropriated by the Government and was not returned to the aggrieved parties. Complaints of oppression and on all other points were likewise heard and investigated, and redressed to the extent which accorded with the views and habits of the Soobadar.

All these matters having been gone through the Soobadar addressed the cultivators and others assembled in the Cutcherry in terms of encouragement, telling the former the amount at which the whole Pergunnah had been assessed, for it does not appear to have ever been the practice to acquaint each Putail or Gowteeah what the exact sum his village was to pay, although he might, by attending the Cutcherry, pick up that information. He then dismissed them, sometimes giving them all Paun, at others that form was omitted, but to the head Putails and Gowteeahs he always gave cloths informing the rest that a remission of $1^{7}/_{8}$ per cent on the leen Ank (about 2/5 of the whole Revenue) would be granted to them in lieu of Sirpau, as this annual present of cloths is here termed.

Thus the Soobadar completed his tour in eight or ten weeks, when he commenced to close the annual accounts, and to prepare those to be sent to Nagpur. He also took the measures before described for realizing the last Kist.

On the expiration of the Fussily year in June he sent off Takeeds to call the Furnaveeses of Pergunnahs with the accounts of the year.

On their arrival they were compared with accounts of the Soobah Muskoor, differences explained and reconciled, the expenditure of Commavisdars finally examined, and either their receipts required payable in a certain time or an order given on them for all sums not admitted, as well as for any balance of revenue remaining due, unless they had applied for an extension of time in favour of certain individuals whom particular circumstances prevented from immediately liquidating the demands against them, and could state that they were in possession of their receipts for the amount; in which cases from one to three months was granted.

The revenue was classed on the Dufters under a variety of heads. The form was as follows:—

Bakee of Last and Former Years.

Mahalance.

Soobah Muskoor.

Total Bakee.

Sall Muskoor (a) *Commavish*

Jeen Commavish

- *Kalsa*
  - Mall consisting of the leen Dowl or original Jumma and Seewayee Dowl or various impositions subsequently added under the denominations of Babtees Puttees and Teekahs Zahat or Pandree
  - Syer including Koots
    - Seway Mahlka: Contracts for Ferries, rents of topes of trees, etc.
    - Duffay Mahlka – extra collections, Nuzzers, etc.
- *Zemindari*
  - Prant Chutteesghur
  - Prant Kaondwan

Seway Commavish

- Nurmeenah or tax on certain articles not included in the Syer Taingah Putty or tax on Bunjaries.
- *Dand etc.*
  - Goonaigaree,
  - Chorie Pairawun,
  - Murkee,
  - Mooar,
  - Gyar,
  - Javah,
  - Chowtye,
  - Mussala,
  - etc. etc.

Total Commavish

(b) Duffaty Femma	*Babtee Mahalance—*
	Nuzzers.
	Chundali Durmadow, etc., etc.
Ieen Duffay	*Baptee Soobah Muskoor—*
	Kussur Brustunka, profit or Koownee Batta, deduction of 4 per cent from the pay of the troops where so agreed upon.
	Nuzzer Dussarah ka, presents made to the Soobadar at that Festival. Chillerah, extraordinaries and Sundries.
	Sowkaree money borrowed from Sowkars.
	Berratdhar, money due on berrats the total of which had been entered in the accounts as paid.
	Mahlance—Money borrowed by
Kurruje	Commavisdars of Pergunnahs.
	Tullub—Balance of pay due to public servants, whose entire salaries had been entered in the accounts as paid.
	Kussurkee Kurruje—Money due on a doubtful account and which there is no intention of paying.
	Total Duffatay Jemma.

Total of Sall Muskoor

Total of Bakee and Sall Muskoor.

The Mahl or assessment on the Kalsa Land was, as observed, sub-divided into two great heads, the leen Dowl, or original Jemma and the Seway Dowl subsequent impositions. These were generally in the proportion to each other of 2/5ths and 3/5ths.

The Seway Dowl consisted of near thirty Babtees. Teekas and Putti which will be particularized in a subsequent part of this report. They were put on at different times and under different pretences and were limited in the operation to certain Pergunnahs. But it was only whilst they were new that they were known to the ryots or distinguished by them from the general assessment. They usually paid the revenue under the following appellations and knew of no other sub-divisions.

The *sall*, or produce of the rice crop, which the ryots so called, although on the dufters it signified the revenue of the whole year.

The Oonally (Unhari) or produce of the wheat crop.

The Gowteeah and Kurree Putty, the first a tax on Gowteeahs proportioned to the land they cultivated, the last a tax on the houses of all cultivators one of which was collected yearly and alternatively [*sic*].

The Teekay of Nuzzers presented at the Raka and other festivals to Commavisdar on account of the Circar.

The Revenue Servants were paid partly by acknowledged salaries, which were entered in the public accounts and partly by perquisites fixed by custom, but which did not appear in the public accounts and were collected extra to the Government Revenue. The principal of these was a Rupee from each village to each of the following officers:—

The Soobadar of the Province.

Furnavees of the do

Pretty (? Prithi] of the Province when there was one, and he was not paid by an additional tax on the Zemindars.

The Cammavisdar of the Pergunnah.

Furnaveese of the Pergannah.

All these officers were likewise entitled to a similar fee from each individual who was fined, but generally took as much more as they could contrive to obtain.

The Furnaveese and Pretty of the Province also withheld for themselves each one per cent on all payments to the Government Troops.

Besides these and the Nuzzers which all inferiors presented to their superiors on every occasion of visiting them there appears in times of common regularity to have been no collections beyond those acknowledged and entered in the public accounts, unless the practice called Chundaw Dirmadow be considered in that light. It was as follows. If a needy Bramin came to the Soobadar and requested assistance, he with the other servants of the Soobadar gave him something in charity out of his own pocket, and arranged with Cammavisdars of Pergunnahs by a private and unofficial communication that they should in their respective limits collect from such village and give to the distressed individuals, one, two or three annahs. Sometimes also the Soobadar received these half voluntary contributions and distributed them in charity to poor Bramins.

The military were paid either in cash out of the Treasury or by orders on the country.

With respect to the Zamindaries their Tribute does not appear in most cases, to have been considered as fixed, but to have depended on the state of the country and means of the chief. It was payable in Kists, but these were seldom attended to. Indeed great arrears were generally due, and payments seldom made until troops were sent to exact them.

For the Zemindaris of Kaondwan there was a separate collector, or Commavisdar, and a Karkoon with an escort was sent annually to receive the tribute of Bastar.

The expenses were classed on the Dufters as follows:—

JIRTEE OR EXPENSES

Ersall or expenses chargeable against Nagpur

Kuzzoorat
- Burnak, Sawkaree given to Sawkars on Bills.
- Nugdee, ready cash sent to Nagpur.
- Berrats, orders in favour of troops and other Sewaye.
- Berrat-expenses defrayed for the Government otherwise than on bills and which did not attach to Chutteesghur.

Sebundy
- Tynautee
  - Sowar
  - Pydul.
- Soobah Muskoor
  - Sowar
  - Pydul

Ieen Taywel

Perricharika -	Female servants of the Rajah's household
Raka	Concubines ....do.............
Boslay	Sons of the female household servants.
Kangee	The Rajah's own expenses.

Taywel Kursh — *Karkanah*

- Paugah
  - Servants
  - Food, etc.
- Feet Kana
  - Servents
  - Food, etc.

Naimnookdar —	Danistan (Here enter all particulars) Dermadow (Here enter all particulars). Ballah Loak, Moolsuddy, etc. (Here enter all particulars)

(Total of Eersall)

Prant Muskoor Kursh (*Chuttesghur expenses*)

Soobah Muskoor.

Buddull Mooshara —	Karkoon Mundally. (Here enter the pay of the Soobadar and all the other Soobadar Servants). Shagird Paisha. Do. of Baldars, Patedhars, and all the inferior servants of Soobadar. Sebundee— Pydul with all particulars. Sewars, etc., etc.

Kairedge Moosharah —	Dufter Kursh with particulars.	
	Dermadow with	
	Byaz Batta	do.
	Dussarah Kursh	
	etc.	etc.

Buddul Mooskara —
- Balance Mall Muskoor
- Karkoon Mundelly with particulars being the pay of Pergunnah servants.
- Sebundee

Kairije Mooskara —
- Dufter Kursh
- Dermadow.
- Byaz Battas.
- etc. etc.

Total of expenses of Prant Muskoor.

Total of Eersal and of Prant Muskoor or Ieen Jertee

Duffatay Fifty.

Rut kursh Goozishtay ka

Sowkaree
Berratdar.
Muhlance
Tulbuldhar.
Total

General Total of Ieen Jirty and Duffatay Jirty.

The balance or difference between the two foregoing accounts of receipts and disbursements was explained in a third account the form of which was as follows:—

Bakee (particulars of balance)

Malance —
- Kalsa
- Zemindaree

Soobah Maskor — [Selluck / Assameewar]

Total of Bakee

Changes that have been introduced and their effects. — In the foregoing system few changes of any importance were made by the Soobadars who succeeded Veetul Dinkur, and those which did take place arose more in irregularities than from intention. Thus some Soobadars contented themselves with a general settlement with each Pergunnah and looked little into the distribution of the assessment on villages and otherwise neglected many parts of their duty. The amount of the Kists and the periods when they were paid, were also often changed. The Soobadar Caishoo Pandit made the first, equal to one-half of the annual revenue, and the remaining two equal to one-fourth each. The first, he made payable on the 5th Baderpud (September), the second on the 5th Kartick (November) and the third on the 5th Poos (January). Bickajee Gopaul made each payment ten days later and did away [with] the sub-division of the Mahl upon the Dufters into Babtees, Puttees and Teekas as well as the distinction of the Ieen Dowl and Seway Dowl, classing the whole collections from the land under the general head of Kallee.

It was in his time that the Bakee first became large. The cause seems to have been the excessive increase of assessments under the heads of Doanna, Josah and Sowaree Putties ordered from Nagpur by Appah Sahib after the death of Nana Sahib in 1222 Fusselee.

Beecajee Gopaul could not safely to himself resist the directions he received, he therefore nominally increased the revenue, to an extent greatly exceeding the means of the country, but wrote off as Newper and carried to the account of the Bakee all that was not realized. Remissions not being granted from Nagpur and the increased assessments continued, the revenues of the present year were applied to the liquidation of the arrears of the former, and thus a process of accumulating Bakee was commenced which could not fail to proceed rapidly.

He also first commenced the practice of Burguns. These were an additional assessment imposed, extra to the usual Jumma, generally towards the end of the year, and were meant to cover the Newper or defalcations above noticed. They were raised indifferently on the lands or as Seway by arbitrary confiscation and fines. Wherever money was found it was taken. This irregularity once introduced Burguns became common under various pretences, and a practice arose for Cammavisdars of their own authority to collect Burguns to cover what was termed the Seway Bootah or that portion of their own expenses which was retrenched from the public accounts. Such a latitude, when admitted of, had of course no limit, but their own fears of punishment and the poverty of the country.

This last usage was known to the Soobadar but he did not prevent it owing seemingly to the retrenchments in the accounts of Cammavisdars being in part for supplies which the Cirkar Pauga and other troops exacted from them by compulsion, but which would not have been admitted in his public accounts had he charged for them. He also raised Burguns for his own expenses.

Latterly only general instructions respecting the annual assessment came from Nagpur and sometimes none at all.

It also became the practice to take the receipts of Commavisdars for the revenue of the whole year deducting only the expenses of the Mall Muskoor and Mokassa, Namenook Durmadow Dawistan.

A minute description of the Mahratta mode of assessment and collection at the time of our assuming charge.— This has been so fully given in the foregoing part of this report, that a separate reply under this head would be little more than a repetition of what has already been stated, unless indeed, an attempt were made to describe the irregularities of Jadoo Row's Soobadarry, but as these were justified by no precedent, and seem to have arisen out of the confusion of the time and the pressure of Appah Sahib's wants, little advantage would result from detailing them.

His Soobadarry was one uniform scene of plunder and oppression uninfluenced by any consideration but that of collecting by whatever means the largest amount possible. The *system* therefore which existed, if any did exist at the time of our taking charge, was that which has been described as prevailing at the termination of Biccajee Gopaul's authority.

Any changes that have since been introduced and their effects. — On my arrival at Chuteesghur, I found that my predecessor, the late Captain Edmonds, had abolished the collection made under the following heads: Jadoo Row's Nuzzer, Commavisdar's Teeka, Furnaveeses' Farkut Chundah, Dermadow and Seway Boota.

These regulations I confirmed, and did away all distinctions in the revenue except those of the Kalee or the land assessment, the Pandry or tax on the trading and other classes not being cultivators, the Syer and Koot or customs and tolls, the Seway or extra Revenue, the Duffay or extraordinary receipts and the Oobary or tribute from Zemindars.

Finding that the ryots were subject to great loss by the period fixed for the payment of the Kists which so much preceded the reaping of their crops as to compel them to pay a heavy interest on the money they borrowed to meet the demands of the Government, I changed the instalments to the following dates. *Viz.*, one-half of the annual revenue to be paid on the 5th of Aswin (October), one-quarter on the 5th Mang (February), one-quarter on the 5th Chyte (April); and this year have further postponed them to one-half on the 5th Kartick (November), one-quarter on the 5th Mang (February), one quarter on the 5th Chyte (April).

As the best means of giving publicity to the Jemabundy fixed for each Pergunnah, and preventing unauthorized collections, I adopted the practice of fixing the assessment on the Kalsa lands by a proclamation which stated the amount to be paid by each village, and was repeatedly explained to the assembled Potels, Gowteeahs and Ryots, copies being delivered to such as wished for them and could read.

There being no Village Writers or records in this Province and the Dufters of the Soobadarry being very imperfect and furnishing little information of a statistical nature, I thought it essential in view to any improvements which might be hereafter contemplated to remove this deficiency. I consequently appointed Ameens to each Pergunnah with Pundays to every 20 or 30 villages, according to their size to investigate the actual state of the country and to record the information they collected in a form furnished to them.

The Ameens also I made independent of Commavisdars, that they might be a check upon them. And for similar reasons gave them and Furnaveeses access to each other's records. The investigation above alluded to having been completed in all the Kalsa Pergunnahs, Droog excepted which only lately came under my charge, the Pandys have been discharged and the Ameens' duty so far changed that they now keep an entire, copy of the Pergunnah papers and affix their Bhar or mark to all receipts for money. It still, however, is their chief duty to enquire into the actual state of the cultivation, to ascertain what collections are made by whatsoever authority, and how they are disposed of.

I ordered receipts to be taken by Gowteeahs and Putails from Commavisdars for all payments made to them as the best means of ascertaining the truth of complaints of unauthorized exactions, and of preventing confusion in accounts.

Following the principle, commenced by Captain Edmonds, I did away with all unacknowledged perquisites and confined the Revenue Servants to their established pays forbidding them to be engaged in Trade.

To Commavisdars I allowed 1 1/2 per cent on the gross annual revenue of their respective Pergunnahs, the Syer not included.

To Furnaveeses comprehending their assistants 1 per cent.

To Ameens comprehending their assistants 1 per cent.

For the Kairijee Mooshara which includes the Kutcherry expenses and all disbursements at festivals, etc., 1/2 per cent on Do.

For the Sirpow or annual presents to Potels and Gowteeahs 3/4 per cent on the land revenue only.

And I fixed the pay of the Revenue Peons or Boodkurs at 2 1/2 Rupees each per month.

The Pandays were the only public servants whom I allowed to be paid by a collection extra to the Circar Jumma, and, as they have been discharged that is now done away with. They received 100 Rupees per annum which was raised under the orders of the Commavisdars from the villages placed under their investigation.

The only collections now made which do not inter into the public accounts are for the village establishments hereafter noticed or for Jockees [Joshis], Byragees, Goseins, and Fakeers, who have at different periods obtained grants in money or grain in certain villages. But the amount of these is not great and they have all been ascertained and duly registered.

I gradually abolished payments in Cowries, where they had been usual, and productive of loss and inconvenience.

I regulated the weight and measures in reference to those used in this quarter, and at Nagpur.

I reduced the number of Pergunnahs from 27 to 8, by which the business was very greatly lessened, and accounts simplified, besides rendering the situation of the Pergunnah Servants more respectable and lucrative, and consequently more worth the acceptance of persons of character and influence.

In the hope of rendering the Kullaly or sale of arrack more productive, I disunited it from the land revenue, with which it had in some cases been blended, and made it a separate contract. This, however, I subsequently found to cause much distress to the Goand population who live in a great measure upon the fruit of the mowah tree from which arrack is made, and consequently restored the former practice directing that the proceeds should be kept under a distinct head.

After a short experience, perceiving [?I perceived] the necessity of some general rules being established with regard to the advantages to be engaged [? enjoyed] by Potels and Gowteeahs, which, if not immediately inforced with much strictness, might still be the rule for deciding upon complaints. In adopting these, I was wholly guided by what I could learn to be the practice of this country. It is, however, well known to all who have enquired into Indian institutions, that they are directed by a general understanding seldom if ever by precise rules, and that that understanding is so loosely acted upon, that, amongst the innumerable deviations that are met with, it is no easy task to discover the most universal and established practice.

The advantages of the Patail I fixed at 1 anna in each Rupee of Land Revenue, to be collected extra to the bicar [? Sircar] Jumma.

The Gowteeah's duties in assisting his ṛyots I defined, as well as his responsibility for deficiencies of revenue, and allowed him the Ground cultivated by one plough in every 8 belonging to his village free of rent, also as Bahiee [Biyâi]. One Ratta in every Rupee's worth of grain sold in his village, and as Serra Dooly [Serha doli] the land cultivated by one plough in every sixteen to be dressed by the whole ryots of the village, and the produce applied in charity, and in the subsistence of travellers, etc.

The produce of Mango Topes, and other fruit trees, having no owners, were also assigned half to Patails, half to Gowteeahs. Following the established practice, I likewise allowed a Karkoon to keep the accounts of every village yielding a Revenue of 1,000 Rupees, restored the Boodkurs where they had been discontinued, and fixed the following Cowls on waste lands.

Ground that had been waste for one, two, and three years, to be rent free for the same terms; that which had been waste for four years and upwards to be rent free for four years; and after the expiration of these periods of cowl, all ground so held, to be fairly assessed, in reference to the value of the adjoining lands.

The effect of these measures appears to be good; but, as before observed, those which relate to Gowteeahs and Poteles have not been inforced with much severity, it being my wish to bring them gradually into complete adoption.

The share of the gross produce which comes to the Government.—The Revenue being paid in money not in kind, this question can only be answered by comparing the expenses and profits of cultivation with the amount paid to the Government. From that ground of calculation it would appear that $^1/_4$ to $^1/_3$ comes to the Circar, the proportion varying to that extent according to the goodness or badness of the season.

The assessment equal on all or otherwise. — The assessment is meant to be equal on each village that is to say proportioned to its extent, fertility, and means; but from imperfect information as to the actual state of the country it probably bears unequally in some instances. Its subsequent division amongst the ryots of the village I believe to be in general pretty fair, or the oppressed party would quit the place to the prejudice of the interests of the Potell and Gowteeahs. The latter may sometimes take a less share of the burthen to themselves than they ought, but of this since in Chutteesghur I have not had one direct complaint, and in respect to the Gowteeahs, were it to occur as all their profits are laid out in agricultural objects it is doubtful that any injury of a general nature would result.

Assessment whether on the seed sown, the plough, the quantity of land or the produce. — The assessment by the Sircar is on each village and is subsequently apportioned by Gowteeahs on each plough belonging to it. It may therefore be said to be on the plough. But the amount paid by a plough in different parts of the country varies most widely from 6 to 22 Rupees.

If the lands were ever measured how improvements suggested — The lands have never been measured nor does it appear that at present any useful purpose would be answered by their being so, as there is so much waste land in Chutteesghur that the cultivation is constantly changing its situation, and to ascertain its extent an annual or half-yearly survey would be requisite.

Land how classed.— The lands are classed under the following appellations:—

The Kanar, or black soil, which yields both the Rubbee and Kurreef crop and in which everything may be grown. It is however considered most favourable to the Rubbee or wheat crop. It prevails most in the central and southern parts of Chutteesghur.

The Muttassee or yellow clay soil yields the Kurreef or rice crop only, also sugarcane and tobacco. It prevails most in the northern and eastern parts of the Province.

The Doresah or a mixtue of the black and red soils, generally at the point where they meet. It is favourable to the produce of rice and ulsee. There is some in all the Pergunnahs.

The Burrea Batta or a red gravelly soil in which till, oored, moong and cotton are grown. It prevails mostly in the Pergunnahs of Ryepore, Dumda and Simgah and is reckoned an unproductive soil.

The Dhee or sites of deserted villages very favourable to the growth of tobacco.

The Kutchar zameen or soil overflowed by streams during the rains in which till, errundee, tobacco and garden vegetables are produced.

The Batta or rocky barren soil fit only for pasture and mowah tree common wherever hills adjoin.

Statement as far back as they can be obtained of the amount of the Land Revenue with prices of grain for each year, pointing out the causes of extraordinary increases or decreases — The Dufters of the Soobadary having been very ill-preserved, this information as derived from them is imperfect. What however was to be ascertained from that source is inserted underneath; but it may be necessary to observe that the Jumma shown by the Dufters is little more than the nominal assessment much of which never having been realized was carried as *newper* to the Bakee account, and has since been remitted or rather struck out as irrecoverable:-

Years		Revenue of all kins from the Kalsa Lands	Extra Revenue of the Soobah Muskoor	Zemindars.	Syer.	Total	
		Rs. a. p.	Rs. a. p.	Rs. a. p.	Rs. a. p.	Rs. a.p.	
1208 Fusslly	...	2,26,226	11,819 7 6	1,105 0 0	34,502 8 0	1,73,573 13 3	The Zemindaris during these years were not under the Soobadar of Chuteesghu.
1209	...	96,618 3 3	8,922 12 6	19,811 5 0	31,457 0 3	1,56,809 4 9	
1210 "	...	1,57,954 12 6	32,456 2 6	32,414 5 6	31,895 13 3	2,54,721 1 9	
1211 "	...	1,63,498 7 6	29,844 0 0	22,486 14 6	36,145 13 0	2,51,975 3 0	
1212 "	...	1,69,765 2 6	15,201 14 0	12,115 4 0	36,145 11 6	23,332 0 0	
1213 "	...	1,68,205 6 6	58,716 7 0	6,341 5 6	35,295 11 6	2,68,648 12 6	
From 1213 to 1222 no records are to found	...	...	...	...	...		
1222 Fusslly		370,786 3 3	95,938 7 0	22,985 0 0	48,474 8 0	5,38,184 2 5	
1223 "		3,71,974 0 9	94,422 8 3	24,085 0 0	48,773 0 0	5,40,154 15 0	
1224 "		3,46,414 7 0	76,842 3 6	25,188 9 0	47,804 8 0	4,96,247 11 6	
1225 "		3,10,803 1 0	1,10,443 10 6	25,723 3 0	48,025 11 0	4,95,055 9 6	
1226 "		3,21,103 12 6	10,665 4 9	28,349 5 0	42,025 11 0	4,02,244 1 3	
1227 "		3,83,961 5 6	7,034 12 3	15,800 5 0	46,571 8 0	4,53,457 14 9	

From the investigation of the Ameens the following result is obtained, but, as there are no village Karkoons or written records, that has no better authority than the recollections of Gowteeahs. I have also added the price of grain in each year which is likewise derived from recollection:—

Years.	Revenue of every description from the Kalsa Lands Rs. a.p.	Price of Grains Chowoul per Re. Cundies	Gewun per Re. Cundies	Channah per Re. Cundies	Remarks
1217 Fusslly	2,95,902 8 0	3	4	4	
1218 "	3,08,543 6 9	3	4	4	
1219 "	3,27,569 15 3	3	$3^1/_2$	$3^1/_2$	
1220 "	3,50,562 15 3	3	3	3	
1221 "	3,70,742 10 9	$2^1/_2$	2	2	
1222 "	4,09,022 8 0	$2^1/_2$	1	1	
1223 "	4,31,973 1 6	2	2	2	
1224 "	4,05,734 8 9	$2^1/_2$	3	3	
1225 "	3,95,641 8 9	3	4	3	
1226 "	3,34,323 14 6	$2^1/_2$	3	4	
1227 "	3,92,198 10 9	$2^1/_2$	3	3	
1228 "	3,33,674 13 9	$2^1/_2$	$1^3/_4$	2	*
1229 "	3,53,682 3 6	$1^1/_2$	$1^1/_2$	$1^1/_2$	

* These years are taken from the Superintendent's papers and are inserted as a means of comparison.

Three and one-eight Chutteesghur Cundies are equal to one Nagpore Cundy.

The increases or decreases in the prices of grain were caused partly by the goodness or badness of the seasons, but chiefly by the demand for grain in the adjoining country which always raised the price in Chutteesghur.

The different Burguns when put on, what of them abolished, what included in the fixed assessment. —As there is no very material difference between Burguns, Puttys, Teekas and Babtees I shall insert underneath all that has had general or partial operation in this Province.

Names	In whose time established	Abolished or otherwise.	Whether included in the fixed assessments.	Where inforced
Rakee Teeka	Hyhywunce Rajahs	Subsequenly blended with the fixed assessment in most places	included	Generally but with some exceptions
Dussarah Teeka	d0	do	do	do
Poos Teeka	do	do	do	Ruttunpore
Kooel Teeka	do	do	do	Ruttunpore and Ballodah
Oonally Putty	do	do	do	Ruttunpore and Balodah Pergunahs excepted
Mohur Putty Bimbajee	do	do	do	Ruttunpore and Ballodah
Chownee	do	do	do	In 4 Pergunnahs
Oorud Kolah	do	do	do	Ruttuopore
Kuree Putty	do	Blended by Major Agnew with the Kallee or land assessments	do	
Gowteeah Putty	do		do	In 9 Pergunahs
Serdaishmookee	do	Subsequently blended with the general assessment	do	Ryepore
Teeka Derdia	do	do.	do.	In 9 Pergunahs.
Gaum Guhnah Jasood	do	do.	do.	In 7 do.
Puttuck Teeka	do	do.	do.	In 12 do.
Nowah Moolayemut	do	do.	do.	Kyepore
Bundaree Putty Bimbajee's...	do	do.	do.	Dumterry.
Warrar Pandiah	Myputrow Dinkur Soobadar.	do.	do.	Ryepore and Ruttunpore

Names	In whose time established	Abolished or otherwise.	Whether included in the fixed assessments.	Where inforced
Koat Putty	Myputrow Dinkur Soobadar	Subseqneutly blended with the general assessment	Included	Ryepore
Doondah Putty	do	do.	do	do
Chawtur Putty	Veetul Dinkur	do	do	Moogailee
Burgun Quilay	do	do	do	Ruttunpore
Maiswance	Kaisho Govind	do	do	Ryepore
Beetry	do	do	do	Moogailee
Sowary Putty	do	do	do	Dumterry and Jazeghee
Byaye Batta	do	do	do	Jazeghee
Dooma Putty	Beecajee Gopaul	do	do	Generally
Pooah Putty	do	do	do	do
Sowary Putty	do	do	do	do
Dussorah Kursh	do	do	do	do
Nuzzer Dewry	do	do	do	do
Tope Kunah Putty	Jadoorows	Done away	do	do
Seway Bootah Burguns collected by the Soobadar for his expenses	Beecajee Gopaul	do	No included	do
Seway Rootah Burguns collected by Commavisdars of Pergunnahs for their expenses	do	do	do	do
Chundah Doramdow Burguns.	Of long standing	do	do	do

	Rs.
The actual amountt of the Land Revenue at present; the amount and cause of any increasse that may be expected. - The amount of the Land Revenue for the last Fussily year was from the Kalsa Lands......	3,29,836
From the Zemindaries the total of their payments considered as Land Revenue	26,792
And adding the Land Revenue of Droog-Sunjary and the whole Oobary payable by the Lanjee Zemindaries lately placed under my superintendence	1,41,138
As well as the balances of Oobary from the Zemindary's of Kowerdah and Pandreeah not received by me in the last year	9,762
The total will be ...	5,07,528

I was in hopes that the revenue of the Kalsa Lands would have increased as in last, for several succeeding years at about 20,000 Rupees annually. But the rains this season having been unfavourable to the cultivation of the rice crop, of which grain one-third less than in the last year has, I imagine, been produced, it would probably cause much future injury to attempt to raise the assessment for the present year. Indeed some remissions may become necessary in those Pergunahs where the last rains have failed.

The expectations I entertain of the revenues of the Kalsa lands being hereafter gradually increased, arise principally in the experience of the past period. I have seen that by the removal of the Toinga Putty or tax on Bunjaries, by the confidence and security given to them and other Traders by the settlement of the country by the opening of new roads, and the comparative safety which has been given to them, that the produce of this Province has more than doubled itself in value and has found a ready sale. Indolent as the inhabitants are these favourable circumstances have not failed to urge them to increase the cultivation and to draw forth a more than usual activity. It is true that a scarcity of grain (which at present is almost the only production of the District) in the surrounding country was one chief cause of the favourable sales which for the last two years have taken place in Chutteesghur, but I have little doubt that if the communication with other quarters continues open, safe, and unrestricted by oppressive duties, the produce of this Province will still find sufficient vent, particularly if the Mahanuddee be resorted to as the means of carrying off the surplus of its consumption to the certain sale which would the afforded by the markets of the Eastern Coast of India.

The want of such a certain sale, when grain has been abundant in the surrounding country, has, I learn, frequently left the produce surplus to the consumption of the District, to rot on the hands of the cultivators, and made their labours fruitless in regard to the profits of export.

But when it is further considered that the climate and soil of Chhuteesghur seem quite favourable to the cultivation in large quantities of cotton, indigo sugar, hemp, tobacco and several other of the most profitable articles of trade whilst the price of labour from the cheapness of grain is very moderate and that it is intersected by navigable rivers, it may be inferred that it only requires the activity and exertion which Trade would give to render the country far more productive than it now is.

EXTRA REVENUE

Explanation of Syer Sall *and other taxes, the period of their introduction, the mode in which they are collected, the amount of revenue they yield.*— On the subject of the *Syer* as I could only repeat the substance of my letter to your address of the 9th March last I trust that I may be permitted to refer to that communication as conveying all the information on that point which it is in my power to offer.

The regular *Syers* appeared to have been established by the Mahrattas very soon after their conquest of the country. The *Koots* or tolls are of more ancient date and existed in the time of the Hyhywunce Rajahs. They are both farmed to contractors who collected them by an establishment of peon maintained by them for the purpose, and stationed at all passes and other suitable spots within their respective limits. The regular *Syers* yielded last year Rupees 53,039 and the Koots 8,235.

The duties upon silks and sugar imported from Benares, Patna, etc., were not included in the *Syer* which was farmed, but under the name Nurmeenah, were collected by the Soobadar and yielded generally about 25,000 Rupees a year. The route to Nagpore by Chutteesghur being now abandoned for the more direct one by Jubblepore and Sewny to Suppara this source of revenue has ceased.

The largest source of extra revenue is the *Pandree* or tax upon those classes who do not contribute as cultivators to the land revenue, the following castes excepted, Bramins, Rajpoots, Girewars, Koots *[sic]* and Mussulmans who are exempted apparently on account of their rank; Carpenters, Potters, Barbers, Lumhans, Gonds, Hulbas, Moungs and Gussheahs being useful to or the servants of the cultivators and others; and Byragees, Goseins, Faquirs, etc., being beggars. This tax, some say, existed in the time of Hyhywunce Rajahs, but it seems more probable that it was introduced by the Mahrattas.

It is collected in the same way as the land revenue by Gowteahs of villages in two kists and paid to the Commavisdars, the assessment upon each house or family being determined by ancient usage, modified according to the present circumstances of the parties. It yielded last year Rupees 7,373. As a rule by which complaints might be decided, I directed that it should not exceed ten per cent on the income of each family.

The *Kullaly* or tax on intoxicating liquors and drugs, as before noticed, I separated from the land assessment and made a distinct source of revenue. Last year when sold to a Single Contractor it yielded at the rate of 4,000 Rupees a year or 2,916-11-0 for the broken period during which it was so rented. This year it will be collected by Commavisdars of Pergunnahs.

Goonaigary is a fine imposed on adulteries and fornications. Dand on other offences, and Mussalla on those who do not attend to the summonses of the Sirkar. They yielded last year Rupees 3,090, but formerly they amounted, under the most just of the Maharatta rulers, to about 10,000 and when made, as they generally were, a means of oppression and extortion they brought as much as 25,000. These taxes, as well as those hereafter mentioned, were introduced soon after the Maharatta authority was established, and all are collected by Commavisdars.

Chooree Perawan is a tax on the remarriage of widows to other than their late husband's younger brother, *Goochaonee* on their remarriage to their late husband's younger brother, *Sawun* on, leave to the widow's father and mother to keep her with them unmarried. *Pytoo* on the dissolving of marriages amongst the lowest castes and new contracts being formed by the parties. These impositions last year, all compulsion in regard to the remarriage of widows being prohibited, produced Rupees 3,569.

Mooar as now regulated, is the amount realized from the appropriation by the Circar of the property of deceased persons, who may have no heirs within the following degrees of consanguinity, *viz.*, sons, brothers, sons of brothers, father, mother or daughters. *Gyar* is the amount arising from the appropriation by the Sircar of the property of persons who have absconded or of property to which there is no claimant. Last year they yielded Rupees 517.

Mundonah is a tax on marriages taken in part from both parties. It last year produced Rupees 174.

Bhat Kowayee is a tax paid by all persons restored to their castes by the usual process of feeding others of the tribe. It produced last year Rupees 33.

Chowtye arises from the Circar taking one-fourth of all property recovered through its means; last year it produced Rupees 94.

Ghaut Gara is a tax on ferries and is generally farmed; it yielded last year 90 Rupees.

Zeddeed teeka is a nuzzer paid by persons on being appointed Patels or Gowteeahs. It produced last year Rupees 214.

Fooah is a tax on gambling of generally one or two annas in each rupee won. It produced last year Rupees 7-8-0.

Coassa Barree (*Kosu Bari*) is a tax on the topes where tussur worms are bred. It produced last year Rupees 6.6.0.

Amrie and *Emlee* are taxes on mango and tamarind topes belonging to the Government. It produced last year Rupees 15.

Tumbacco and *Nuss* are contracts at certain places for the exclusive right to sell tobacco and snuff. It produced last year Rupees 104.

Eejara Fattra is a tax on bazars assembled at places of worship on days when pilgrims visit them.

Kurkee is a tax said to be voluntarily paid by those who obtained favourable decisions from the Circar.

Suggestions for improvement in the manner of collecting or for the abolition of such as may be peculiarly oppressive or very unproductive. — With respect to the *Syer* no arrangement can be very effectual which does not form part of a general system operating as well in Chutteesghur as in the adjoining portion of the Rajah's territory. A bag of grain now pays duties to the amount of one Rupee in its transit from hence to Nagpore which is collected by 10 or 11 different zemindars and renters and Shirona 2 Rupees and 1 anna. As commencement of a reform I should conceive it best to take the *Syer* into our own hands, that we may get an insight into the accounts which we do not now possess and, according to the understanding of the contractors, cannot claim. The present contractors, when good men, might be allowed to continue is charge with a salary, but the Department must be placed under the supervision of Karkoons on the part of the Superintendent to inforce the system ordered and to keep a copy of the accounts.

The system which would appear to me preferable would be that of having but one *Syer* within the limits of the Superintendent's authority regulated on the principle of taking 2 per cent on all goods, valued according to Nerrick [nirakh] to be established annually, which pass the frontier either as exports or imports, a lattitude being allowed to the Superintendent to increase or diminish this scale of duties as he sees cause, and enirely to remit them on those roads which it is desirable to open. All internal duties it will be very essential wholly to abolish. In this district, by a practice which however is unsanctioned by any regulation in sanad held by the renter, they have gone to such a length that, extraordinary as it may appear, there are no public markets for any articles of value. The whole of the vegetables, grass, wood and other trifles, which are brought into the bazars of Ryepore or of any other of the larger towns might all be bought for a few rupees. Buying and selling goes on privately between friends, and chiefly by barter. This may a good deal be owing to other causes, but I have no doubt that the duties levied upon every article which quits one village to go to another, have greatly promoted it.

The Koots might without any difficulty be done away with in the Kalsa Lands and the measure would, I am of opinion, be productive of the greatest advantage. It would also appear to me advisable to purchase them by small remissions of rents from all the Zemindars, who do not command some difficult pass or jungly tract of considerable extent, in which case it probably would be preferable to allow them, as a means of interesting them in the safety of Traders, a toll of one or two annas on each bullock-load without any reference to the contents.

By these arrangements, if adopted, the regular *Syer* would ultimately, it is probable, be increased in value; but a considerable loss would, I think, occur for the first two or three years.

With regard to the manner of collecting the other taxes mentioned under this head I have no improvements to suggest.

The tax on spirituous liquors has been already adverted to, and the Kullals are so numerous a class, and the mowah fruit so much an article of food to the Goands, that I conceive the sale must remain with the inhabitants of the country, the tax being regulated and its amount received by Commavisdars of Pergunnahs and carried to a separate head in the account.

Goonigary and *Dand* are now imposed only in cases where they form a wholesome and necessary restraint.

Mussalla has fallen out of use. *Chowree Perawan* has been divested of its worst character by the removal of all compulsion in the remarriage of widows, and *Sawun* has, in consequence of that rule, been discontinued. *Mooar* has been modified so as to be less repacious and unjust seizure than formerly. *Chowtye* on account of its tendency to give the character of partiality and unfairness to decisions and for other reasons sufficiently apparent, has been abolished; as well as *Zeedeed Teeka* which I found to be made a pretence for acts of injustice; and *Kurkee* has fallen into disuse. The other taxes do not appear materially objectionable although some are little productive.

AGRICULTURE

Mode of cultivating the different productions and time of reaping and sowing.— The cultivators commence to prepare the ground for the Khuree (here called Dhan) in the middle of Jait (June) by ploughing the land twice, once lengthways and once across and repairing the banks of the rice field. They do nothing else to it.

Immediately after the first showers of the rains they sow, by scattering the seed with the hand, rice in the low grounds, ooreed, till, moong, cotton, too codo and kootkee, in the high grounds. The seed is not covered in any way in some parts of the District. In others the *Copur* or Drag is passed over it. There are three kinds of rice distinguished by the names given to the manner of their cultivation and which are called *Becassy, Lie (Lehi)* and *Ropa.* The Becassy process is as follows: — In about a month when the rice has grown to the height of about eight inches, it, and the weeds which have come up with it are rooted up together either by passing once over the field a plough, what is called here a *Pun* or rude. Harrow with one row of teeth about six inches long sloped to the front.

The water is then drawn off for about eight days by which the weeds are killed but not the rice which shoots out again although much of it has been deep in the mud.

The water is then readmitted. In another month, or rather more, when the Rice has risen to the height of one and half feet, the weeds are again removed But on this occasion that is done with the hand and principally by the women and children. In Kartick (November) it is ready for reaping when it is cut down with a hook, the grain being seized with one and whilst the instrument applied to the bottom of the stem about two Inches from the ground. It is collected first in small heaps within the reach of the reaper and two or three days after when quite dry it is carried away and put into *Kurries* (Karhi) or large heaps near the *Kootar* (Kothar) or place where it is to be separated from the straw and husk.

The *Lie* manner of cultivation is as follows:— The seed is first soaked water until it begins to shoot which it does in two days, it is then taken to field which has been previously worked into fine mud, and is sown by being scattered with the hand, a person being stationed to keep the birds off. If weeds grow up with the rice, they are removed by the hand but by this process few weeds appear. When ripe the rice is reaped in the same way as the *becassy.*

By the *Ropah* process a small spot of ground previously worked into a fine mud and well manured is sown with a large quantity of dry seed. When the plants are six Inches high they are taken out with the hand but in small bundles and immediately replanted in fields which have been previously cleared and were worked into mud. Weeds seldom appear. When ripe the rice is reaped as above described.

The best rice is produced by the *Ropah* plan and the worst by the *Lie.*

There is also an inferior rice called here Heronah (Haruna) and Sated (Sathya) which requires little water and is grown in high places where it can receive no moisture but that which falls. It is sown in the Becassy manner the weeds are once removed by the hand.

Ooreed, till, moong, toor, bunnee, cuppas, codo, and koothee are sown in fields twice ploughed, and several are frequently sown in the same field. They are reaped in Kartick except the moong which is one month later. The ooreed and moong are torn up by the roots, the cotton picked off the bush which is left to decay, and the rest are cut. All are removed to the threshing places and piled in separate heaps.

To the middle of Aswin (October) the ground when the cultivators can spare time is prepared for the Rubbee (here called the Oonallee). It is ploughed three times in different directions and smoothed, and the clods broken by the *capur (Kopar)* or kind of Drag. The seed is sown before the Dassorah (October) by the plough being passed a fourth time over the ground prepared with a hole through the wood behind the share, in which a hollow bamboo is fixed, the top of which is split so as to afford a rest for the hand. The man who directs the plough then takes a hand full of seed and lets it fall into the bamboo as the plough proceeds. Thus gewn, ulsee, mussoor, battana, chenna and erendee are sown. Tewara Wullia Guppas, Wulla Moong and Wulla Ooreed are sown by the hand and by broadcast. These grains do not require weeding as they are exposed to little rain. In Paug (March) they are reaped, and carried to the threshing place. Ghewn and chenna are cut, the rest are torn up the roots, the Cotton and Errundee excepted which are picked off the plants.

Tewra, buttana, mussoor, chenna, ooreed and ulsee are frequently sown in the ground which has previously yielded the rice crop.

It will be observed that there are two kinds of cotton, ooreed and moong, the one grown during the rains the other in the cold season. The seeds are different but the plants have the same appearance. The cotton produced at the Rubbee and the ooreed and Moong produced at the Kureef are preferred.

There are no enclosures to the fields and they are of most irregular shapes indeed the whole appearance of the cultivation is slovenly and unsightly. Little injury is done by birds and much by the cattle belonging to the cultivators themselves.

Most grains are separated from their stems and husks by being tread by bullocks. Ulsee and toor are previously beat with a heavy stick. The errundee seed is separated wholly by that method. The till is tied in large bundles and put up on its stems until it is perfectly dry when the pods open. Then a cloth is spread on the ground and the bundle being reversed over it the seeds fall out. This operation through a superstitious idea is generally performed at night. The cotton is separated from its seed by being passed between two Maunds cylinders of wood.

Description of the instruments used. — These are few and rude, and are as below. — The *Nangur* or plough of a very rude kind and which does not penetrate more than six inches below the surface, as in this country it is said that the fertility of the soil lies on the top, and that all the experiments which have been made of ploughing deep, have failed.

The *Copur* is a Drag formed of a thick board five or six feet long which is attached by two bamboos to the bullock's yoke, and the side of which bearing perpendicularly on the soil, smoothes it and breaks the lumps.

The *Wukur* is something similar to the above. It is a Drag composed of a beam of wood having two pegs projecting downwards from near the extremities, between which is placed a piece of iron. This latter scrapes along the ground as drawn forward and answers the same purpose as the Copur.

The *Pun* is a rude harrow composed of one log of wood, armed with 8 to 10 prongs of iron sloped to the front.

The *Hussesh* (Hasiya) is a rude reaping Hook.

The *Koorpee* is used in weeding, and resembles a very small reaping hook flattened in the curve and sharpened on the outside.

The *Rapah* is what is elsewhere known by the name of the *Momuly.* It is the Indian shovel.

The *Koodlee* (Kudali) is the Indian pickaxe.

The *Chetwar* is a wooden spade used for cutting turf to repair the banks of the rice fields.

The cultivation is irrigated chiefly by water from tanks, but in some cases water is drawn from wells by the lever or balanced beam here called *Tainde (Tenrha).* The *Moat* or leather bag raised by bullocks is not usual.

Expenses of raising and rates of returns of the different sorts of grains. — All the agricultural labourers being paid by one-fourth of the Grain and one-fifth of the sugarcane they assist in cultivating (as will be hereafter more particularly noticed), that with the cost of seed, tear and wear of implements and cattle and the hire of occasional weeders constitutes the expense of raising; and may, those who employ labourers and are already provided with cattle and implements be estimated as one-third of the produce. To those who perform the labours is the field with their own hands, assisted by their family, it is probably less than one-quarter.

The rates of return of the different sorts of Grain has been variously reported to me from the different Pergunnahs, that it is very difficult to strike an average that would be likely to be correct. I therefore annex a statement showing the greatest fluctuation between good and bad years and barren and rich soils, although it can be littlc satisfactory:—

Quantity of Seeds

Grain	Sown	Produce
Dhan	I Cundy	8 to 15 Cundies
Ghawn	"	5 to $7^1/_2$ "
Chennah	"	5 to $7^1/_2$ "
Mussor	"	4 to 6 "
Battana	"	4 to 10 "
Till	"	10 to 20 "
Ullsee	"	10 to 20 "
Codo	"	15 to 20 "
Toor	"	10 to 20 "
Ooreed	"	8 to 15 "
Moong	"	8 to 15 "
Errudee	"	10 to 20
Kootkee	"	15 to 20 "
Tewra	"	5 to 10 "
Cuppass	1 Cundy of 20 Maunds ...	5 to 25 "
Sugarcane	1000 Plants	40 to 50 Paparies of Goor

Rate of profits on agricultural capital. — In a country like this where degree of natural fertility or sterility possessed by the ground selected for cultivation and the goodness or badness of the season determine the abundance or scantiness of the crop, the science of husbandry being too little understood and the population too indolent materially to modify the effect of those great moving causes, it is very difficult to arrive at satisfactory results on points of this nature. The various information all apparently well founded, which you receive defeats every attempt at calculation. It is, therefore, with much uncertainty that I give the following reply:—

Money actually laid out in cultivation by a Ryot who understands his business and can himself labour, for which interest is not paid, implements and cattle being already possessed, might yield in the most favourable years after paying the expenses of tillage and the Government demands a clear profit of one-half and in unfavourable years of less than one-third.

If however cattle, implements and seed are to be bought and interest paid on the Money, it seems to be the general opinion that, under the most fortunate circumstances, no profits can be expected until the third or fourth year.

With regard to other persons entering into speculations of this kind they appear as frequently to meet with losses as with direct profits, but they have the satisfaction of growing what they themselves consume, and the labourers employed by them bring in wood, leaves, grass and otherwise assist in the business of the house.

There are, however, two modes of laying out money in agricultural speculations which are almost certain of being advantageous. Those are the lending of money or grain to the agriculturists, and the buying up of grain when it is cheap to sell when the prices rise.

The usual rate of interest on money borrowed by the cultivators is from 2 to 3 per cent per month. It is sometimes also half an anna per month on each Rupee, which would be $37^1/_2$ per cent per Annum. The repayment likewise seldom being in money, but in grain, a further advantage is gained on the bargain. Various practices in this respect exist in different parts of the Districts, but the most general may be said to be to calculate the interest due on the money from the period of its being lent, to that of the crop being reaped, and then to strike a bargain for the payment of the whole sum due in grain, which is generally given on these occasions half a Kundi cheaper than the price of the day.

Another practice is peculiar to sugarcane to give money or plants at the commencement of the season and at the period of cutting the cane to receive back one-half more in money, or in goor at a cheap valuation.

By purchasing grain at the harvest when it is cheap and keeping it up until the rains when the price is raised, a profit of 50 per cent is generally made.

Hire of agricultural labourers. — There are three different classes of labour in Chutteesghur, the *Saunjeeahs* in the Southern quarters and the *Cummeeahs* and *Poandhars* (*Ponrhars)* in the Northern.

The Saunjeeahs receive one-fourth of all grains and one-fifth of all sugarcane reared by their labour, also a Cumbly (blanket) each every second and sometimes every year. On first being taken into service they likewise receive 2 Rupees as a kind of deposit for if they change their place it must be returned, and they are supplied with grain by their employer as they require it, which is taken back from their share at the harvest, as well as an increased quantity proportioned to its dearness when supplied and cheapness at the season of repayment.

It is a condition with each Saunjeeah that he build 12 *Huts* [haths] of mud wall;, make a Chupper of 20 *Huts* long and, of moderate breadth, supply 20 small straw brushes and bring in for his employer's use 1,000 Pullies of grass.

The Cummeeah and Poandhars have assigned to them for their own benefit a portion of the ground the cultivation of which is entrusted to them. This portion varies greatly in extent in different Pergannahs. It is sown with their own seed but tilled with the implements and cattle of their master. The produce of their ground is their own, the repaying out of it 11/2 Kundies for each 1 Kundi of grain which their employer had supplied them with for food. After they have ploughed, sown, and rudely dressed their master's ground their engagement is fulfilled and they are paid at the rate of 1 or 2 Kattas of dhan or codo for each day on which they may afterwards be employed.

As may be supposed the Soumjeeahs are greatly preferred to the Commeahs and Poandhars.

Women for weeding, etc., generally receive 1 Katta of dhan or codo per day and boys something less according to their size.

At harvest time in some places men receive 2 Kattas, and women and children 11/2.

Lands how affected by constant cultivation, manures and fallows; would it be expedient to provide for the latter in making settlements. — Alternative years of fallow are always allowed in the cultivation of sugarcane, but no regular system in this respect is observed with regard to other grains.

This probably arises from the abundance of unoccupied ground fit for tillage, and the practice which is common of occasionally changing the situation of the cultivation. There can, however, be no doubt that the land would be impoverished by constant cultivation and would yield bad crops. For the reason however, before noticed it would not appear necessary to provide for fallows in making settlements.

Manures, where resorted to supersede the necessity of fallows. Those used are cowdung for the muttassee red clay soil, Ashes and village sweepings for the Kanar or black soil, and the refuse of the Ulsee after the Oil has been extracted for sugercane and paun. The ashes of other Dungs and in the jungles the ashes of wood are also common.

Twenty Cart-loads to the ground cultivated by one plough is the usual quantity, but manures are not very frequently used.

Mode and rate of supplying Beej Potga. —The Ryots are not supplied by the Sirkar with grain on their accounts. They take it from whom they please from Potels, Gowteeahs, Sawkars, or others and the rates are very various. For *Beej* or Seed, however, the general rate for the Kurreef is for one Kundi $1^1/_4$ or $1^1/_2$ at the harvest, and for the Rubbee for 1 Kundi $1^1/_2$ or 2 Kundees. For *Poatga* or food for 1 Kundi $1^1/_2$ at the harvest.

How much of the different kind of grain sown in a given quantity of land.— The following quantities of grain are sown in the space cultivated by one plough or in a square of 160 yards:—

Becassee Dhan	...	12	Kundies $3^1/_8$ equal to one Nagpore Kundy
Lie ”	...	8	”
Ropa ”	...	6	”
Heronah ”	...	14	”
Codo ”	...	1	”
Moong ”	...	$1^1/_2$	”

Ooreed	"	...	3	"
Till	"	...	1	"
Ghewn	"	...	7	"
Chennah	"	...	5	"
Buttanah	"	...	5	"
Mussoor	"	...	7	"
Ulsee	"	...	2	"
Kothee	"	...	$^{3}/_{4}$	"
Toor	"	...	$1^{1}/_{2}$	"
Tewra	"	...	5	"

How much land can be cultivated by one plough. — A plough with four good bullocks should cultivate a square of 160 yards.

VILLAGE ESTABLISHMENT

List of the village officers, their duties and emoluments hereditary or otherwise; their castes and the nature of the Potulty tenure; what originally, what changes have taken place in it; hereditary or saleable; if hereditary by what rule.— The village officers are the Potel where one has been appointed, and the Gowteeah; and the servants here called Eikeerry, are the Taihloo, the Nigh, the Gyrah, the Dobi, the Lowar, the Chumbar, the Baigarrees.

The situation of Potel is not of ancient origin. It was established by the Maharattas soon after their conquest of the country, as a means, there is every reason to suppose, of providing for the needy Bramins of their own tribe. They are generally of the higher castes, but some are of the lower. They are the Superiors of several villages or of a Talook, having Gowteeahs at those villages where they do not themselves reside. They settle the assessment with the Sirkar and are responsible for its payment at the established periods. They supply the Ryots through Gowteeahs with money, seed, cattle, etc., when they require it and the Gowteeahs cannot do so, and ought in all ways to promote the prosperity of the tract under their control. Their acknowledged emoluments are one Anna in each Rupee paid through them to the Circar, or 16 per cent on the whole amount and their [un-]acknowledged emoluments are interest on the money they lend to the Ryots, repaid in grain at a cheap rate as before described and cultivating portions of land themselves under the advantage of being their own assessors and the chief authority on the spot. They formerly took more than anna in the Rupee, but without authority. The situation is not hereditary and cannot be sold but the son of a Potel, if fit for the duty, has the claim to succession which his father's previous serevices give him, and which are attended to or disregarded as suits the chief authority in the Province.

Some Potels who understand the business of cultivation and particularly those who are natives of Chutteesghur are useful and improve the fertility of their Talook, but in general the appointment is made merely a source of emolument to the individual holding it, to the injury of the public revenue and often to the disadvantage of the ryots. Potels are generally the Gowteeahs of the villages where they personally reside.

The situation of Gowteeah is of ancient standing and existed in the time of the Hyhywunce Rajas. They are the superiors of one village only, and are of all castes down to Goands and Chumbars. Where there is a Patel it is the duty of the Gowteeah, under his directions, to assign to each Ryot his share of the public revenue according to the number of ploughs he possesses and to aid the Ryots to the extent of his means with money, seed, cattle, etc., and to apply to the Potel for what he cannot command. To collect from them the revenue when due and pay it to the Potel, to allot to each family a dwelling place and the ground they are to cultivate. To cherish the Ryots, to hear all their complaints and redress them when in their power, also to settle their quarrels, to see that the Taihloo provides travellers with what they require and with Baigarries, to report through the Potel all crimes and offences committed in his village, and finally to satisfy all, and make himself beloved. Where there is no Potel the Gowteeah performs both duties, but his emoluments are the same in either case and are as follows:— One plough rent free in every eight which belong to the village and pay revenue, for his own personal advantage; the Serra Dooly or the ground cultivated by one plough in every 16 free of rent and which being sown with the Gowteeahs seed and tilled by the Ryots generally, the produce is applied by the Gowteeah in charity and in food to travellers, the Sircar Peons, etc.; and the Bahyee or established custom of the Gowteeahs taking from the buyer one Katta in every Rupee's worth of grain sold in the village. Formerly the Gowteeah took what was called Punpeeah which was a small annual imposition on certain of the Pandry assamees, also a small donation on marriages (Beeah and Choore Pairawan) in the village, but neither of these are now authorized. The office is not hereditary or saleable but, as observed in regard to the Patel, the son of a Gowteeah has that kind of claim to succeed which may be attended to as a matter of favour, but is not one of right. Gowteeahs hold their situations upon what is called a Torun Chitty, to which the seal or the Commavisdar of the Pergunnah is attached.

The Taihloo are two persons under the immediate orders of the Gowteeah and who assist him in all his duties, the one of the Gandah the other of the Chowan Caste. They go his errands, inform him of the state of the cultivation, what new Ryots arrive and what old ones depart, what offences and improprieties occur, and what travellers pass and repass. The call the Ryots to pay the revenue, they dun those that are tardy, they confine such persons as are subjected to that punishment. These duties they perform in common. The following are distinct:— It is the Province of the Gandah to attend to the accommodation of travellers, to procure them Baigarries, etc. The Chowan is the guard of the village, goes rounds at night and during the day and is responsible for thefts. The manner of remunerating these servants is different in almost every village. They in some cases receive a share of the Serra Dooly in grain or a part of the ground is assigned to them to cultivate, in some receive annually 2 Kundees of grain from the Gowteeah and ten Kattas from each Ryot, in some there is a contribution in money made for them, and in some they are paid in part by all these methods. They have also a handful of grain in the Bahiee for the trouble of measuring. The office is not hereditary or saleable.

The Nigh or Barber is to be at the call of the Gowteeah, shaves him and the Ryots, shampoes the Gowteeah and travellers, rubs them with oil, prepares the plates made of leaves for eating off and the Gowteeahs' hooka, paun, etc.,

etc., and at marriages washes the feet of all the bridegroom's party. His wife also attends the females of the Gowteeah's family. He is paid generally by two Kundees of grain from the Gowteeah and 10 Kattas from each Ryot annually or 20 cowries (a Boory) for each time he shaves them. At marriages also he has perquisites. The office is not hereditary.

The *Gyra* or cowherd acts a good deal as a servant to the Gowteeah. When he moves he accompanies him and carries his baggage in a Cower on his shoulders, cleans his brass vessels, cowdungs his Chauka, brings him water and assists travellers in these respects, he is paid partly in l*ansut* [? land out] of the Serra Dooly partly in money and grain. The office is not hereditary.

The Doobee or washerman washes the Gowteeah's cloths and those of the Ryots and cuts firewood; he is remunerated by payments either in grain or money.

The Lowhar or blacksmith makes and repairs the implements of hhusbandry and does also the other work of the village in his way. He is supplied by the Ryots with charcoal and is paid as above.

The Chumbar or Shoemaker mends the bags with which water is raised, furnishes the thongs used about the ploughs, gives the Gowteeah two pairs of slippers annually and removes dead animals. He is paid in money or grain as above.

The Baigarees are of all the low castes and carry loads for travellers, for the Circar and for the Gowteeah and Ryots. They are paid partly in land and partly in grain.

Besides these persons there are in some villages religious Bramins of this country, here called Ooproohets, who celebrate marriages and other rites, and who are supported by the Ryots.

There are also astrologers at most of the large villages who are Maharatta Bramins and were named by Bimbajee; they possess sunnads entitling them to small contributions in money and grain from the country.

In some villages there are carpenters who are paid in the same way as the blacksmiths, but there are few of this craft in the district.

Have the common Kirsons any rights in the Lands they cultivate.— According to the present universal understanding and practice the Kirsons have no rights in the land they cultivate, nor can I learn that an order of things ever existed on which such a claim could be founded. There are no Wuttundaries in this Province.

POLICE

How administered under the Maharatta Government, the power of the Patels and Mamlutdars in support of it, improvements introduced or proposed. — There appears under the Maharatta Government to have been no separate police in this Province, at least no system or establishment for the purpose. It has however, been seen that the Gowteeah of each village according to long-established usage exercised a kind of patriarchal authority over the whole of the inhabitants, and that it was his duty to report to his superiors all great crimes and offences; also that the Chowan (although himself of a caṣte much addicted to thieving) was its guard and was responsible for thefts. Besides the supervision of these Officers, the Boodkurs or Revenue Peons under the immediate authority of the Commavisdar and who were either stationary in different parts of the Pergannahs or constantly moving about it, took cognizance as a source of Revenue of all offences and irregularities which were subject to be punished by fine. The Commavisdar thus heard of most offences, but he acted in respect to them more according to his discretion than to any fixed rules laid down for his conduct, except that it seems to have been understood that no opportunity was to be lost of raising the revenue by fines. These means appearing as well suited to the great objects of all Police, the prevention and detection of crimes, as the formation of a new and distinct establishment every member of which would in one way or other have oppressed and extorted money from the inhabitants, no change has been made by me. But the outline of the duties of Gowteeah and Commavisdar has been defined as will be hereafter shown.

A policy of having the villagers armed and encouraged to defend themselves. — No circumstances seem at present to call for this measure, and none to be likely that would render it necessary. There is now no restriction upon the villagers carrying arms.

CIVIL JUSTICE

How administered under the Maharatta Government. — There were no courts for the administration of Civil Justice under the Mahratta Government and there is but too much reason to believe that in this branch of judicature there was a total failure of all substantial justice, and that where redress was sought beyond the village Gowteeah, interest or bribes were the general if not the only means of obtaining it. It would be difficult to define the authority which decided on civil cases. Sometimes it was the Gowteeah, sometimes the Potel or Talookdhar, sometimes the Punje, sometimes, the Furnavees, sometimes the Commavisdar, sometimes the Soobadar, sometimes persons about the court of Nagpur and sometimes the Rajah himself. But the higher the appeal was carried as much the greater was the number of inferior persons who were to be intrigued with bribes and cajoled.

No success was expected without patrons, and they were only to be bought.

Plans for improvement of it.— This is I fear with our present means very difficult, but will probably be attained to the greatest extent practicable by encouraging private arbitrations, and by referring civil cases to the decision of Panchayats formed with impartiality and subject to appeals where corruption or other unfair dealing can be proved against the members composing it.

A particular description of Punchayats.— Punchayats are of very ancient date in this Province. They probably from the name consisted originally of five members, but in more modern times that seems to have been regulated by accidental convenience or the degree of importance attaching to the case to be determined. Sometimes they consisted of two members, at others of as many as ten. Neither the complainant or defendant had any voice in the selection of the members. They were fixed upon by the principal local authority not unfrequently by his assigning the duty to some of the persons sitting in the Kutcherry at the time the complaint was made. When Commavisdars or any other higher authority ordered Punchayats, Razeenamas or agreements to abide by the decision were taken from both parties, but this form was not usual in the village Punchayats regulated by Gowteeahs.

As in some measure connected with Punchayats it is proper to advert to the office of Punje which appears to have existed under all the ancient Government(s) of this quarter. Judging from duties now discharged by persons called Punjees in the surrounding zemindaries, they would appear to be the counsel of the Zamindar and to aid him in all duties of importance. If a negotiation is to be undertaken a Punje is sent. If a civil case is to be decided a Punje superintends the Punchayats, if any internal arrangement is to be effected a Punje is entrusted with the duty. In short where a Zemindar delegates any authority it always seems to be a Punje.

The situation of Punje under the Hyhywunce Rajahs previous to the Mahratta conquest was it may be inferred such as it now is in the Zemindaris, the internal Government of which has not been interfered with. After the introduction of the Maharatta authority, however, they appear to have been almost entirely suppressed, and persons under that title were only occasionally nominated at the heads of the principal Pergunnahs to superintend arbitrations, a duty to which their former avocations were by no means limited.

The character of their decisions, how far the substantial ends of Justice are answered by them, in what estimation held by the Inhabitants. — The loose, casual and sometimes partial manner in which Punchayats were formed would induce much doubt as to the enlightened nature or strict justice of their decision, and equally so as to the substantial ends of justice being answered by them. But on the other hand Punchayats were held in such veneration by the people that they commonly compared their awards to the decrees of the almighty, and thus from the force of habit and long-established impressions a contested point was probably more effectually set at rest by the decision of a Punchayat and in a manner more satisfactory to all the parties concerned than could have been accomplished by any other means whatever.

It is also likely that Punchayats held respecting disputed property in a village or amongst the inhabitants of several adjoining villages under the authority of Gowteeahs were in all respects equitable.

What are the most common subjects of litigation. — Litigation on any subject is not yet common in this Province, but references on the subject of debts of longstanding are numerous.

CRIMINAL JUSTICE

How administered under the late Government. — As in the case of civil justice, so in that of criminal justice there were no courts or established system. The practice is all that can be referred to. It seems to have been understood that the only person who had the power of life and death was the Soobadar of the Province, and he generally referred all cases of an aggravated nature to Nagpur. If an order came to execute a criminal it was the form that it should be repeated three times before it was carried into effect. But highway robberies and rebellion were frequently punished with immediate death by the Soobadar without any reference to other authority. When capital crimes were committed at a distance from where the Soobadar was, it was the duty of Commavisdars of pPergunnahs to send the delinquents in irons to the place of his residence, and a short investigation by the Soobadar decided the fate of the prisoners. It would not appear that the decisions so passed were erroneous, but the evidence on which they were given was, it is to be apprehended, of the most imperfect kind, generally little more than the letter of the Commavisdar stating the circumstances and a few questions put to the prisoner himself. The practice of sending the witnesses with the prisoner and of confronting them with him certainly did not prevail, and it is with the utmost difficulty that I can now enforce the rule. Distinctions not reconcilable to our notions were also made in reference to the caste of the parties, as well in determining the quality of the offence as the punishment with which it was to be visited. For instance if a Bramin killed a low caste man he was at most fined. If, however, a low caste man killed a Bramin he lost his life. And a distinction of the same kind was preserved throughout all the other castes. Bramins, Gosains and Byraggees never appear to have been put to death. They were punished by fine and imprisonment, and when very criminal their houses raided, their property confiscated, and they themselves expelled the country. The killing of a cow intentionally by the above favoured castes cause their expulsion from their tribes and was death to all others. The act when unintentional was to all expulsion from their caste. Women were never put to death. Some crimes likewise which we regard in the gravest light were scarcely noticed or considered to call for punishment. Like duelling with us, they appear to have been thought a necessary restrain on the community. Such were murder to avenge the infidelity of a wife, daughter, or mother, or supposed acts of witchcraft. The vindictive principle of blood for blood was also acknowledged, and a murder committed in retaliation even for an act of manslaughter was rarely noticed. Deaths likewise which occurred in affrays between persons of the same caste were not punished more severely than by fine.

Defects of it. — The defects of this system were that the detection of capital crimes was left a great deal to chance, that the investigation was, to our notions, unsatisfactory, and that all were not punished alike. But although these are unquestionably defects they are probably aggravated by our ways of thinking beyond the acutal evil which these occasioned.

Plans proposed for its improvement. — The measures which I have adopted, as well for the improvement of the police as for regulating the administration of civil and criminal justice, are so blended together that I have been obliged to postpone until this place a detail of them.

That will be best given by extracts from the two proclamations which I issued on the subject. The first was dated the 30th June 1819 and was as follows:—

1. Commavisdars are vested with judicial authority in their respective Pergunnahs.
2. All treasons and offences against the State, murders, thefts of property beyond the value of Rs. 5 and other great crimes will be reported for decision of the Circar.
3. In regard to small offences the Commavisdar, having investigated the matter in public Kutcherry, will inflict the punishment sanctioned by usage, but will not without the authority of the Circar cause more than 10 stripes to be given or impose a fine beyond 10 Rupees.
4. Every month the Commavisdar will transmit to the Circar an amount of the causes he has decided specifying the fines and corporal punishments inflicted.
5. Gowteeahs are charged with a judicial Superintendence in their respective villages reporting everything to the Commavisdar and acting upon his orders.

6. In every Pergunnah Commavisdars and in every village Gowteeahs will, at the request of the parties concerned, assemble Punchayats according to custom for the decision of disputes connected with property and a record of its decision will be preserved to be produced when required by the Circar.
7. All complaints are in the first instance to be preferred to Gowteeahs of villages, if he does not redress them, they are next to be preferred to Commavisdars of Pergunnahs, and should he not redress them, they are to be referred to the Circar when justice will be done. If complaints are not first preferred to Gowteeahs and Commavisdars, they will not be attended to by the Circar.
8. Where there are Cutwalls it will be their duty to take measures for discovering and reporting to Commavisdars all offences committed within the limits of their charge.
9. If any public offender absconds a "*dalee*" will according to former usage be sent off in every direction and the person described must be seized and brought to the Circar.

The second was dated the 4th December 1819 and was as follows:—

1. Agreeably to ancient usage a Punjee will be named to each Pergunnah who will receive a salary from the Circar.
2. All complaints which may be made to Commavisdars regarding property, disputes of castes, etc., which he may consider it proper to refer to a Punchayat will be so investigated under the superintendence of the Panjee.
3. A Punchayat will be constituted as follows:—

   The complainant will name two members, the defendant two, and the Punjee will form the fifth— these persons being assembled in the public Kutcherry will investigate and decide on the matter in dispute.
4. The evidence given before every Punchayat as well as the decision will be duly recorded and submitted to the Commavisdar who will subsequently return the papers for deposit with the Punjee.
5. The Commavisdars will confirm and enforce the decision of the Punchayat unless one of the parties interested complains that the Punchayat has received

a bribe from the other side. In such case the Commavisdar will enquire into the matter, report on the subject to the Circar, and suspend the award of the Punchayat until the orders of the Circar be received.

6. It is the express order of the Circar that the Punjee shall receive no money from those applying for redress and they are required not to give any. A disobedience of these directions will be severely punished.

7. The Commavisdar will assemble the Gowteeahs, Ryots, Mahajeins, Baipaus, etc. at the Cutcherry, and having informed them that the person they may choose as a Punjee will be named to the office for one year will call upon them to make the selection which being reported will be confirmed by the Circar.

8. At the end of each year a similar proceeding will be adopted in order to the nomination of the new Punjee.

9. If any complaints are preferred against any Punjee the Circar will without much enquiry direct another to be appointed."

These rules have appeared to me to answer well, and as they are founded on the practice of the country, and habits of the people, I have no alterations in them to recommend. There is, however, one improvement which constantly presses itself on my attention, and that is the advantage which would be derived by the superintendent having the aid of an European Officer to assist him particularly in this Department. The various and numerous complaints and offences to be investigated; the often tedious process of procuring all the evidence that can be adduced to elucidate the question; the correspondence necessary for that object and for ascertaining the merits of a case; and the labour of examinations now all press hard on the time of the superintendent and compel him to limit the scope of his investigations and to dispense with enquiries which would have been satisfactory to himself as well as publicly beneficial.

What crimes most prevalent. — None can be said to be very prevalent, but acts of violence arising out of jealousy and intrigues or to avenge supposed injury from witches are the most common.

What punishments awarded for particular crimes. — The intentional killing of a cow or a Brahmin was death to all except Bramins, Gosains and Byraggees who for the offence were expelled their castes until they had by pilgrimages expiated the crime, when they were often readmitted. Where the act was unintentional and occurred by accident, all were punished alike by expulsion from their castes.

The murder of a high caste man by a low caste man was generally punished by death. The murder of a low caste man by a higher caste man was punished by fine.

Rebellion and highway robberies were punished by death.

Stealing and the other lesser offences were punished by cutting off hands, noses, ears and fingers, branding on the forehead, flogging with a Zairbund-confinement [in] the stocks, and fines.

Women were not punished more severely for any offence than by cutting the nose off. Their lives were never taken.

Hanging and blowing away from guns were the usual modes of execution, and torture does not appear to have been common.

What best calculated to prevent the commission of Crimes with reference to the opinion and feeling of the people.— Death, severe mutilations, and fines are the only punishments which appear to be much dreaded by the people of this quarter, and there is reason to fear that our practice of sentencing criminals to work in irons on the roads for life, or for a limited time, carries with it but few terrors.

MISCELLANEOUS

Information and suggestions on any subjects not mentioned above.— I am not aware that there is any subject of importance which has not been treated of in this report, or that I can add materially to the information it contains.

I annex, however, a statistical *table which gives the result of investigation which has been made in the Kalsa Lands by the Ameens and Pundays appointed by me; also a second* table showing the average proportion which the assessment bears to each village and plough.

From these papers it will be observed that there is a very extraordinary variety between Pergannahs and even Talooks on every point on which comparison can be made, and that circumstances combined with the undoubted habit of the Ryots to migrate from place to place renders it indispensable that every statistical enquiry to be correct should be recent in date and narrowed in locality. General results to any practical purpose would be fallacious.

The same causes, and the general poverty, and fluctuating state of the country seem to render annual assessments necessary and to oppose any more permanent settlement.

I have the honour to be,

Sir,

Your most obedient Servant,

Raipur. P. VANS AGNEW, Major

The 23rd December 1820. *Superintendent of Affairs,*

Chutteesgurh.

REFERENCES

* [NOTE. - The first few pages are missing from the one copy of this Report recently found in the Secretariat Record Room, Nagpur. The spelling of the original has been retained. Any words not in the original added to complete the sense or as an explanation are shown throughout within square brackets.]

[† ? Pali, in Lapha Zamindari, where a famous temple stands, with which is connected the name of Jajalla Deva].

[*See Hunter's Orissa Volume II, page 8.]

† [? Heowunsee.]

* Apparently an attempt to give the old classification of Brahmins, Kshatreyas, Vaishyas and Sudras.

† A local battalion organized for the purpose of collecting the land tax. See Hunter's Orissa's Volume II, page 54.

APPENDIX-2

Some Notes concerning the People of Mungeli tahsil,
Bilaspur District by E.M. Gordon
Published in the *Journal of the Asiatic Society of Bengal*
Vol. LXXI, Part 3, No. 21902, 1903 pp. 38-49; and
Vol. LXXXIII, Part III, No. 1, 1904 pp. 1-20
[Read 6th August, 1902]

A. NOTES ON CASTES

1. *Dalit*

The dalits of this Tahsil are divided into four distinct sections:—

1. Satnāmi.
2. Chuṅgiyā.
3. Kanaujiyā
4. Ahirwār.

Satnāmī:— The *Satnāmīs* take the first place in consideration because of their numerical importance and also because of their interesting peculiarities. In the *Journal of the Asiatic Society of Bengal*, Volume LIX, Part I, Nos. 3 and 4, 1890, will be found a brief historical sketch regarding this people. The assassination of one of the *Satnāmī* gurūs at Aurābandā near Mungēlī has been merely mentioned in the above sketch. The *Satnāmīs* invariably accused the Rājputs of having murdered their gurū. This gurū had exasperated the Hindūs by wearing the janevā. He died at a village named Nāri on his way to Raipur where he was being taken by the Police Dārogā from Mungēlī. The following is the list of *Satnāmī* Gurūs in order of succession:—1. Ghāsī-dās, 2. Bālak-dās, 3. Agardās, 4. Sāhib-dās, 5. Ajab-dās.

The practices and views noted below are peculiar to the Satnāmīs:—

The Tabu.—Ghāsidās enjoined his followers to abstain from the use of intoxicating drinks, from flesh of every kind, and from the use of tobacco. The *Satnāmīs* taboo *masur-ki-dāl* (*Ervum Lens*) and *lāl-bhāji* because of the reddish appearance resembling blood. The use of *taroī* (*Luffa Acutangula*) is forbidden because of its supposed resemblance to the horn of the buffalo and *brinjal* (*Solanum Molongena*) is repugnant because of its resemblance to the scrotum of the same animal. During the recent years of famine these restrictions have been given up to a great extent. In the out-lying villages of Bilaspur District the *Satnāmīs* will be found much more staunch in their beliefs and practices than along the Railway line. A great change is coming over these people who unanimously state that they are quickly drifting away from the position taken up by their first gurū, Ghāsidās.

Yoking Cattle.—Ghāsidās forbade the yoking of oxen for ploughing purposes after the mid-day meal. This injunction is still heeded by great numbers of *Satnāmīs.* In cases of necessity I have known them to continue ploughing from early morning to late in the afternoon in order that they may not break away from the old practice. The original idea seems to be that of compassion for their cattle.

Jahariyā:— Amongst the *Satnāmīs* there may be found a select few who are known as *Jahariyās.* The prevailing opinion in regard to them is that they are the best of the *Satnāmīs.* According to one story when the Dalits were being boiled in the rice caldron, the Dalits who stuck to the bottom of a cauldron and were burnt are the *Chuṅgiyās*. Those who were boiled in the centre are the *Satnāmīs*, while those at the top are the *Jahariyās*. They are held in high esteem by the *Satnāmīs*. They have the chief characteristic of never sleeping on a bed but always on the ground. They are said to wear coarse, uncoloured clothes, and some say that they eat only *dāl* and rice. The children of *Jahariyās* intermarry with other Dalits and are not necessarily of the same section as their parents. This seems to be a vow taken by certain *Satnāmīs*. The Order is said to have arisen after the time of Ghāsidās. When one is found fastidious in food and drink he is taunted with the saying "You wish to be a *Jahariyā*."

Chuṅgiyā:— 2. The *Chuṅgiyā* Dalit may also be termed "the smoking Dalit" for it is principally in regard to smoking that they differ from the *Satnāmīs*. The word 'Chuṅgiyā' is applied to a pipe made of a rolled leaf. It is said the *Chuṅgiyās* are back-slidden *Satnāmīs*, those who found the restrictions imposed by Ghāsidās altogether too severe for practice. A *Chuṅgiyā* may become a *Satnāmī* by breaking a cocoannut in the presence of the gurū and by the payment of a rupee (more or less according to status). The *Chuṅgiyās* consider the *Satnāmīs* as superior to themselves and sometimes endeavour to pass off as *Satnāmīs*. As a matter of fact these two sections of Dalits intermarry frequently but the more strict *Satnāmīs* are opposed to intermarriage with *Chuṅgiyās*. Smoking and idolatry are the chief points of demarcation between these two sections. The *Chuṅgiyā* village invariably contains stones covered with vermilion while no settlement of staunch *Satnāmīs* will show any signs of idolatry. Both the *Satnāmīs* and *Chuṅgiyās* wear the necklace of wooden beads known as a *kaṇṭhī* (from the word meaning 'neck'). This neck-lace is said to be placed round the child's neck soon after birth and it is broken immediately a person expires. It may be renewed when it is old. The glass bangles worn by women are also broken before burial.

Peculiarities of the Chuṅgiyā:— They rear no poultry, goats or pigs. They eat the flesh of cattle which have died a natural death. I know many who use intoxicants. They may be considered to represent the *Satnāmīs* in their former state, that is, as Ghāsidās found them before his great reformation. Together with the *Satnāmīs*, the *Chuṅgiyās* are chiefly agriculturists. These two sections of Dalits are Dalits only in name for they do not work in leather as in other parts of India. They call themselves *Chuṅgiyā* and *Satnāmīs* respectively. A *Chuṅgiyā* calls himself Dalit, Dalit *Sitāramiya* and *Chuṅgiyā*. The Kanaujiyā calls the *Satnāmīs* and *Chuṅgiyās*, *Jheriyā*, a word which I think may have come from the word *jhāri*. Is it not probable that when the Kanaujiyās immigrated into these uncivilized parts they found other Dalits in these places whom they called the Jangli or Jhāri? This term is very much disliked by those to whom it is applied and it is a term of contempt used by the Kanaujiyās only. It may be noted here that there are also Jheriyā Telīs, Jheriyā Marārs, etc.

The Hindūs term all the Dalits alike as Chamārs. Of the different kinds of Dalits, the Hindūs appear to hold the *Satnāmīs* in higher esteem because of their many restrictions as to food and their general cleanliness of person and habitation as compared with the other Dalits; this is worthy of notice when we consider that the *Chuṅgiyā* and Kanaujiyā are religiously more closely allied to the Hindūs and worship the same deities which the *Satnāmīs* entirely ignore. While *Satnāmīs* observe most of the Hindū festivals I find that they do not take part in the Holī. It should be remembered, however, that my remarks with regard to the *Satnāmīs* apply only to the staunch members of this sect. As I have already noted, there is an increasing indifference amongst them.

Kanaujiyā:— 3. The Kanaujiyās are the Dalits proper, for, they are the leather-workers. Their villages and houses are invariably most dirty and disagreeable. In appearance these Dalits are far inferior to the *Satnāmīs* for they usually have a dissipated appearance. They are much given to the use of intoxicants and during a marriage or after a burial they meet together and drink large quantities of liquor. They eat pigs' flesh but do not rear the pigs. They make shoes of a peculiar type. In some portions of the Bilāspur District, I am told, there are Kanaujiyā to whom the above remarks do not apply. My observations are mostly confined to the Mungēlī Tahsil.

Ahirwār.- 4. Ahirwārs are very similar to the Kanaujiyās though they do not intermarry. I have not made very detailed enquiries into this section. They appear to be small in numbers. I am told that they make shoes of a different type to the Kanaujiyās. The Kanaujiyā shoes are of one single piece of leather. The Ahirwār shoes have a separate portion for the front. The Ahirwārs moreover make shoes with much fancy work, silver thread worked in red cloth. This work is done by the women. Before an Ahirwār girl can be taken in marriage she must show herself efficient in this kind of needle work. The Kanaujiyā fancy work on shoes is not as elaborate as the Ahirwār work. Kanaujiyā shoes are named "Nirjāhi" (probably from *Nirjor*, meaning without joint) also Munda, meaning plain or bare. Ahirwār shoes are called "Salāhi." The Ahirwār shoes are considered the more lasting.

2. *The Kurmīs*

The sub-castes are as follows:—

1.	Deśā	5.	Manwā
2.	Chandaunā.	6.	Ekbahiyāñ
3.	Gabel.	7.	Kanaujiyā
4.	Sarāti.	8.	Phuljhariyā.
		9.	San-boyā

1. The Deśā Kurmīs are found mostly in the Mungēlī Tahsil. They are peculiar in that they do not rear poultry and avoid residing in villages in which their neighbours would keep poultry. They will not tease cotton, their women do not wear a *nath* (a nose ornament). The Deśā Kurmī may not have two wives who are sisters. If a Deśā Kurmī should purchase a pair of shoes which prove too small for him he cannot on any account sell the shoes to another. He may make a gift of the shoes to some poor Brāhmaṇ. If he should sell the shoes his caste people will demand a *Bhāt* for this offence. The Deśā Kurmīs are all of one *Gotra*, known as Kāshi *Gotra* (this word may be a corruption of Kaśyap).

Amongst Ekbahiyāñ Kurmīs, as their name signifies, the women wear bangles on one arm only, glass bangles on one arm and metal bangles on the other.

Phuljhariyā. This word means the withering of the flower; phūl, flower and jharnā, to wither, or droop.

The Sanboyā Kurmīs are those who cultivate *San* (or hemp). This cultivation is usually confined to the Mulhā and Gond castes but the Sanboyā Kurmīs are also permitted to engage in it.

The Kurmīs both burn and bury their dead. If in good circumstances the Kurmī will undoubtedly be burnt.

3. *Telī.*

Mr. Risley in his "Tribes and Castes of Bengal" mentions two distinct kinds of Telīs. The one soaks up the oīl from the *ghāni* (oil mill) and the other allows the oil to trickle down through a hole in the side of the *ghāni.* The former he says regards the latter as greatly inferior. The Telīs of Mungēlī Tahsil appear to be entirely of the latter class, and they know nothing of the Telīs who soak up the oil from the *ghāni.* The Telī sub-castes are:—

1. Jheriyā, most numerous in Bilāspur.
2. Ekbahiyāṇ, who wear glass bangles on the right arm and Rāng bangles on the left.
3. Madpotwā, in former days used to distil intoxicants. They are found near the hills. They keep pigs and poultry. Jheriyā Telīs do not rear poultry and pigs though they keep goats and eat their flesh. If a Telī should have worms in a sore he will call together the Telīs of the Sanwāni *Gotra* and give them a feast, for by so doing he removes his impurity. When the g*hāni* is first placed in the ground five pieces of *haldi* (turmeric), some cowries and a *supāri* (areca nut) are placed under it. The Telīs *ghāni* or oil-press, in common with mills of every kind amongst all the castes, is invariably turned from the right to left.
4. The Crī Bāsnā Telīs and the Ekbahiyān Telīs in marriage processions take the bridegroom on a p*ālki,* whereas the Madpotwā, the Deśā and the Dhimar Telīs take the bride and bridegroom in a g*āṛā* or cart.

4. *Marār*

The sub-castes are as follows:—

1. Kosariyā.
2. Bhoirā.
3. Hardiyā.
4. Kāchi.
5. Jheriyā.
6. Pabiyā.

The Marārs are gardeners or vegetable-growers. The Kosariyā Marārs do not eat *Rengaiyā bhāt*, that is, food which has been carried from one place to another. Most Marārs are obliged to employ a *dolā* or *pālki* in their marriage processions even when the bride's house is next door. The Marārs do not rear poultry but they may rear goats. They use tobacco but not intoxicating drinks. A Brāhmaṇ's presence and service are required at the marriage ceremony. Both burial and cremation are practised in this caste. The Bhoirā Marārs are considered the lowest. They use intoxicants freely and do not necessarily employ a *pālki* in the marriage procession. The favourite gods in this caste are Dulhā Dev and Thākur Dev.

5. *Garariyās*

The sub-castes are as follows:—

1. Jheriyā.
2. Deśā.
3. Nikhar.
4. Dhengrā.

The Garariyās are the shepherds of this Tahsil. Their sole occupation is to tend sheep and to weave blankets of the wool from their flock. The Jheriyā Garariyās weave blankets in three separate *patis* or strips and these are sewn together length-wise. They use only a small loom. The Nikhar and Dhengrā Garariyās weave the whole blanket on a large loom. The Garariyās do not keep poultry and pigs. They will not eat the flesh of sheep which have died a natural death.

6. *Kumhār*

The sub-castes are:—

1. Deśā
2. Jheriyā.
3. Phuljheria

The Kumhārs make earthen vessels and also tiles. I am told that no Kumhārs keep poultry and that only the Deśhā Kumhārs use intoxicants.

7. *Baret.*

There are four sub-castes, viz:—

1. Jheriyā.
2. Kanaujiyā.
3. Deśā.
4. Dhobahā.

The Barets are the washermen and are found in every village where there are Hindūs. The Kanaujiyā Barets are considered the best. The keeping of poultry and goats is not forbidden in this caste. They use both intoxicants and tobacco. They may both burn and bury. They wash for all the castes except Dalits and Ghasiyās. The Barets all employ Brāhmaṇs in their marriage ceremonies. The Kanaujiyā Barets require his presence at the circumvention of the marriage pole but the other Barets employ a Brāhmaṇ merely to fix an auspicious day for the marriage ceremony.

8. *Baḍhaī.*

It is worthy of notice that there is no Baḍhaī (carpenter caste) in these parts. The Dalits have many of their own people practising carpentry but those who belong to the true Baḍhaī caste are all of them immigrants from the United Provinces. I am told that the few *pardeśi* (foreign) carpenters in this District came from up-country together with the Kāyasths after the Mutiny of 1857.

9. *Ghasiyā.*

The sub-castes are:—

1. Lariyā.
2. Rāmgariya.
3. Oriyā.
4. Dingkuchiyā.
5. Mandarchāwā.
6. Dolbohā Lariyā.

The Ghasiyās are also known as the Thanvārs. The chief occupation is that of a groom or grass-cut. They also trade in baskets and *supas* (winnowing fans), combs made of bamboos and marbles. They do not make these articles but carry them a long distance in order to make a small profit. Lariyā Ghasiyās are considered the best. Together with all the other sub-castes, they rear pigs. The Oriyā Ghasiyās often do the work of sweepers. The Dingkuchiyā Ghasiyās as their name intimates are employed chiefly to castrate bullocks, buffaloes and horses. The word kuchiyā means to crush, while the first syllable in this name probably means the testes of an animal. The Mandarchāwā are employed in making drums. They do not object to disposing of the carcasses of cattle. Dolbohā Ghasiyās as their name indicates carry the *dolā* or *pālki* for several castes. The Ghasiyās mostly worship Dulhā Dev, whose altar is invariably found near the cooking place. The Rāwats will not wash the plates of the Ghasiyās. This caste is very much given to the use of intoxicating drinks and drugs. Their women frequently go out as midwives. There is one peculiarity amongst the Ghasiyās which requires special notice. They will never take salt from the house or hand of the Kāyastha. If a Ghasiyā should be employed as a syce in the service of a Kāyastha he will not, on any account, hold the stirrup for his master, neither will he handle his master's bedding or clothing. The Ghasiyās say that these restrictions are due to some Kṛyā or vow taken by their ancestors in connection with the Kāyasthas.

The Ghasiyā may take salt from the house or hand of a Dalit but he would be out-casted if he should take salt from the Kāyastha.

Since writing the notes concerning the Ghasiyās, I have heard the following story in two widely separated portions of the Tahsil. It explains the cause of the feeling of the Ghasiyās towards the Kāyasthas. It is said that away back in the distant past the Kāyasthas invited all the Ghasiyās to a feast with the object of poisoning them. The Ghasiyās responded to the invitation in large numbers. During the feast, in some way, two of the Ghasiyās, a man and a woman (some say a boy and a girl) discovered that the Ghasiyās were being poisoned and they made their escape and hid themselves under the loom of a weaver, or Pankā. It is from these two who escaped that all the Ghasiyās have descended and they have taken a vow never to receive even a pinch of salt from the treacherous Kāyasthas, who all but exterminated their caste.

10. *Rāwat.*

There are seven sub-castes, *viz.*:—

1. Jheriyā.	2. Deśā.	3. Kanaujiyā.
4. Phuljhariyā.	5. Kosariyā.	6. Kauriya.
7. Dharbhol		

The Rāwats are the watermen and cattle-grazers. Excepting the three last-named sub-castes the Rāwats may cook for each other but one may not add salt to the food for another. Each kind of Rāwat will add the salt for himself. The Kosariyā, the Kauriya and the Darbhol Rāwats are said to eat with the Gonds and to rear pigs. These three sub-castes are found mostly in the hills. The Kanaujiyā Rāwats are considered the best. They do not fill water for others, nor will they wash plates. A Kanaujiyā Rāwat will not graze the *Bardi.* They will graze only the *Gorhi.* The *Gorhi*, I am told, contains no bullocks or buffaloes while *Bardi* means an indiscriminate herd of cattle. *Pāhat* is a term applied to a herd of cattle owned by one man and the Rāwat who grazes the *pāhat* is called the *pāhatiyā.*

B. *Some Beliefs and Practices Common to Various Castes*

1. *Marriage by Capture.*— During a Dalit wedding I noticed the remains of the old practice of "Marriage by Capture". When the bridegroom's party was approaching the house of the bride for the marriage ceremony there was a sham fight between the friends of the bride and bridegroom. The boy's friends lifted him up on their shoulders and, surrounding him on every side, approached the bride's home swinging around their *lāṭhis* in a threatening manner. On reaching the bride's house they crossed sticks with the bride's friends who gradually fell back and allowed the bridegroom's friends to advance. The women of the house gathered with baskets in their hands and some threw about rice or Murrā in pretence of self-defence. When the cudgels of the bridegroom parties struck the

roof of the bride's home (or the Madwa) her friends considered themselves defeated and the sham fight was at an end. This practice is known as *Parghauni dhātā*. It is common to all castes in the Mungeli Tahsil.

2. *Marriage restrictions.*— When a husband dies his wife considers it proper to go to her Dewar, her husband's younger brother. She will never go to her husband's elder brother whom she respects as a father-in-law. Amongst the Dalits a man may have two wives who are sisters. Except amongst the Gonds and Ghasiyās the marriage of cousins is forbidden. The Ghasiyās and Gonds allow the marriage of cousins on the mother's side because they are of different *gotras*, but the cousins on the father's side are considered as brother and sister. They are of the same *gotra*, and may not intermarry.

3. *Māmā Bhācā.*— It is said amongst the ordinary people of this District that Māmā and Bhācā (maternal uncle and nephew) should never cross a river in the same ferry. During a storm if they should be in the same house there is a danger of the place being destroyed by a thunderbolt. The nephew must not touch the uncle's head nor must he touch his shoes, nor eat the food left by his uncle. The uncle should never strike or beat his nephew. If he should stumble against him by accident the uncle will ask the nephew's pardon. I know a man who is afflicted with palsy and it is attributed to his having beaten his sister's son.

4. *Twelve-and-half Castes.*— In these parts all the different castes are said to have $12^1/_2$ sections. The Dalit unanimously declare that there are $12^1/_2$ kinds of Dalit but they are unable to name the whole number. They say that fallen women make up the half.

5. *Aversion to killing a cat.*— There is a strong aversion to the killing of a dog or cat. A dog may be killed, but to remove a dead dog will out-caste the remover. A sweeper alone should do this. To kill a cat means that the offender makes himself responsible for all the sins committed by that animal, and these are numerous because of the many lives of birds and rats which have been taken by the offending cat. The killing of a cat will out-caste the offender.

6. *Graves.*— Amongst the people of this Tahsil the grave is always dug from north to south. One reason assigned is that the head of the earth is to the North. Another reason is that, in the *Satyuga*, the sun rose in the North and in each succeeding era it has risen at a different point of the compass till, in *Kaliyuga*, it rises in the East.

7. *Names.*— Despicable names are very frequently given to children especially when the parents have lost one or more by sickness or miscarriage. A woman expecting a child will sometimes go through the performance of the sale of a child to a neighbour. She is given five or ten *cowries* for which she promises to make over her child on its birth to a neighbour. The child is nominally her neighbour's child and is named Pāchkāur or Daskāur as the case may be.

It is considered inadvisable to expose a young child to the gaze of a large number of persons. There is a desire to secrete a child up to a certain age. The result is frequently disastrous to the health of the infant who pines for light and fresh air. In this connection it may be mentioned that the giving of nick-names after some chief characteristic is exceedingly common and hence we find the following names of men and women:— Kanwā (blind), Bhirā (deaf), Kondā (dumb); Khorwā (lame), Kariyā Kāri (black), Bhurwā, bhuri (fair). It does not follow that one who is named dumb is speechless. He may have been late in speaking.

8. *Miscarriage.*— Miscarriage is almost invariably attributed to the *Tonhi* or witch. If the supposed witch should touch the woman with child, or hand her some eatable, or in bathing if a drop of water should splash, on to the expectant woman, from the garment being washed by the *Tonhi*, the results are said to be disastrous. This last cause of miscarriage is said to be most common and may be attributed to a woman having injured herself while bathing or washing at the riverside or tank.

9. *Birth practices.*— Midwives are mostly Dalits of the Kanaujiyā and Chungiyā sub-castes or Nagārchis. Ordinarily a woman receives two annas for

delivering a girl, four annas for a boy, as well as a piece of cloth. The barber and the washerman also receive presents. Amongst the better class of Dalits and farmers, it is customary for the new-born infant to be placed in a *supa* or winnowing fan. A bed is made of rice and the infant is placed in the nest of rice and thisgrain is then given to the nurse. The nurse will also go to the house of the head-man of the village, and to the near relatives of the new born infant, and make a mark with cow-dung before the main entrance. On seeing this sign the master of the house presents the nurse with grain or money. It is usual to withhold food for six days from a woman after confinement. Liquid of every kind is withheld for three days.

10. *Bhandārnā.*— The still-born infant or one which passes away before the *Chatti* or sixth day, the day of purification, is not taken away to be buried. It is placed in an earthen vessel or *ghara* and is buried in the door-way or in the yard of the house. By so doing some say that the mother is likely to bear another child, but others give no reason for this practice; a prominent *Satnāmī*, who undoubtedly knew of this practice, stoutly denied all knowledge and declared he had never heard of it. A feast is required of the relatives of the deceased only if the body is taken to the burial ground, and the idea of burying in the yard may have arisen from a desire to avoid giving a feast. Others maintain that the still-born or young infants are especially sought after by the *Tonhi* or witch and to avoid their being made into Mukhā Dev (or the dumb spirit) the infants are buried in the house or yard. This practice is known as Bhandārnā. It is common to all castes in this Tahsil. I am not prepared to say that it has any connection with infanticide.

11. *Witches.*— The fear of evil spirits is very firmly fixed in the minds of the people. Some declare that spirits are not as numerous now as they were formerly. They are not so much talked about; in other words, the people are finding more topics of conversation; the belief in the evil-eye is still prevalent and a volume might be written on this fruitful subject. Those who practise witch-craft are nearly always women. The *Gunai* or remover of the evil-influence, on the other hand, is almost invariably a man. The witch is said to do her work

with two and a half letters "Aṛhā'ī Akshar". The *Gunai* requires seven letters. I do not understand the force of this saying. Any one who is practising witch-craft is said to experiment on trees by causing them to wither and revive according to his will. He first throws some rice at a tree and mutters certain words which will cause it to wither. He should then revive it. This is the crowning test of having acquired the tricks of witch-craft. If one should try to learn the practices of a witch and fail he is said to become insane and is called *anshiki.* In order to bring a familiar spirit under control the spiritualist is said to go and sit near the grave of a recently buried person. He must go there naked and, lighting a small lamp, must sit near the grave, nodding the head, in fact swaying the whole body, most persistently and perseveringly till the spirit of the dead appears. The spiritualist then commands the spirit to come under his control to obey his slightest wish of inclination. From that time forth the familiar spirit may be used for any purpose, even for the killing or sickening of a neighbour. Both the old and young women are said to have familiar spirits, but the evil influence of the young women is much greater than that of the old. With advancing years the power of the witch is said to diminish. A clod of earth taken from a newly dug grave will suffice to enable a spiritualist to call up the spirit. Hence for three days after a burial graves are closely watched and women are never found attending a burial. The witches are said to prefer, as familiar spirits, those who have been hanged, or such as have had the head severed from the body. There is a spirit of ghost known as *Murkātā* or the headless ghost. There is a spirit or ghost known as *Matiyā* (See Crooke's *Folklore*, Vol. II, 266). He is said to be very short in stature, and of a fair, reddish appearance. He appears with a *kāwar* or bamboo with suspended ropes for carrying goods. This *Matiyā* is sent by a witch to destroy the prosperity of certain homes. He has but to carry away a small portion of the food of the house and from that time forth, however much grain may be prepared, it will always prove insufficient. In order to keep away the *Matiyā* a small *kāwar* is made of an empty pumpkin and this is suspended from the roof of the house. It is supposed that the *Matiyā*, on entering the house, will see the *kāwar* and depart with the impression that the house is occupied by one of his own kind. The belief is very prevalent that the spirit of the deceased returns to the house the first night after burial, and, in order to know whether he or she has been to the house, there is a practice of spreading ashes in the door-way so that the foot-prints may be seen in the morning.

12. *Botlagānā.*— I find a practice amongst the Dalits which is known as Botlagānā. Before a prominent member of a family is buried, it is customary amongst the Dalits to make a mark on the body of the deceased, with either *ghī* or oil or soot, and this same mark is sought for on the body of infants who may in the near future be born into the family. If a child should be born with a mark similar to that made on the ancestor's person he is considered a reincarnation of that individual.

13. *Sickness.*— The belief is very prevalent that if a woman during her period of sickness should take part in any affair it will undoubtedly prove unfortunate. If she should approach a man with opthalmia it is believed that he will lose his eye-sight by ulceration. This superstition applies to small-pox also, though in this case it is on account of the *Dēvī* being annoyed and giving her victim increased suffering by greater violence in the symptoms. A woman in this condition will also avoid entering the house of one in labour. Her presence is said to increase, unnecessarily, the labour pains and, if the child is born, it is said that her presence will bring on infantile jaundice.

14. *Burhā Māi.*— A person with small-pox is said to be troubled by the *Dēvī* or goddess, *Mātā* or Burhā Māi, hence outsiders, if they approach the house of one with small-pox, do so with much reverence, taking off the shoes and turban, holding their hands together in a supplicating manner and doing obeisance.

15. *Iron and Cholera.*— During a cholera epidemic there is a desire to avoid the use of the name of the disease. This sickness is often called Hāwā (wind) or simply *Bimārī* (sickness), or *Duhkhī.* The idea prevails amongst the lower castes that the presence of iron wards off the disease or the goddess, hence during the epidemic people are frequently seen moving around with an axe or sickle.

16. *Pregnancy.*— Pregnant women are considered specially liable the evil influence of witches, because of there being two lives "Dojivan." They therefore

take special pains to avoid them. In the event of a woman having died in child-birth or during pregnancy, her spirit is considered to be specially sought after by the witches. Increased precautions are therefore taken after the death of a woman in child-birth.

17. *Worms.*— Amongst all castes if worms should be found in a sore or ulcer the person so afflicted is considered an out-caste. It is necessary to feed the caste people and to perform various other rites to be re-admitted to caste. When there are worms in a sore, the expression used is "Phul par gayā".

18. *The Winnowing Fan.*— There is a firm belief that if a "Supā," or winnowing fan, should be placed on a cart, it will cause the cart to move slowly, and will considerably increase the weight. Hence all household goods are placed on a cart, excepting the "Supā" which is carried in the hand of those going on foot.

19. *Salt.*— There is a general belief that it is unfortunate to spill salt. One who does this will in Patāl gather up each pinch of salt with his eyelids. It is also considered inadvisable to hand salt to a friend or neighbour in the bare palm of the hand, for this will cause enmity between the parties concerned. Salt is therefore received, not in the bare palm, but in a cloth or vessel. (See *Macedonian Folklore,* by G.F. Abbott, page 103.)

20. *Rats' flesh fattening.*— The eating of rats' flesh is a common practice amongst the children of the lower castes. Since the pastime of children is often the remains of the earnest life-work of adults in an earlier stage of culture, this practice of eating rats seems to point back to the time when rats formed a staple article of food amongst the people. Even now, in times of scarcity, the people of the district have been known to live on field rats when they were obtainable. I am told that rats' flesh is considered fattening and is given to emaciated children and to cattle in order that they may put on flesh.

21. *Horses and the monkey.*— "Ghorā kā rog bāndar meṇ jāe." This saying appears to have originated in the belief that if a monkey is tied in the stable

of a horse, any disease which may be likely to attack the horse, will go to the monkey instead. The saying is now repeated when one person has to suffer for the offences of another. It may be that in time this practice will be discontinued and forgotten and the saying will still be current and will arouse questions as to its origin.

22. *Owls.*—These birds are known as the priest of the witches "Tonhi kā guru." They are considered extremely unlucky birds and are associated in the minds of the people with misfortune and death. It is considered inadvisable to call aloud at night to anyone by name. The owl will hear the name called and will take to calling that name till the person sickens and dies. A clod of earth or a stone is never thrown at an owl, for it is believed that the owl will take up the stone and drop it in some stream; and as the earth or the stone dissolves in the water, the person who threw it will go into a decline and will die.

23. *Whirlwinds.*— These phenomena are supposed to be caused by *bhūts* or evil spirits. I have also heard them called "a knot in the wind." Tylor has truly said—"What is poetry to us was philosophy to early man."

24. *Small-pox, etc.*— Diseases of this group are all associated with the *Mātā* or Mother, the Devi or goddess of these diseases. Those who have been attacked by the disease, and have recovered, are said to have been wedded by the *Mātā*. "Mātā usko bihāyā hai." It seems probable that this expression arose from the resemblance of one attacked by the disease to the bride or bridegroom covered with turmeric and oil during the marriage ceremony.

25. *The horned kettle-drum.*— Amongst the numerous musical instruments used in this district is the Nishān or the horned kettle-drum, which is largely, if not entirely, used in marriage processions. It has two long deer horns attached to it on either ride. The drum hangs in front from the waist. It has the usual shape of a kettle-drum. To the metallic portion are attached the horns which are often decorated with long strips of coloured cloth. Some time ago I saw a drum which was brought from the Nāgā country. It was made of human skulls. Having previously seen this form of drum I was led to think that the horns attached

to the kettle-drum in this district are but a "survival in culture" reminding us of the time when drums were made by stretching skins over the skulls of deer with the horns intact. The original skull has now been replaced by the more durable metallic portion, while the "law of copy" has continued the horns as ornamental. I have seen a drum in which for some reason the horns were replaced by long pieces of iron. Possibly in time the horns may be entirely forgotten and the long iron projections on a drum will be the only remains of a drum originally made from the skull of a deer.

26. *The mark of the hand.*— "Hāthā denā" is the term applied to the mark made by the out-stretched palm of the hand. (*a*) The agricultural cart of the district is known as the *gāṛā*. It is made of solid wooden wheels, with no spokes, and is well adapted for crossing the fields and embankments. During the rainy season these carts are taken to pieces and are put together at the close of the wet months. When the *gāṛā* is put together for use after the rainy season, it is sometimes bathed in milk for good luck, but almost always the wheels are marked with the impress of the hand dipped in oil. I once met a cart on the roadside which had come to grief, and the driver sat disconsolate with the bags of grain lying around him on every side. I asked if the owner of the cart had "hāthā diyā" when he put the cart together, and the reply was that he had not, and this was believed to be the cause of the misfortune. (*b*) Before the birth of a child it is also usual for the nurse in attendance to dip her hand in oil and make an impression on the wall, and it is supposed by the way the oil trickles down, that she can tell whether the new comer will•be a boy or a girl. (*c*) During a festival towards the end of the year, it is the practice of the women of the herdsmen (the Rāwats) to go to each house in the village and with red and white paint to make a mark on the wall which bears a faint resemblance to a hand. I doubt, however, if the resemblance could be seen except by one who had heard that the mark on the wall is called a "hāthā." Schoolcraft says: "The figure of the human hand is used by the North American Indians to denote supplication to the Deity or Great Spirit, and it stands in the system of picture-writing as the symbol for strength, power, or mastery thus derived." On the same subject, Sir Daniel Wilson says that, "Among an interesting collection of mummies recovered by Mr. J.H. Blake, of

Boston, from ancient Peruvian cemeteries on the Bay of Chacoata, one is the body of a female wrapped in parti-coloured garments of fine texture and marked on the outer woollen wrappings with the impress of the hand. The same impress of the red hand is common on Peruvian mummies."

27. *Threshing floor practices.*— It is considered unlucky for one who has ridden on an elephant to enter a threshing-floor, and on the other hand if one who has ridden on a tiger should enter he will bring good luck. The Gonds and Bhumiyās, who may capture a young tiger, will lead it around the country amongst the agricultural people, who pay a small fee to have their children placed on the tiger. To enter a threshing-floor with shod feet is also considered unlucky. When the grain has been threshed and is awaiting measurement, some branches of the Baer tree (*Zizyphus vulgaris*) is placed on the stacked grain in order to keep off the *Matiyā* or goblin who takes away the grain and makes it measure less than was expected. Grain is never measured at noon in the threshing-floor but usually at the morning and evening hours.

28. *Close relationships.*— It is considered highly improbable that there will be immoral relationship between those who are closely related. Public opinion on this subject is such that it is considered improper for a man to marry a woman who bears the name of his mother, sister, aunt, etc. In fact, I think that on no account would a marriage be arranged between those who bear the names of near relatives. Parents, names are never given to children.

29. *Taboo as to days and months.*— The Hindūs will not shave themselves on certain days. Others observe not the days but the dates in this particular. During the fifteen days of the *pitra pāk* or the fortnight of the Manes, a Hindū will never be shaved. A woman will not put on new bangles during this same period. In the month of Jeṭh, May-June, it is against the custom of the people in these parts to perform the marriage ceremony of a first-born son, the *Jeṭh putra.* A pundit tells me that the restriction applies only when a *Jeṭh putra* is wedded to a *Jeṭh putri.* But the common people have narrowed down the restriction and make it apply to the marriage of every firstborn son, whether married to a first-born

daughter or not. This self-imposed restriction of the people reminds one of the restriction placed on themselves by the Jews. They were forbidden by the Law to give more than forty stripes, but they thought it desirable to stop short of the full number in order to avoid exceeding it, and hence gave "forty stripes save one".

30. *Pāch lakriyā (five sticks): a funeral practice.*— There is a custom amongst those who bury their dead known as *pāch lakriya.* From the name it is undoubtedly originally connected with the practice of cremation. When the grave has been filled in and the mound has been made to mark the spot, those who are present at the burial each make five small balls of earth and place them all in a heap at the head of the grave. While doing this they address the deceased and say, "Jāo, mājhi ke kok meṇ avatār leo." This being interpreted means: "Go, become incarnate in some human being." Regarding the *pāch lakriyā* practice it should be noted that it is stated that originally it was the practice of those who attended a cremation to take with them five sticks to place on the funeral pile; this practice seems to have disappeared and the only remains of it, in these parts, seems to be this custom at a burial of making balls of earth and calling them the five sticks.

It is considered meritorious to assist in a burial, and there is a saying that if one could bury a hundred persons, all by himself, he would be made a rājā in the next birth. Another interesting custom in connection with burials is that which is known as "kāṇdh utārnā" (kāṇdh, meaning shoulder). Those who have carried a bier, after the funeral, each take a clod of earth and with this they will touch first the shoulder, where the bier rested, next the waist, then the knee, and finally drop the clod to the ground. They suppose that by so doing they remove from the shoulder the weight of the corpse which would otherwise be felt for some time.

31. *Pitra pākh or the fortnight of the Manes.*— During the fortnight of the Manes there are two days set apart for the coming of the deceased. The Manes are supposed to visit the homes of their relatives on the date of their decease,

i.e., if a father died on the third of any month in the year he will be expected on the third day of the fortnight of Manes. The women all come on the ninth day of the fortnight, and on the thirteenth come all those who have met with a violent death—by a fall, snake bite, or any other such cause. A monitor, in one of my schools, once asked for a day's leave. On inquiry I learnt that it was the ninth and he was expecting his mother, long since dead, to visit his home that day. In order to perform some ceremony he was asking for leave of absence.

32. *The howling of dogs.*— The weird, unearthly noises made by dogs, especially at night, are attributed to the animals seeing ghosts and evil spirits invisible to man. It is interesting to note that Bachelor in his very entertaining work on the "*Ainu of Japan*" says that this same belief is prevalent amongst that distant and primitive people. Amongst them, however, this belief appears to have had a further development, for they do not only say that dogs of this world see the inhabitants of the next, but that the dogs of the next world howl on seeing the inhabitants of the earth. It may be noted, just here, that in two other particulars I noticed a resemblance between the Ainus and the Hindūs. They follow their dead in single file to the burial, and the widows have their heads entirely shaved just as they do in India.

33. *Sadhouri, a birth practice.*— Before the birth of the first-born child, at the seventh month (?) it is customary for the woman's nearest relatives to prepare some specially tasty dishes and bring them to the house of the woman who is expecting that she may partake of them. The more wealthy will bring along pieces of clothing also, and these will be presented to the woman. On the birth of the child, the parents will make gifts of clothing to those who gave them in the first place. The food brought at this time to the woman who is expecting is called the "sadhouri." I am told that this word is connected with the word "sādh" (meaning desire) and may have some connection with the longing of the pregnant woman for certain kinds of food.

34. *The Gourd.*— Or the calabash, is used in many different ways. Frequently it is seen as part of the simple fiddle or other stringed instrument.

It is also in use as a water-vessel; some are large and measure a foot in diameter, others are small and can be tied to the waist for a long journey. Some gourds are used as floats in the flooded streams.

There is also the gourd rattle, small in size and filled with seeds or pebbles; this is shaken in the hand in certain exorcising rites. Tylor in his "*Primitive Culture*" more than once refers to the gourd rattle used in Africa for divining and exorcising purposes.

35. *Position in burial.*— When the Hindūs bury their dead they place the body of a man with the face downwards, whereas a woman is buried with the face upwards. In a work on Stanley in Africa I remember reading of a certain people in that country who bury their men placed on the left side, while the women are placed on the right side in the grave.

36. *The Tijā or the women's fast.*— This takes place on the third day of the light half of the moon, in the lunar month of Bhādon, corresponding with our Aug.-Sept. It is very widely observed by women only. On this date and during the following night the women will keep a strict fast. They make images of sand of Māhādev and Pārbati and worship these images, for it is in remembrance of Pārbati's fast in the forest that the festival is observed. It is said that Pārbati's father, Himāchal, wished her to marry some one besides her own chosen Māhādev, and she went away to the forest and there made an image of her lover, Māhādev, and worshipped it. Māhādev found her worshipping his image made of sand, and he then decreed that all women, for all time, should fast on that day in memory of Pārbati's fast; and the women who did not fast, should be barren throughout seven successive incarnations.

37. *Sacrifice to Rāt Māi, the Night Mother.*— Of the many sacrifices required of the Hindus this one seems to me the most striking and remarkable. It is confined, I think, to the low caste Hindus and is spoken of with contempt by the Brāhmaṇs. It is observed in connection with the first-born only. It is made about a year after the birth of a son who is the first-born son of a father, who

must himself have been an eldest son. The sacrifice takes place once only in each generation. Only the members of the family are present. They fast for the previous day and the sacrifice takes place at night. A hole is dug in the house near the main entrance to one side. The sacrifice is a black goat, but amongst the Gonds or Ghassias, a pig. After the animal for sacrifice has once entered the door of the house it must not go out again nor must any portion of the sacrifice be taken out. Daughters who are married into other families may not take part in the sacrifice, but girls of other families who are married into this one, may take part. The animal is slain in the house at night, it is cooked and eaten and all the refuse portion is buried in the hole previously dug. The points of resemblance between this sacrifice and the Jewish passover are somewhat striking.

C. *Folk-Tale and Fable*

1. THE STORY OF ĪR, BĪR, DAU AND I.

1. *Īr kahis chal bāṇs kāte, Bīr kahis chal bāṇs kāte, dau kahis chal bāṇs kāte, hamun kahen chal bāṇs kāte.*

   Īr said come let's cut bamboos, Bīr said come let's cut bamboos, Dau said come it's cut bamboos, I said come let's cut bamboos.

2. *Īr kātis īr bāṇs, Bīr kātis bīr bāṇs, Dau kātis tīn bāṇs, ham kāten kanai.*

   Īr cut one bamboo, Bīr cut two bamboos, Dau cut three bamboos, I cut small bamboo.

3. *Īr kahis chal gulel banāi, Bīr kahis chal gulel banāi, Dau kahis chal gulel banāi, human kahen chal gulel banāi.*

   Īr said come make a gulel (pellet bow), Bīr said come make a gulel, Dau said come make a gulel, I said come make a gulel.

4. *Īr banāis īr gulel, Bīr banāis Bīr gulel, Dau banāis tin gulel, ham banāin guleliā.*

   Īr made one gulel, Bīr made two gulels, Dau made three gulels, I made a small gulel.

5. *Īr kahis chal chirāi māre, Bīr kahis chal chirāi māre, Dau kahis chal chirāi māre, hamun kahen chal chirāi māre.*

   Īr said come kill a bird, Bīr said come kill a bird, Dau said come kill a bird, I said come kill a bird.

6. *Īr māris īr chirāi, Bīr māris bīr chirāi, Dau māris tīn chirāi, Ham māren liṭiā.*

   Īr killed one bird, Bīr killed two birds, Dau killed three birds, I killed a litia (a small black bird).

7. *Īr kahis chal chhenā bine, Bīr kahis chal chenā bine, Dau kahis chal chenā bine, hamun kahen chal chhenā bine.*

   Īr said come gather fuel (lit. cow-dung cake), Bīr said come gather fuel, Dau said come gather fuel, I said come gather fuel.

8. *Īr binis īr chhenā, Bīr binins bīr chhenā, Dau binis tīn chhenā, ham binin kaṇdoṇ.*

   Īr gathered one fuel-cake, Bīr gathered two fuel-cakes, Dau gathered three fuel-cakes, I gathered a small cake.

9. *Īr kahis chal chirāi bhūṇje, Bīr kahis chal chirāi bhūṇje, Dau kahis chal chirāi bhuṇje, hamuṇ kahe chal chirāi bhuṇje.*

   Īr said come broil the bird, Bīr said come broil the bird, Dau said come broil the bird, I said come broil the bird.

10. Īr *bhuṇjis īr chiraī, Bīr bhuṇjis bīr chirāi, Dau bhuṇjis tīn chiraī, ham bhuṇjen liṭia. (Jatke athkā baṛ bāchis).*

    Īr broiled one bird, Bīr broiled two birds, Dau broiled three birds, I broiled a small bird: it was burnt and so much remained (here a gesture is made with the finger to indicate a small quantity).

11. *Īr kahis chal piḍhwā lāye, Bīr kahis chal piḍhwā lāye, Dau kahis chal piḍhwā lāye, hamaṇ kahen chal piḍhwā lāye.*

Īr said come fetch a stool, Bīr said come fetch a stool, Dau said come fetch a stool, I said come fetch a stool.

12. *Īr lānis īr piḍhwā, Bīr lānis bīr piḍhwā, Dau lānis tin piḍhwā, ham baiṭhe waisnech.*

    Īr brought one stool, Bīr brought two stools, Dau brought three stools, I sat just so.

13. *Īr kahis chal chirāi khāi, Bīr kahis chal chirāi khāi, Dau kahis chal chirāi khāi, hamun kahin chal chirāi khāi.*

    Īr said come eat the bird, Bīr said come eat the bird, Dau said come eat the bird, I said come eat the birdie.

14. *Īr khāis īr chirāi, Bīr khāis bīr chirāi, Dau khāis tin chirāi, ham khāyen liṭiā.*

    Īr ate one bird, Bīr ate two birds, Dau ate three birds, I ate the liṭiā.

15. *Īr kahis chal ghoṛā lihe, Bīr kahis chal ghoṛā lihe, Dau kahis chal ghoṛa lihe, hamun kahen chal ghoṛā lihe.*

    Īr said come buy a horse, Bīr said come buy a horse, Dau said come buy a horse, I said come buy a horse.

16. *Īr leis īr ghoṛā, Bīr leis bīr ghoṛā, Dau leis tin ghoṛa, ham leyan gadahī.*

    Īr bought one horse, Bīr bought two horses, Dau he bought three horses, I bought a she-ass.

17. *Īr kahis chal ghoṛā pahaṭāi, Bīr kahis chal ghoṛā pahaṭāi, Dau kahis chal ghoṛā pahaṭāi, hamuṇ kahen chal gadahi pahaṭāi.*

    Īr said come race my horse, Bīr said come race my horse, Dau said come race my horse, I said come race my ass.

18. *Īr pahaṭāis īr ghorā, Bīr pahaṭāis bīr ghoṛā, Dau pahaṭāis tin ghoṛā, ham pahaṭāin gadahī.*

    Īr galloped one horse, Bīr galloped two horses, Dau galloped three horses, I galloped the ass.

19. *Īr kahis chal pāni piyae, Bīr kahis chal pāni piyae, Dau kahis chal pāni piyae, hamun kahen chal pāni piyae.*

Īr said come now to water, Bīr said come now to water, Dau said come now to water, I said come now to water.

20. *Īr gais īr ḍabarī, Bīr gais bīr ḍabarī, Dau gais tin ḍabarī, ham gayen gadahī ḍabarī. Temā, hamār gadahī saṭakage.*

Īr went to one pond, Bīr went to another (*lit.* two) pond, Dau went to a third pond, I went to ass-pond—in which my ass became entangled.

21. *Īr ke ghorā hoṇ, hoṇ, hoṇ, hoṇ, Bīr ke ghorā hoṇ, hoṇ, hoṇ, hoṇ, Dau ke ghoṛā hoṇ, hoṇ, hoṇ, hoṇ, hamār gadahī chīpon, chīpon*

Īr's horse cried hoṇ, hoṇ, hoṇ, hoṇ; Bīr's horse cried hoṇ, hoṇ, hoṇ, hoṇ; Dau's horse cried hoṇ, hoṇ, hoṇ, hoṇ; my ass cried chīpoṇ, chīpoṇ.

22. *Īr kahis chal āmā khāye, Bīr kahis chal āmā khāye, Dau kahis chal āmā khāye, hamuṇ kahēn chal āmā khāye.*

Īr said come let's eat mangoes, Bīr said come let's eat mangoes, Dau said come let's eat mangoes, I said come let's eat mangoes.

23. *Īr khāis īr āmā, Bīr khāis bīr āmā, Dau khāis tin āmā, ham khāyen kochalaiyā, pahuchage gosaiyā.*

Īr ate one mango, Bīr ate two mangoes, Dau ate three mangoes, I ate small mango, then came the gardener.

24. *Īr lā māris īr lāthi, Bīr lā māris bīr lāthī, Dau lā māris tin lāthī, ham gayen bochakaiyā.*

Īr was beaten one stripe, Bīr was beaten two stripes, Dau was beaten three stripes, I came off scot-free.

2. THE STORY OF MAHĀDEO AND THE JACKAL

[The writer of these lines was at one time travelling at night across country accompanied by some villagers when the cry of the jackal was heard in the distance. One of the villagers remarked, "There's Māhādeo's Watchman." On inquiring as to why the jackal was called Māhādeo's watchman, the villager narrated the following story, which appears to be very widely known in the Mungeli Tehsil.]

Once upon a time the elephant and the jackal made a covenant of friendship. They agreed to go out together in search of pasture. The elephant told the jackal to mount his back and look around in search of something to eat. The jackal spied a sugarcane field from the elephant's back and they both resorted thither to have a feed. The jackal having a small stomach was soon satisfied; so he said to the elephant, "Friend, I am thirsty, let us go in search of water." The elephant replied, that his stomach being large, he had only begun his meal, but he told the jackal to again mount his back and look around if he saw cranes flying, for where the cranes went there would surely be water. The jackal replied, "Friend, I can see no cranes and I am dying of thirst. I must have a drink." Then said the elephant, "In my stomach there is always water enough to satisfy you: if you enter my stomach you may drink as much as you please, but first promise me one thing—promise me that you will not look upwards, while you are inside of me." The jackal promised faithfully to do as he was told, to have his drink inside the elephant and to come out without looking upwards. The elephant then allowed his friend, the jackal, to enter his stomach by his mouth, and the jackal quenched his thirst. Before coming out, however, he thought, "Why should the elephant tell me not to look upwards?" He was so overcome with curiosity that he looked up to see what was above him. There he saw the elephant's liver and heart and other organs all covered with blood and very tasty in appearance for a jackal. He then thought to himself, "Here is water and here is food for many days, why should I leave so good a place and go wandering over the country in search of my food?" So the jackal took up his abode inside the elephant and ate and drank every day as much as it pleased him. In time the elephant sickened and died, for the jackal was daily eating away his inside. When the elephant died the jackal was entrapped in his carcass which dried and shrank in around him. The jackal then found himself in a sad plight and loudly he cried for some one to help him to get out. Now it so happened that Māhādeo and his wife,

Pārbati, descended from heaven to walk on the earth, and in their wandering they came near to the carcass of the elephant in which the jackal was entrapped. On hearing the cries inside the elephant, Mahādeo drew near and asked who it was that was making a noise inside. The jackal replied, "Who are you that question me?" Māhādeo then said, "I am the great god Māhādeo, but who are you?" The jackal replied that he was Sahadeo, the father of Māhādeo. The jackal then said to Māhādeo, "If you are really and truly the great god Māhādeo, now you will show your power by causing a heavy shower of rain." Māhādeo then caused it to rain in torrents, and the rain fell as it never had fallen before. Because of the damp and the moisture the hide of the elephant began to swell, and thus the jackal was able to make his escape. Māhādeo then took an oath that he would avenge himself of the jackal for this act of deception.

After some time Māhādeo learned the place where the jackal used to go to the river to drink, and he hid himself in the water that he might lay hold of him when he came for his daily drink. When the jackal was drinking at the stream then Māhādeo lay hold of one of his legs and drew him into the river and tried to drown him, but the jackal cried aloud to Mahādeo that he had not laid hold of his leg but that he was holding the root of a tree. Māhādeo then let go the jackal's leg and the jackal made his escape, and so he deceived Māhādeo the second time.

Again Māhādeo determined to seize the jackal, and this time he feigned himself dead and lay like a corpse where the jackal would be sure to see him. The jackal came near him, but first he wished to make sure that he was dead. So he said aloud that a corpse recently dead passes flatus, but this corpse had passed no flatus. Māhādeo hearing this allowed gas to escape, and the jackal ran off saying, "Oh, you are no corpse and you will not deceive me."

After a time Māhādeo hit upon another device of catching the jackal. He made a large figure like that of a woman, all of bees-wax. In the hands of this figure he placed a basket of sweets such as children like, and inside the figure of wax he placed a weaver's spinning wheel, so that the arms of the figure might work back and forth as controlled by Māhādeo at a distance. When the jackal came near he thought the figure of wax was an old woman with a basket of sweets in her hands. So the jackal came nearer still and tried to steal the sweets from the woman, but when he came within striking distance the figure struck him with one arm and then with the other, so that the jackal was covered with wax and stuck to the figure; then Māhādeo came near and laid hands on the jackal and made him his prisoner. The jackal was kept bound in Māhādeo's yard, and every morning and evening Māhādeo would go to the jackal and give him a sound thrashing. This he did for many days, and the jackal in consequence became greatly swollen in appearance. One day a strange jackal came into Māhādeo's yard, and seeing the bound jackal so fleshy in appearance, he asked what he was given to eat that he should be so fat. The jackal who was bound began to praise Māhādeo and his treatment of him. He did this to such an extent that the strange jackal became desirous of trying Māhādeo's hospitality. Then the imprisoned jackal offered to exchange places with the stranger. With his help the one jackal was set free and the new one was bound in his place. In the morning Māhādeo came as usual to beat the jackal he had bound. The strange jackal instead of getting good food as he expected was given a severe beating. He thought he would wait till evening and then he would get his meal. But when evening came Māhādeo again approached him with a stick and was about to beat him when he asked Māhādeo about the good food and the good treatment of which the other jackal had told him. Then only did Māhādeo know that the jackal which had deceived him so often had deceived him once again. So he gave the strange jackal his freedom and told him, "You go now and be my *pāhāredār* or watchman, and I must hear your voice in the night keeping watch for me." From that time forth the jackal has been Māhādeo's watchman.

3. THE LITTLE BLACK-BIRD

There was once a little black-bird (the litia) who was the proud owner of three *kauries.* This bird used to come to a king and repeatedly say, "I have three *kauries,* O king, I have three *kauries,* O king." The king was so much annoyed by the continual chirping of the little bird that he ordered his servants to take the three *kauries* from the bird and to drive it away. But the bird would not leave the king and so it began to say, "My wealth has made you rich, O king, my wealth has made you rich, O king." The king then ordered that the three *kauries* should be returned to the little black-bird. The bird then took the three *kauries* and went to the seller of parched grain and with the three *kauries* she bought three grains of parched gram; taking the gram the bird flew off and sat on a new cart which a carpenter was making, and there she was eating the gram. Having eaten two grains she was about to eat the third, when it dropped from her beak and fell into a joint of the new cart where she could not get at it. In great distress she appealed to the carpenter to take to pieces his cart that she might get at the grain she had lost. "You silly little thing," said the carpenter, "do you suppose I am going to take to pieces my new cart to get at a single grain which you have dropped into the joint of the wood-work." The little black-bird then went to the king and said to him that she had lost her grain, and asked him to order the carpenter to open up his cart that she may get at her grain. "You silly little thing," said the king, "do you suppose I am going to order the carpenter to open his cart that you may get one small grain. "The little black-bird then went to the queen and begged of her to persuade the king to order the carpenter to open the cart to let her get at the grain. But the queen also said, "Get away, you silly little thing." Then the little black-bird went to a deer and said, "Come, O deer, I wish you to graze in the queen's garden, for she will not persuade the king, and the king will not order the carpenter, and the carpenter will not open the cart, and I cannot get at my grain." But the deer would give no heed to the bird and called her: "You silly little thing." Then said the bird, "I will go to the *lāthī*" (the strong stout stick). And to the *lāthi* she went and said, "Come, stout stick, strike the deer: for the deer will not graze in the queen's garden, and the queen will not persuade the king, and the king will not command the carpenter, and the carpenter will not open his cart, and I cannot get at my grain." But the stick also would give no ear to the cry of the little black-bird, so she went at once to the fire; and she begged the fire to burn the stick, for the stick would not beat the deer, and the deer would not eat the queen's garden, and the queen would not persuade the king, the king would not command the carpenter, the carpenter would not break up his cart, and she could not get at her grain. But the fire also made light of the little bird's prayer; so she went next to the lake and implored the lake to quench the fire, for the fire would not burn the stick, and the stick would not strike the deer and the deer would not destroy the garden, and the queen would not persuade the king, and the king refused to command the carpenter, who also refused to open up his cart, so that the bird could not get at her grain. But the lake refused to help the bird. She then went to a place where there were thousands of rats, and to the rats she presented her prayer that they should come and fill the lake with their diggings, for the lake would not quench the fire, etc., etc. But the rats also gave no attention to the wishes of the small black-bird. Then the bird went to a cat, and of the cat she implored that she should attack the rats, for the rats would not fill in the lake, and the lake would not quench the fire, etc., and she could not get at her grain. But the cat also was deaf to the prayers of the small black-bird. Then she went to the elephant, and of the elephant she implored that he would crush the cat, for the cat would not kill the rats, etc., etc., and she could not get at her grain. But the elephant treated her as did all the others. Then she went to an ant and begged the wee ant to crawl into the elephant's ear, for the elephant would not crush the cat, etc., etc., and she could not get at her grain. But the ant also gave no heed to her prayer. Then at last she came to the crow, the most greedy of all creatures, and of the crow she begged that he should eat the ant; from sheer greed the crow consented to eat the ant; but the ant seeing the crow about to eat it went to crawl into the ear of the elephant; and the elephant fearing the harm which the ant could do him went to crush the cat; but the cat slipped away and was about to destroy the rats, and they at once began to fill in the lake; and the lake becoming alarmed was about to quench the fire, when the fire began to burn the stick, and the stick began to beat the deer, so that the deer was about to destroy the queen's garden, when the queen began to persuade the king, and so the king commanded the carpenter, and the carpenter opened up his new cart; and the little black-bird found her grain and happily taking it up she flew away and quietly enjoyed her repast and lived very happily ever after.

4. THE DEER AND THE JACKAL

Once upon a time a deer and a jackal went to a well to drink. The jackal said to the deer, "Friend, I will first go down and have a drink and afterwards you may drink also." So the deer held the jackal by the tail while he hung over in the well and quenched his thirst. When it was the deer's turn to drink, the jackal held him by the tail, and while he leaned over to drink, the jackal pushed him over into the water. Close by there were some men harvesting peas, so the jackal called aloud to them that there was a deer fallen in the well, and the men all hastened to look into the well. On seeing the deer in the well the men set to and hauled out the dead body of the deer. They then took it away to a short distance and began to cut it to pieces. Just then the jackal came on the scene and said to the men: "Friends, will you not give me some of the meat also?" But the men replied that they had taken out the deer with great difficulty, and they refused to give the jackal a portion of the flesh of the deer. The jackal repeatedly begged of them for a portion, but the men positively refused to share the meat with the jackal. Then said the jackal to the men, "If you cannot give me meat, you can at least oblige me with a few sparks of fire." The men then handed him the fire. The jackal taking the fire set ablaze the stacks of peas which the men had been harvesting. The men, in great alarm, left the deer which they were dividing between themselves and came to save their burning stacks of peas. The jackal then helped himself to as much of the deer as he pleased, and he ran away laughing at the stupidity of the foolish men who refused to share with him the flesh of the deer.

5. THE LOUSE AND THE CROW

Once a louse and a crow made a covenant of friendship. The louse said to the crow, "Go, friend and bring me some fire." So the crow brought his friend, the louse, some fire. Then said the louse, "Now, friend, I will broil and eat you." The crow replied, "If I strike you once with my beak you will disappear: how then can you talk of eating me?" But the louse broiled and ate his friend, the crow. Passing on the louse came across a loaf of bread which a man was cooking on the fire. Then said the louse to the loaf of bread, "I will eat you, my friend." But the bread replied that the louse would be scorched in the fire, and how could he eat the bread. But the louse ate the bread also. Passing on the louse met a she-goat. To the goat he said, "I am about to feast on you." The goat replied that if she would trample on the louse he would be reduced to nothing. The louse replied that he had eaten the crow and the loaf of bread, and he could eat the goat also. And he quickly finished the goat. Passing on the louse met a cow. To the cow he said, "I am about to eat you, O cow." But the cow replied, "If I trample you under foot you will be reduced to nothing." The louse said, "If I have eaten the crow and the bread and the goat, what then can hinder me from eating you." So he ate the cow also. Passing on the louse met a buffalo. To the buffalo the louse said, "I will eat you also." But the buffalo replied, "I have but to trod on you and you will be nowhere." Then the louse ate the buffalo also. The louse next met five strong sepoys. To the sepoys the louse said, "I am about to eat you five men." The sepoys replied, "You will lose yourself in the head of but one of us, and here you speak of feasting on us five warriors." But true to his word the louse ate the five sepoys. Next the louse met a wedding procession in which there were one lakh of peopie. Addressing them, the louse said that he would eat them. The men replied that the louse would be lost in the head of but one man, and how then could he speak of eating a lakh of people. But the louse replied that he had eaten first the crow, then the loaf, then the goat and the cow and the buffalo and the five sepoys, and he would certainly eat the lakh of people in the procession; and he quickly devoured the whole number. Next the louse came upon an elephant, and to the elephant the louse said, "I will eat you in no time." The elephant replied that he could blow away the louse with but one puff of breath from his trunk. The louse then related how he had eaten the crow, the loaf, etc., etc., and accordingly he ate the elephant also. Now the louse being thirsty came across a huge tank of water. Said the louse to the tank, "I am about to drink in all of your water." The tank replied that the louse would be washed away with but one wave from the waters of the tank, and how then could he talk of drinking in the waters of the tank. The louse again proceeded to narrate how he had eaten the crow, the loaf, the goat, etc., etc., and the louse then drank in all the waters of the tank. Now it so happened that some women came as usual to fill the vessels of water at the tank, and to their great astonishment they found that the waters had disappeared. While they were looking around one of the women who had but one eye spied on the bank of the tank a small shining object which proved to be the louse. Said the woman, "This surely is the creature which has drunk the waters of our tank." Just then a strong sepoy came along to have a drink at the tank. The women showed him the louse which had taken up all the water. This strong warrior immediately drew his sharp sword and with one stroke he cut in two the greedy louse. Immediately the crow appeared, and the loaf, and the goat, the cow, the buffalo, the five men, the one lakh of people, the elephant also and the waters of the tank. Each of these went to their respective places, and the women after thanking the brave sepoy who had befriended them, filled their water-pots as usual and went to their homes.

6. THE TIGER AND THE BARBER

A barber was at one time going through a jungle and he had with him nothing but the implements of his trade. Not knowing how to save his life he quickly devised the following scheme. Taking out his small looking-glass he boldly went up to the tiger and held up the glass before the tiger. Addressing this wild beast he said, "I have promised the king to slay twelve tigers and have accepted trust-money for this task. Now I have found only two tigers (meaning the real tiger and its reflection in the glass): can you direct me to ten more." Hearing this the tiger was so alarmed that he quickly disappeared thinking that the barber was truly a tiger-slayer. Thus by his cunning the barber saved his life.

7. THE PILĀ AND THE PILI

Once upon a time a Pilā, a large grain measure, had a quarrel with the Pili, a small grain measure, and the Pilā beat the Pili so that the Pili ran away from her husband in a temper. When the Pili was on the road-side she met a crow seated in a neem tree. The crow said to the Pili, "Where are you going to, Oh Pili." The Pili replied that her husband, the Pila, had beaten her, and she was running away from him. Said the crow, "Well, come and stay with me: do not go away in anger." The Pili replied, "What will you give me to eat and what to drink, what to wear and what to spread?" The crow replied, "I will place one wing under you and the other above, and the food left over by others I will bring you to eat." But the Pili said she would not stay, and so saying she went on her way. On the side of a tank the Pili met a bagulā, and the bagulā also begged her to remain with him. The Pili said to him, "What will you give me to eat, what to drink, what to wear, and what to spread?" Said the bagulā, "I will place one wing below you and the other above, and I will feed you with fishes." But the Pili would not stay with the bagulā and went on her way. Next the Pili come to a place where a Rājā was holding his Durbār. Then the Rājā asked of her, "Where are you going to, O Pili?" The Pili replied, "The Pila beat me so I am going away in a temper." But the Rājā begged of her to remain with him. The Pili asked him what she would get to eat and what to drink, what to wear, and what to spread. The Rājā said, "I will place one cushion below you and one above, and whatsoever you desire you may have to eat." But the Pili refused to stay with the Rājā. As she went on her way she met a dog coming from the river after having had a bath. The dog said, "Where are you going to, O Pili," and the Pili replied that the Pila had beaten her and she was going away from him in a temper. Then the dog also asked the Pili to stay with him and the Pili said, "What will you give me to eat and what to drink, what to wear and what to spread." The dog replied that in the Rājā's store there was a quantity of *gur* (raw sugar), and they would eat from that as much as they pleased. Then the Pili consented to stay with the dog. And they both lived in the Rājā's store-house. One day the Rājā sent his daughter to bring *gur* from his store. So the daughter taking the scales and weights went to the store to fetch the *gur*. First she threw the scales into the store and was about to follow herself, but the scales struck the dog on the head and the Pili jumped out saying:—

Lim bharābhar kauwā chhārev,	On the neem tree I left the crow,
Tāl bharābhar bagulā,	On the tank I left the bagulā,
Hai re mor buchā kukur,	Oh now my wounded dog,
Paseri mur kuchā.	The weights have crushed your head.

8. THE STORY OF BAHURĀ, THE COW

Once upon a time there was a great king named Rājā Chandrāgetu. He had a herd of one thousand cows, and amongst these was one which was the best of them all named Bahurā. This cow was large and beautiful to behold, and she gave milk continually without ever ceasing. One day the herd of cows was out grazing when the great cow Bahurā became separated from the rest and wandered away into the cave of a tiger. Just then the tiger came out of his den and was greatly delighted at seeing so delicious a feast awaiting him. Addressing the cow he told her to prepare to die, for he was about to feast on her. The cow Bahurā begged of the tiger not to commit so great a sin as to kill a cow, but the tiger replied that since she must die at some time, why should she object to becoming a portion of so great a being as a tiger. The cow then said to the tiger that since he was determined to eat her, she asked his permission to go and see her young calf to whom she had not yet given milk, and after once feeding the calf she would return to the den and allow herself to be eaten. The tiger laughed at the cow and asked her if she thought that he was going to let so sweet a morsel get away from him. Again the cow begged of the tiger and took a vow that if she should not return, the curse that comes on one who kills a Brāhmaṇ should come on her. Again she vowed that if she did not return the unhappiness which that woman has who knows that her husband loves someone better than herself would be hers. The tiger seeing that the cow had taken these great and terrible vows, and promised to return, allowed her to go and give milk to her young calf. When the cow had fed her young she said to the calf, "Now I am about to leave you and fulfil my promise to the tiger." But the young calf declared that if the mother was to die he would die with her. Not all the persuasions of the mother could deter the calf from following her to the cave of the tiger. The tiger on seeing the cow had come back was greatly amazed at her fidelity, but nevertheless he was preparing to feast on her. Just then the chariots of the gods descended from the heavens to take up the faithful cow and her calf. But the cow refused to go: she said: "First let this tiger be taken up to heaven; then I wish my keeper, the herdsman, to be taken; after that let all the cattle in my herd be taken; then I wish the king of my country to go and all his subjects;

last of all I will go myself." The gods were so overcome with unselfishness of the cow that they gave orders that the whole country should immediately ascend to the heavens with the faithful Bahurā. And so to the present day a festival is observed in memory of Bahurā, and at this festival an earthen image of a cow and a tiger is worshipped.

D. *Some proverb and sayings, showing the thoughts of the people.*

1. *Bāl ukhāre le murdā haru nahin hoy.* By pulling out the hair you will not lighten the weight of the corpse (*i.e.*, a little makes no difference).
2. *Khoṛi moṛi, taṇg tori, khoṛi ke laikā pāch koṛi.* The lame, the maimed, the broken-legged, the poor have children five score.
3. *Ultā pultā bhāu sansārā tab nau ke mūr mūrai lohārā.* When the world is turned upside down the blacksmith will shave the barber.
4. *Nāche lā āwai nahin marwā lā doshi.* He who cannot dance blames the roof (or the temporary canopy made at the weddings).
5. *Bhaisā ke singh bhaisā lā garu.* The buffalo alone knows the weight of its horns.
6. *Dahi ke bhorā kapsā lilbe.* Instead of curds he swallows cotton.
7. *Bareṭ ke kukur na ghar ke na ghāt ke.* The washerman's dog stays neither at home nor at the washing place. (This saying is applied to those of wandering, unsettled habits, especially women who leave their husbands often).
8. *Tāwā garhe lā āwai nahin sāi kābar jhoke.* He (the potter) cannot mould a plate, why does he take an advance?
9. *Teli ke tel rahhe to pāhar nahin chupre.* The oilman has oil in abundance but he does not grease the mountains.
10. *Khāye ke dari ghaṭ ghat jae, pīse ke dārī paċhīte lukāi.* At the time of eating on the scenes, at the time for grinding hidden away.

11. *Bakrā kā jiv chhuṭis, khawaiyā lā anonā.* The goat has given its life and still the dish is considered insipid.

12. *Jar gae bhitri nahin āwai sisri.* When one is burning within he cannot whistle.

13. *Jānwar mā kolihā, pakshi mā kauwā, manukh mā nauā.* Amongst beasts the jackal, amongst birds the crow, amongst men the barber (these three are the most cunning).

14. *Wakt pare bākā to gadhe ko kahe kakā.* In time of necessity one will call an ass his uncle.

15. *Ghar le nikel roshi ke rosh, ek din mā tin kos.* He starts from his house at very great speed, but goes only three *kos* (nine miles) in a day.

16. *Gānṭh ma nahin kauri, nāk chhede lā douri.* Not a *kauri* at her waist and she runs to have her nose pierced (for a nose ring).

17. *Sau ko sūli, chor ko pūri.* For the good man the gallows, for the thief a feast.

18. *Angarā ke roti lā dhangrā khāi, khaprā ke roṭi lā bihāta khai.* The bread from the ashes (considered the best) for the stranger, the bread from the tile for the husband. (Said when a woman pays more attention to a stranger than to her own husband).

19. *Bhalwā ke deh mā rowā kā dukāl.* On the body of the bear a famine of wool.

20. *Rājā ke marge hāthi, prajā ke marge ghor, rāṇḍi ke marge kukur, tinoṇ barābar hoy.* The king has lost his elephant, the subject has lost his horse, the widow has lost her dog; the loss of each one is the same.

21. *Dāl nā pisān, khaṭāi binā udās.* He has neither dal nor flour and yet he is sad for want of sour.

22. *Tiryā mirtini bānjhli, dhani lagāwe dosh, yeh to likhnā Brahma kā, bālak kahāṇ se hoy.* The wife is childless, barren; the husband thinks the fault is with her, but this is decreed of Brahma: whence then can she have a child?

23. *Deshi kuti, bilāyti bhāk.* A country dog with a foreign bark.

24. *Dūbar lā do Āsādh.* For the needy there are two Āsādh. (Āsādh is the month before the beginning of agricultural operations; when the poor are out of work this month seems to them to pass very slowly).

25. *Rājā kā rāni luwai kāndi, rājā pahinau son chāndi.* The king's consort goes to cut grass, the king adorns her with silver and gold.

26. *Chatur lā kekrā nahin chābai.* The crab cannot bite the prudent.

27. *Bhukh nā mānai juthā bhāt, piās na mānai dhobi ghāṭ, nindh na mānai marghat ghāṭ, jawāni na mānai jāt kujāt.* Hunger regards not unclean food, thirst minds not the washing place, sleep objects not to the bier as a bed, and youth (desire) regards not caste or out-caste.

28. *Kauri na bouri ludak de louri.* He has neither one not many *kauries* and yet he swings around his stick (in a grandiose style).

APPENDIX-3

Extracts from Charles Grant : *The Gazetteer of Central Provinces,* Bombay I ed. 1867, II ed. 1870, pp. 56; 100-03; 412-13.

The population, as distributed above, shows Hindus seventy-six per cent, Aborigines twenty-three per cent, and Mohammadans one per cent. Under the designation of Hindus are included all those classes who are of Aryan origin—the division has been made with reference to race, not religion, for it so happens that, in this district (Bilaspur), among the Aryan tribes there are prominent castes who do not conform to Hindu religion. They may be termed Hindu dissenters. The *Dalits*, who are twenty-one per cent of the population, call themselves "Satnamis" and are followers of their own priest Ghāsī Dās. The Pankās and Gāndās, who are nine per cent of the population, are "Kabīrpanthīs." This same "Kabīr" has numerous followers in other castes, viz. among Ahirs, Kurmis, Telis, and c, but their number it is impossible to compute. Approximately it may be stated that of the seventy-six per cent of recorded Hindus, half are so in race only. Turning to the Aborigines, the most numerous section consists of Gonds. They are the fifteen per cent of the population; then follow "Kanwars," who are four per cent. All other castes are limited in number. The Mohammadan element is insignificant, being but one per cent, and in the aggregate counts for little. Arranged according to creed, the population would stand as follows: Orthodox Hindus, thirty-six per cent; dissenters, thirty-eight per cent; worshippers of local deities, twenty-three per cent; and Mohammadans, one per cent.

Dalits

In describing the specialities of the more important classes of the community, the *Dalits* should be named first, for almost every fourth man in the district belongs to this section of people. They have been so long settled in Chhattisgaṛh that they seem to have no kind of tradition, even in the remote past, of any other home. As a body they possess active and well-set figures, are more brown than black in colour, and are less marked in features than the easy and higher classes. They are fairly energetic and industrious cultivators, are somewhat tenacious of their rights, and considerable numbers of them have attained a position of comfort and respectability. A description of the religious movement, which has given prominence to the *Dalits* of Chhattisgaṛh may not be out of place. Ghāsī Dās, the author of the movement, like the rest of his community, was unlettered. He was a man of unusually fair complexion and rather imposing appearance, sensitive and silent, given to seeing visions, and deeply resenting the harsh treatment of his brotherhood by the Hindus. He was well known to the whole community, having travelled much among them, had the reputation of being exceptionally sagacious and was universally respected. By some he was believed to possess supernatural powers, by others curative powers only, by all he was deemed a remarkable man. In the natural course of events it was not long before Ghāsī Dās gathered round him a band of devoted followers. Whether impelled by their constant importunities, or by a feeling of personal varity, or both causes combined, he resolved on a prophetic career, to be preceded by a temporary withdrawal into the wilderness. He selected for his wanderings the eastern forests of Chhattisgaṛh, and proceeded to a small village called Girod on the outskirts of the hilly region, bordering the Jonk river, near its junction with the Mahanadi. He dismissed the few followers who had accompanied him, with the intimation that in six months he would return with a new revelation, and mounting the rocky eminence overhanging the village, disappeared into the distant forest. Meanwhile the followers, who had accompanied him to the foot of that henceforth mysterious hill were active in spreading through the whole *Dalit* community his farewell message, with that warning that all should appear at *Girod*, as the termination of the six months interval approached.

Among a superstitious people these tidings worked marvels, and created a perfect ferment expectation. During the period of suspense nothing else was talked of, and the public mind anxiously looked for some revelation. As the close of the appointed time drew near, *Dalits* from all parts of Chhattisgaṛh flocked to Girod. The scene as described by an eye-witness was strange and impressive. The roads leading to this hitherto unfrequented hamlet were traversed by crowds of anxious pilgrims. The young and the old of both sexes swelled the throng—mothers carrying their infants, and the aged and infirm led by stronger arms. Some died by the way, but the enthusiasm was not stayed. At last the long-looked-for day arrived, and with it the realisation of the hopes of the hitherto despised community. In the quiet of the early morning their self-appointed prophet was seen descending the rocky eminence overhanging Girod, and, as he approached, was greeted with the acclamations of the assembled crowd. He explained to them how he had been miraculously sustained for the period of six months in the wilderness; how he had held communion with a higher Power; and how he had been empowered to deliver a special message to the members of his community. The message absolutely prohibited the adoration of idols, and enjoined the worship of the Maker of the universe without any visible sign or representation, at the same time proclaiming a code of social equality. It appointed Ghāsī Dās, the high priest of the new faith, and added the proviso that this office would remain in his family for ever.

The Satnāmī religion

The simple faith thus enunciated may best be termed a "Hinduised deism," for there were mixed up with it certain social and dietary regulations copied from Brāhminism. The movement occurred between the years 1820 and 1830, and is scarcely half a century old. It includes nearly the whole D*alit* community of Chhattīsgaṛh, who now call themselves "Sat Nāmīs," meaning thereby that they are worshippers of "Sat Nām" or "The True One" —their name, and a very appropriate one, for God. They would fain bury the opprobrious epithet "Chamār" among other relics of the past, did it not with traditional pertinacity, and owing to the hatred of the Brāhmans, refuse to forsake them. In the early years of the movement an effort was made to crush its spread, but in vain, and Ghāsī Dās lived to a ripe old age to see the belief he had founded a living element in society, constituting the guide, and directing the aspirations, of a population exceeding a quarter of a million. He died in the year 1850, at the age of eighty, and while the work he accomplished by our clearer light seems darkened with prejudice, ignorance, and imposture, yet there can be no doubt he did a good fight in demolishing, even within a small area, the giant evils of idolatry, and thus perhaps preparing his community for the reception of a higher and purer faith. On the death of Ghāsī Dās, he was succeeded in the office of high priest by his eldest son Bālak Dās. This Bālak Dās carried his feeling of equality to so high a pitch, that he outraged all Hindu society by assuming the Brāhmanical thread. Wherever he appeared he offensively paraded the thin silken cord round his neck as an emblem of sacredness, and hoped to defy Hindu enmity under cover of the general security against violence afforded by British rule. So bitter, however, was the hostility he raised, and so few the precautions he took against private assassination, that his enemies at last found an opportunity. He was travelling to Raipur on business, and remained for the night at a roadside resthouse. Here a party of men, supposed to be Rājputs, attacked and killed him, at the same time wounding the followers who accompanied him. This occurred in the year 1860, and the perpetrators were never discovered. It exasperated the whole *Dalit* community, and a deeper animosity than ever now divides them from their Hindu fellow-citizens.

Bālak Dās was succeeded nominally by his son Sāhib Dās, a child, but really by his brother Āgar Dās, who is now virtually high priest. The duties of this office are more of a dignified than onerous character. The high priest decides finally all questions involving social communication, and prescribes the penalties attending restoration. For those who can attend on him personally, or whom he can arrange to visit, he performs the ceremonies at marriage and on naming children; at the latter ceremony a bead necklace, in token of entrance into the Satnāmī brotherhood, is placed round the neck of the child. It is not absolutely necessary, however, that the high priest should officiate at any ceremonies. They are sufficiently solemnised by meetings of the brotherhood. Most *Dalits* once a year visit the high priest, and on these occasions a suitable offering is invariably made. They have no public worship of any kind, and consequently no temples; they have no written creed, nor any prescribed forms of devotion. When devotionally inclined, it is only necessary to repeat the name of the deity, and to invoke his blessings. No idol of wood or stone is seen near their villages. They have a dim kind of belief in a future state; but this does not exercise any practical influence on their conduct. Their social practices correspond for the most part with those of Hindus. They ignore, however, Hindu festivals. As a rule they are monogamists, though polygamy is not specially prohibited. Their women are not in any way secluded from public gaze, and are, equally with men, busy and industrious in home and field pursuits. In fact in most of their arrangements, to a superficial observer, the *Dalits* present nothing peculiar, and it is only after inquiry that many of their distinguishing features are discovered.

Satnāmī practices

The account thus given has been gathered from oral testimony—a source of knowledge liable to error and exaggeration. In its main features, however, it is accurate; disputed points have not been touched. One is whether Bālak Dās was accepted as an incarnation. Most of Satnāmis deny regarding him as such. Another is whether Satnāmī brides associate with the high priest before being taken to their husband's home. No Satnāmī will acknowledge this, and the columny is attributed to Brāhminical ingenuity. Some forms of prayer, collated from Hindu authors, are said to exist among the teachers, but they are quite unknown to the people, and the only act of devotion which a Satnāmī practices is to fall prostrate before the Sun at morn and eve and exclaim, "Sat Nām," "Sat Nām," "Sat Nām," translated literally "God ! God ! God ?" or perhaps implying "God have mercy ! have mercy !" Turning to their social practices, it is found that they eat no meat. They will not even drink water except from one of their own caste, and liquor is prohibited. They marry ordinarily at the age of puberty, the parents selecting a bride; the marriage itself is purely of a civil nature, being celebrated by elders, with a feast given to the friends of the family. They bury their dead without any religious ceremony, and in everyday life their moral notions are not rigid. A fatal split in the community has arisen from a most trivial cause—the use of tobacco. In the first outburst of religious enthusiasm, which animated the followers of Ghāsī Dās, it would seem that drink and tobacco were simultaneously forsaken. The use of liquor apparently was a weakness which was essentially and effectually overcome, but the strange solace which smokers appear to find in tobacco, and more especially a labouring population, possessed irresistible charms. A reaction set in, and finally a considerable portion of the community turned to their pipes. To talk of pipes in connection with an eastern people seems an anomaly, but in Chhattisgaṛh it is strictly correct. The *hooka* of Northern India is unknown here, and in its stead the broad "*palās*" leaf is folded into a pipe-like shape with a bowl at one end, in which dry tobacco is placed. It is called a "*Chūngī*," is universally indulged in by all classes, and field labourers, by its use, break the dull monotony of their daily toil. The Satnāmīs who again took to "*Chūngīs*" come to be opprobriously designated as "Chūngiās" by their brethren, and retain the appellation. They maintain their orthodoxy, and urge that Ghāsī Dās had a subsequent revelation conceding the use of tobacco to his people, and that consequently in his later years he absolutely withdrew his original prohibition. The Satnāmīs thus remain divided into two great sections—the "smokers" and "non-smokers." It is said that the smokers eat meat, and are not real Satnāmīs, but as a body they perfectly repudiate the insinuation. The Satnāmīs thus described are a strange and interesting people, and as a special mission has lately been inaugurated for their enlightenment and instruction, they are perhaps destined in the future to exercise an influence proportioned to their numbers and position in the annals of Chhattisgaṛh. *There is no class more loyal and satisfied with our rule than this community, and if it should happen, that, like the Kols, they are favourably impressed with Missionary teaching, a time may come when they will be a source of strength to our government.*

* * *

The *Dalits* lay claim to a very high antiquity among the inhabitants of Raipur district; but the truth of their assertions appears open to doubt. They call themselves Raidāsīs—a name which none of them can explain, but which evidently comes from Rai Dās—a Dalit reformer and disciple of Rāmānanda, who is said to have lived about the fifteenth century in the country lying to the south of Oudh and in Rewa. The creed he preached seems to have been very similar to that of Ghāsī Dās, the celebrated Satnāmī teacher, who started the great movement among the *Dalits* fifty years ago, which has excited so much attention, and who seems rather to have revived the teaching of Rai Dās than preached a new religion. The name of Satnāmī was that assumed by the followers of Rai Dās, and the constant reference to his name shows that his doctrine must have sunk deeply into their minds before they came to Chhattīsgaṛh, as there is no trace of Rai Dās having ever visited the country. Again, the *Dalits* are chiefly found in the north-west of the district, there being very few south of the Raipur tahsil, and they have never, like the Gonds, Telis, and Ahīrs, spread all over the district—a fact which seems to show that they are immigrants of a comparatively late date. It is generally supposed that the names of "Satnāmīs" and *Dalits* are synonymous; but this is by no means the case, as the Satnāmī religion does not refuse to receive proselytes from any class. But as the *Dalits* form the majority of the sect, and as no distinctions of caste are admitted among the members, all converts of other castes become, in the eyes of Hindus, *Dalits*. Under the influence of Ghāsī Dās a considerable number of men of other castes became Satnāmīs especially Ahīrs and similar accessions must have taken place from time to time, otherwise it is hard to account for the very large numbers of *Dalits* found in the district. As a class, too, they do not present the same degraded appearance as their brethren in other parts of India, and as a rule they are lighter in colour than the members of other cultivating castes, while some of the men, and many of the women, are remarkable for good looks. Although the *Dalits* are, in the parts of the district where they are chiefly found, by far the most numerous of all the castes, they have failed in securring a leading position in any part of the country. They are looked down upon by the Hindus; the Satnāmī, and Hindu "Pārās" in villages where both classes are found, being always separate and distinct; but at the same time the Satnāmī ryots are a power in the land. As a class they always act together, and are persistent assertors of their rights, real and fancied, and a terror to encroaching mālguzārs, few being found bold enough to stand up against the resistance of *Dalit* ryots to unpopular measures. Outwardly though, as Satnāmis, scrupulous about their eating, they are slovenly and untidy in their habits, and the houses of even the wealthiest of them are generally miserable hovels. They are generally industrious though careless cultivators, and frugal in the extreme, indulging in no extravagance in dress or jewellery. The dress of the men is usually a single cloth, one end of which encircles their loins and another their head, and the women wear little or no jewellery; yet they rarely make money, and seem to want the talent of getting on in the world. Their villages are seldom prosperous, though there are some few mālguzārs, who form conspicuous exceptions to the rule. Though this apparent inability to improve their position is partly due to Hindu opposition, yet one great cause of the phenomenon seems to be their individual fickleness and want of perseverance. A very slight cause will send a *Dalit* cultivator away from his village, and though they generally return after a short interval, yet these migrations must necessarily hinder the accumulation of property.

* * *

Bhanḍār is a village in the Raipur district. It is the headquarter or sanctuary of the Satnāmis of Chhattisgaṛh, and came into importance about twenty-seven years ago (1840), when Ghāsī Dās, the founder of new faith, became proprietor of the village. He built in the centre a large square of temple-like house, and to this place his followers flock three times a year for confession and absolution.

APPENDIX-4

Chhattisgaṛ : *notes on its tribes, sects and castes.—By* P.N. Bose, B.Sc. (Lond.) F.G.S. *Deputy Superintendent, Geological Survey of India.*

[Received 3rd October:—Read 5th November 1890].

1. A BRIEF ACCOUNT OF CHHATTĪSGAṚ

Name.—The Bengal-Nagpur Railway will open up a tract of country which is now but little known to the public. In the Central Provinces, it is called "Chhattisgar." Two derivations of the name have been proposed. According to the Central Provinces Gazetteer,* Chhattisgaṛ owes its name to thirty-six (*chhattis*) forts (*gar*) included within it. Serious objections, however, have been urged against this interpretation by Mr. Beglar of the Archaeological Survey.† While in Bihar he heard a tradition, that ages ago, in the time of Jarásandha, thirty-six families of dalits had emigrated from that country and settled in a country far to the south of it, which was called "Chhattisghar" (thirty-six families). He was not at the time aware of any country which bore that name, and his inquiries with regard to it being ineffectual, he became rather sceptical about its existence. When, however, official duty brought him to Chhattisgaṛ, the tradition he had heard in Behar came back to his mind. Here was a country far from Bihar, and south of it, the people of which appeared to him to be singularly like the Biharis in language, dress, manners, and customs—a people, too, of which the dalits formed very important element. Mt. Beglar suggests that Chhattisgaṛ derives its name from the thirty-six families of Bihari dalits who settled there; according to which interpretation 'Chhattisghar' should be spelt 'Chhattisgar' Considering, that long intercourse had made Mr. Beglar perfectly familiar with the Beharis before he visited Chhattīsgaṛ, his interpretation becomes authoritative. Besides, it promises to throw some lights on the history and affinities of one of the most remarkable peoples that inhabit India—the Chhattisgari dalits. We must say, however, that as the word is pronounced by the people, it is difficult to make out whether "Chhattīsghar" or "Chhattīsgaṛ" is the correct spelling; we have adopted the latter as the one in current use.

Physical and political Geography.—Chhattisgaṛ as an administrative division of the Central Provinces comprises the districts of Raipur, Bilaspur and Sambalpur, and including Bastar, covers an area of about 53,000 square miles. But Chhattīsgaṛh proper includes Raipur and Bilaspur only; and we shall use the term in this restricted sense. It comprises a central plain covering an area of about 10,000 square miles surrounded by a forest-clad hilly country of a somewhat wider extent (about 12,000 square miles); strictly speaking, the plain country alone should be called Chhattīsgaṛ, and it is only for the sake of convenience that we have included the surrounding hill tract within it. The contrast between the hill and the plain country is sharp and striking. The former is clothed with thick jungle, little cultivated, and sparsely populated, the population consisting chiefly of aboriginal tribes. To the *shikari*, it affords sport in abundance; the tiger is especially abundant in the southern, and the wild buffalo in the eastern jungles, while in every direction, the antelope, the spotted deer, and other varieties of game may be found. The plain, on the other hand, is almost flat, perfectly denuded of jungle, well cultivated, and thickly populated. With the exception of a small narrow strip in the western portion, it is what is called *khalsa*, that is, under the direct management of the British Government. The hill tracts are partitioned amongst a number of zamindars and feudatory chiefs, who pay an annual tribute. The zamindars maintain their own police. The feudatory chiefs, whose gross revenue in most cases does not exceed that of second-class zamindars in Bengal, are invested with authority equal to that of a Holkar or Nizam. They not only keep their own police, but also have their Jails and civil and criminal courts.

Geology and mineral resources.—The configuration of the country well illustrates the intimate connection between geological structure and physical features. The plain is formed of Vindhyan sandstones, marls and limestones, which have been but little disturbed from their normal horizontal position. The hills surrounding it are, on the other hand, composed of older rocks which have undergone considerable disturbance and metamorphism. At the north-eastern extremity, about Korba there is a considerable outcrop of the coal-bearing strata (Gondwana System). The results of the coal-exploration conducted by the Geological Survey are not very encouraging with regard to the ground traversed by the Bengal-Nagpur railway; but, not very far from it, there is one tract near Korba where workable coal of good quality has been found. In the hills to the north, west, and south extensive iron-ores of exceptionally good quality exist. Iron-smelting is still carried on there to some extent in the primitive fashion. But with the opening of the railway, the industry already on the wane, will probably be nearly extinct. Copper and lead-ores exist; but their extent is not yet known. The sandstones of the plain are largely used for building purposes; and the limestones are quarried chiefly for road metal. In places the limestone is tolerably pure and would yield lime of good quality.

Jungle produce.—Of forest produce, lac and *Hurra* (Haritáki, *Terminalia citrina*) are the most important. The former flourishes best on Kusam (*Carthamus tinfosius*) and Palás (*Butea frondosa*). But it is also grown, though to a very subordinate extent, on Baer (*Ziziphus jujuba*) and a few other trees. The lac is mostly taken to Mirzapur. The *Hurra* is exported to Europe, through Bombay.

Agriculture.—Chhattisgaṛ is, or rather has been the land of plenty. To the people of the neighbouring districts, it has long been known as *khalauti*, or the "Land of the Threshing-floors." Rice, wheat, and linseed are the chief crops. Rice and wheat were formerly sold—and that too not so very long ago—at fabulously cheap prices. Only five or six years ago, after the opening of the Nagpur-Chhattisgaṛ Railway, rice used to be sold, at some distance from its terminus at Nandgaon, for Re. 1-4 or less per maund. But the price in 1889 was Rs. 2-8, and will no doubt go up still higher when the Bengal-Nagpur Railway system is completed.

In the southern and eastern portion of Raipur, as well as in Bilaspur generally, rice is the principal crop. In the western portion of the plain, wheat appears to be more largely grown than rice. Wherever there is black soil (*kanhár*) wheat is preferably sown on it; whereas rice is chiefly grown on sandy soil. Rice, however, is the principal crop. The area on which rice is grown in the districts of Raipur and Bilaspur amounts to nearly two million acres, whereas the wheat area does not amount to more than 130,000 acres.

History.—The earliest traces of man we found in this district are some bone and pottery mounds by the Seonath river. They invariably occur in the plain country. Who the men were, it is difficult to surmise. But, whoever they were, they had passed the stone age, and had been in the habit of using iron implements. In the south-western portion of the district of Raipur, away in the jungles, there are remains of rude forts and temples which tradition ascribes to a race of Gauli kings. No reliable information, however, is available about them. To a later period, belong the ruined temples and *Sati* pillars of Balod, Gurur, Sirpur &c., some of which date back to the beginning of the Christian era. Mr. Beglar of the Archaeological Survey finds evidence in an inscription of the extension of the Chalukya power right into the heart of the modern district of Raipur.*

The authentic history of Chhattisgaṛ dates back only to the middle of the eighth century, when Raja Suradeva of the well known Haihai family ruled at Ratanpur† in the district of Bilaspur. The place is now overgrown with jungle; but, extensive tanks and ruins testify to its former grandeur. Nineteen kings of the Haihai line had preceded Suradeva, but all that is known about them is of the vaguest character. Surrounded by barriers of high hills on all sides, Chhattisgar entirely escaped the Muhammadan invasion, and the Haihai dynasty ruled undisturbed till the middle of the eighteenth century when the country came under the sway of the Bhonslas of Nagpur.

Of less antiquity than the Haihaibansi rulers of Ratanpur were the Gond kings of Garha Mandla, Lanji and Chanda. The western portion of Chhattisgaṛ, included in the zamindaries of Sahuspur-Lohara, Gandai, Dhundi-Lohara &c. belonged to one or other of these dynasties.

In 1818, Chhattīsgaṛ came under the superintendence of British officers; and in 1854, on the lapse of the province of Nagpur to the British Government, it was formed into a Deputy Commissionership with head quarters at Raipur. Since then a separate Deputy Commissionership has been established for Bilaspur.

2. GENERAL REMARKS ON THE TRIBES &C.

I have left out the higher Hindu castes, Bráhmans, Rájputs, Káyasthas and Beniyás; the Muhammadans too and such castes as Dhobi, Mehter &c., who are chiefly met with in towns, have been omitted from these notes as they do not present any special features of interest, being settlers from Northern or Western India. Even of the specially Chhattīsgarī people, these notes do not pretend to be exhaustive, as they treat of those only with whom I came into personal contact. In thus restricting myself I hoped to have avoided errors into which second-hand information often leads,* and to have attained correctness by sacrificing completeness.

The people, as elsewhere in India, may be broadly divided into Aryan and non-Aryan, or, perhaps less logically into Hindu and Aboriginal . Either of these methods of classification would answer well when we have to deal with such well-marked Aryan or Hindu castes, as Bráhmans, Káyasthas, and Beniyás, on the one hand, or such well marked non-Aryan or Aboriginal people as the Jungly Gonds on the other. But, it is difficult exactly to define the ethnological position of a good many of the castes treated of in these notes. The Satnāmīs, for instance, one of the largest and most interesting castes in Chhattīsgaṛ are looked down upon by the Hindus, and in their faith they are rather aggressively anti-Hindu—the word Hindu being used in its popular sense. Yet, physically the Satnāmīṣ resemble their Aryan more than their non-Aryan neighbours; and it is impossible to place them in either of these categories without giving rise to serious objections. Similar difficulties are experienced in classifying such castes as the Kanwá'rs, the Pankás and Hálvás. In the present state of our knowledge a rigid system of classification would, I think, be rather disadvantageous than otherwise; I have not, therefore, adopted any. I may, however, mention in passing, that the Gonds have unquestionable Dravidian affinities, and that the Bhunjiyas, the Baigás, the Komárs, and the Saonras probably belong to the Kolarian group. Whether the Sudra castes such as the Telis, the Márárs, the Koshtás &c., are Aryan or non-Aryan, or a mixture of the two, it is difficult to say exactly. I do not think any of them is of purely Aryan blood, some of them may be Hinduised non-Aryans. The process of transformation is still going on. The greater number of the Gonds who have settled in the plain country amongst the Hindus have adopted the manners and customs of the latter. They are proud to be called Hindus, and are ashamed to own affinity with their brethren of the jungles; and some few have succeeded so far as to be recognised as Hindus. Some of the castes are probably of mixed descent. The Dhur Gonds appear to be such.

Some castes or sub-castes are due solely to differences of habitat and environment; others to inequality of social position. The castes into which the Gonds are subdivided seem to be mostly explicable by one or other of these causes. Those who have settled in the plains have been greatly affected by their Hindu environment. They have entirely forgotten their own language, have taken to Hindu manners and customs; and will on no account have social intercourse with their brethren in the jungles. Thus we have two great castes, one comprising settlers in the plain country, and the other dwellers in the jungles. Amongst these, again, minor castes would be formed owing to geographical and social causes. A barrier, such as a range of hills, would prevent intercommunication and social intercourse and give rise to castes. People of high social position, those, for instance, who claim kinship with the once powerful Gond kings of Garhá-Mandla, Lanji &c., would not associate with those of an inferior status, and would thus form a caste by themselves.

The sects of the Satnámis, the Kabirpanthis and the Mán Bhains are very interesting. The followers of the last named sect were not separately entered at the last census; they are not, in fact, mentioned. This is an omission which it may be hoped, will not recur at the next census. In the districts of Raipur and Bilaspur the Kabirpanthis number 230,526, and the Satnámis 356,533. At the last census the population of these districts including Hindus and Aborigines, numbered nearly three millions. The Kabirpanthis and the Satnámis, therefore, together form about 24 per cent. of the entire population. The Kabirpanthis do not appear to believe in any God beyond their Guru to whom they accord divine honours. The Márárs and the Bhunjiyas also did not express their belief in any God. They have *sthápanás* in their houses for their ancestors to whom they give offerings periodically.

The Satnámis are Monotheists, but like the Kabirpanthis they worship their Guru. The Mán Bháins are Vaishnavas.

All these sects, the Kabirpanthis, the Satnámis and the Mán Bháns, abjure caste and eschew flesh and fish and spirituous liquors. A section of the Satnámis abstain even from smoking.

Rice is the principal food of the people in the plain country, and *kodo* that of the Gonds and other tribes living in the jungles. Spirituous liquor (prepared from mhowa flower) is indulged in chiefly by the Gonds, especially those who live in the jungles.

The clothing of men is usually of the scantiest possible dimensions; but, that of women is, as a rule, ample and decorous. In the interior, strong, coarse, indigenous cloth is still largely in use; but with the extension of railways it is to a large extent giving way to cheaper, more showy, though less durable cloth of Manchester make. The fate of the weaving castes like that of the iron-smelters is sealed.

There are certain practices which are common to most of the tribes and castes described in this paper, and which may be conveniently mentioned here.

Re-marriage of widows is a general practice. A widow is allowed to wed herself to the younger brother of her deceased husband—a custom which appears to have largely prevailed in ancient India. She can, however, marry almost anybody she pleases in her own caste. The essential part of the ceremony of such marriage consisting, I am told, in making presents of *churis* (thin glass or earthen bracelets) to the bride—who, in her widowed condition, remains without any ornaments whatever—is called *churi* marriage. Being inexpensive, it is often resorted to by impecunious wife-hunters in preference to regular marriage which is rather costly. Marriage is certainly not allowed to be a failure in Chhattisgaṛ. A man can of course take to himself as many wives as his means will allow; and a wife can leave her lord for anybody else provided the latter compensates the injured husband, the damages being rated according to the customary marriage expenses of the caste.

The practice of worshipping the Thákur Deo and Mátá is almost universal. The former is the village god, and is worshipped by all the villagers twice a year, in the months of Paus and Chaitra. The Deo consists of a collection of peculiarly shaped stones usually placed on a sort of *dais* under an umbrageous tree. In Drug Subdivision (Raipur district), stool-shaped stones with two legs (supposed by General Cunningham to be Buddhist remains) take the place of the Thákur Deo. Elsewhere, he is supposed to be embodied in characteristically shaped pebbles. Besides the stones strictly representing the Thakur Deo, numbers of others are placed by their side. In fact, the seat of the Thákur Deo is a sort of local museum. Any curiosities found in the neighbourhood, either pebbles or other rock specimens or remains of old temples &c. are carefully deposited there. Before leaving a village, I always made it a point to pay my respects to the Thákur Deo, and the visit was always interesting, and sometimes instructive as well.

The worship of the Thákur Deo consists in sacrificing goats and fowls, and having a good feast. In some villages the headman (malguzar) collects subscriptions from the villagers, and the expenses of the festival are met from the fund so raised.

Mátá, called also Bhaváni and Kálikà at places is the well known goddess of smallpox. She is greatly dreaded, and universally worshipped, being carefully lodged in a thatched shed in the outskirts of the village. She is usually represented by a pebble; a trident, an earthen lamp, and a pot for milk or water being its necessary adjuncts. She is worshipped in Baisakh with sacrifices of fowls.

Bhim Sen represented by his celebrated club, a large piece of stone daubed with vermilion, is universally venerated. Mr. Hislop says* that "his worship is spread over all parts of the country, from Berar to the extreme east of Bastar, and that not merely among the Hinduised aborigines, who have begun to honour Khandoba, Hanumán, Ganpati, &c. but among the rudest and most savage of the tribe." This universal popularity of Bhim Sen (who cannot be any other than the well known Páṇḍava) is a rather curious fact.

Belief in witchcraft is universal. People coming from Jabalpur and other places are in mortal terror of the Chhattisgarhis who are supposed to be past masters in the black art. A Jabalpur servant of mine—a Christian to boot—would ascribe his fever from which he suffered greatly to the malice of a fellow Chhattīsgari servant. I have been told many stories about the doings of supposed witches. At one time they were punished by the villagers rather heavily, but since the establishment of British rule, the witches have had a rather easy time of it.

3. DESCRIPTIONS OF THE TRIBES, SECTS, AND CASTES

*The Gonds**

Distribution.—The Gonds extend from Hoshangabad on the Narbadá to the Godávari south of Bastar, a distance in a line of over 400 miles. The area of the country occupied by them is about 120,000 square miles. According to the last census they number 2,040,355 souls. Scattered over such an extensive country through no less than 18 districts, generally separated from one another by difficult natural barriers, it is no wonder, that we should find important local differences among them in language, religion, manners and customs. The account given here relates chiefly to the Gonds of Chhattīsgaṛ with whom the writer had personal intercourse.

Whence the Gonds came and when they settled in India are points on which but little light has been thrown as yet. From their language they appear to belong to the Dravidian section of the aboriginal population of India, and to be more closely allied to the Tamil than to the Telugu subsection.†

Gondi Songs.—The late Mr. Hislop, to whom Indian science owes so much, collected some highly interesting songs of the Gonds. These have been published with an abstract English version in a work entitled "Papers relating to the Aboriginal Tribes of the Central Provinces." They had never before been committed to writing, but have been handed down by tradition. It is probable, therefore, that we have not got them in their original form; indeed, embellishments from Hindu mythology are clearly discernible in their present garb. Still, the main structure of the songs is clearly recognised to be Gondi. They are five in number, but are linked together into one story, in which the gradual social evolution of the Gonds may be distinctly traced. The first song treats of the creation of the world and of the Gonds. It presents a very life-like picture of the primitive condition of the Gonds. When they were born:

"Hither and thither all the Gonds were scattered in the jungle;
Places, hills and valleys, were filled with the Gonds.
Even trees had their Gonds. How did the Gonds conduct themselves?
Whatever comes across them, they must needs kill and eat it;
They made no distinction. If they saw a jackal they killed
And ate it; no distinction was observed; they respected not antelope, sambar and the like.
They made no distinction in eating a sow, a quail, a pigeon,
A crow, a kite, an adjutant, a vulture.
A lizard, a frog, a beetle, a cow, a calf, a he- and she-buffalo,
Rats, bandicoots, squirrels—all these they killed and ate.
So began the Gonds to do. They devoured raw and ripe things;
They did not bathe for six months together;
They did not wash their faces properly, even on dunghills they would fall down and remain.
Such were the Gonds born in the beginning.
A smell was spread over the jungles.
When the Gonds were thus disorderly behaved.
They became disagreeable to Mahadeva,
Who said; "The caste of the Gonds is very bad;

I will not preserve them, they will ruin my hill Dhavalagiri;
I perceive here and there smells'."

In a note on this passage, the editor observes: "This somewhat sarcastic description... of the habits of the Gonds is probably of Hindu origin." But, the description is not at all sarcastic; nor is it even exaggerated. I have personal experience of Gonds whose habits are exactly the same as those so vividly depicted in the above passage. In fact, the present normal condition of the Gonds living in jungles is not far different from the primitive condition described in it.

The song then goes on to relate how for their misbehaviour all the Gonds except four were imprisoned by Mahadeva. The four Gonds who escaped the fate of their brethren,

> "...travelled onward over hills.
> Thence they went and saw a tree rising upright as a date tree, which they climbed and looked about.
> They said: 'There is no hiding place for us'.
> But, one of them looked and saw a place named Kachikopa Lahugad.*
> They went by the jungly road and searched that place."

The second song relates how the four runaways first lived by hunting alone and then gradually learnt rude cultivation. Lingo, who is worshipped by some classes of Gonds as a god, was brought into existence by Bhagavan to better the condition of the Gonds. He went to the four Gonds who had taken refuge at Kachikopa Lahugad, and was kindly received by them. They had been living on game which they ate cooked or raw. Lingo told them to cut down trees and get a field ready. But,

> "...Their hands were blistered, and each blister was as large as an Aola fruit.†
> They threw down their hatchets and came to Lingo,
> (And said): "Our hands are blistered, therefore we threw down our hatchets."
> They went aside and sat down. Then arose Lingo and held a hatchet in his hand,

And went on cutting trees; the trees fell, their roots were dug up.
Thus he began to cut down jungle. In an hour he made a good field.
(They said): "Our hands are blistered and not one tree have we cut down.
But Lingo in one hour has cut down several trees;
He has made the black soil (appear), and has sown rice and hedged it round."

This is the sort of cultivation which the Gonds learnt, which in many parts they still practise, and which they would not leave for any other if they could help. It goes by the name of *Dáhi.* Since the prohibition of the reckless cutting down of trees in British territory, the Gonds have had to take to the plough in some parts, but nowhere do they appear to have done so with a heart as yet.

The four Gonds of Kachikopa Lahugad were unmarried. Lingo set out in search of wives for them. An old giant of the name of Rikad Gawadi had seven daughters, Lingo inserted a bamboo stick in the hollow of a gourd and made a guitar.

"He plucked two hairs from his head and strung it.
He held a bow and fixed eleven pegs to that one stick, and played on it.

* * *

He approached the fire where Rikad Gawadi was sleeping.
The giant seemed like a log lying close to the fire; his teeth were hideously visible.
His mouth was gaping."

The effect of music on the mind of a savage is well described. The old giant had, in fact, been so charmed that he gave Lingo free permission to take his daughters away. Lingo brought them and married them informally to the four Gonds of Kachikopa Lahugad. In time, however, they got jealous of Lingo, though most unreasonably, and killed him.

I have not space for any more extracts from the songs, enough, however, has been quoted already to show how interesting they are, and how valuable from an ethnological point of view.

The third song relates the revival of Lingo, and his delivery of the Gonds who had been imprisoned by Mahadeva on account of their filthy habits. The fourth song treats of the subdivision by Lingo of the Gonds into tribes, and the institution of the worship of the Gond gods; and the fifth takes another step towards civilisation—the institution by Lingo of the rites of marriage among the Gonds.

Distribution of the Gonds in Chhattīsgaṛ—The Gonds try to avoid the plain country where they have to compete with the Hindus and Satnámis Dalits, and prefer to live in the jungle-clad hills, especially in the feudatory states and zamindaries where they can satisfy their natural propensity for jungle produce, and where they can to a certain extent avoid using the plough which they hate. In that portion of the district of Ráipur which is called *khalsa* (*i.e.*, managed directly by the British Government), and which consists chiefly of an open plain country, the Gonds form only 18.6 per cent of the total population and the greater majority of them more or less Hinduised, whereas they muster strong in the feudatory states, especially in Kanker, which is entirely a hilly country, where they form no less than 62 per cent of the total population. In the feudatory states of Khairágar, Nándgaon and Chhuikhádán, which, in their physical features combine the characters of Kánker and of the khalsa portion of Raipur, the Gonds form about 24 per cent of the entire population.

Types of Civilisation.—There is another feature about the distribution of the Gonds which is noteworthy. Those who have settled in the plain country approximate to the Hindus; indeed, aspire to pass as such. They have forgotten their dialect, and are often ashamed to own affinity with their brethren of the hills whom they hold in undisguised contempt. Like their Hindu neighbours they eschew beef and pork. Some of them worship Hindu gods, such as Mahámái, Mahádeo, and entertain Brahman priests; and some assume the holy thread. The chiefs of Kawarda and Khairagar, though, I am informed, of Gond origin, call themselves Kshatriyas; and the chief of Khairágar has succeeded in forming alliances with needy Kshatriya families. Most of the plains Gonds, especially those who are well-to-do, call themselves Hindus, and are proud to be recognised as such. They worship, however, almost invariably, the great Gond god—the Buḍha Deo.

The farther one goes away from the plains, the more Gonds are found unaffected by Hindu influence and approximating to the primitive type. In fact, the stages of civilisation represented historically in the songs referred to above, are here represented in space, the comparatively civilised Hinduised type prevailing in the cultivated plain country, and the primitive type in the wildernesses bordering it. The hill Gonds are more or less omnivorous; and altogether in their habits approximate very closely to their primitive ancestors, who, as related in the song quoted above, were imprisoned by Mahadeo for polluting the hill Dhavalagiri. They never have anything to do with Hindu gods or Brahman priests.

From the vocabulary of the Gonds it is possible to form some idea of their primitive civilisation. They not only have names for most wild animals and forest trees with which they must have been well acquainted, but there are special Gondi terms for such domesticated animals as the elephant, the horse and the camel. The only weapons for which there are Gondi names are the hatchet, the trusty and constant companion of the hill Gond, and the bow and arrow, which most aboriginal people are very expert in using. For barber, carpenter, and weaver, they have no Gondi names; and they still stand in little need of such differentiated professions. Plough they call *nágar*, a Hindi word; and as, already observed, they have not taken to it with a heart as yet. They have their own terms for iron, and for workers in iron—iron smelting is still largely practised by them. But for copper and gold the terms are Hindi. They appear to have been in the habit of bartering in kind as they have no special term for any kind of coin. They can count in their own dialect only up to ten, beyond that they count in Hindi. They have Gondi terms for sun, moon, stars, day, evening and nights, but none for week, month, and year. Altogether the social progress which the Gonds attained was of a very low type; and it is no wonder, that as soon as they came in contact with the more civilised Hindus, they should have endeavoured to take to the ways of the latter.

Physical appearance, character, &c.—The physical features of the hill Gonds are distinctly Mongolian. I found the Mongolian characters most pronounced in the wild country on the borders of Chhattisgaṛ and Mandla—thick lips, scanty hair, compressed nose, and short stature. But in the plain country, it is often difficult to tell a Gond from a Hindu, the former having approximated to the latter not only in habits, but also in appearance. The men are slim, well built, and active (on occasions), dexterous in the use of the hatchet, and in the jungles, of the bow. Like most other aboriginal tribes, the Gonds are very strongly addicted to intoxicating drinks. When not under the influence of fear, they are lively, frank, and truthful. One could not wish to have more agreeable and more useful companions in the jungles than they are. The clothing of the men is of the scantiest possible dimensions; but the women are as a rule decently clad. Both are very fond of ornamenting themselves with trinkets.

Deities.—Buḍha Pen is the great god of the Gonds. He is universally worshipped, even by those who have become Hinduised. Two grand festivals appear to be held in his honour, (in the months of Mágh? and Bhádra?) when the usual offerings of coconut, betelnut &c., are made, and cows, goats, and fowls are sacrificed. The sacrifice of the cow is considered an essential part of the worship by the hill Gonds. A few stones daubed with vermilion represent the god. Serpent worship is prevalent to some extent. There are images of serpents at Sahuspur, in Sahuspur-Lohara zamindari, and at Ambagar in Chauki zamindari. I was told at one place, that the serpent is worshipped every three years when a vessel of milk is left for him. Lingo is held in great veneration in some parts; but, elsewhere, the very name is unknown. Dulha Deo, who is the great god of another aboriginal tribe, the Baigas, is also greatly esteemed in some places, as also the Hindu god, Mahadeo.

Besides these, there appear to be special minor deities for each *got.* The Gonds are divided into 5 *gots.* One of these *gots* comprises worshippers of three deities, another of four deities, a third of five deities: and so on. The three deities of the first of these *gots* are, I was told, the bull, the tiger, and the crocodile! These animals are considered sacred by, and would not contribute towards the food of, those who belong to this particular *got*; but the members of the other *gots* would not scruple to eat the flesh of any of these animals! I cannot, however, vouch for the correctness of this information; I often inquired about the *got*-gods, but never got any satisfactory answer. The four deities of the four-god *got* are, I was informed at one place, the Buḍha Deo himself and his three brothers, Aginkumár, Rausárna, and Áudia Singha; at another place I was told, the four gods were the tortoise, the crocodile, a kind of fish called *bodh*, and a ferocious bird the name of which was given as *sarewá.*

The Gonds of course believe in evil spirits and witches. But they do not appear to have any clear idea of a next world. Notwithstanding repeated questioning, I failed to ascertain if they had any word for it.

There is no regular priesthood amongst the Gonds. The nuptial, funeral, and similar ceremonies are performed under the lead of aged relatives. But generally in every village there is a man who is supposed to have the power of charming tigers, or preventing by *mantras* such calamities as drought, cholera &c. He is called "Baigá." The name is derived from a tribe called Baigas to be mentioned later on who are especially credited with these powers.

In some parts, a group of villagers acknowledge a head called *Sonwani* who presides at panchayets to settle disputes.

Ceremonies.—After a period varying from a few days to one month, the child is named and caste people are fed.

Marriage usually takes place after puberty. There is no restriction as to the number of wives which a man may take to himself. But, marriage being a costly concern, it is only the well-to-do who can indulge in polygamy. The ceremony consists of four stages, at each of which the bridegroom has to spend according to his social status. In the first stage called *sagái* (a kind of betrothal), the bridegroom has to make a present of rice, liquor, and some cash to the father of the bride, and of *churi,* and *phunri* (silk) tape for the hair) to the bride. The second stage (*barokhi*) consists in bringing the bride to the home of the bridegroom—a reversal of the ordinary Hindu process—when presents of grain, clothes, and cash have to be made to the father of the bride. At the third stage, the bride and bridegroom are anointed with oil and turmeric and they go round a pole seven times. The ceremony takes place with great feasting and the usual drunkenness. The fourth stage of the ceremony consists in sending the bride to her home.

When the bridegroom has not the means to make the necessary presents to the father of the bride, he serves the latter as a labourer for a period varying according to the price set upon the lady.

Burial and Cremation.—The dead are usually buried with head to the north and feet to the south. Great care is taken of the graves of distinguished persons. Earthen mounds are raised over these, which are kept very clean, and protected from the sun and rain by a shed. Rude clay figures of men and horses are kept on the mound, symbolic probably of the way in which the departed have gone to heaven. A few days after death, the *srádh* takes place, when caste people are fed.

When cremation is practised—as it is by those who are somewhat Hinduised—mounds are sometimes raised over the ashes of the dead. These mounds usually point north-south, but sometimes east-west. Quantities of paddy are sometimes put on the mounds, as offerings to the spirits of the dead.

Castes.—The Gonds, like the Hindus, are divided into castes, of which I have met with the following:-*

1. Ráj.
2. Kureti.
3. Khatalwár.
4. Dhur.
5. Koitor or Jháriá. (Sometimes also called Rávanvamsi).
6. Pardhán (including Pátharia, and also Ágariá?).

The first three castes have conformed more or less to Hindu customs, and count among their members a large number of well-to-do Gonds, such as the zamindars of Chauki and Sahuspur-Lohara. They take the holy thread, and, as a rule, venerate Hindu gods. But they may be distinguished from the Hindus, by their worship of the Buḍha Deo, either openly or in secret. The plains Gonds belong almost exclusively to one or other of the first four classes. The hill Gonds belong almost quite as exclusively to the Koitor or Jháriá class.

Jharia literally means 'jungly'; and Mr. Hislop observes[†] that the meaning of '*Koitor*' is "evidently associated with the idea of a hill"; so that, the name of the fifth class would appear to signify simply Gonds who inhabit the jungle-clad hills. Those who settled in the plain country, and imitated the manners and customs of the Hindus, began to look down upon their brethren of the hills. Hence the former would have no social intercourse with the latter; and thus two great classes would be naturally formed. A further subdivision of the plains Gonds is probably due to social and local causes. The Raj Gonds, for instance, claiming kinship with the royal families of Garha-Mandla, and Lanji, would naturally form a caste.

The Dhur Gonds, who are very numerous in the plain country, occupy a lower status in society than those mentioned above. I suspect the name is of Hindu origin, being corrupted from 'Bidur,' which signifies the mixed descent of the caste. Amongst the peculiarities mentioned to me of the caste, one is that their marriage is consummated in one day, whereas that of the others takes several days.

The *Pardháns* form a small caste. Their social status is considered lower than that of the other Gonds. The *Ágarias*, who are iron smelters, appear to form a subsection of them, as also the *Pátháris* who correspond to the *Bháts* of the Rajputs.

The village 'Baiga' mentioned before not unoften belongs to the Pardhan caste. The name Pardhan appears to be of Sanskritic origin, signifying 'chief'; and it is rather strange that the caste should be held in such low estimation. "About the Mahadeva hills" observes Mr. Hislop[*] "the higher Pardháns act as Pujaris, and the lower as rude musicians, the Koitors seeming to look down upon both offices as somewhat menial."

The members of the castes mentioned above belong to one or other of the following *gots*:—

I. Worshippers of three Deities.

(1) Markám.

(2) Sori.

(3) Khosro.

II. Worshippers of four Deities.

(4) Tekam (a kind of tree, the teak)

(5) Neitam. (Nei = a dog).

(6) Kariám. (Charcoal? or from *kar*, cock?).

(7) Singram (or Sindram? after a variety of fish).

(8) Malgam.

III. Worshippers of five Deities.

(9) Gháore.

(10) Pureti.

(11) Kibuáká.

(12) Porte.

(13) Purám.

IV. Worshippers of six Deities.

(14) Wikká.

(15) Kattam (Kachlam?).

(16) Karám.

(17) Erkárá.

(18) Paoli.

(19) Marrapoi.

(20) Kuroti.

(21) Tumrekke.

(22) Selám.

(23) Etti.

(24) Otti.

V. Worshippers of seven Deities.

(25) Kunjam.

(26) Márai (Mára = tree).

(27) Dhurua.

&c.

It would be interesting to know the signification of these terms. The meanings of a few I could gather are given. It will be seen that they refer to some tree, or animal. The names of some of the special gods of the five groups just mentioned have been given before. They refer mostly to animals, such as the crocodile, the bull, the tiger &c.

The *gots* into which the worshippers of the three deities (which are the bull, the tiger, and the alligator) are divided are what are called *Bhaibunds*, and they cannot intermarry; they must form alliances with other *gots*. Similarly the worshippers of the four deities are *Bhaibunds* : and so on. It is interesting to note in this connection, that the "Kols are subdivided into two or three hundred groups each of which is called after an animal or a tree; and the rule is that a member of a particular animal group, such as the snakes, the tortoises, the eels or the mangooses, may not marry within that group."*

Select Vocabulary

ENGLISH OR HINDI.	GONDI.	REMARKS.
(*a*) Cereals &c.		
Wheat	gok	
Peas	batrala	
Ashar	rahari	Appears to be a corruption of the Hindi word.
Urid	pupul	
Kodo	koda	
Gram	nadai	
Arsi	arsa	Corruption of Hindi.
Paddy	wanji	
Rice	nuka	
Tilli	nung	
Bread (*Chapati*)	sádi	
Flour	pindi	
Salt	haor	
Tobacco	máku	

	Sugarcane	elouda	
	Liquor	dáḍngo	
(*b*)	Domesticated antimals &c.		
	Cow	tháli	
	Calf	páiá	
	Dog	nái	
	Cat	bilár	Hindi.
	Sheep	bhedal	Corruption of Hindi.
	Goat	bakrá	Do. Do.
	Pig	paddi	
	Horse	podá	Do. Do.
	Elephant	háti	Do. Do.
	Camel	hutum	Do. Do.
	Cock	wágoti	Ghoghoti (Hislop).
	Hen	kar	
	Egg	mench	
	Milk	pál	
(*c*)	Wild animals		
	Tiger	puliál	
	Leopard	chital	
	Bear	arjal	
	Nilgai	dhumoi	
	Sambar	mán	
	Deer	kodrá	
	Wild dog	kherá nái	
	Jackal	kolhiál	Corruption of Hindi.
	Rabbit	malol	
	Peafowl	mal	
(*d*)	Wild and cultivated trees.		
	Teak	teká	
	Sáj	mardi	
	Dhowra	werma	

Mhowa	idu	
Bija	bija	
Peepul	gáhma	
Tendu	tumri	
Schara	doudera	
Mango	marká	
Brinjal	singihápa	
(*e*) Metals, implements, &c.		
Iron	kachi	
Copper	tám	Hindi.
Silver	kuro	
Gold	sona	Do.
Hatchet	márs	
Spear	gorká	
Matchlock	banduk	Do.
Sword	talwár	Do.
Bow	wil	
Arrow	káun	
Fort	gar	
Battle	ladái	Do.
King	rája	Do.
Army	mal	
Sport	háwing	
Plough	nágar	Do.
(*f*) Miscellaneous		
Barber	mán	Do.
Carpenter	badái	Do.
Weaver	mehrá	(Name of a caste.)
Smith	kháti	
Shepherd	kopa	
Village	nár	
Pice	paisá	Hindi.
Rupee	rupeá	Do.

Kaudi	kaudá	Do.	
Leaf	áke		
Flower	pungár		
Fruit	pádi, káia		
Marriage	maḍmi		
Bridegroom	duláh		
Bride	duli		
Infant	chháwá	Do.	
Boy	chudur	Addressed as Bábu.	
Girl	tudi	Do.	Nuni.
Middle-aged man	reiá	"	
Middle-aged woman	nun		
	man		
	máju		
Old man	seda		
Old woman	sedo		
Sun	din		
Moon	nalench		
Star	sukkum		
Evening	din udit	Hindi.	
Month	máhiána	Do.	
God	pen		
Goddess	pedi		
Witch	dhuki, pasro		
Truth	thauka		
Falsehood	fándi		

The Bhunjiyas

Distribution.—The Bhunjiyas are found in the south-eastern portion of the Raipur district, in the Khariar and Bindra Nawagar zamindaries. At the census of 1881, they numbered 4,721.

Language.—The language of the Bhunjiyas is curiously like Bengali, as the following vocabulary will testify:

English		*Bhunjiya*
Hair	...	kesa.
Head	...	muda.
Face	...	mukha.
Eye	...	ámkhi.
Nose	...	nása.
Thigh	...	jánu.
Horse	...	ghodá.
Dog	...	kukura.
Tiger	...	bágha.
Bear	...	bhálu.
House	...	ghara.
Rice (uncooked)	...	chála.
Rice (cooked)	...	bháta.
Road	...	márga.
Sun	...	suraj.
Moon	...	chandra.
I	...	ámi.
You	...	tumi.

Worship.—The Bhunjiyas do not appear to have any gods. They venerate the sun and the moon, and have *sthápanás* for their ancestors to whom offerings are made. There is a Pujári for a certain number of villages, who corresponds to the Baigá of the Gonds. He is supposed to possess the power of checking epidemics and the ravages of tigers, and receives voluntary contributions from the villagers.

Ceremonies, food, &c.—The marriage ceremony lasts for three days, and presents are made to the father of the bride as usual. After marriage, the cooking utensils are thrown away. If the wife visits her father's home she appears to get a very cold reception, at least so it would seem to a stranger; for she is not allowed to enter the house, but has to live outside and cook for herself.

The kitchen, which is invariably detached, is kept scrupulously clean, ornamented on the outside with red paint. There is a sort of veranda attached where the male members (who are not allowed to enter the kitchen) partake their meals. The ladies of the household carry their scruples to such an extent, that should anybody (not a Bhunjiya) even touch the kitchen, it becomes polluted and must be burnt down! The Bhunjiyas never use any metallic vessels, which are considered impure.

The men are allowed to drink liquor and to eat fowls, but they appear to be very slow about availing themselves at least of the former privilege. For a most wholesome check is exercised by the fair sex, which more civilized people would do well to imitate. I am informed that the ladies of the house who never touch spirits, would not admit the men into the sleeping apartments if they smelt of liquor, and as they are forbidden entry into the kitchen, the fate of inebriates must be a very hard one.

I was told by one informant, that on festive occasions, the invited guests are given uncooked rice and dál, which they cook separately and eat. I learnt from another source, however, that on such occasions the male guests would be allowed to eat together, but not the female. All the observances of the tribe are evidently meant to preserve great purity amongst the fair sex.

The dead are buried. A hatchet and vessels for drinking water are left on the grave.

I am told, curiously enough, that the *gots* of the Bhunjiyas are similar to those of the Gonds.

Saonras

Distribution.—A branch of the great Savara tribe. Like the Bhunjiyas the Savaras are found in the south-eastern portion of the district of Raipur. At the last census they numbered 3,849. They are good cultivators, and not expert at woodcraft like the Bhunjiyas and the Kamárs.

Worship.—The Savaras have sthápanás in their houses for Mahálachmi to whom offerings of fowls &c. are made in Chaitra. Dulhá Deo also is worshipped.

Language.—From their language they appear to be allied to the Bhunjiyas. A few English words and their equivalents in the Savara tongue are given below.

Sun	bela.	Rice	chál.
Moon	yon.	Wild boar	baráha.
Water	pán.	Pig (domesticated)	ghusrá.
Bird	chiri.	Cloth	dhuti.
Tiger	bágh.	Mouth	tuṇḍ.
Bear	bhálu.	Tooth	dánt.
Dog	kukur.	Son	pilá.
Cat	billi.	Daughter	tugil.
Cow	gáyá.	Eye	áhkh.
Paddy	dhán.	Nose	nák.

Ceremonies.—The young are buried, and the old cremated; caste people are fed three days after a death.

Unlike most other tribes in Chhattisgaṛ, no money present is made to the father of the bride.

Gots: Khutia, Juriá, Jhákar, Májhi, &c.

Kamárs

Distribution.—These are found in the same parts as the Bhunjiyas, and numbered 3,641 at the last census.

Worship.—Dulha Deo, Bhaváni, and the Earth, besides Ráur Gosám and Kachna Dhuma, who are represented by stones put up in jungles are venerated.

Vocabulary

Father	bábá.	Foot	putoá.
Sister	bái.	Leg	redi.
Wife	mántin.	Hand	putoá páte.
Son	noná.	Finger	ántakhá.
Daughter	cheḍa.	Arm	dhmut.
Piece	cháu.	Ear	kána.
Dál	dáu	Nose	nási.
Wheat	pit.	Mouth	tomuḍa.
Bullock	bailá.	Head	muḍa
Arrow	káuṇda.	Hair	wán.
Bow	dhanu.	Beard	goch.
Tobacco	dhungiá.	Tiger	bágh.
Wood	dáru.	Leopard	durká.
Bird	litto.	Sámbar	jiváḍ.
Dog	kmeklo.	Boar	baráha.
Cat	biláo.	Sun	suraj.
Iron	lohá.	Moon	jond.
Thigh	jam.	Go	jáo cheḍá.
		Give	dihá.

The general term for addressing women is "*nágráin*," that for addressing wife is "*jhi.*"

From this vocabulary, it will appear, that while certain words are common to the Bhunjiya and Savara dialects, there are others which are peculiar.

Manners and Customs.—For marriage the bridegroom has to serve the bride's father for a certain period (4 years or so)—a custom which is met with also amongst the Gonds and some other tribes when the father of the bridegroom is not in a position to make the needful presents to the father of the bride. Amongst the Kamárs, however, there does not appear to be any alternative. This is probably owing to their chronic impecuniosity, as they are bad cultivaṭors, worse than the Gonds, and subsist mainly upon sport and woodcraft.

The men drink, but not the women. As amongst the Bhunjiyas, greater purity is expected of the women, than of the men. The latter, for instance, are allowed to partake of food cooked by Gonds, whereas the former are not.

The young are buried, and the old cremated.

Gots.—As in the case of the Bhunjiyas, it is rather strange, that the names of the *gots* should be similar to those of the Gonds, from whom they appear to be radically different in language. Some of the *gots* named to me are *Neitam, Sori, Markam, &c.*

Names of men—Lachman, Jharia, Budhu, Bahadur, &c.
Names of women—Nari, Lachmi, Dukhdei &c.

***Baigás* (Bhumias)**

These are most numerous in the wilds of the Mandla district and there is only a sprinkling of them in the north-western portion of Chhattīsgaṛ in the feudatory state of Kawarda. Like the hill Gonds, they are strongly averse to cultivation and prefer living on jungle produce. In their features, they have not the marked Mongolian characters which the Gonds have. They shave their head in front; and the long back hair is tied in a knot behind. They speak the Chhattīsgar dialect in Chhattisgaṛ.

Dulhá Deo is the great god of the Baigás. But Bhavani is also worshipped. The Baigás are greatly respected by the other tribes and are sometimes called Bhumias. Some of them are supposed to be gifted with supernatural powers, especially in checking the ravages of tigers. The priests of the Gonds (who are themselves Gonds), are called Baigás. Hence some confusion has arisen; and the Baigá tribe in Bilaspur was probably owing to this reason included amongst the Gonds at the last census. The tribe, however, is quite distinct physically as well as in language and other characters.

The essential portion of the marriage ceremony consists (as in the case of the Gonds and most other tribes) in going round a pole 7 times.

Gots.—Mārai, Dhurna &c.

The Binjáwárs

There is only a sprinkling of these in the eastern portion of Chhattisgar. From the fact that Dulhá Deo is their principal deity, they appear to be closely allied to the Baigás.

Gots.—Limni, Manji, Endja, Láen &c.

Kanwárs

The Kanwárs claim descent from the Kshatriyas, and worship the Jaghrapháud, whom they consider their chief deity. But they also appear to recognize Dulhá Deo, the great god of the Baigás, and Buḍha Deo, the great god of the Gonds. The dead are also buried, an essentially non-Hindu practice. In fact, the Kanwárs combine in themselves partly aboriginal and partly Hindu characters.

Ceremonies.—Five days after a birth, the caste men are fed. At marriage, the bride and bridegroom, both anointed with oil and turmeric go round a pole 7 times at the bride's as well as at the bridegroom's. The bridegroom puts on the holy thread at the marriage ceremony.

When parents die, the head is shaved clean, and after 5 days caste-men are fed: on the death of other relations, the head is only partly shaved.

With regard to food and drink, the Kanwárs, at least professedly, are strictly Hindu, fowls and pigs as well as intoxicating liquors being prohibited.

Gots.—Bag-dehria, Dhankul, Khanrádhar, Banjári &c.

The Hálvás

Mr. Hislop classes the Hálvás with Gonds.* Following him, Mr. Sherring does the same; but the latter has them also amongst non-aboriginal tribes.† Their affinities are doubtful, but whatever they may be, I doubt the kinship of the Hálvás to the Gonds.

The Hálvás are an agricultural tribe found in the southern portion of the Raipur district. They speak the Chhattigarh dialect and profess to have come from Bastár. Their chief deity is Kanhálin who is worshipped with sacrifices of goats &c. The chief reasons which lead me to think that they are not Gonds, are (1) the fact, that they do not venerate the Buḍhá Deo, which even the most Hinduised Gonds do; and (2) the fact, that the *gots* of the Hálvás are quite distinct from those of the Gonds.

In the Central Provinces Gazetteer,‡ the Hálvás are said "to gain their living chiefly by distilling spirits, and worship a pantheon of glorified distillers, at the head of whom is Bahadur Kalál." This statement has also been quoted by Sherring. But, there must be some confusion, as I have not come across a single Hálvá who earns his living in the way represented here; nor are the Hálvás aware of any members of their caste doing so anywhere.

Except on occasions of marriage and similar festivities, they profess to abstain from drinking.

The dead are buried.

Gots : Mahla, Raut, Pátae &c.

***Dalit* (Satnami Sect)**

The Dalits form the largest caste in Chhattīsgaṛ, numbering 248,429 in the Raipur, and 95,020 in the Bilaspur district, that is to say they form about 12 per cent of the total population of these districts which is estimated at 3 millions.

The Dalits, except a few to be mentioned later on, all belong to the Satnámi sect. They are a fine, sturdy race of agriculturists, rather tenacious of their rights, and, as they are united, quite capable of holding their own against the Hindus who look down upon them with great contempt. They also sometimes call themselves Rai Dásis after Rám Dás, "a Dalit reformer and disciple of Rámánand who lived in the 15th century; the modern Satnámi creed is a revival of the doctrines of Rám Dás preached by Ghási Das in the early part of the present century."* Ghási Das, an unlettered but thoughtful Dalit, was deeply impressed with the degraded condition of his community, who were strongly addicted to drink and other vicious habits. He gradually acquired considerable influence by his wisdom and high moral character, and gathered round him a handful of devoted followers. One morning he collected them, and telling them to assemble all the Dalits at a particular spot after six months, himself retired behind the hills in the south-eastern portion of Chhattisgaṛ to meditate and hold communion with God. On the appointed day a large concourse of the Chhattigari Dalits was brought together to receive God's word from Ghási Dás. The reformer slowly appeared with the rising sun and gave them the message: which was to the effect, that there is only one true God (the Sat Nám), that all men are equal, that the idols of the Hindus are false, and that meat, intoxicating liquors, and smoking are interdicted. The assembled Dalits received the message with great enthusiasm and the Satnámi sect was established. Ghási Dás became their Guru or Primate and declared the office to be hereditary.

The Dalits gradually found out, that it was hard work abstaining from all the good things of the world, and those who wished to indulge in smoking, formed themselves into a sub-sect called *Chungiá*. A *chungi* is a leaf (preferably that of Palás, *Butea frondosa*) rolled into the form of a pipe in which tobacco is smoked: hence the name of the sub-sect. The *Chungias*, however, appear to have unrestricted social intercourse with the more orthodox members of the community.

The dissemination of the Satnámi doctrines infused new life into the Dalits and they rose to positions of comparative influence and respectability, which apparently made them an eye-sore to their Hindu neighbours, to whom the very name of Dalit is a byword for all that is degraded. Besides, the protest of the Satnámis against the idolatrous practices of the Hindus aggravated the enmity of the latter. Several attempts were, I am told, made against the life of Ghási Dás, but none succeeded. But, his son and successor Bálak Dás was murdered in 1860. Persecution to any serious extent is of course impossible under British rule, but affrays between the Hindus and the Satnámis, now and then occur. Where the latter are in the minority, the former, I am informed would not allow the guru of the latter to ride on an elephant and go in procession through their villages.

The guru goes on tour in great state, with elephants, camels, and a large following. The name of the present guru is Agar Dás. The Satnámis prostrate themselves before him and give him presents according to their means. He has his deputies called Bhándáris scattered all over the country, who collect his dues; sometimes, villages are farmed out to them at fixed amounts. The Bhándáris represent the guru in all social ceremonies. It is said that the bride associates with the guru or his representative before entering her husband's home. But the Dalits stoutly deny this, and assert it to be a calumny invented by their Hindu enemies. It is difficult to get at the truth in this matter: the bride appears to be presented before the guru or his deputy, and she has to make a present to this functionary.

The Hindus assert that the Sátnámis do not act up to their doctrines. There are, of course orthodox and heterodox people amongst all castes, and some Sátnámis certainly do not abstain from meat.

The Sátnámis salute by bowing low, lifting up their left leg, and exclaiming 'Sat Nám, Sat Nám'. Their worship consists in exclaiming these sacred words at sunrise and sunset. ['Sat Nám' means 'the right or true name,' i.e., the true god.]

The dead are buried. Relations are fed on the third, fifth, tenth or fifteenth day.

The Sátnámis do not observe any class distinctions amongst themselves and are a very compact body.

Gots: Kusariá, Bhatbahari, Banjára, Jarkaria, Aril, &c.

Mochi

The Satnámi Dalits have no intercourse with those who prepare hides or work in leather. As in other parts, carcasses of animals contribute to the food of the Muchis.

Worship Dulhá Deo once in two or three years with offerings of rice, &c.

Kabirpanthis

These are followers of Kabir, a disciple of the reformer Rámánand, who preached in Northern India in the fifteenth century. The doctrines of the Kabirpanthis are similar to those of the Sátnámis: like the latter they are enjoined to abstain from flesh food and spirituous drink, to observe no caste distinctions and not to worship idols. Both forms of faith are protests against the idolatry and caste-system of the Hindus on the one hand, and the vicious habits of the aborigines on the other. There is, however, one point of essential difference. Sátnámism forcibly enjoins belief in one God, whereas Kabirpanthism does not do so. Indeed, beyond the guru, and the ordinary village deities like Thákur Deo, and the goddess of smallpox, I am not aware if the Kabirpanthis have any other object of worship. All the Kabirpanthis I questioned did not certainly declare their belief in one God, as the Sátnámis invariably did.

Kabirism notwithstanding its anti-Hindu tenets is not in such bad repute amongst the Hindus as Sátnámism is. This is probably due to the fact, that the latter is professed by Dalits only, whereas the former counts amongst its followers many Hindus, not excepting even Bráhmans and Rajputs. The Pankás form the greater majority of the Kabirpanthis of Chhattisgaṛ; I have not met a single Panká who is not a Kabirpanthi. The Gandas, Telis, Márárs, Kunbis, &c., contribute large numbers, the Telis especially. In these cases, those who become Kabirpanthis are not excommunicated, but continue to live with their caste people: for instance, a Teli's becoming a Kabirpanthi would not interfere with his marrying into a non-Kabirpanthi Teli family. The Brahmans and Rajputs, on becoming Kabirpanthis, are renounced by their castes. Their number, however, is small and they are amply compensated by the bestowal on them of all the fat posts of the order.

Though the Sátnámis and the Kabirpanthis equally profess disregard for caste distinctions, the latter do not carry their disregard into practice or do so to a limited extent. Though Kabir, the founder of the sect, preached the equality of all men and had Muhammadan as well as Hindu followers, I have not come across a single Muhammadan member of the order in Chhattīsgaṛ; and it is certain that a Dalit will not now be admitted. The Kabirpanthis I have met, usually observe caste restrictions; a Teli Kabirpanthi, for instance, would not eat food cooked by a Panká belonging to the same order.

The ceremony of conversion is very simple, consisting in blowing the *mantra* into the ear of the convert, and placing a necklace of wooden beads round his neck.

The constitution of the order is similar to that of the Sátnámi sect. There is a guru who is venerated, worshipped I should say. The guru lives at Kawarda, the capital of a feudatory state of the same name, in the north-western portion of Chhattīsgaṛ. Like the Sátnámi guru he occasionally goes out on tour in great pomp. He has got his deputies called Bhándáris and Mahants dispersed all over the country, who make converts, collect contributions, and officiate at social ceremonies.

The dead are buried. A grave is dug, and the corpse laid in it with the head to the north, and a Mahant or, in his absence, some elderly Kabirpanthi blows into its ears some sacred names, and pours into its mouth some coconut oil, after which every member of the party with his back to the grave, throws a handful of soil into it, then he turns towards the grave and fills it up. Those who can afford raise a memorial over it. After three days the head is shaved entirely by near, and partly by remote, relations. The kinsfolk assemble at the house of the deceased and squatting round a raised *dais* (called *chauká*) sing sacred songs.

The Mán Bháu Sect

This sect is similar to the Kabirpanthi and Sátnámi sects, in that they all abstain from flesh and spirituous drink and disregard caste. The Mán Bháus believe in Vishnu, and the Bhagavadgitá is their sacred book. They are, in fact, Vaishnavas. There are monks and nuns who are vowed to celibacy; but the larger number are Grihasthas, *i.e.,* householders. The followers of the sect are most numerous in Berar. In Chhattīsgaṛ there are not many, and those I met are all householders. The Kátiás (a weaver caste) appear to have been converted *en masse*; there are also followers of Mán Bháu amongst the Telis, Kunbis, &c. I was told, that their guru lives at some place near Ramtek in the district of Nagpur. The process of conversion is very simple, consisting in blowing the *mantra* into the ear of the person who desires to be initiated.

In Chhattisgaṛ, Bráhmans are respected by the Mán Bháus, and I did not notice any ill-feeling between the two which is said to exist in Berar.*

Kunbi

An essentially agricultural class, allied to the next caste the Kurmi. In the last census returns, the number of the latter for the districts of Raipur and Bilaspur is given as 99,620. But the Kunbi is not separately mentioned, and must be included in this number.

A good many of the Kunbis belong to the Mán Bháu sect just described. They worship Vishnu, abstain from flesh food and intoxicating liquors, and bury their dead. The others worship Mahā, eat goat's flesh and fish, and practise cremation. The two classes can intermarry if they belong to the same clan.

There are two clans,—1, the Jháriá; 2, Puroli, the former being, as the name signifies, restricted to the jungles, and the latter to the plain country. The division is evidently due to habitat. The two clans do not intermarry.

Those who practise cremation preserve a few bones, and, in the case of the old and well to do, take them to some sacred place and deposit them there.

Bones are so deposited in the Mahánadi at Rajim, and in a stream called the Narbada near Chuikhádán.

Caste men are fed 10 days after death.

Kurmi

Allied to the Kunbi.

Gots: Charnáha, Manáha, Singror, Pátaria.

Teli

A large agricultural and trading caste numbering at the last census 203,503 in Raipur, and 61,324 in Biláspur.

The Telis are divided into five clans, viz.—

I. Garbária—those who have come from Garbá, Mándlá.
II. Kanojia—those who have come from Kanoj.
III. Jháriá—those who live in the jungles.
IV. Ekbanhiás.
V. Háliás—Distillers.

The Garbárias are divided into 32 gots: Boir, Bágh, Sanichára, Hirwani &c.

Gots of the Kanojia Telis: Sonsat, Sirsat, Souger, Jomkátar, &c.

Gots of Jháriás: Átbháiá, &c.

Ahir

Also called Ránt and Gairá. Number at the last census in Raipur 141,983; in Bilaspur, 85,546. Shepherds, servants, cultivators.

Worship Dulhá Deo, Buḍha Deo, &c. The Áhirs have a great festival about Dewali time, when they go about dancing and singing, richly bedecked with strings of *cowri* shells.

They are divided into three clans based I believe, on habitat:

I. Jháriá—those who live in the jungles.
II. Kusuriá.
III. Kanojiá—those who are said to have come from Kanoj.

Gots of the Kusuriás: Amádár, Bághwá, Markám, &c.

Kalár

The Kálárs are a rather numerous class, and met with throughout Chhattisgaṛ as distillers, traders and cultivators. They appear to derive their name from 'kal' which is Gondi for liquor, distilling being their main occupation. At the last census they numbered 20,307, in the Raipur district.

Worship—The chief deities are Dulhá Deo, Rátmá, the latter being represented by a flat piece of gold or silver. One informant told me that Bhagaván is the only *pákká* god they worship, the others being what he quaintly expressed as *kátchá*. In the southern portion of Chhattisgaṛ, Báhádur Kalaria and her son Sasan Chábári are worshipped in the Holi time. They were evidently very successful distillers, and lived at Sorar and Gurur, where the remains of their distilleries are still said to be preserved.

Subdivision—The Chhattīgarh Kálárs are subdivided into two classes:

I. Darsená.
II. Gajbhátiá (jungly Kalárs).

The Darsená are further subdivided into the Chhota and the Bara Darsena, of whom the latter are said to abstain form liquors.

Some of the Kalárs belong to the Kabirpanthi sect.

The dead are buried with the head towards the north.

Gots: Neora, Nág, Dhurná, Sonwani, &c.

Márár

Called also Pátel and Máli. At the last Census numbered 35,096 in Raipur, and 24,541 in Bilaspur. Gardeners and cultivators.

The head of the Márárs is usually shaven in front in the form of a semicircle. The hair is kept long and tied behind in a knot.

They do not appear to have any special objects of worship except their ancestors, to whom they offer *hom.*

The Bastariá Márárs, who appear to be of Gond origin, and with whom the other Márárs have no social intercourse, worship the Gond gods, Buḍhá Deo, and Dulhá Deo.

There is no special ceremony for marriage, beyond that kinsfolk are feasted at the time. The bride comes to the house of the bridegroom with her relations and stops there for five days. One wife only is allowed.

Fish is eaten; but meat and intoxicating liquor are prohibited. Some Márárs become Kabirpanthis, when they are said to abstain from fish also.

Panká

With the next named caste number 35,128 in Raipur. They earn their livelihood as watchmen and weavers, and make but indifferent cultivators.

They all profess to belong to the Kabirpanthi sect.

Gándá

Closely allied to the Panká, and follow the same professions.

A good many become Kabirpanthis. These have no social intercourse with the Sákat (Sákta) Gándás, whose chief deity is Dulhá Deo.

There are three clans: (1) *Bajauia*, those who play on tomtoms &c., (2) Mohariá (3) Bastariá.

Banjárá

An adventurous class of traders. Before the opening up of the railway, the Banjárás used to carry on a roaring trade. Even now strings of Banjárá pack-bullocks are to be met on the highways leading from Chhattīsgaṛ towards Mándlá and Jabalpur. The Banjárás are an essentially nomadic tribe, scarcely ever settling down at any place for a considerable time. They are, however, now taking to agriculture at places, as their hereditary occupation does not any longer pay, as it used to do a few years ago.

At the last Census, the Banjárás numbered 8,518 in the Raipur district. They worship Banjárí, a goddess represented by a piece of stone daubed with vermilion during Dewali. No priests are required except at marriage, when the services of a Bráhman are put into requisition. The Banjárás, I am told, make converts of Gonds and other tribes. For some time before, and during the Holi festival, the Banjárá women, old and young, in gala dress, go about in batches from house to house, and village to village, dancing and singing, expecting, of course, presents of money or grain.

The women put on a large peculiar, conical bonnet. by which they may be easily recognised.

The Banjárás are divided into 18 Gots of which I could get names for ten only. Bhuktiá, Urtiá (Bartia?), Ráuriá (or Láuriá), Jharbolá, Trie, Kent, Korrá, Pálthiá, Mur, Bádant.

Keot or *Kewát*

Numerous in the plain country; at the last Census their number for the districts of Raipur and Bilaspur is given as 85,690. Fishermen, cultivators. Chief god—Deví or Durgá (with four hands). They eat pork.

Bhuí

Allied to Keot, and very likely included in it at the last Census, as I do not find it separately mentioned.

Mehrá

A large class, numbering 26,796, in the Raipur district at the last Census. The Mehrás act as koṭwáls (watchmen) of villages in the western portion of Chhattisgaṛ. They also follow agricultural and other occupations such as weaving.

Worship Náráyana and Mahádeo. Some are followers of Mánbháu. There is one class of Meharás callings themselves *Beid* who worship Bhagaván or Súrajnáráyana, and are said to abstain from beef and intoxicating drinks. They have no intercourse with the other Mehrá who will eat anything they can get hold of, carrion not excepted and who are considered very low in the estimation of the Hindus.

The dead are buried with the head to the north. Some selected spot in the house is consecrated to the dead. Caste people are fed three days after death.

Kátiá

A small caste of weavers. They are mostly followers of Mánbháu. The dead are buried.

Koshṭá

A rather large class. Mostly weavers. At the last Census they numbered 17,438, in the district of Raipur.

Gods Dulhá Deo, Rátmái (represented by a flat piece of gold or silver, also worshipped by the Kalárs).

There are two subdivisions (1) Chhattisgari, (2) Mahratti. The former must have been long settled in Chhattisgaṛ, and the latter must be newcomers. The two clans have no social intercourse with each other.

Burial and cremation are both in vogue.

REFERENCES

1. Published in JRAS. B, 1890, pp. 269-300
* *op cit.,* p. 88.
† Arch. Surv. Rep. Vol. VII.
* Arch. Surv. Rep. Vol. VII. p. 141.
† Central Provinces Gazetteer, p. 90. Mr. Beglar would not allow this town any greater antiquity than the middle of the 15th century. (*Op. cit.*, p. 165).
* I may illustrate this by an instance, which will be referred to later on. The Central Provinces Gazetteer (to which I am greatly indebted) describes the caste of Hálvás to be distillers; and Sherring quotes this description in his great work on "Hindu Tribes and Castes," (Vol. II, p. 147). I did not, however, come across a single Hálvá who was a distiller; and I was told, that there was no such Hálvá in Chattisgar or anywhere else. There is, however, a clan of the Telis called Háliás, who are distillers by profession. It is this similarity of name which probably led to the confusion.
* *Op. cit.*, p. 16.
* Mr. Hislop observes: "The name of Gond, or Gund, seems to be a form of Kond, or Kund, the initial gutturals of the two words being interchangeable.... Both terms are most probably connected with *Kondá*—the Telugu equivalent for a mountain—and thereore will signify the 'hill people'." (Papers relating to the Aboriginal Tribes of the Central Provinces, p. 3).
† Caldwell's "Comparative Grammar of the Dravidian Languages." 2nd edition, pp. 513-516.
* "The meaning in Gondi is the 'Iron Valley—the red hills'; a nomenclature very applicable to the mineral products and external aspect of many hills in the Gond country." (Hislop, *op. cit.*, part III, p. 6, foot note.)
† Sanskrit, Ámalaki, *Phyllanthus emblica* (Wild.)
* Mr. Hislop mentions the following division into twelve and a half classes in imitation of the Hindus: Ráj, Raghuwál, Dadave, Katulyá, Pádál, Dhobi, Ojhyál, Thotyál, Koilabhutál, Koikopál, Kolám, Mádyál, and an inferior sort of Pádál, as the half-caste. These divisions probably hold in the country about Chándá and Nágpur. Katulyá is probably identical with the Khatalwár of Chhattisgar. Padál, is identical with Pardhán or Páthári; Kureti and Dhur cannot be identified with any of the classes mentioned by Hislop, and appear to be peculiar to Chhattisgar.
† *Op. cit.,* p. 14.
* *Op. cit.,* p. 18.
* Abstract of Mr. H.H. Risley's paper read before the Anthropological Institute of London.—*Nature* for July 31, 1890, p. 335.
* *Op. cit.,* Vol. II, p. 147.

† *Op. cit.*, Vol. II, p. 108.

‡ *Op. cit.*, pp. 221-222.

* Hunter's Gazetteer, Vol. XI, p. 372.

* Gazetteer of Barar, quoted by Sherring, *op. cit.*, Vol. II, p. 164.

GLOSSARY OF CHHATTĪSGAṚHI TERMS

aṇkwār, embracing, one of the placid forms of Chhattísgarhi women depicting the same sex in an embracing posture.

añjurī, folded hands; a type of *mudrā* or gesture. In this gesture the two hands are clasped against the chest, palm to palm, and extended upwards with all fingers erect or slightly bent.

añjor, light, heat or fire; one of the five *mahābhūtas*. Prior to creation the *añjor*-power remains latent in the Supreme Being.

añjorī-pākh, bright moon-day.

andhiyārī-pākh, dark moon-day.

akās, aggās, sky; *ākāśa* is that which gives space and makes room for existence of all extended substances.

agam, deep, mysterious.

agamjānī, prophet. Guru Ghāsidāsa is depicted as *agamjānī.*

acruj, surprise.

aconā, wash one's hands; sipping water which is one of the *sandhyā* prayer. The ritual is to be performed in sitting posture.

aṭpaṭ, topsy-turvy, reversal. Widespread nostalgia for the past, and dreams of Chhattīsgaṛh returning to a mythical golden age are built into the very fabric of religious belief.

aṭārī, upper storey of a substantial village house. It is from that the shy heroine of many ballads looks down and sees the hero; it is in such lofts, with their comparative remoteness and privacy, that lovers find a convenient meeting place.

aṛhā, illiterate, stupid, sceptic and agnostic.

aṛhā-baid, a little knowledge is dangerous thing.

atmaytī, intimacy which is a form of pure consciousness manifested in every thing.

anakh, jealousy. It is a widespread factor affecting behaviour.

ancinhār, unknown, non-comprehension of truth. It is due to the impressions of the previous perceptions.

antas, inner, heart, *antahkaraṇa*. The *Sāṁkhya* system calls the *buddhi, ahaṁkāra* and *manas* as *antahkaraṇa*, the inner organ, in contrast to the five sense organs and five organs of action which are external organs, the *bāhyakaraṇa*. In brief, this is the psychological contribution of the *Sāṁkhya* system. It starts with the fundamental experience of the knower and the objects known. It shows that all mental processes arise from the evolutes of *prakṛti*. It is the *puruṣa* who is the psychological reality. Consciousness is not a product of the material or mental processes. It postulates an empirical self, the ego which cognises with the help of *puruṣa*, the principles of consciousness.

anbhal, evil.

anācār, *tyranny*.

aniyāv, injustice.

apkhayā, one who eats forbidden food.

apaṛh, illiterate.

apayā, infamy.

abhāg, ill-luck.

apariddhā, selfish. It is the lower self according to *Gītā* (VI. 5-6). The self of reflexes and bodily needs is described as the lower self.

aphāns, ridicule.

amarbel, *Cuscuta reflexa*, a parasite with long golden thread like stems usually found on the *boir* tree; symbolizes lovers.

amriṭ, nectar, immortality; the ultimate goal of life in the form of self-realization.

ammar, immortal. It is also conceived of in terms of nectar-essence, which according to Tāntric tradition, may be consumed from the body itself by *yogic* processes.

arath, meaning. *Satnām* has its own definition of meaning and logic, because it operates in myths and legends.

alkar, obstacle.

alkarhā, unconceived.

albelī, carefree woman.

alhan, calamity, evil.

awaiyā, one who is to come.

avtār, incarnation. In the *Mahābhārata* and *Rāmāyaṇa*, the popular view is frequently expressed that God comes down to Earth. It is explained in *Bhagavad Gītā*.

awāj, sound. *Satnāmī* life interaction is a symphony of vocalization and a melodic line of movement at times punctuated by speech segments, at times punctuated by silence—perhaps to dance—or to think.

asgun, bad omen.

asat, false, non-existence.

asādh, unclean, impure. Before we can attempt to concretize the full structural complexity of the *Satnām*, we must examine the conceptual meaning of purity and pollution. Because of the magico-religious ideas of Guru Ghāsīdāsa, the reader may find the Satnām obscure. In fact, the whole question of pollution is of the greatest importance, and obscure as are some ideas connected with it, it cannot be ignored if we are to elucidate the consequences of magical thought on the psychology of the *Satnāmis.*

asīs, blessings.

asudhahā, impure.

ahiwāt, good-fortune, wifehood.

ahiwātī, lucky, husband alive.

ānknā, to tattoo. Tattooing being more or less permanent mutiliation of the skin, is essentially badge of allegiance Less.

ānkhī, the eye. When we do not want to see something, we logically close our eyes and remain in symbolic ignorance of what we are looking at. The most obvious examples of this are shutting the eyes for a second or two, to exclude the outside world from vision. Guru Ghāsidāsa's sketch in this book reduces the amount of visual information while coming in concentration.

āñjar-pāñjar, skeleton.

ānwlā, Phyllanthus emblica. The tree is worshipped by Hindus to promote fertility in women and cattle. It frequently occurs in *Panthī-gīt. āmalaka* in *Skanda Purāṇa* (II.4.12.13) represents the earth: *āmalakī samantāt pāpam mardayati iti.*

ānsū, tears.

āgī, fire. Oblations thrown into fire are supposed to reach the Sun that sends rain which produces crops, the sustenance of all beings.

āchar, letter, alphabet. One of the forms of *brahman,* the others being *Kāla* (time), *Karma* (action) and *svabhāva* (nature) according to Vallabhaites. *Akṣara* appears in the forms of *Prakṛti* and *Puruṣa,* the former developing through many stages.

āṛ, barrier, the veil which keeps the soul away from freedom. According to certain *Vedāntic* schools *jīvas* or individuals are said to be constituted by the *āvaraṇa-*

power of *avidȳa* or *māyā*. In *Tāntric* tradition *āvaraṇa* sometimes means enclosure. In Buddhism there are two such veils in regard to the impurities—*Kleṣa* and *Jñeya*. (b) People feel safer behind some kind of *āṛ* (physical barrier). If a social situation is in any way threatening, then there is an immediate urge to set up such a barricade (as in *Rāmāyaṇa* Rāma sets up barricade for Bāli). For a tiny child faced with a stranger, the problem is usually solved by hiding behind its mother's body and peeping out at the intruder to see what she or he will do next. The most popular form of barrier signal is the body cross. The *svastika* is one of them.

āmā, mango. Mango and other fruits are often used to describe women friends. The *āmādūdh* or mango-breasts are very much admired. In Chhattīsgaṛhi folklore child-giving mango is a common theme.

ārati, ceremony to adore god. It revolves the waving of lights before the Supreme Being and is performed to the accompaniment of music.

indri, sense-organs. Religious behaviour with its varieties in the sensory channels involved, and the subtle shades of semantics, constitutes a well-structured system of *Satnām*. According to *Satnam manas* is also an *indriya*. The five external ones are sound, sight, touch, taste and smell.

irkhā, jealousy. It is regarded as one of the six enemies (*ripu*) of man.

isārā, sign, signa. The patterns of behaviour of Ghāsidāsa were special triggered events and may be called "sign stimuli". We use sounds and postures signalling anger or fear to warn off aggressors or alert each other to possible danger. If emotions are so basic it is not surprising that their expression is universal. Any other system would cause too much confusion so that survival might be threatened. If you could not tell roughly what another person's facial expression meant, you could fall into danger or miss a great opportunity. At a very basic level, it is important for emotion to be expressed obviously and clearly—it helps in survival.

īsar, īswar, Supreme Being.

ukhrū, sitting on heels.

ugtī, sunrise.

ujiyār, light.

uttī, East

ud, ghost. Ritual events are important in ritual communication. An example of this may be provided by cases in which a spirit medium may suddenly go into possession-trance, a state most definitively marked by the emergence of prophetic speech style in utterances.

udelaī, to raise questions.

updarā, turmoil. It may be called *prakṛti kopa* in Kauṭilyan terminology. People revolt against the government because of disaffection and anger. In *Jayapurarājavaṁśāvalī* we find that Bastar tribes revolted against their king: *upādravana vanavāsinaḥ prajāḥ*. People suffering from "obsessive–compulsive neurosis" may complain of unwanted thoughts which erupt repeatedly into their minds.

uprohit, purohit, priest.

upās, fasting. According to *dīkṣā* rites the Renouncer retreats to a hut, fasts, and submits to a *rite de passage* involving imitation of the foetal posture and the complete dependence of the infant. The psychology of purification is at the root of caste segregation, though different in intensity and motive among *Satnāmīs*.

ubārnā, liberate; liberation from bondage to the fleeting world of appearances *(mayā)*; it is not bravery but wisdom which is the key to the mystery of life.

urid, the pulse, *Phaseolus radiatus*. The oil expressed from this is offered by Hindus to Saturn, an inauspicious planet, and for this reason the pulse is regarded as vaguely unlucky.

ekṭak, gaze. Gaze-behaviour regulates the beginning and ending of speech. It serves to initiate and terminate social interaction. When two people meet and make eye-contact, they find themselves in an immediate state of conflict. They want to look at each other and at the same time they want to look away. The result is a complicated series of eye movements, back and forth, and a careful study of this gaze behaviour can reveal a great deal about their friendship.

To understand why the rules of human 'glancing' are so complex, it is necessary to appreciate that there is not one, but several reasons why we may want to look at someone, and several other reasons why we may want to look away.

ojhī, reply to an abuse.

olī, two ends of *dhōtī* cupped together.

aukhāt, power. The cult of political power and the cult of mystical power were rooted in a single tradition: *yoga.* Kauṭilya's idea of disciplined manipulation of kingly authority is indeed chilling: "It is power and power alone which, only when exercised by the king with impartiality and in proportion to guilt, either over this son or his enemy, maintains both this world and the next."

aughaṛ, a tāntric ascetic. A class of ascetics who are beyond all restrictions (*Kulārṇava Tantra* XVII).

autār, incarnation.

kapilā-tarpan, rite of Godān. A sacrament which consists in shaving the head and also the hair on the other parts of the body; see. *Śat.Br.* III. 1.2.4.

kaṇṭhā, string of *tulsī* used by *Kabīrpanthīs.*

kaṇṭhī, one-*mankā* string worn after *Guru*-dakṣiṇā.

karsā/kalas, earthen pitcher which is filled with rice ceremonially and closed with small earthen plate on auspicious occasions, often with a lamp placed over its mouth.

kalaū, the Kali Age and its climax. The prospect of *Śūdras* practising *dharma* in the manner of upper *vaṛnas* is envisaged in Chhattīsgaṛhi oral literature as a sign of the cataclysmic advent of Kali. *Vāyupurāṇa* (*Tarkaratna,* 1910.58-59) also incorporates it: *Śūdrāḥ dharmam cariṣyanti yugānte puryupasthite.*

kasbātī, the urban man, uncultured.

kāchan, divine experience, divine inspiration. It is attained through the *Sāttvika* purification, the opposite is *rākas* (demoniac treasure).

kājar, lamp-black often used to underline the beauty of a girl.

kāy-baurā, dump corpse.

kumat, ill-will, false knowledge.

kuriā, cottage, room, hut. Place where wandering ascetics congregated for religious discussions. *kutūhalaśālā* in Sanskrit.

kuru-asnān, incomplete bath. Bath for purification.

kusuwā, red and white.

kerā, plantain; it is generally regarded lucky and auspicious in Chhattīsgaṛh. Hindus believe it to be abode of goddess.

kes, hair has magical significance in Chhattīsgaṛh, as in many other parts of the world. It is shaved at a funeral or when some one is to be admitted into caste after excommunication.

koilī, cuckoo. The Chhattīsgaṛh attitude to cuckoo is more sympathetic than that common in Europe; it is regarded as rather pathetic because it cannot hatch its own eggs and rear its own chicks. It is the symbol of a bride or a beloved.

korā, lap.

kauwā, the crow is a very natural symbol of the human beings in whose company it lives so intimately.

khanjrī, small tambourine.

ganuṭiyā, landlord, zamindar.

gaū, Cows are married women who work scattered over countryside.

gaūkī, oath by cow.

gaṇgājal, friendship by exchange of holy water.

gajbel, boyfriend, the *gajbel* is one of the many types of friendship made by villagers in Chhattīsgaṛh.

gajāmūng, friendship through the exchange of *gajāmūng.* It should be analyzed on the psychological theory of associationism.

garhan, eclipse.

gārī, abuse.

ginyā, companion.

girhā, planet.

gīd, song.

gun, quality (a quality associated with one of five elements). A common term in Indian religio-philosophical tradition which is generally understood to mean some unchanging essential characters of a substance, although the word is variously interpreted.

gunaī, imagination, thought, remover of evil influence.

guniyā/ojhā, spirit-doctor, magician who understands magical charms. People seek the help of magicians in the diagnosis of the supernatural causes of disease, and in propitiation of those forces which brought it about. The primary duty of magician is to fight disease and death, but he must also stimulate the growth of crops and protect them from hail and storm.

guru, teacher, a religious preceptor, spiritual guide.

Guru Ghāsīdāsa, the leader of one of the mightiest peasant revolts who spoke in the inspired language of a prophet and reformer. The politics of peasant rebellion was almost invariably expressed in sacred idioms and it ended up, apotheosized, as sect (Guha 1966.251).

gokhī, deceitful.

goṭh, talk.

goṛdhoī, the rite of washing the feet.

got, lineage.

gotiyār, having same lineage.

godanhārī, a woman who tattoos.

godnā, tattoo.

godharin, a woman employed as a tattooer.

gohār, call, cry; *gohār* is the cry for help, it could bring a positive change in Ghāsīdāsa.

gorarnā, mark.

goras, cow's milk.

gosāī, sage, a religious leader.

gawntarī, village-journey.

giyān, knowledge; Guru Ghāsīdāsa has emphasized on the knowledge because his *achūtattva* (birth impurity) could be done away through knowledge according to *Manu* (V.150). The verse V.109 of *Manu* identifies the various parts of the person and their respective purifiers. The body is cleansed by water, the mind by truthfulness, the soul by learning and austerities, and the intellect by knowledge. This shows the importance which Manu and Ghāsīdāsa attach to knowledge.

gwālin, lamp-holding dolls.

gharī, time, hour. Like space, time is also inferred, though not perceived.

ghursī, the village warming-pan, an earthen bowl which is filled with smouldering scraps of cow-dung carefully damped down.

ghoṛ, horse, the horse is not only an object of religious veneration connected with ecstatic trance, lucky and pure, but is also has important sexual properties. To the Gond and Pardhān a horse is full of sexual associations.

caunk, picture made of dust; known as *dhūlicitra* in *Śāstras.*

candainī, moonlight.

canwar, chowrie-fan or the fly-whisk consisting of the tail of a yak. It is used during the performance of any worship.

ciksā, body-plaster.

cinhā/cinhār/cinhārī/cīnhā, mark, sign, identification. Our individual consciousness is virtually irrelevant to an understanding of socially and culturally organized phenomena of sign-systems.

cuṛelin, the usually dangerous ghost of a woman who has died in pregnancy or childbirth.

colā, body, a mystical term; the muscular body of the Guru portrayed in folksongs conveys dominance and self-assurance.

caunkā, a religious festival of Kabīrpanthīs.

chaṭhī, sixth day after birth ceremony.

chatraṇgī, man with umbrella.

chāpā, a colour print; the husband literally is as fine as photograph or probably a coloured print of Kṛṣṇa.

chutihā, untouchable.

chercherā, a festival of children.

chohar, labour (at birth).

janwārā, friendship during *Navarātri* festival.

jagar-jagar, dazzling light.

jagwārī, watchfulness.

jaṭ, long hair of a Sādhū, matted hair.

jatrā, pilgrimage.

jaduhā, sorcerer.

janaulā, riddle.

janewā, sacred thread. Sacred thread worn by the *Satnāmis* during the initiation. It is a symbol of *dvijatva* and is worn in the opposite side of the Brāhmanic tradition. Religious acts done without wearing it are futile.

jap, muttering, devotion. To internalise and mutter the *Satnam* relating to the identity of *guru* It is conceived as the easiest process of spiritual attainment.

jamghaṭ, gathering.

jāntā, throughout Chhattīsgaṛh *grindstone* is put in front of the bride and bridegroom when they sit for ceremonial greetings during their wedding.

jānwar-jiyā, twins.

jānwar-joṛī, a friend of the same age sharing the same interests and delights.

jāmun-ḍārā, name of ceremonial friendship.

jichuṭṭā, impatient.

jingī, life; the life of Ghāsīdāsa was a turning point—an emotionally significant event changed his life.

jiwrā, soul.

ji, Sir!

jug-jug, age to age.

jugjugī, coloured glass beads.

jewārā, a festival of goddess Kālī.

jogan, an invisible creature, hardly to be ranked as a godling or demon, said to be light and delicate as a firefly. *Jogan* usually moves in swarms and may be of great help to human being. Often appears as a symbol of woman-lover.

jogī, ascetic. He is the *Bairāgi Sādhū* or *sādhu,*who is supposed to be very embodiment of renunciation and chastity, often appears as a symbol of lover. At a marriage the bridegroom is abused by his mother-in-law as a *jogi* with matted hair full of scorpions. The symbol is appropriate not so much because the ascetic often has a very bad reputation among the aboriginals because he is always wandering on from place to place and never remains attached to a fixed abode. So too the aboriginal lover changes from girl to girl and can never remain in one place.

joṛī, yoke-fellow. It is often used both for a lover who expects an attachment to become permanent husband. A *joṛī* is something definitely more than a casual attraction. It is the person in whose company one will pull the heavy plough of life.

jot/Jotī, light, the divine light.

jotsī, astrologer.

johār, salute. Variations in greetings within Chhattisgaṛhi culture is extremely informative and communicates attitudes towards the person greeted. In general, acts of intimate association between persons of unequal status will exert forces towards the equalization of status.

jhaṅhaṭ, problem.

jhankul, hidden place.

jhamak-jhamak, graceful walk.

jhārnā, exorcism.

jhūlnā, swing, sexual symbolism.

ṭarrānā, to use obsinate language.

ṭiklī, ornamental paint (circular) or coloured paste on the forehead of women.

ṭimṭimī, a kind of drum.

ṭonā, sorcery; e.g *māraṇa, vaśikaraṇa, stambhana, uccāṭana,* vidveṣaṇa; see *Śāradātilaka* XXIII.

ṭonhā, sorcerer (m). The *Satnāmis,* like many Indian people, were much pre-occupied with witchcraft, and their thinking in this sphere is extensively dealt with (Gordon 1903-4, Appendix II). However, in conducting their lives witchcraft was secondary to their major concern with the verdicts of the oracles, which was consulted for all important decisions. In fact, when the oracle was consulted on the command of a guru, the outcome had the force of law. The general background of ideas and beliefs against which the working of the oracle must be viewed is of a kind of 'mystical'. *Ṭonā* was related to patterns of the thought that attribute to phenomena 'supra-sensible qualities' that can neither be based upon, nor logically inferred from, observation. The questions asked of the oracles mainly concern the operation of mystical forces so that they might be counteracted if they presented a threat.

ṭonhī, sorcerer (f).

ṭhepā, abusive language.

ḍaṇḍāsaran, prostration, bowing, reverential salutation.

ḍahariyā, a sub-caste of *Satnāmī.*

ḍūmar, Ficus Glomerata, fig. The milky sap is regarded as having magical and medicinal properties. It is very rare to see a wild fig flower, but it is thought exceedingly lucky to do so. People say to a friend who is seldom seen, "You are like a wild fig flower, we never see you".

ḍhaṅg, manner.

ḍhekī, rice husker—has a magical significance. It is waved round the heads of bride and bridegroom during a marriage.

ḍhong, pretence.

ḍhoṅgī, deceitful. A pregnant girl supposed to get very *ḍhoṅgī* she pretends to be in pain, demands attention, 'craves' for a lot of things that she could be without. The husband has a very tender love for her at this time.

ḍhopṭan, turban.

ḍholkī, a small drum.

tamūra, guitar of one strip.

taraī, stars.

tāmas, anger; *tāmas* may sometimes signal a loss of control, but in the case of *Ghāsīdāsa* it equally signalled a determination to oppose what he did not accept and made his influence felt.

tirath, tirith, pilgrimage place.

tirsūl, trident, the weapon of Śiva.

tiriyā, woman. Woman, says the Pardhan poet, is *nārī, nāhar* and *nāgin* — wife, tiger and cobra. A woman is a snake because, 'once she desires a man she chases him and bites him, thus making to love her. To love a girl is like poison in the body.' There is a story that a Rājā had a lovely daughter, so beautiful and auspicious that she was Lakṣmī herself. One day, four rich men came at the same time wishing to marry her, and the father angry at their importunity made his daughter into four girls, one her original Lakṣmī- like self, one a cobra, one a bitch and one a cat, and to each married one of the four suitors. So it was that there are four kinds of women. Some are Lakṣmī, fortunate, beautiful and adored; some are bitches; some are cats; and some are cobras.

tihār, festival. Though festivals may be secular, in many cases, they are inevitably observed with religious rites, ceremonies and observances.

tījā, Hindu festival observed on the 18th day of Vaiśākha.

tulsī, Ocymum Sanctum, the basil, sacred to Viṣṇu and the infant Kṛṣṇa.

tulsīdal, friendship through exchange of *tulsī* leaves.

tūmā, guard. A guard is a favourite symbol of a girl and the people sometimes speak of the *tūmā-dūdh*, or the breasts that are like gourds.

terahī, a rite after thirteenth day of the deceased person.

tel, oil, obvious symbol for devotion and sex.

telmāṭī, a rite when oil is poured on the body of the bride.

dadariyā, a tune.

darsan, seeing, view, the auspicious vision of a god or great man. The vision and realisation of truth by which a man becomes free from all fetters and attains liberation.

dasrahā, a Hindu festival.

dahikāndo, a festival during Janmāṣṭamī when curd is looted.

didī, elder sister.

diyā, lamp. Symbol of love, used as a sexual symbol. The wick, the oil, the bowl of the lamp all have their place in symbolism.

dīwār, wall of a house. Man is like the wall of a house: once it is loosened, it falls.

dukhiyā, sufferer. The first of the four truths preached by the Buddha is *dukkha.*

deur, a palace.

deva, god or godling.

devatallā, abode of god.

devar, husband's younger brother.

doniyā, food for the departed.

dauntelā, rite to pour oil on the icons during marriage ceremony.

dagadev, the elder son authorized to kindle the pyre of his father.

dhanvṛa, the *dhāṭakī* in *Bhaviṣyapurāṇa* (I. 10.35-43) which bestows heaven.

dhajā, flag on the religious place.

dharam, religion, law, prescribed duty, right; Ghāsīdāsa realized the purpose of his life, so instead of creating unnecessary stress in society, he found the meaning of life in religion, so that *Satnāmīs* may live happier.

dharmin, religious. In Puranic tradition *dharma* as a moral order was in the pristine glory in *Kṛta-yuga* the earliest of the traditional ages. It then had four feet but lost one foot in each succeeding *yuga.*

najar, the evil eye, is the eye of envy, and it is an inevitable feature of a world in which men set store by looks, or health, or goods, or any pleasant thing. Even if, as is likely, one sets no store by one's mere subsistence, the very deprivations of others give grounds for fear. Since there is no one who cannot find someone whose plight is in some way worse than his own, so there is no one who is completely immune to envy and so to *najar.* Let me describe some typical *najar* situations. Doors should always be closed while eating, otherwise hungry men may look in. Thus, if one is eating out of doors, and someone passes, one should offer him food. If food is offered, and can be accepted on caste grounds, some, be only a little, should be eaten to demonstrate goodwill. A man in the village once suffered a fever because when he was drinking tea outside his house a stranger to whom he had offered some, had refused it. The fever was only cured after he had given a coconut to the goddess. The stranger in this case was presumed to be deliberately malevolent.

nanjatiyā, lower castes, due to pollution theory.

nanad, husband's younger sister.

nandī, river. In Chhattīsgaṛh the use of streams and rivers to symbolize love is of course, very common.

narag, hell. The word may be derived in two ways : *ni* and *araka,* as meaning 'going below' (the earth) or *na* and *ra* and *ka,* meaning 'where there is not the slightest place for joy.'

nariyar, coconut.

nahāvan, purificate rite for ten days after the death of a person.

nācā, dance.

nāndiyā bailā, bulls of Mahādeva.

niyāy, judgement. The system of logic which became the basis of one of the six traditional systems of Indian philosophy.

nirwār, decision.

neng, the word *'neng'* is a social custom and attitude of mind that is characteristic of Chhattīsgaṛh. On all ceremonial occasions — it may be birth, marriage, festival, funeral — certain privileged persons, relatives, or officials of the rite, hold the proceedings and demand a present. Nothing can proceed until the ceremonial tax is paid. This is a fruitful source of dispute in weddings; for on such occasions there are many relatives to be bought off. Here, after the birth of a child, the midwife, barber and washerman refuse to fulfil their proper functions until they are given the proper dues. This is a word of greater importance for understanding the Chhattīsgaṛhi mind.

panjrī, consecrated food.

pailagī, to touch the feet in salutation, lit. 'I touch your feet'.

paṭhaunī, bride's first going to her husband's house.

patiyānā, to believe; beliefs and judgements gave Ghāsīdāsa's emotions specific flavours — a way of flooding back.

panghaṭ, bathing-*ghāṭ* of a pond, or well or river practically gives an outsider the only opportunity of meeting a girl in village India.

pañca-lakaṛiyā, a rite to cast five pieces of wood in a pyre; known as *'pañca-kāṣṭha'* in *Smṛti.*

panthī, a dance-cum-song of the *Satnāmī* sect. *Pantha* is group or sect based on a common religious bond or on certain ideals. In medieval reformistic religious movements this term acquired a wider significance.

parcār, publicity, preaching.

partīt, trust, due to his environment, Ghāsīdāsa developed a balance between trust and mistrust and finally developed a basic trusting nature in *Satnām.*

parthī, earth, woman is the earth: she is the field tilled by the man. Earth as the mother is worshipped in a score of different forms. "Woman is like earth: you may dig again and again, but she remains firm".

pardes, a foreign land, other, may mean for a girl the husband's house, may mean Chhattisgaṛhia a resident of Uttar Pradesh and Bihar. The Chhattisgaṛhi view of otherness, in spatial terms is an element of the territoriality of the protest. This self-differentiated is due to the exploitation.

parbudhiyā, one acts according to other's advice, depending on someone.

parabhū, the Lord, the Supreme Being.

permesar, the Highest Person. The concept of an all-powerful supreme being arose mainly from the masses; the god who would bestow grace and forgive human weaknesses and limitations.

parwār, family.

parsā, Butea frondosa; the *palāśa* or *ḍhāk.* Its large trifoliate leaves represent the Hindu Trinity and are used in worship. This is the 'Flame of the Forest'.

paretin, a female ghost, spirit of a departed woman.

pānw pakhārna, to wash the feet, a rite of showing reverence.

pākh, fortnight; especially in relation to the moon. Rites for gods and for prosperity must be performed in the bright *pākh* and for *pitṛs* and magic in the dark *pākh.*

pāp-dharam, good and evil. The notion of man's life as *pāp-dharam,* a mixture of good and evil, of vice and virtue, is common among the aborigines. *Pāpa* is a sinful act. It has evil effects on knowledge, intellect, sight, slumber and so on. It affects the beings to be born in the next incarnation in many ways. It results in personal ugliness of many kinds, in the loss of bodily strength and in various deformities of the human body. The commitment of certain sins condemns the soul to be born in the next life in the class of an inferior species. Other sins prevent the soul from acquiring the full powers and senses which are the right of the class in which it is born.

pālāgi, a salutation with the touching of feet.

piyrī, yellow garment, auspicious.

pīpar, *Ficus religiosa,* a sacred tree, the abode of the *Brahmā.*

purkhā, person, the primaeval man as source of universe, ancestors. When gratified by *śrāddha* they bestow on their descendants long life, progeny, wealth, learning, happiness, heaven and liberation.

purkhautī, traditional, the way of fathers, see *Chāndogya Upaniṣad* V.10.

Purwaī, East wind.

purohit, priest.

paikarmā, walking around in rituals, the first attempt which a *Satnāmī* aspirant to spirituality makes at the going round the *Jait Khambha.*

paiṭhū, means that a girl enters to a man's house and declares herself wife.

paurukh, vigour; when Ghāsīdāsa applied his energy and creative attitude to *Satnām,* the resulting success increased his vitality.

poṭārnā, to embrace.

posā, costume, dress. The rural masses use it as a measure of their own deprivation and as objectives worth fighting for when roused to do so.

phaūt, death.

phalphalahā, not able to keep a secret.

phundrā, an ornament for tying the hair: it consists of balls of red, green and blue wool held together by coloured cords.

baiṭkā, assembly.

batras, conversation, gossip.

barihār, coolie.

bandan, vermilion for the goddess.

bapurā, unfontunate, poor.

bahrū, broom. To the Chhattīsgaṛhīs broom is primarily something that sweeps away refuse. For this reason brooms are carried out to the boundary of the village and hung up there as a sign that poverty and disease have been swept away.

bāns, bamboo; a girl is often compared as bamboo.

bān, arrow, sorcery, promise, habit. In the Tantric concept it is said to reside within the triangle of the *anāhata cakra*; see *Ṣaṭcakranirūpaṇa* XXV.

bāsī, food left over from a previous meal and served again. Chhattīsgaṛh is known for it.

bidiyā, knowledge of sorcery. It denotes knowledge; female deities and their *mantras;* the female partner of the aspirant. As knowledge it is *parā* and *aparā.*

bintī, prayer. The art of surrendering one's own self to the Supreme Being. The word also stands for devotional songs. In the second sense it has a twofold significance — praise of the Lord and music of a particular type.

birhā, sorrow. The word *'birhā'* is said to mean sorrow and the songs are used by Gond and Baiga while a bridegroom takes a girl to his house.

bihāv, marriage.

berā, time.

buṛtī, west.

baigā, sorcerer, also name of tribe. He is *vijñāta* in the sense that he possesses three kinds of *vidyā* — reading, visualising and perceiving.

baihā, madman; the idea of lover as a madman is very common. The people do not say, 'He is in love with her'; they say, 'He is mad for her'.

bor, the *badarī* plant, the abode of *Viṣṇu* (*Matsyapurāṇa* 153.512-13) under which Ghāsīdāsa performed penance.

bhanwarī/bhānwar, the ceremonial procession of bride and bridgroom round the sacred pole in a wedding.

bhains, buffaloes are men who work hard when they have to, but are happiest in company joining horn to horn.

bhaujī, elder brother's wife. The relationship between a girl and her husband's younger sister are intimate and tender. A young wife is a stranger in her husband's house; everyone is very critical all the time; she generally is nervous and afraid of the new family. But two people beside her husband, console her. One is her *dewar,* the husband's younger brother, with whom she has every right to a romantic and humorous connection; the other is her *nanad*, the younger sister, probably unmarried and a favourite in the house, and to whom she can turn for support and confidences.

bhakati, devotion as a cult challenged traditional moral values and attitude.

bhagwān, God.

bhajnahā, a chanter.

bhaṛrī, wandering astrologer.

bhaṇḍārā, social dining.

bharam, doubt, illusion, error-impression.

bhalbhalhā, one who cannot keep secrets.

bhawānī, goddess.

bhāt, rice, symbol of social solidarity.

bhākhā, language.

bhutiyār, labourer.

bhūt, a ghost or demon, a class of mischievous spirits or hobgoblins.

bhojlī, friendship by the exchange of sprouted barley.

manjūr, peacock. In traditional Indian mythology the peacock is represented as sufferring from the heat and delighted with the first drops of rain; used in magic the feathers are a potent demon-scarer. The aboriginals also use peacock feathers as symbols of the gods. The peacock is an apt symbol for expressing delight and vitality of a man's beloved.

machrī, fish. Fish as a set of fertility symbol is old. The use of fish as a sexual symbol is worldwide. It occurs in life and tradition of Chhattisgaṛh. The double fish is found on bronze bowls, bells and gongs from Tibet to Chhattīsgaṛh. This is a Buddhist symbol, one of the light auspicious signs. The same sign was regarded as lucky when put on the walls of Chhattīsgaṛh. The place of fish in the Tāntric ritual is well-known. Oraon use fish as symbols of married girls. In Chhattīsgaṛh the ritualistic use of fish is more common at funerals.

macher, honey-bee, is a symbol for the lover and his love.

maṭmaṭhī/maṭakko, to waggle. The expression is used of a flirtious girl who walks about with hips swinging.

maṭiyā, a kind of devil.

maṛaī, celebrated market.

maṇḍala, an address to *Satnāmīs.*

mansubhā, intention.

mayā, illusion, attachment, love. The term is used in many senses. The masses feel that the *māyā* is the only cause of the world, feeling strongly. They hold that whole *brahman* is the cause, *mayā* is auxiliary. It is the power of *brahman* like heat in fire. So it is an attachment.

marghaṭ, graveyard.

marjād, chastity, limit.

maram, secrets.

masān, devil, cremation-ground.

mahant, a leader of religion.

mahāparsād, the highest of the various grades of conventional friendship. The reference of the word is to the blast food distributed at the great pilgrim centre Jagannāth Puri.

mahuā, the tree *Basia latifolia* which provides the aboriginals with food, oil and ardent spirits.

māyājāl, the net of love.

mitān, friend.

milbhenṭ, embrace.

mukati, release, liberation, setting free. The final liberation (mukati), according to Guru Ghāsīdāsa can be attained directly through knowledge (giyān) alone; this is what Śaṅkarāchārya conceived: *Shrībhagavadbhaktirasāyan.*

mulukh, country.

mainā; In fact *mainā* is, after the parrot, probably the most popular bird among the villagers of Chhattīsgaṛh. In folk-tales, the *mainā,* like the parrot, is sometimes a go-between of lovers. The suitability of the bird as a woman-symbol needs no emphasising.

mohgaṛh, the fortress of love. It is regarded as one of the six enemies of man. According to Buddhism it is regarded as belonging to the category of four universal bad properties. According to Jainism it is an *āvaraṇa* (cover) which generates worldly attachments and passions.

mohnī a love-charm, enchantment. Charms and spells were common throughout Chhattīsgaṛh. In the compound *Jugti-mohnī* it means a living but invisible creature which can give powerful aid to human beings.

raichat, demon.

raī, death; at the final life crisis, when *Ghāsīdāsa* would have looked back on his life with a sense of self-fulfilment and satisfaction, he would have rejoiced on the new identity of his folkman.

raksā, demon.

raksel, north, the northern people according to Chhattīsgaṛhi image are demons.

raṇg, colour-symbolism. The colour red frequently appears in Chhattisgarhi poetry of every kind. It is said that its popularity among the Hindus is due to the fact that it is the colour of blood, and that the *sendur* or vermilion powder, so often used in Hindu worship, on the parting of a woman's hair and in marriage ceremonies, is a blood substitute. The vermilion is part of what is known as *sohāg,* the lucky gift which is given at the marriage of a Hindu girl in parts of India and which also includes *kukkum* or red powder, and *mahāwar* or red balls of cotton wool. It is also said that a red *sāṛī* or red turban at once awakes desire. The blossoming of the red flower is the onset of menstruation.

rangrailī, exciting and colourful.

ramāyan, the Great epic *Rāmāyaṇ,* haunts in *Satnāmi* mind.

raruhā, poor.

ras, juice, essence, flavour. In Chhattīsgaṛh a youth who is full, or over-full of *ras* is nicknamed *rasiā* : the implications are not polite. In this *ras* the sole aim of the devotee is to have the closest embrace of his beloved. He lives in and for his beloved. He drinks deep in beauty, but thirst quenches not.

risi, sage, one of the inspired persons to whom the oral tradition is known.

rākhī, a Hindu festival called *rakṣābandhana.*

rāgi, companion.

rīt, rite, custom.

rukh, tree. It is considered both meritorious and exciting to plant trees. The Chhattīsgaṛhi who does this generally has a greater desire to perpetuate his name, and looks forward a prosperous old age. In a poem the old man who planted mango and tamarind trees in his youth finds himself jealous of the vigour of their fresh green leaves and compares it to the lack of strength and life in his own limbs.

rūp, face, appearance, outward form, figure, shape or colour. One of the two broad divisions of the five constituents (*skandhas*), the other being *nāma* in Buddhist belief. It denotes the material elements.

roṭi, bread, an obvious sexual symbol.

rautiyā, name of the *Satnāmī*-clan.

laṇgṭā, naked, one who has no money.

lachmī, Goddess Lakṣmī, cow.

lamsenā, a youth who serves for his wife instead of paying the bride: price.

lahrī, emotional; Ghāsīdāsa's emotions became increasingly complex and served deeper purposes of life.

lāg, cost of a marriage.

lāgmānī, relationship.

lālbhājī, name of ceremonial friendship.

limaū, is a simile fr the breast.

lunj, insensitive, not involved with others.

lehrā, the wave with its swinging movement is natural sexual symbol and is used frequently in the songs.

lokhan, famous.

wāh de, look! there.

wāh re, bravo!!

sanedoha, messenger. Guru Ghāsidāsa is a messenger of truth; see *Paraśurāmakalpasūtra* X.63.

saitā, truth, honesty, patience.

saūkhi, net.

sugun, good omen.

sangī, friend.

sat, truth, being, term for the truth or Divine which Ghāsīdāsa understood to be personal.

satnām, knowledge of Brahman, the truth; a *Satnāmī* salutation to *Satnāmīs, Satnāmī* may be excommunicated if beaten. This is a reversal of the old tradition when he was not supposed to raise the voice on being beaten.

satnāmī, followers of the *Satnām* sect. Previously before the rise of *Satnām-panth* *satnāmīs* were branded on the buttocks and turned out of the village.

satmahin, the *Satnāmī* woman.

sataurī, ancestors up to seven generations.

sandes, news. The source of message of Guru Ghāsīdāsa is necessarily identifiable from the *Panthi*-songs.

sansā, sorrow

sapnā, dream, symbolism in Ghāsīdāsa's dream, unconscious acts of his personality.

saparihā, companion.

sarag, heaven. It is a source of unsurpassed joy according to the epics and *Purāṇas* where an individual can reach after death in consequence of meritorious actions performed in worldly life.

saragwāsī, heavenly. It is imagined as a place of thousands of *yojanas* above the earth. According to *Mīmāṁsakas, svarga* is the reward of all sacrifices for which no reward is expressly provided by the *Vedas.*

sāī, title of sādhu. Ascetics belonging to the non-orthodox orders. They challenged the authority of the Brāhmaṇaṣ.

sānth/sānthia, the *Swastika*-mark. *Svasti* is benediction, c.f. RV X. 178 is a *svastyayana* hymn.

sākhī the witness. The kind of devotion in which God is looked upon as a friend, as between Kṛṣṇa and Subala. *Sakhya bhaktas* are comrades who consider themselves equal to God in every respect. It develops into *anurāga* (intense love).

sākhoccār, chanting of *mantras* during marriage ceremony.

sājā, Terminalia tomentosa; the sacred tree of the *Gond,* the traditional abode of Baṛādeva.

sādh, liking, faith or conviction which is the means for developing the highest reverence for the preachings of the Guru.

sādhu, a Hindu ascetic, holy person whose life is dedicated to the search for God. Sādhus are often compared to cotton, as dry (i.e. unattached) as the cotton pad and as useful for protecting common men as cotton-clothes for body.

sāl, Shorea robusta; a tree at once sacred and useful.

sāheb, gentleman, the divine body. It is the all pervasive reality in *Santa*--tradition.

sidhaurī, this is a little ceremony intended to satisfy cravings. The woman is visited by her mother or brother, who brings seven different kinds of food. She sits on her mother's lap and is ceremonially fed.

sirton, true.

suā, parrot. The parrot is an ideal messenger between lovers in Chhattīsgaṛhi folklore. The parrot is famous in Indian folklore as a bird of learning, a go-between of lovers and a sex-symbol. A girl is symbolized as usual as parrot.

sumarnī, the *japamālā* in Sanskrit. The string of beads carried by saints or religious minded persons, the most popular of which is a kind of dried seed called *rudrākṣa.*

sumiran, recollection.

suraj/suruj, the Sun; it symbolized Supreme Being to Ghāsīdāsa.

surtā, memory; Ghāsīdāsa's emotions and moods affected the way he remembered and what he remembered affected his mood. Dramatic 'state dependent', effects may be seen in the *Panthī* songs.

surāj, self-government.

sūpā, the winnowing fan is one of the most domestic implements. The winnowing fan is everywhere associated with magic. There is quite enough of itself to make a winnowing fan sacred but there is another cause. It is used as a sort of planchette by the *guniyā* magician.

sendur, vermilion powder used in Hindu marriages.

sembal, Bombax malabaricum; the cotton tree, sacred to the Hindus and used in many aboriginal ceremonies.

sewāgīt, prayer of gods and goddesses, religious prayers. Authentic religious folk-songs are not very common in Chhattīsgaṛh and they have a habit of turning into love-songs in their concluding lines. Rāma, Lakṣmaṇa and Sita are described as members of an earthly family, and it is not always possible whether a name denotes a legendary or an actual lover.

son, gold; for the people of Chhattīsgaṛh the word 'gold' awakens the memory of Golden Age now sunk to iron, of the days when monarchs handled gold *mohurs,* of exquisite fabled ornaments made of the precious metal. Gold has always had a high place in the poetic imagination of Chhattịsgaṛh.

saunsār, the world. The manifestation or opening out *(unmeṣa)* of the unmanifested.

haṁsa, swan, goose; in fact, it is a fabulous bird of great beauty, that lives on pearls and is often used as a symbol of the mysterious invisible life of man.

hajārī-dūlhā, is a word used in both flattery and derision. It can mean 'son of a thousand fathers' or 'son of a marriage that cost a thousand rupees'.

hathjorī, folding hands.

hathwā, palm-prints.

hathauī, astrologer, palmist.

hardī, turmeric, the powdered root is used to colour water in *Holi* festival, as a demon-scarer, much used in weddings, symbol of love.

har-har, repeating of Mahādeva's name.

harhī, wandering wife. It is usually used of a cow or she-goat that will stay in the shed, but is always wandering abroad. So are some wives. The epithet is applied to a wife.

hānkā, a beat for game; magicians use the word in their charms to drive away evil spirits.

hār, garland.

hīrā, diamond. To the people of Chhattīsgaṛh the diamond simply means something rare, beautiful and precious. The singers of *Panthī* are some of the poorest people in the world and it is safe to say that not one of them has ever seen a precious stone. Yet references to the diamond, the ruby and the pearl are common in their songs and folk-tales. Motilal, or the Pearl Boy, is a common name and a Pardhan hero is called Hiraman Ksatri, the Diamond warrior. 'A woman', says a proverb, 'is a diamond because she gives you one'.

The use of these symbols is probably a literary convention that has been acquired from wandering Hindu ministrels or has come down in the tradition of Gond kingdoms. The five precious things of a Hindu story are gold, diamond, sapphire, ruby and pearl.

What is remarkable here is its use by people to whom the objects of comparison are so unfamiliar.

hajī, exclamation calling attenion.

homnā; offering, burnt offering. Offering made to fire in the name of different deities. It is necessary in numerous ceremonies and rites. To perform *homa* a raised square form is built. Offerings are thrown into the fire with *mantras.*

horī ke āgī, the Holi fire is regarded as 'virgin fire' and has the magical value.

NOTES TO CHAPTERS

CHAPTER 1 — INTRODUCTION

1. In the wake of the Dalit movement in the late seventies, the expression of subordination and domination through lexical means became more than a mere tracing or symbol or ritualistic affirmation of the social hierarchy. So the expressions like *chamār* or *Harijan* considerably constitute the hierarchy; they are the shadow and substance. If the total picture is biased over a period of time, the cumulative impact will be considerable. The term should give a correct picture of reality, because the lexicon ought to reflect reality as it is. From these different terms of social role portrayal, one gets the impression that the role of the lower caste people is limited to their traditional occupations. So in India, codes exist for proper 'names'. Accordingly the use of the word *chamār* is prohibited through the legislation. Due to the negative evaluation of the word, I have replaced it with Dalit. I apologize those authors from whose writings the word has been replaced for positive evaluation. The author should take care that his writings are not in conflict with the equality between the elite and non-elite and that they do not give the impression of a negative impression of one of the social groups or show a man or a woman in an offending way.

2. There are seven spatial myths known as *rāwṭi* which are concerned with seven places (Dentewāṛā, Kānker, Pānābaras, Dongargarh, Goṇḍaī, Bhoramdeva, and Dalhjapoṇḍī) depicting the charismatic personality of Guru Ghāsidāsa.

CHAPTER 2 — THE PROCESS OF SEMIOTIC BREAK (ADHAROTTARA) IN CHHATTĪSGAṚH

1. The *Kabīr-panth* of Chhattīsgaṛh is descended from Muktāmani, the younger son of Dharmadāsa of Bāndhavagarh. The main rituals in this *panth* are *Chaukā* (four types) and *ārtī.* The main actors are guru (*mahant*), *dīwān* (priest), *gāyak* (*bhajan-maṇḍalī*) and *yajamān* (the householder) along with the audience.

2. He was born on 18th December 1756 A.D. from Manhagū (F) an Amrautin. His wife Saphurā gave birth to four sons and one daughter.

3. Girodpurī is repeatedly recited in *Panthī*-songs:

nar-nārī gāvain amar pad pāvain
giraudpurī jāwain re dukh bisrāwain.

It is just like *Kāśī* in the *Purāṇas.*

CHAPTER 3 — GURU GHĀSIDĀSA AND SATNĀM-PANTHA

1. Kishan Lal Kurre has collected *rāwṭīs* and *amṛtavāṇī* of Guru Ghāsīdāsa. The *amṛtavāṇī* collected by Kurre in Chhattīsgaṛhi are of universal nature: such as (a) *mankhē mankhē mā bhedabhāva nāhī, kariyā ho yā goriyā;* (b) *dāī hā dāī āy;* (c) *murhī gāy ke dūdh lā jhan pībē;* (d) *gāy-bhains lā nāgar mā jhan jotbē;* (e) *tor pīrā otkec āy, jatkā mor pīrā hē;* (f) *konē jīb ka jhan mārbē;* (g) *māns la jhan khābē;* (h) *paṇḍit ho yā moulavī, mūllā ho yā sant, sāṭīdār-bhaṇḍārī ho yā mahant, ye sab sant lā sante jaun;* (i) *sabai bhagwān hā barābar mān;* (j) *ḍhog jhan kar;* (k) *banāyec bar hai tab dariyā banā, kuā banā, nāthālaya banā, mandir-masjid jhan banā,* etc.

2. The following *Panthī*-song depicts their way of life:

sādā sādā khānā aur saral sādā rahnā hai
colā lā bigaṛē taisē khānā pīnā tajnā hai
māns-madirā ke to choṛ de adhār gā
jehī khānā-pīnā mā bigre samsar ga

3. *Satnāmīs* claim their lineage from the sun. Their houses are built facing the sun. The sun has been one of the most impressive phenomena of nature, which has evoked admiration and reverence from religious and scientific minded people alike, all over the world as a divine being or as a source of life and all energies in this world. Right from the time of *Ṛgveda, Sūrya*, the sun is being extolled as a divine entity:

tatsavitur vareṇyam
bhargo devasya dhīmahi
dhiyo yo naḥ pracodayāt (*RV*. III. 62.10)

CHAPTER 4 — THE SEMIOTICS OF SATNĀM

1. His depiction of *Satnām* may be seen in the *panthi*-song:

tor haṁsā phanse he māyājāl sāheb
Satnām le lo ho.
jīnā-marnā naiye kuchu hāth sāheb
Satnām le lo ho.
duniyā mā āke dhartī mā āke
Satnām le lo ho.
nartan pāke mānus-cholā pāke
Satnām le lo ho.
māṭī ke tan more ye sapnā adhūre
Satnām le lo ho.
dukh ke gharere sukh bahu thore
Satnām le lo ho.

* * *

satya karma-dharma ho satya-haḍḍī-charm ho
satya swarg-nark ho satya pāpī-gark ho
satya nadī-nālā ho, satya māyājāl ho
duniyā re melā he, haṁsā akelā he
satya he ātmā satya he parmātmā

satya guru-nām he gāye he mahātmā
satya bhagwān he jātpāt nāhī ho
ohī prabhu pāī jo Satyanām gāhī ho.

2. The means to approach the knowledge is means to attain the light, according to *Panthī*-song.

Sūnya gagan bīch bāsā ho
nirmal gyān ke prakasā
nivāsā ho Satnām ke nivāsā
ātam ke ghaṭ ke rājā
hirde palang bichāye ho
dayā-dharam doū chanwar ḍolāye
mohinī lubhāye ho
ye de ho vo lok jahān na pānī
na pavan prakāsā ho
anhad rāg chhattīson bājen
dason dwār chaprāsī ho
chhanan-chharan Indra-parī nāce
achraj au kauwāsī ho
gyān ke gaṅgā ghaṭ bhītar ma
kāhe bhaye piyāsā ho

3. *Haṁsa* finds major-place in the *Panthī*-songs:

Chal haṁsā amarlok jaibo
ihān hamar saṅgī kono naiye
ek sangī hābe bar ke tihāī
dekhe ma jiyrā juṛāī
ek saṅgī parbhū Satnām he
pāpī manlā manāye
janam-maran ke sabodin saṅgī
ohī swaraṭhā amrāye.

CHAPTER 5 — THE MODEL OF JAIT KHAMBHA

1. *Jait-khambha* along with white flag occurs in the *panthī*-folksongs

Sundar gobar mā aṅgrā lipāye he
jeker ūpar chaukā-chandan purāye he
kanchan ke thārī ghī ke ārti sajāye he
nariyar supārī laung lāychī magāye he
jaise ē khambhā gāwn-gāwn lahrāye he
taise dil mā Satnām upjāye he

* * *

Sat ke pavittar ēhī khambhā la gaṛāye he
binā raṅg-chal ke dhajā phah rāye he

2. For the publicity of *Satnām*, see the following lines from *Panthī*:

alīn-galīn ma Satnām ke prachār he
gānw-gānw ma bhare Lachhmī-bhaṇḍār he

CHAPTER 6 — SATNĀM PARADIGM OF SATLOKA

1. The *Satnām* paradigm of a conscious cosmos may be seen in the following lines of *Panthī:*

baṅgalā ajab bane re bhāī
banglā ajab bane re
naynā me panmesar dekhenw
baṅglā ajab bane re
e baṅglā ke das darwājā
pawan chalāvay haṁsā
āwat jāt konī nahi karthe
iswar ke ī mansā
hāṛ-chām ke ịṛtā banāye
lahū rakat ke lohe
ronwā kēnwā chhānī bane he

haṁsā rahe sukh soī
ihān mārā koī nahi ejī
e des ma hamar kono nai e gā
e phūl lage he e phulwārī lage
jahān bhanwrā baserā kare
phūl jharige bhanwrā uṛige
pachtāwā hāth re
chalo re haṁsā
amarlok jānā hai jī

CHAPTER 7 — SATNĀMI SPEECH BEHAVIOUR

1. The following *Satnāmī dadariyā* depicts the same:

Hindū la rām-rām,
Paṭhān la salām,
panikā la bandagī
Satnāmi la Satnām

CHAPTER 8 — THE FOREST OF SYMBOLS

1. The *chaukā-songs of* Kabīrpanthis have birds as the symbols of souls:

nikal calew re ciṛiyā
tan ke chiṛiyā nikal chalew re
khaṭiyā ke murdā la utāre bhuinyā
hardī-tel lagā ke
chār muhāsī boh ke lege
ab ghaṭ ma utāre re

* * *

ḍehrī lag tāre mehrī ke rowe
pharikā lag sab bhāī
jāt-kuṭum marghaṭ ma robay
haṁsa akelī jāt re.

CHAPTER 10 — PANTHI: THE SECTARIAN DANCE AND SONG

1. Some of the excerpts from the *Panthī*-song are as follows:

(a) *Jasodā maiyā jaise krisna la khelāye he*
godī ma baiṭhaṛ ke mātā palnā jhulāye he
taise amrautin dāī ghasiā la pāye he
bār-bār chūmai mātā godī ma khelāye he
Kausilyā ke godī jaise rāmchandra khele he
taise tor aṅgnā Ghāsīdās khel he.

(b) *ho lalnā dhanya amrautin*
tore bhāgya sohar-pad gāwat he
dān-punya howat he apār
sohar-pad gāwat he
ānand-maṅgal manāw
sohar-pad gāwat he.

(c) *tāre ho tāre gurijī koṛhī kejīwla*
satya-bhavan ke ho rākhe he nīnwla
gaṇḍaī ma melā bhare sādhu-muni-gyānī ke
āye hāvai narnārī des-desānī ke
koṛhī ke dal āye girat-paṛat rowat ho
baṛe-baṛe sạdhu manke charan la jāwain ho
ro-ro ke koṛhī kahai haṁsā la ubārā ho
hamre janam lā bābā lewā sudhārā ho
korhī ke dukh dekh sab tiriyāvain ho
sādhu-sannyāsī sabe bhāg-parāwain ho
bolat he sādhu ek koṛhī ke dal le
guru Ghāsīdās ke batāwthe bal le

(d) *chīnhat hai tolā*
ṭhagwā ḍongarī ke rājā
bhārī bhūkh lāge hohī
āke molā khājā

ram-ram-ram
ye dhuni tor jalthe
dhuni ke āghū ma
baghwā hā kindarthe
baghwā haunhāwe
garje bar lāgthe
dhiyān bhaṅg hoge
mor gurujī nihārthe
antarjāmī he
Ghāsīdās bābā mor
baghwā ke āghū ma
ṭhāṛhe dūnō hāth joṛ
āghū-āghū baghwā renge
pāchhū-pāchhū ghāsī ho
dhan more mahimāla
'achraj au kauwāsī ho

BIBLIOGRAPHY

Agnew, P. Vans. 1820. *A Report on the Subah or Province of Chhattisghur* written in 1820 A.D., Nagpur 1922.

Baden-Powell, B.H. 1899. *The origin and growth of village communities in India.*

Bajpai, K.D. 1984. *History and Culture of M.P.*, Ahmedabad.

Bajpai, K.D. 1985 *Cultural History of India*, Kanpur.

Behar, Sharad Candra. 1986 Daliton ke Masīhā (Hindi), unpublished, typed pages 1-8.

Bettelheim, Bruno. 1976. *The Uses of Enchantment*, New York.

Bhattacharya. 1896, *Hindu Castes and Sects*, Calcutta.

Boas, Franz. 1911. *The Mind of Primitive Man*, New York.

Bose, P.N. 1890. "Chhattisgar: Notes on its tribes and sects and castes", *Centenary Review of the Asiatic Society of Bengal* (from 1784-1883).

Briggs, Geo. W. 1920. *The Chamars*, Oxford.

Cassirer, Ernst. 1944. *Essay on Man*, New York.

Chaturvedi, Parasuram. 1986. "Satnāmis-Sampradāya", (Hindi), unpublished, typed pages 1-6.

Chisolm, J.W. 1868. *Report on the Land Revenue Settlement of the Bilaspur Distt. in Central Provinces,* Nagpur.

Crooke, W. 1986. *The tribes and castes of the North-western Provinces and Oudh,* Madras.

Dube, V.N. 1983. *Regional and class-variations in Chhattisgarhi,* unpublished Ph.D. thesis, Raipur University.

Dundes, Alan (ed). 1978. *Varia Folklorica,* Mouton.

Durkheim, Emile. 1961. *The Elementary Forms of Religious Life,* Trans. by Joseph Ward Swain, New York.

Elwin, Verrier. 1946. *Folksongs of Chhattisgarh,* Oxford.

Elwin and Hiwale. 1944. *Folksongs of Mekal Hills,* Oxford.

Frazer, J.A. 1915. *The Golden Bough: A Study of Magic and Religion,* New York.

Freud, Sigmund. 1946. *Totem and Taboo,* New York.

Grant, Charles C. 1870. The *Gazetteer of Central Provinces of India,* Calcutta.

Grierson, G.A. 1885. *A Bihar Peasant Life .*

Grierson, G.A. 1904. *The Linguistic Survey of India,* Vol. VI, Calcutta.

Guru, Vijaya. 1986. Naslavād va sāmājika avamānanā ke khilāph (Hindi), unpublished, typed pages 1-4.

Hewitt, J.F.K. 1869. *The Bilaspur Settlement Report,* Nagpur.

Hiralal, Kavyapadhayaya. 1880. *A Grammar of Chhattisgarhi Dialect.*

Hiralal, R.B. 1921. *The Census of India,* C.P. and Berar, Pt. I.

Hiralal, R.B. 1933. *Indian Antiquary,* Vol. 62.

James, E.O. 1917. *Primitive Ritual and Belief.*

Jevons, F.B. 1908. *An Introduction to the Study of Comparative Religions.*

Jung, Carl G. 1958. *Psychology and Religion,* New York and London.

Kantikumar. 1969. *Chhattisgarhī Bolī Vyākarana aur Kosh,* Delhi.

Ketkar, S.V. 1901. *History of Caste in India* (2 Vols).

Keyur Bhushan. 1982. "Sant-Siromaṇi Guru Ghasidas" in *Chhattisgarh kī vibutiyān* (Hindi), Bhopal.

Keyur Bhushan. (undated). 'Shoshita aur Pathabhraṣṭa Samāj ke Prakāshstambha', in *Kawardhādarpaṇa* (Hindi).

Khare, G. 1990. Guru Ghasidasa in *Jnānaḍhārā* (Hindi magazine), Bilaspur.

Lawlore, M. 1867. *The Gazetteer of Central Provinces,* Nagpur.

Levi-Strauss. 1969. *The Raw and the Crooked,* New York.

Levi-Strauss. 1978. Myth and *Meaning,* New York.

Lipner, Julius. 1986. *The Face of Truth,* Oxford.

Lyall, Alfred C. 1899. *Asiatic Studies,* First series.

Malinowski, Bronislaw. 1926. *Myth in Primitive Psychology,* London.

Martin, Janet. 1985. *Metaphors and Religious Language,* Oxford.

Manzel, E.M. 1932. *Chhattisgarhi Lexicon,* Nagpur.

Mukerjee, A.C. 1916. *Hindu Fasts and Feasts,* Calcutta.

Neitzsche, Friedrich. 1967. *Human, All Too Human,* Berlin.

Nelson. 1909. *Bilaspur District Gazetteer,* Nagpur.

Nelson. 1909. *Raipur District Gazetteer,* Nagpur.

Oudh Gazetteer, 1877, Vol. I. Calcutta.

Panthīgīt: Oral poetry of *Satnāmī* sect of Chhattisgaṛh, Field-collection.

Report of the Census of Central Provinces for the year 1872, Calcutta.

Russel, R.V. 1908. *Imperial Gazetteer of India,* Vol. X.

Russell, R.B. and Hiralal. 1916. *The Tribes and Castes of the Central Provinces of India.*

Shering, M.A. 1879. *Hindu Tribes and Castes,* Vol. II, Madras.

Shesh, Shankar. 1973. *Chhattisgarhī kā Bhāshāshāstrīya Adhyayana*, Bhopal.

Shukla, H.L. 1977 (a) *Lankā kī khoj*, Allahabad.

Shukla, H.L. 1977 (b) *Kosalānandam* (ed), Raipur.

Shukla, H.L. 1985. *Social History of Chhattisgarh*, Delhi.

Shukla, H.L. 1994 (a) Semiotica Indica, 2 Vols, Delhi.

Shukla, H.L. 1994 (b) Guru Ghāsīdāsa (in Hindi); Bhopal.

Shukla, H.L. 1994 (c) Guru Ghāsīdāsa Charitamahākavyam (in Sanskrit).

Shukla, Tara. 1976. *Impact of Chhattisgarhi on Muria*, Ph.D. thesis.

Tailang, B.R. 1966. *Chhattisgarhi, Halbi and Bhatrī*, Bombay.

The Bijak of Kabir, Trans. into English by Rov. Ahmed Shah, 1917.

The Religious Sects of Hindus, Christian Literature Society, 1904.

Thurston and Rangachari. 1909. *Castes and Tribes of Southern India.*

Vaidya, C.V. 1940. *History of the Hindu Mediaeval India*, Vol. I.

Verma, N.D. 1979. *Chhattisgarhī Bhāshā kā Udvikāsa*, Allahabad.

Verma, Shrīkānt. 1986. 'Akar Se Vidroh' (Hindi), Unpublished, typed pages 1-4.

Watts, Alan W. 1953. *Myth and Ritual in Christianity*, London.

Wheelwright, Philip. 1965. 'The Semantic Approach To Myth' in *Myth: A Symposium*, T.A. Sebeok (ed), Baloomington.

Westcott, G.A. 1907. *Kabīr and Kabīr Panth*, London.

Yadu, M.L. 1979. *Chhattisgarhi Lokoktiyon kā Bhāshā-Vaigyānika Adhyayana*, Raipur.

INDEX

NAME INDEX

SUBJECT INDEX

ILLUSTRATIONS

(MAPS & PLATES)

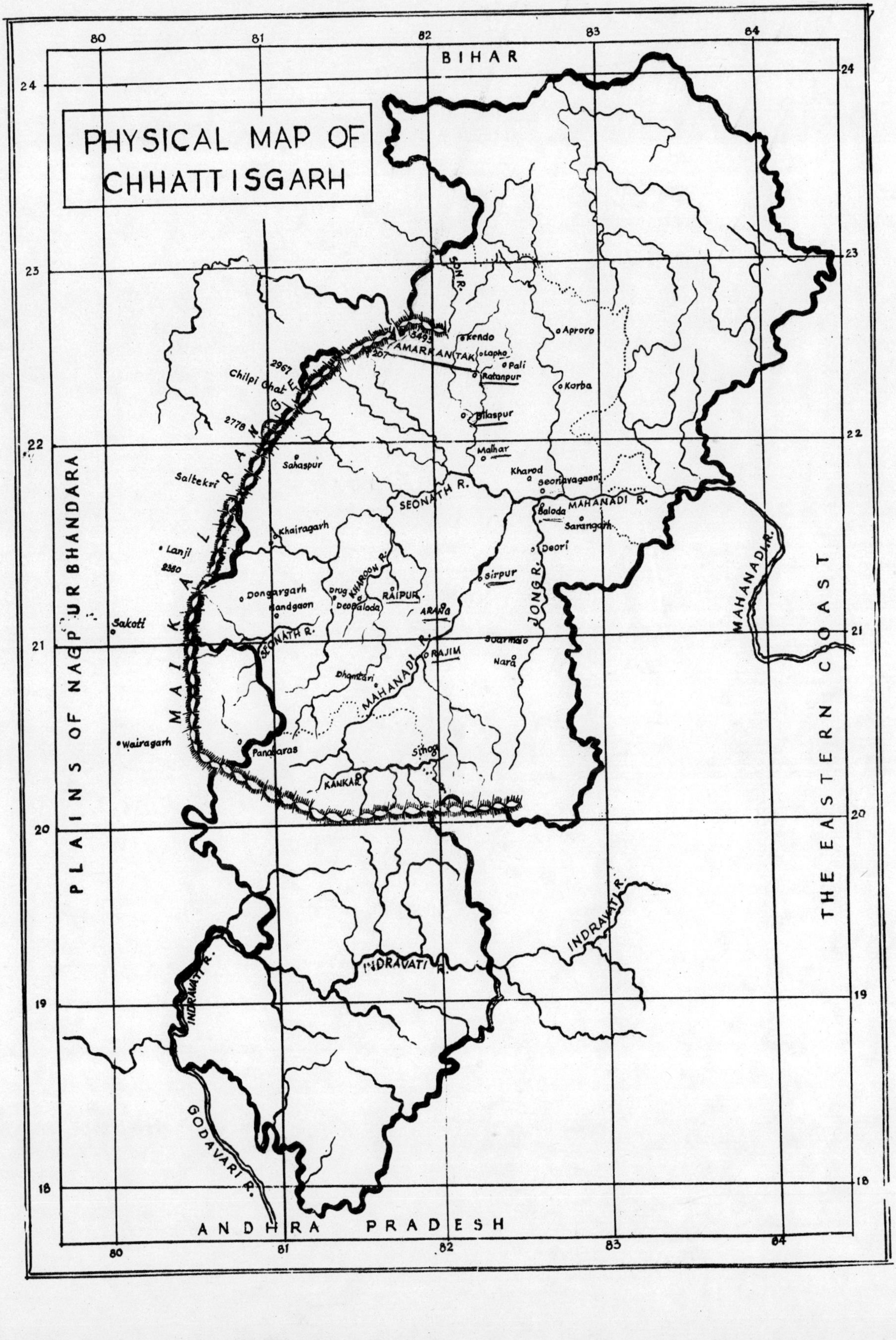

PHYSICAL MAP OF CHHATTISGARH
BIHAR
ANDHRA PRADESH
PLAINS OF NAGPUR BHANDARA
THE EASTERN COAST
MAIKAL RANGE
SON R.
AMARKANTAK
3493
2967
2778
2350
207
Chilpi Ghat
Kendo
Lapha
Pali
Ratanpur
Aproro
Korba
Bilaspur
Malhar
Kharod
Seorinarayan
Sahaspur
Saltekri
SEONATH R.
MAHANADI R.
Baloda
Sarangarh
Deori
Khairagarh
Lanji
Sirpur
JONG R.
KHAROON R.
Dongargarh
Drug
RAIPUR
Nandgaon
Deobaloda
ARANG
Sakoli
Soarmal
RAJIM
Nara
Dhamtari
MAHANADI R.
Wairagarh
Panabaras
Sihoa
KANKAR
INDRAVATI R.
GODAVARI R.
80
81
82
83
84
24
23
22
21
20
19
18

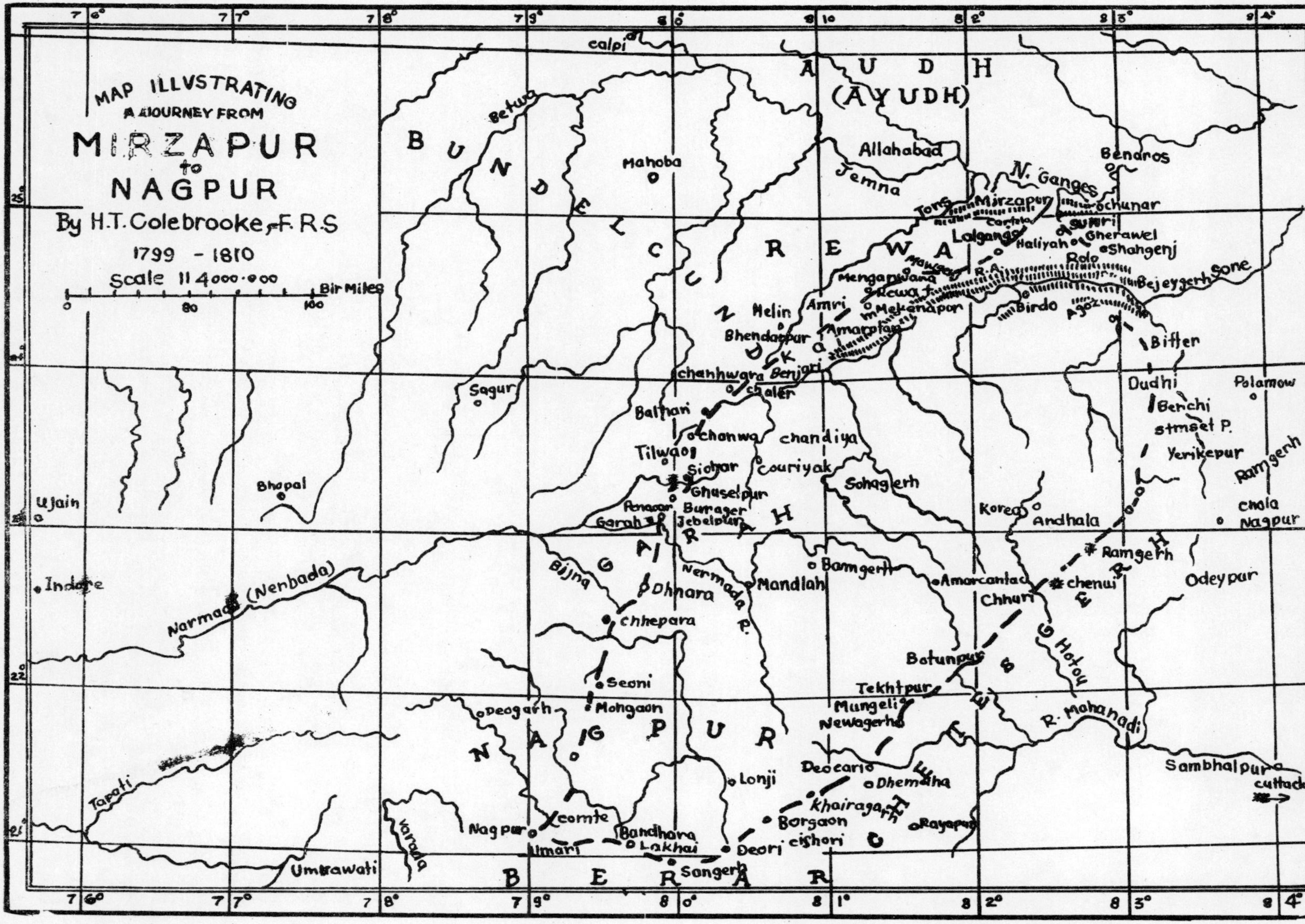
MAP ILLVSTRATING
A JOURNEY FROM
MIRZAPUR
to
NAGPUR
By H.T. Colebrooke, F.R.S
1799 - 1810
Scale 1 | 4000·000
Bir Miles
0
80
100
AUDH
(AYUDH)
BUNDELCUND
REWA
GARHA
NAGPUR
BERAR
GOERH
calpi
Betwa
Mahoba
Allahabad
Jemna
Benaros
N. Ganges
Mirzapur
chunar
Tons
Lalganga
Haliyah
Gherawel
Shahgenj
Rolo
Sone
Bejeygerh
Birdo
Bitter
Amri
Melin
Bhendappur
Amarpatan
Mekendpur
Rewa
Menganwana
chanhwara
Benjari
chaler
Sagur
Balhari
chanwa
chandiya
Tilwaos
Sichar
Couriyak
Sohagerh
Ghuselpur
Buragar
Jebelpur
Garah
Bhopal
Ujain
Indore
Narmada (Nerbada)
Bijna
Dhnara
Nermada R.
Mandlah
Bamgerh
Amarcantac
Chhuri
chenui
Ramgerh
Korea
Andhala
Dudhi
Benchi
Polamow
Yerikepur
Ramgerh
chala Nagpur
Odeypur
chhepara
Seoni
Mongaon
Deogarh
Batunpur
Tekhtpur
Mungeli
Newagerha
R. Mahanadi
Hotou
Sambhalpur
cuttack
Deocari
Dhemdha
Lonji
khairagarh
Borgaon
Rayapur
Deori
Nagpur
comte
Umari
Bandhara
Lakhai
Sangerh
Varada
Umbrawati
Tapati

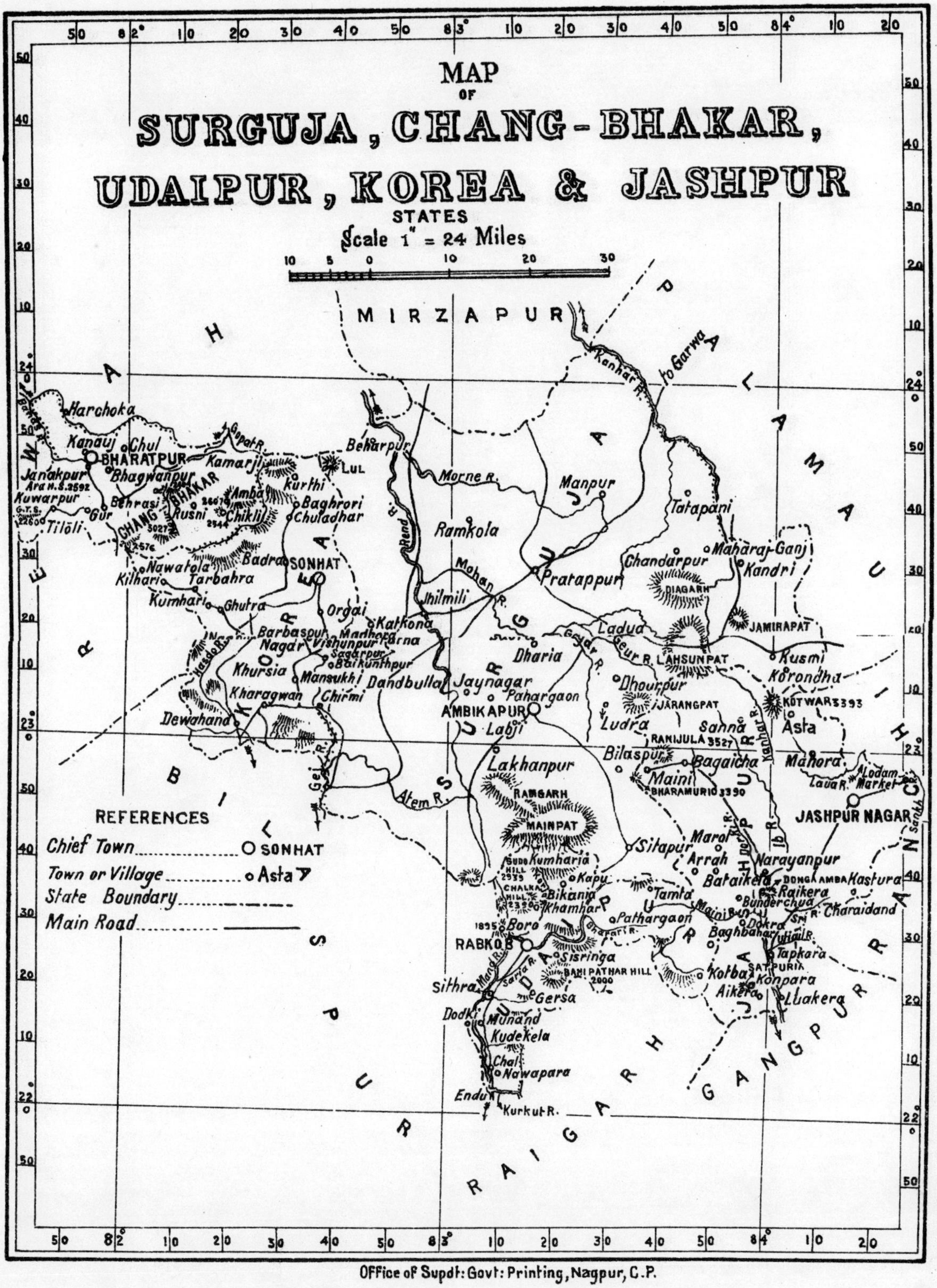

Office of Supdt: Govt: Printing, Nagpur, C.P.

Pl. 1: The place where Satnām was revealed

Pl. 2: Rāmnāmī procession

Pl. 3: Rāmnāmī festival

Pl. 4: Rāmnāmī ritual

Pl. 5: Woman totooed with rām-rām

Pl. 6: Rāmnāmī male in his attire

Pl. 7: Jait-Khambha: The symbol of truth

Pl. 8: Jait-Khambha in temple-yard

Pl. 9: Guru Ghāsīdāsa temple

Pl. 10: Sārangarh Inscription of Maha-Sudeva

Pl. 11: Rānījhūlā temple

Pl. 12: Kewṭin temple

Pl. 13: Mahāprabhu from East Pujārīpāl

Pl. 14: The temple of Rāmgaṛh Hills